THE
DEVIL'S
PADDLE

By Beau Hays

ISBN: 9781080969746

First Edition

Cover photo by Dan Marshall
danmarshallphoto.com

For Mary Pat Elsen & Jean Moelter

Red Wing...
Fall, 2016

1

And breathe deep, he did, the gathering gloom.

The darkness around him stood in stark relief to the small pool of light in which he stood. The majority of his body was tensed, his dominant arm pinned tight behind his back, his hand clutched tight around the contents therein. His left arm, the weaker of the set, an issue with which he took much umbrage, was not tensed but hung loose at his side.

He stared into the black beyond the netting.

The aforementioned netting was strung tight on all sides. Taut like chain-link, it spread across the entirety of his field of vision. Remnants of old duct tape that had once formed a target upon the surface still clung to it. The top corner of one of the few remaining pieces of tape was peeling and hung down askew with its back showing. It was marred, black with crud, long stuck to the formerly tacky surface. But the tape and its intended purpose was nothing to him. It was a crutch meant for amateurs. His focus was pin-point and finite and instinct would guide his hand as it had a thousand times before; he would need nothing more.

The babble from the radio behind him disappeared into the night air, unheard for the moment. When the broadcast returned from commercial so too would his interest in it but now all was lost to him but the sweet spot beyond the netting.

The outside world encroached and his concentration broke.

Not broken by the radio but by voices from the house. He looked in that direction but the single floodlight that supplied him his small swath of light shone into his eyes eclipsing all else. He chose the spot he stood intentionally. The feel of the light helped to achieve the atmosphere he strived for, but now he wished that he could see into the kitchen. He had been distracted by the voices from that direction because the cadence and intensity of the conversation had spiked.

His dad and Lisa were arguing.

An occurrence that was not exactly rare as of late. His dad had told him that they weren't fighting, he said that he didn't even like to call it arguing. What was going on between them wasn't necessarily combative. It was much more complex than that. So his dad had said, but to a ten-year-old boy it seemed like fighting. Or at the very least, arguing.

He put his dad and Lisa and their complex adult issues from his mind and returned his focus to the task at hand. The arm behind his back had not slipped but the tension had drained. He rotated the ball in his hand and replaced his fingers on the raised seams. Then he waited. He waited for the radio.

Major League Baseball had recently gone to the new wildcard format for the playoffs and his favorite nine, *his* Boys of Summer, were playing game 163. A one game playoff to see which wildcard team would advance. And now he waited for his favorite player, *his* Closer, to take the mound in the top of the ninth and put an end to someone's season. To salt away a one-run victory.

The darkness that surrounded him outside of his little circle of light and beyond the patio at the back of the house was, in actuality, a large darkened forest. But he could not see the outline of a single tree. To him, the encompassing woods had ceased to exist. In his head he could hear the crowd up in Minneapolis, not quite a roar yet, but building to it as the moment approached. He could smell the ballpark, the brats, the peanut shells, even the beer. He thought that beer was gross but it was part of the experience and he wouldn't strike it, not even from an alternate atmosphere created solely in his mind.

Then the radio was back.

The roar of the actual crowd coming through the radio mixed with the din coming from the crowd in his head. Provo and the Dazzle-Man cracked the microphone and announced that Jack Mavis had taken the mound. Both crowds ratcheted up the volume another notch. The guys did some light radio analysis while Jack finished his warm-up tosses. He adored Jack Mavis. Jack was the best pitcher that he'd ever seen. He rotated the ball that was in his own hand one last time, realigning the seams and placing his fingers appropriately across them. Now he waited for Jack.

The Dazzle-Man wrapped up his analysis and Provo took up the call.

He heard every word that was said and yet he heard nothing. He shook off the first sign put down by the catcher in tandem with the description of what Mavis did on the mound. Everything he did, every piece of his ten-year-old mechanics was based on Jack. He nodded again in perfect time with the call and in unison they went through their wind-up and let the fastball fly. His follow-through pulled him forward off of his imaginary mound. He immediately set his feet and whipped his glove up in front of his face.

"Swing and a miss!" came the call from the radio.

The ball rocketed off the netting of the pitch-back and thumped solidly into the glove that was set right before his eyes. He dropped the glove, switched the ball back to his throwing hand, and stepped back to his makeshift mound. He resumed his stance and again waited for Jack. He waited while the batter stepped out, adjusted his gloves and stepped back into the batter's box. The batter dug in and he and Jack set their stance.

And then they were in motion again.

"Swing and a miss! Strike two."

The ball rebounded and smacked his glove again in the exact same spot as the previous pitch, right in front of his eyes. He went back to the mound. Set his stance, and waited.

And repeat.

"Strike 3! Mavis blew it right by him!"

Thump. The carom hit his glove again.

He switched the ball back.

Three strikes on three pitches. Up in Minneapolis Jack was feeling it. Here in Lisa's backyard, he was feeling it. They were in the zone. He went back to the mound to wait. The next batter stepped into the box and it began anew.

"Swing and a miss, Mavis touched ninety-eight on that fastball."

Thump. The ball hit his glove.

Again.

"Strike two! He chased on the slider."

Thump.

And again.

"Locked him up! Called strike three! That's two down on six pitches!"

Thump.

He switched the ball to his throwing hand but didn't return to his makeshift mound. He walked around it instead. Here in the backyard, some fifty miles south of the ballpark, he could feel the pressure. He couldn't even fathom how guys like Jack could handle it. It must be intense, but that was what made the game great. He devoured anything that had to do with baseball and he knew what an immaculate inning was. Three strikeouts on nine straight pitches happened, but it was rare. It was like being witness to a triple play, or an in-the-park homerun.

But he was getting ahead of himself.

In the time that he had been roaming around his makeshift mound the opposing manager had opted for a pinch hitter to avoid the lefty-on-lefty matchup and now the new hitter stepped into the batter's box and dug in. Along with Mavis, he took his own place and prepared to pitch. In unison they took the sign, nodded, and went into the wind-up.

"Another swing and a miss!"

Thump.

The intensity of the crowd kicked up yet another notch. They were on their feet but he didn't need the radio to tell him that. He could see it. His fantasy had blended with the reality seamlessly and Lisa's backyard was no more.

Jack went into his motion. He did the same.

"Strike two! Mavis elevated the fastball and Escobar swung at a pitch that was up in his eyes!"

Thump.

Again, he stepped off the mound. He removed his ball cap and wiped his brow with his forearm. They were one strike away from not only an immaculate inning but moving on in the playoffs as well. He replaced his ball cap and fought down the excitement that was trying to engulf him. He took his spot and waited. Provo announced to him that Jack toed the rubber and shook off the first sign again.

Together they shook off the second one.

"Come on Hardy, give him the fastball," he muttered into the night air.

"Hardy sets the sign and Jack gives him the nod, and here's the pitch."

They went into their wind-up. They kicked their legs in tandem, their arms come over the top, and then the ball was in flight.

As the pitch came out of his hand, Danny Boyd knew it wasn't right. Time slipped and it took forever for the orb to travel the sixty feet to the plate. He could hear the crowd roaring through the radio. The entirety of the world stood still and the rubber band that was time stretched. It stretched right up to the breaking point, but it held, it did not fracture. And then it shot back into true and the ball crossed the plate.

"Strike three! Strike three!" Provo screamed through the radio. "Mavis burned him with the flamethrower! We're moving on and Jack Mavis just tossed an immaculate inning to make it happen!"

Danny's own ball hit the pitch-back wrong.

It had dropped from high to low in the strike zone and missed the sweet spot. It rocketed up in the air and over his head. He whipped around and watched it go, like a home run ball, sailing off into the darkness of the woods.

He walked, dazed, out to the edge of the throw of light and stopped.

Provo and the Dazzle-Man were going nuts on the radio behind him but now he felt detached. He was excited, and glad there would be another game in a couple of days, but that last pitch altered him somehow, blunting the enthusiasm that he should be feeling. He looked back at the radio, at the pitch-back, at his imaginary created environment, and then he returned his gaze to the woods.

He stared out into the dark, into the heart of the night, a land of shadows.

And then he stepped out of the light.

2

Danny had a rough idea of how deep the ball should've gone based on its trajectory when he lost sight of it, unless it had hit a tree. It could've ricocheted in any direction if that had happened. He hoped it hadn't. About twenty yards into the woods the terrain started to drop, becoming a hill. If the ball had landed this far out it could've rolled, down, further into the murky dark. At the top of the descent he looked around.

There was no sign of the ball, just trees.

Dark, gnarly-looking trees.

Danny turned back toward the house. The forestry was obscuring his view but he could still see the light from the patio. He gave another quick look around him for the baseball but saw nothing. He turned and faced back down the hill. The shadows began to creep and his skin began to crawl. He didn't like it out here, out past the warm comforting glow of the light. He let out a long slow breath, muscled up his courage, and started down the hill.

There was nothing to be afraid of. It was just trees after all. And the dark.

Just as he began to scuffle down the incline, he thought he saw something move on his right. He snapped his head around in that direction. In that first moment, as his vision settled, the dark played all manner of nasty tricks on him. Danny Boyd saw a wicked variety of potential, half-formed horrors. But then his eyes adjusted and those awful momentary visions settled into the shadows they were.

Just shadows.

But was any shadow really *just* a shadow? The apparitions of the night changed and morphed in a constant scrum around him, never settling enough for him to truly trust his eyes. He knew in his head that there was nothing there, that it was just his mind tempting him to follow the clearly blazed trail that descended into irrational fear. His head knew that, but his heart seemed unable to decipher the difference.

It began its attempts to race its way out of his chest. Again, he breathed deep and attempted to rein in its gallop. He managed a degree of success and it slowed, or at least he was able to convince himself it had slowed.

He started down the slope again.

And then he slipped.

His feet came out from underneath him as if propelled. His tether to the earth severed for the moment. He then reconnected seconds later with a jarring force. He landed hard on his butt. The impact on his tailbone reverberated up his spine with an intensity that he could feel in his teeth. He slid a few more feet down the hill, scraping his sides. Sticks and twigs and other debris clawed at his skin as his shirt pulled up toward his armpits. Moments later the slide ended and he came to rest breathing hard. He squeezed his eyes shut tight against the sudden sting of tears.

Danny cracked his eyelids the slightest bit but the world was awash and he could feel wetness running over and down onto his cheeks. He clamped his eyes shut again and turned his head to the side. He could feel the unforgiving ground on his left cheek and focused on it, willing the tears away. After a few hard, halting breaths he felt some semblance of control return. He opened his eyes again and his vision was no longer obscured.

And his baseball lay on the hill, no more than a few feet in front of him.

He scrambled to his feet and shuffled over to it wiping at his eyes. His backside was causing him some serious discomfort. He walked back and forth a couple of times in an attempt to alleviate some of the pain and had a modicum of success. Looking back up the hill, he found the warm glow of the patio light was now nothing more than a memory, the grade of the land effectively extinguishing it from his view. A glance around at the forestry enveloping him raised his heart rate again and he had to remind himself that there was nothing to be scared of.

It was just those trees. Something about the disjointed nature of the branches caused his skin to tighten and the little hairs upon it to stand on end. He physically shook off these symptoms and that's when he heard it.

It was the soft, slow, rumble of water rushing in the distance and drifting up to him from further down the slope.

The river.

Danny knew that Lisa's land butted up against the Mississippi but he'd never been this deep into the woods before. He'd never seen it. He also knew he was not supposed to be out this far, not without his dad. But that sound, it seemed to have its own gravitational pull and against his better judgment he started down towards it, the literal pain in his butt forgotten for the moment.

He shuffled his way down the slope until the land levelled out. Following the soft rushing sound of the flowing water he travelled deeper into the woods. He stopped well short of the embankment where it dropped off, leading down to the riverbank.

The Mighty Mississippi spread out below him.

It rolled gently, but his dad had told him about the

current. About how it could grab you and pull you. Pull you with it even though the water seemed so calm, so serene. He stared into the deceptive black water and watched it as it slipped on by, running south on its way to warmer climes.

<u>3</u>

Tim Boyd sat at the little café booth in Lisa's kitchen that served as her breakfast nook. He sat and waited. And as he waited, his patience waned.

He couldn't see Danny outside but he could see the ball popping up off the pitch-back and out of his view from the kitchen window. The game had to be between innings as Danny's pitches would never arc like that if the action was on. The kid had some skills. Not that he thought his boy would be going pro or anything like that but he could maybe play college ball, possibly get a scholarship. Assuming he could keep his child-like love of the game for that long, that his love for baseball could outlast the various pitfalls of adolescence.

He checked the score on his phone and saw that the boys were holding a one-run lead going into the ninth. He smiled to himself, forgetting Lisa and his frustration for a moment. The lead meant that Jack Mavis would be taking the mound and Danny would be losing his little mind. The ball stopped popping up and he knew Danny was preparing for Jack to take the field.

From the other room he heard Lisa signing off of the call she was on and the small smile slipped from his face.

She walked back into the kitchen and sat down across from him. He drained the rest of his beer and got up. He walked to the sink to rinse the empty bottle and toss it in the recycling.

"You want another beer?" he asked.

"No, I'm good."

"Great." The response bordered on sarcastic.

He returned to the table and sat down.

She gave him a look, a look that he knew better than to

press but he just couldn't bring himself to let his slow smoldering anger go. Not just yet.

"Sorry," he said, but with only slightly less sarcasm than the previous statement.

That look, the one that should have been heeded in the first place, hardened and he knew he'd pushed his luck. Further than was necessary, probably, if the truth were to be told.

He softened his stance and attempted a more genuine apology.

"Look, I am sorry. I don't mean to be a jerk about him, but when you're throwing him in my face—"

"Throwing him in your face?" She didn't raise her voice, but voiced her displeasure with him all the same. "I took a phone call, a phone call from one of my best and oldest friends."

And so they'd found their way back to a topic they had exhausted countless times, her best friend, Stanley 'Stas' Mileski. The two of them had been friends since they were kids but the tenure of their relationship mattered little when weighed against Tim's mounting frustration.

Stan Mileski was a Pole from the old Nordeast neighborhood of Minneapolis. Stas was short for Stasiu which was Stanley in Polish. He could have just gone by Stan but he didn't, he was called Stas. Tim found it all a little too precious.

But Stas was Lisa's best friend. And in his head Tim knew that was just what they were, friends and nothing more. But in that spot where that little coal of anger had been forged, forged and stoked by the bellows of jealousy, that which his head knew to be true held little water.

Against better judgment, he continued.

"Yeah, you took his call, like you always take his calls. No matter what, whether I'm here or not, if we're in the middle of something, whatever, you take his call."

He had elevated his voice, just a little, but it was enough. Unbeknownst to him, outside Danny had noticed and it had broken his concentration. Inside, across the table from him, Lisa's gaze changed. It lost intensity but didn't soften. It steeled.

"I think I'll have that beer after all," she said, slowly rising from the table and going to the fridge. She didn't ask him if he wanted one as well. She didn't look at him. Instead she grabbed her beer, popped the cap off and walked to the sink. She took a long pull from the bottleneck and looked out the window, out into the night, out into nothing. The window at the sink faced the side yard, not the back where Danny was playing. She probably wouldn't have been able to see him even if she was looking right at him, though. Her mind was elsewhere.

"I'm sorry," Tim said from the table. "And I mean that, I *am* sorry, but I also meant what I said. We've talked about it a hundred times..."

"That's just the problem, Tim, we have talked about it a hundred times and it never seems to make a difference." She didn't sound exactly angry, a little maybe, but exasperation was the overriding factor coloring her tone at the moment. "And my relationship with Stas is not going to change. I understand that it's difficult for you but I don't know how else to tell you. He's no threat to you or any relationship we have."

"If you understand that it's difficult for me, why is it so goddamn hard to compromise a little and not take his phone calls when I'm here?"

She turned to him and the steel in her eyes had cooled further and hardened, becoming something even less malleable and more immovable. She leaned her butt back against the counter and took another sip of her beer but her eyes never moved from his. It was the moment to let this go, to let it go and move on. Move on as he had countless times before, every time in fact that the tiresome topic of his girlfriend's best friend inevitably arose.

And it was inevitable. It would always be back. *He* would always be back.

And Tim had just maybe had enough.

He was on the precipice, teetering on the ledge. A ledge they had formed together slowly over the last year and a half.

First as friends, then growing and shaping into something much more than that over the last few months. But now the footing beneath him had grown untrustworthy. He could feel it wanting to give, to let go beneath his feet. Without even realizing it on a conscious level, he made the decision to step off into the abyss of his own accord. He wouldn't wait for the foundation to just let him go, crumbling to nothing and catching him by surprise.

He opened his mouth to say something. Quite possibly to verbalize the dagger that would strike their beautiful but fragile courtship down.

He was waylaid before he could drive the knife in.

Her eyes had shifted away from his and the words died in his throat as he watched her. The steel ran out of her in an instant and was replaced with an immediate concern. She was now looking out the window that faced the backyard.

"Where's Danny?" she asked.

Any anger Tim Boyd had been harboring evaporated. He stood and looked out the window as well and realized his boy was nowhere to be seen. The pitch-back stood alone in the pool of light, punctuating the otherwise empty space of the illuminated patio area. It created a stark relief against the darkness of the forest enveloping it.

"He knows better than to be off in those woods," Tim said to himself as much as anyone else. The momentary paralysis caused by Danny's absence from the yard passed and they both moved at once for the back door.

"Danny!" Tim called as he came through the door. He put a tone of irritation into his voice to let his son know he was displeased with this variance to the well-stated rules.

"Danny!" he shouted again when no response came. His voice was now tinged with a slight urgency that had not been affected intentionally.

From what seemed a far-away distance, he registered the hubbub coming from the radio. The level of jubilation and histrionics coming from the announcers led him to believe that the outcome of the game had been favorable. That only fueled his consternation. There was no fathomable reason that Danny would have abandoned his station and missed the post-game celebration.

"Danny!" His and Lisa's voices rang through the darkened wood as one. They looked to each other and without the necessity of words struck off into the woods in different directions calling his name.

With every few seconds that passed the level of fear gripping Tim, no matter how potentially irrational, ratcheted. First to what he would've thought an inconceivable plateau, and then bounding beyond. He stumbled and went to a knee as the panic began its slow squeeze in his chest. He rose quickly and hollered Danny's name again. Horrendous images and dark ideas that he wouldn't have normally entertained scurried about on the periphery of his mind, attempting to find purchase.

Threatening to tense and bite, and begin to tear.

Then Lisa's voice, full and rich, boomed out from somewhere to his left.

"Tim, he's here. I've got him."

"Danny!" Tim yelped as he changed direction and bolted through the trees toward the sound of her voice.

He reached them in a matter of seconds. Lisa stood with her arm around Danny. They were a reasonable distance from the embankment leading down to the river, but too close for Tim's comfort nonetheless. When he saw Tim, Danny broke from Lisa and ran to him. Tim dropped to a knee and engulfed his son in his arms, hugging him tight. He looked at Lisa over Danny's shoulder and his heart lurched. Her emotional state, the care and love in her eyes, made him feel a little pathetic for whatever petty qualms he had been giving voice to just moments ago.

He could afford it no more thought than that, though, before his attention returned to Danny.

"Are you okay?"

"I'm fine, Dad."

"What are you doing out here? Why didn't you answer us?"

"My ball flew out into the woods and I went to find it. I heard the river and I couldn't help it, I just had to look. I know I'm not supposed to, I'm sorry, Dad." The last came out in a rush as Danny buried his head in Tim's shoulder, stifling tears.

"It's alright, buddy, you just scared us for a second."

Lisa stepped over to them and gently rubbed Danny's head while Tim held him. After a moment Danny released his father and leaned back, wiping a few tears from his eyes.

"Did you hear we won the game?" he asked, a slight grin skirting its way across his little face.

Tim couldn't help but smile. "I did, buddy. Jack shut her down, eh?"

"Sure did, just like always."

"Alright, let's go back to the house."

They turned and walked away, leaving the river to rush on behind them, and strode off toward the house. Lisa a little in front, Tim with his arm still around his boy, trailing slightly behind her. An easy calm started to settle down around them now that the momentary scare had passed. They walked together, like a family, back towards the house. They weren't yet, there were still many hurdles to be cleared, but it seemed possible to Tim that they might still be able to get there.

They walked through the silent woods resembling, in many ways, a little familial unit.

As they walked, Lisa looked straight ahead or sometimes back at the boys, tossing a quick smile in their direction. She never cast even the slightest gaze to her left, which gave them no reason to look in that direction either.

Not that there was anything to see over there.

Just an old shed, running to ruin.

A rickety old outpost that seemed to have seen no love in decades.

Except maybe that wasn't exactly accurate. It did look rickety. It did *look* like it was running to ruin. But there was a brand-new padlock clasped on the door shining in the slight moonlight. A brand-new padlock keeping whatever was locked away inside shut out from the rest of the world.

Red Wing...
Spring, 2017

<u>1</u>

The winter passed as they do in the deep north - long, quiet, and cold. But the calendar flips, eventually. Crushing, frigid temperatures and short days at last begin to give way and the hibernation slowly comes to an end. A higher and closer sun begins to melt the snow pack encasing the earth and the slough can be heard running from the eaves of homes and back into the softening soil. Spring, as the calendar defines it, is no guarantee that Old Man Winter will loosen his stranglehold at once, but hope springs eternal. For the trio that included the two Boyd boys and Lisa Lathrop the slow nature of the winter season had been good. It mellowed and blunted emotions that might have been driven too hard by the stifling heat and humidity of summer. The time spent in close proximity and the relative isolation from the outside world had strengthened the bond between them that had seemed so tenuous a few short months earlier.

The lack of proximity to one Stas Mileski did much to help as well.

Not that he was out of the picture, that would never happen, but his presence was less palpable. Whether she had heeded Tim's request or something had just changed, contact between she and Stas had become infrequent, or at the very least was handled out of Tim's purview. And on the flipside, the slow months spent together and the relaxed comfort they had developed in their own atmosphere had dulled his jealousy as well.

Stas on the periphery was something that he found he could handle, that he could accept even. And once acceptance had been solidified, the baggage he had shouldered and carried had begun to slip away. On a beautiful March morning Tim decided to take a step that he previously wouldn't have been able to fathom. He would take an interest in her old friend.

Outside, the sun was shining.

Sunny and pushing fifty degrees on a late March morning in Minnesota could be magical. Nowhere near that which most would consider idyllic, but the contrast to the freezing wind chills and frigid temps they had just weathered was so glaring that it suddenly felt like the heart of summer was upon them. Any small piles of snow still hanging on were melting. Another dumping of snow was not only not out of the question, it was probable, but this time of year it wouldn't last long.

Spring Training was in full swing, pushing toward the season opener, and Danny was ready to get out and play ball. After the epic performance that had propelled them on in the playoffs last year the squad had fallen short, but a new season was upon them and with it came new hope. Tim had pulled the pitch-back out of Lisa's garage first thing that morning and Danny was already out in the yard warming up. Starting with a slow toss and working his arm back into condition.

Tim and Lisa were again sitting at her breakfast nook.

Across the table he faced the woman he was quite possibly coming to love. He looked her in the eye and prepared not only to accept the inevitability of her best friend in his life, but to go a step further and attempt to invest.

"I want to ask you something," he said.

"Okay," she replied, but tentatively. Something in his

tone must have tipped her off that it wasn't going to be a frivolous question.

"It's about Stas." He smiled in an attempt to telegraph that there would be no aggression in the question but something in her eyes contracted and he knew her guard was coming up. "It's nothing bad," he added but she still wasn't buying it. "I promise." The worry line at her eyes smoothed but he had the distinct feeling she had to make it do so, it hadn't happened naturally.

"Alright." She was unable to cover the hesitancy that was still quite present.

"Seriously, I just want to know about him."

"You want to know about Stas?"

"Yeah. It's just..." He stumbled over his words for a moment, the right ones eluding him. Her gaze softened as she realized he really was trying and that this wasn't necessarily easy for him. "Look, I know I have two choices," he said. "I can keep being jealous and childish about him and risk eventually losing you or I can accept that he'll be a part of my life if I'm going to continue to be a part of yours. And I intend to remain a part of your life for as long as you'll put up with me, so I guess I should probably make an attempt to learn a little bit about the guy."

She smiled, and it was genuine. She reached across the table and took his hand. She held it tight. It was actually a fair amount of expression for a woman who in general went pretty light on the touchy-feely affairs of their romance.

"What do you want to know?"

"I don't know. I guess we should start at the beginning. I know you've known him forever, but how long *is* forever?"

She wiped at her left eye. No tear had actually tumbled but a glassy sheen had filled them both, the emotion of the moment trying to get the best of her. "I met him in 1987," she started. "I was ten years old, he was eight. My parents worked for a summer resort, a lake place, up north and in '87 his family started spending summers there. For two years we spent almost every waking moment of every summer together."

"Two years?"

"Yeah. They were good times; long idle days, making our own fun because there was nothing else to do." She faltered. "And then they stopped coming." She drifted off and seemed far away for a moment.

When he realized she wasn't going to continue, he attempted to help, to fill the space. "But you guys stayed in touch, even at such a young age? That's pretty cool."

"No, actually we didn't see or talk to each other for ten years." She was still distant, her focus elsewhere, lost perhaps in a time long ago. And again, she seemed disinclined to continue, leaving Tim to fill the void.

"So…did you just run into him again ten years later?"

"No." She paused and struggled for a moment for the right way to put it. "I guess you could just say we found each other."

"Okay…and you guys laughed about the good ol' days and the rest was history, or what?"

"Not quite." Her voice took on a slight underlying tone of bitterness that seemed to him to be incongruent.

"Not quite?" he asked and expelled a short, confused laugh.

Lisa looked away again as she was obviously preparing to tell him something, something that was of great import to her. The moment that had bonded her to a man called Stas with such strength that he would now and forever be a part of Tim's life as well. Tim was surprised to find that Lisa did not seem pleased to be ruminating on that moment. He was also surprised to find that he sincerely did not like the idea that whatever she was about to say caused such a reaction in her.

And that was when he realized he probably had the whole thing wrong.

That whatever it was that had cemented them to each other for the rest of their lives had not been some joyous magical moment at all, but probably quite the opposite. It was going to be something terrible or tragic. He was about to tell her to stop, that he didn't need to know, but before he could spit it out, she went on.

"It happened that last summer. He was almost the same age that Danny is now and he nearly drowned. It was pretty early in the morning, I don't even know why he was out by the pond that early. I just happened to have woken up early as well. When I couldn't fall back asleep, I decided to go out for a walk… And if I hadn't, he would've died."

She stopped. Tim thought about interjecting again but this time the empty space between her words seemed necessary.

"It was not long after dawn. It wasn't dark outside but not like full daylight either. It was ethereal, like the darkness was still finishing the process of sneaking away." She spoke with such clarity and recall of the moment that it sent a small shiver down Tim's back. He thought again about trying to stop her but he couldn't deny that part of him did want to hear it.

"I was walking along the lake. Past the end of the beach there were trees that filled in along the shoreline, and from there a little path ran off through the woods. At the end of that path, on the other side of the little stand of trees, was a pond with a small dock for fishing. For whatever reason, I walked back towards it. As I approached the pond, I heard light splashing. At first, I thought it was just fish jumping but it kept happening, rapidly. When I got there, I don't know what I expected to see…but it most certainly wasn't a human hand breaking the plane of the water. It kept shooting up and slapping at the surface."

She stopped speaking for a moment. She was no longer present in her kitchen. Her mind was years and miles away. Tim kept his mouth shut and waited until she was ready.

"For a moment I just stood there, paralyzed by fear and surprise. But then, with a suddenness I will never forget, everything went silent and the slapping stopped. The surface of the lake rippled and then smoothed and I snapped out of it. I ran to the end of the dock and dove in fully clothed. He was fully clothed as well. I don't know what the hell he was doing out there but he must have fallen off the dock and then had somehow gotten tangled in the tall weeds at the bottom of the little lake. They were tangled all around his legs and ankles, holding him under. I had my fish knife on me and was able to cut him free. We made it back to the little dock but he didn't have the energy to climb up so I dragged him to the shore and ran for help. He'd swallowed some water but otherwise was basically fine. Had he been down there for another couple of minutes though…"

She trailed off and the tears she'd been stifling brimmed and slipped over, running down her face. She made no attempt to curb their flow. "His parents collected their stuff and put him in the car. A bunch of the adults had convened in the main lodge. I wanted to talk to him but everyone told me to go to my room. I left, but didn't go to my room. I stayed close enough to eavesdrop. His parents came back in and I heard them yelling at mine, I heard my name and for years I thought they blamed me."

"Blamed you? For what?"

"Oh, I don't know. I was twelve years old. Rational thought wasn't playing a part in it."

"For ten years you thought that?"

She nodded and put her hand up to cover her eyes as the real onslaught of tears began. She sat that way, crying hard but without the dramatics of sobbing, as silent as the breeze. He squeezed her other hand, the one still holding his, and thought about going to her side of the table. To hold her tight, as tight as he had ever held anyone with the exception of Danny, but he knew her well enough to know that would be way too much attention paid to her in this moment of weakness. So he sat, sat and held the one hand that she had offered him and he waited.

It didn't take long, but for Tim it was an eternity. She took a deep breath, wiped her eyes with the hand covering them and looked away. After another deep breath she turned to him achieving a moderate level of composure. Not much, but some.

"I'm sorry," she said through a sad little laugh.

"Jesus, Lisa, don't be sorry. I'm sorry, that's a terrible

story. We don't have to talk about this anymore."

"No, you deserve to know. The hard part is over, saying it out loud. I just hate thinking about that moment." Tim said nothing; there was nothing to say. He had seen first-hand just how much she hated it. She went on. "I didn't know it at the time but that terrible morning formed a bond between us that, like it or not, we were stuck with. Ten years later, my parents had died and my life was in shambles. That's when we reconnected."

And just like that they had stumbled into another topic on which she was generally mum. Tim had always wondered about her parents. She never spoke of them. Apparently, they had both died, and relatively close to each other if it was within ten years. Intrigue tried to get the better of him but he decided that now was not the appropriate time to press her into another trip down memory lane. Maybe she'd get to it herself.

"Stas helped me through that time. I was just twenty-two years old." She paused again and Tim thought maybe she would actually elaborate on the subject of her parents.

She did not.

Again she did not sob, didn't even hitch, just closed her eyes against a fresh bout of tears but was unable to stop them. Tim had seen enough. Damn her strength and her sensibilities, he dropped the hand he was holding, moved to her side of the bench and folded her into his arms.

<u>2</u>

Eventually Lisa pulled herself together.

While in general her stoic nature had no interest in the outpouring of emotion she had demonstrated or the empathy it had kindled in Tim, she realized that she did appreciate his show of affection and had maybe even needed it.

On some level she found that worrisome.

Once the fountain of tears had been extinguished and a semblance of normalcy had returned, she and the boys had gone into town for lunch. They drove into the township of Red

Wing separately as Tim and Danny would be heading back up to the Cities directly after lunch. It turned out lunch was a continued elixir. Danny had them both laughing until their bellies hurt and when they parted ways it was the same as usual. A bit of sadness at the parting but the overriding emotion was one of profound happiness. They would be together again soon and to be together was what felt most right these days.

Lisa climbed back into her SUV and headed out of town driving south on Highway 61 back toward home. She tossed her phone on the passenger seat; sometimes Danny would send a parting text from Tim's phone and she liked to read them as they popped up on the display.

Ten minutes later her phone chirped. It wasn't the text alert though, it was ringing. She grabbed it off the seat and checked the ID. No contact info was displayed, just a number. Not a random number, though. It bore a 320 area code and the number alone was as good as a contact name. She exhaled a long slow breath and hit the 'accept' button on the display.

"This is Lisa."

She listened.

"I'm in the car now. I should be back to my place in ten minutes."

Again, she listened.

"Tonight, or tomorrow?"

Then, once again, the silence on her end filled the vehicle for a moment.

"I'll be ready."

She pressed the 'End Call' button, terminating the conversation. She then applied a slight increase of pressure to the pedal beneath her right foot. Eight minutes later she pulled up in front of her garage at the end of her driveway. Lisa exited the vehicle and without even realizing it, she shot a quick glance around the yard effectively checking the perimeter. She then entered the house.

In the kitchen she reached her slight hand and wrist into the small space between the refrigerator and the cabinet that housed it. After a moment of fumbling blindly along the back of the appliance her hand stumbled upon that which she sought. Being very careful not to let it fall between the fridge and the wall as she slid it out, she removed a little black box, a magnetic Hide-a-Key. She slipped the key out of the case and walked out the door into her backyard.

Walking down toward the river, again Lisa's eyes darted around her, canvassing the trees as she walked among them. Through the woods she trod, deeper and deeper but not all the way down to the river. Before she reached the Mighty Mississippi she veered to her right and walked down to her rickety old shed.

That rickety old shed with the shiny new padlock.

At the door she stopped and inserted the key, popped the lock open, and threw wide the doors to the darkness inside.

<u>3</u>

Three days later Tim Boyd was walking back to his office from a lunch meeting when his phone rang. He checked it but saw a number he didn't recognize and it didn't have the prefix for Danny's school so he opted for the ignore function. He rarely got calls from people he didn't know. When he did it was usually someone who wanted his money. He was raising a boy on his own. No matter how honorable whatever the cause of the caller might have been, he had very little dough to spare these days for any charity that wasn't he and Danny.

Back at his cubicle the rest of the day passed as most of them did lately, as time killed. Getting through work, getting Danny through school, it was all just killing time, working their way to the weekend so they could get back to Red Wing. Lisa's house was feeling more and more like home to both of them than the little townhouse in which they passed the weekdays. They lived in Eagan, a suburb on the southern end of the Twin Cities metro area, but they were finding themselves drawn to the south and the small town living of Lisa's place as opposed to the north and the urban lifestyle of the Cities.

A real move was something to which he was giving

some serious thought. Danny had friends at school but none that he would be horrified to leave, and he was outgoing. Making friends wasn't hard for him. The longer Tim waited, though, the more difficult it was likely to become. If he waited until Danny was closer to finishing elementary school, he would run the risk of him wanting to stay with his friends and it wouldn't be fair to make him move, not right before starting middle school. It would be an easier transition if it happened sooner. He laughed to himself. It didn't seem that ridiculous to think about maybe moving in with Lisa now, but that night last October when Danny disappeared down to the river, it couldn't have been further from his mind.

He reeled himself back from his reverie, looked at the clock, and saw it was almost 4:30. Time effectively killed. He shut down his computer, grabbed his stuff and headed down to the parking lot. He tossed his bag in the backseat and pulled his phone out as he climbed into the car. He had one voicemail. He barely remembered his phone ringing after lunch. He could probably just erase it but you never know, best to give it a listen.

He hit play and a man's voice addressed him.

"Hey, Tim, this is Stas…Stan Mileski. We've never met but, ah, I was just wondering if you've talked to Lisa lately. I was supposed to get in touch with her yesterday…" Tim felt a stab of jealousy that he hated, but it was there just the same. It vanished quickly, "but I haven't heard from her. I've called her a couple times and got nothing. Have her give me a call if you talk to her, would ya?"

The line went dead. Tim sat there in his car, in the parking lot with the phone up to his ear without moving. When was the last time he'd talked to Lisa? Was it yesterday? No, it was the day before yesterday.

Feeling a slight hint of anxiousness he scrolled to her number and hit 'call.'

He got her voicemail.

He dialed again.

Again, the call went straight to voicemail.

His anxiety climbed a notch. He was probably overreacting but the fact that Stas had resorted to calling him was leaving him feeling uneasy, rattled.

He scrolled to a different number. Tina Lawson, the neighbor who watched Danny after school until he got home, picked up on the second ring. He was in luck and she said she'd be fine to watch Danny for a while. Tim reiterated that he was driving down to Red Wing and that it might be kind of late by the time he returned. She assured him it was no problem. She was a sweet lady. A sweet lady who understood the trials and pitfalls of single parenting, and he couldn't have been more thankful for her help at that moment.

He hit the highway heading south and the speedometer shot to ten over the speed limit. Seconds later it had climbed to fifteen over. He did his best to keep his eyes wide and alert for officers of the law who might impede his progress but his luck would have to hold, his focus was teetering towards freefall.

Thirty-three minutes later he slowed as he came into Red Wing proper. He took the opportunity to call Lisa again. And again, he got only the pre-recorded sound of her voice telling him to leave a message. What were the chances anything had happened to her? Slim; it was probably just some sort of misunderstanding. Maybe something was wrong with her phone. That was most likely the case but he couldn't manage to mount a convincing case for it in his own head. He reached the southern end of town and the speed limit went back up to 55mph from 35mph. The needle on Tim's dashboard jumped.

For the last stretch of highway he gave up what little concern he had for lurking police. He drove as fast as traffic would allow and reached her house in less than ten minutes. He wheeled in hard, passing the mailbox and kicking up dirt and gravel that had collected at the end of her driveway.

Seconds later he screeched to a halt in front of the garage and his hard-hitting heart caught in his throat.

Lisa was sitting in the swing on her front porch.

She looked tired but other than that she seemed to be fine. He hopped out of the car and ran up the steps to the porch. She looked at him and he saw the surprise register in her eyes at seeing him there on a Wednesday evening, but the exhaustion seemed to override the shock.

"Are you okay?" he asked.

"I'm fine, what are you doing here?" She had just claimed to be fine but her voice was thin and reedy.

"I couldn't get a hold of you... I called… Are you sure you're okay? You look beat, honey."

She smiled, "I'm fine." And her voice sounded stronger. A little bit anyway. "I'm so sorry you had to come all the way down here. I've had a long couple of days and I haven't been sleeping and I guess I must have let my phone die. I've been so busy I haven't even looked at it. I'm sorry."

"It's alright." He went and sat next to her on the swing. She took his arm, put it around her shoulders and laid her head on his chest. Another show of affection, maybe her gruff exterior was starting to crack just a bit. He craned his neck to look at her. She was smiling but her eyes were still distant and she really did look exhausted. "What have you been so busy with?"

"Oh, you know, the life of a landscape designer in the spring. It's when all the heavy lifting gets done. I have a client that's a real ball buster. Nothing's working for her."

"I'm sorry, kiddo, and you haven't been sleeping?"

From off in the distance behind her house he heard the receding engine of a motorboat drifting through the air from somewhere on the river.

"No, it's been a little hellish. I really do feel bad that you had to drive all the way down here. How long have you been trying to get a hold of me?"

"Just since I left work. What really got me worked up is that Stas was worried enough to call me. He said he was supposed to talk to you yesterday and hadn't heard from you."

"Sonuvabitch!" she barked and he was relieved to hear she really did sound more like herself. And truth be told, he derived a wee bit of pleasure from the fact that she could be busy enough to forget about talking to Stas. Then she laughed which warmed his heart even further.

"What's so funny?" he asked, smiling a bit now himself.

"So, are you and Stas gonna start chatting now? Are you guys gonna be all buddy-buddy and start excluding me?" She gave him a playful punch in the thigh.

"I wouldn't worry about that. I don't think we're quite there yet." But he said it through a smile and he found that he was happy to be able to joke about it.

"Can I make you some dinner since I made you run all the way down here?"

"I wish I could. The neighbor lady has Danny so I should probably get back."

"I'm so sorry, Tim." She sat up and looked at him.

"I'm just glad you're alright." He gave her a kiss, not a passionate kiss, but it was sweet and it lingered, neither of them really wanting to let go. He pulled back and looked at her. She was beautiful but she really did look worn down. "Get some sleep, kid, and I'll see you on Friday," he said as he stood and stepped off the porch.

"Will do, boss. Oh hey, any chance we could find someone to watch Danny on Friday night? There's a show coming through town I want to see, at the Sheldon in Red Wing."

"That's April 2nd, right?" He took a second to consult his mental calendar. "I bet I can find someone to watch him. That sounds fun."

"See ya then, babe."

"Not if I see you first," he said, laughing as he slid behind the wheel. He rolled down the window. "Oh, and you should maybe give Stas a call and let him know you're still alive." He winked at her.

"I will." She blew him a kiss. He pretended to catch it and waved as he turned the car around and headed back down the driveway.

As his car drifted out of view her smile faltered. She waited another couple of seconds and then pulled her phone, her fully charged phone, from her pocket. She scrolled through the missed calls from Tim and Stas to the number with no name and the 320 area code attached to it and hit 'Call.'

An anonymous voice answered, "Hello."

Into the phone Lisa said, "We're clear for now...but there may be a complication."

"Yeah?"

"Yeah." Lisa paused. "There's more to the package than we previously expected."

Lisa listened while the person on the other end of the line responded.

"It could be good for us," she said, "but there is no longer any chance that our involvement will go unnoticed."

"Do we need to be worried?" the disembodied voice asked.

"We'd be stupid not to be. We're going to have to be very cautious. I'll be in touch when I know more."

She terminated the call and dropped the phone in her lap. The budding but still bare branches of the trees lining the empty driveway rustled in the breeze. She leaned back in the swing and released a long, slow sigh.

4

Friday rolled around. Tim had arranged for Danny to spend the night with one of his friends. He dropped him off, said his goodbyes and hit the road a little after six to meet Lisa at the Sheldon Theatre in downtown Red Wing.

By the time he left town the temperature had begun to slip. The sky darkened, the cloud cover became heavy, and that snow that had disappeared so quickly with the spring thaw was threatening to return. When he arrived at the theatre a little over a half-hour later the temperature had dropped into the mid-thirties and a light sleet had begun to mist the roads, making them slick. If it continued to get colder, and he feared it would, it could make the trip back to Lisa's after the show treacherous.

The Sheldon was a beautifully refurbished opera house

that often hosted touring theatre shows. This evening's performance was a musical adaptation of Howard Mohr's book *How to Talk Minnesotan*, a delightful romp discussing the particular idiosyncrasies of the native folk. Lisa had seen it during its original run at the Plymouth Playhouse in Minneapolis. When she saw that the touring version would be coming through town, she thought Tim would love it. It was one of those things where, if you grew up in the culture represented, you could find myriad examples of your own friends and family.

Tim met her in the lobby and saw right away that Lisa looked better than she had on Wednesday when he'd left her house. She must have gotten some sleep. A healthy modicum of heavy laughter during the show helped even further, for both of them. When they left the theatre arm in arm afterward, they were laughing back and forth and the warmth radiated from within.

And they needed that little flush as well, because they stepped out onto the sidewalk and into a full-blown early April snow storm. Reluctantly they dropped each other's arms, pulled their light spring coats tight around them and put a hustle in their step on the way to the tavern down the street.

They reached the bar and he held the door for her as she rushed through, big fat snowflakes adhering to her hair and coat. They grabbed a booth, ordered a beer and took in the joint. The jukebox was rocking and a small dance floor was partially filled with folks their age and older dancing, or attempting to anyway. It was the kind of place where the people watching was ripe. They'd been here a number of times before. It was probably their most regular spot to grab a drink when someone else was watching Danny.

Their beers were delivered. They saluted each other, clinked glasses and sat back, happy to be spectators for the moment.

A few minutes later the raucous tune that had been pumping through the old tired sound system came to a close. The folks on the floor and a few of the other patrons sitting on the periphery applauded a band that was nowhere near this little small-town dive bar. Lisa clapped loudly as well but not for some band playing in absentia, she clapped for the dancers. Those people who were reliving some of their youth, dancing to some rhythm that only they could hear. At least it appeared that way based on how they swayed and stepped on beats that were never the same and yet somehow always managed to elude the two and the four.

The opening strains of some clichéd slow song filled the room and most of the dance floor cleared. The exception being a few couples who clung to each other as if clinging to life itself, perhaps even in a literal sense when it came to one of the couples. Lisa and Tim turned from the floor and to each other.

They chatted for a few minutes rehashing the show and their favorite parts. The *a capella* ice fishing song seemed to be the favorite between the two of them. They laughed over some of the funnier bits and then settled into a comfortable silence as they sipped their beers. Lisa turned her attention to the dance floor again and Tim to the sudden winter wonderland coming to fruition outside the front window.

"Snow's starting to pile up," he observed.

"Yeah, maybe we should leave your Honda here and you can drive back with me."

"And risk being seen in that gas guzzling monstrosity?" He liked to give her a hard time about the big SUV she drove. It was a little joke between them. He knew she needed it for work. Sometimes she had to haul all sorts of materials to her landscaping jobsites but he liked to poke fun just the same. Tonight though, it might be nice as the snow, while probably short lived, seemed unlikely to cease falling any time soon.

"Suit yourself," she said through a sly smile.

"It's not a bad idea, but I have to get back and get Danny in the morning."

"I can drive you back here in the morning."

He thought for a long moment about that tempting offer but, in the end, balked. "Naw, I'll make it. You need your sleep. Anyway, I don't want to make you get up and drive me back here."

"Suit yourself," she said again, still smiling. "Aren't you sweet?" He felt her toe brush his calf under the table and he smiled back.

The little moment they were enjoying was interrupted as her phone started buzzing on the table. The volume was still shut off from the show but the vibrate function caused it to rattle its way toward her beer.

He could see the display, no name, just a number.

He looked to her to see if she would answer it but she was just looking down at it, a slightly pensive look dampening her features.

"Who is it?" he asked.

"No idea." She clicked 'ignore' and the phone stopped buzzing. She smiled at him again but some of the liveliness had gone out of it.

"Are you alright?"

She gave a tiny shake of her head, not to negate, but as if to clear it. "I'm fine," she said, and looked a little more like she meant it. "I just have no idea who that was." She looked out the window and seemed far away for a moment. She could do that sometimes, he'd gotten used to it but still found it the smallest bit unsettling. But then she turned back to him and the sly smile was back. "We should probably hit the road though if you're going to have any hope of making it to my place in that tin can of yours."

He laughed and they both drank down the last of their beers.

"I've got to run to the bathroom quick," he said. "If you think I have time, that is, and that we won't be completely snowbound when I get back."

"I guess that'll all depend on how long you take."

He was laughing as he walked to the restroom. When he returned, she was standing by the table holding his jacket out to him ready to go. They again made a brisk pace back to the lot where they had parked. Tim noticed the pavement was indeed quite slick under the heavy layering of wet snow.

"Drive safe," he said to her over the roof of his car as they both cleared the snow off of their respective vehicles.

"And the same to you, my dear," then she climbed up into that big SUV and he slipped into his little Honda. She pulled out and he followed behind her, out of town and onto Highway 61 heading south.

Once they had cleared the slight glow of illumination being cast against the night sky by the township of Red Wing the dark enveloped them. The only view in their headlights was the fading tracks of the vehicles that had gone before them and the falling snow. Tim could at least, for the most part, follow in the tracks being plowed by Lisa's vehicle but she was steadily pulling ahead of him.

She's showing off in that thing now, he thought to himself as her taillights were slowly shrinking up ahead of him. Before long they had become little more than small points of red light peeking back through the snow that was falling in front of him. For a second, he goosed his accelerator in an attempt to keep some kind of pace but a moment later the traction of the tires gave way. Just a bit, causing a short little slide, but it was enough to make him slow and let her go on ahead.

It was only a matter of minutes before her taillights were gone and he was alone, cutting quietly through the wall of white like the last man on earth.

Another man may have found it emasculating, his girlfriend tearing off into the deep dark night, leaving him trailing behind. She was blazing her own way in a vehicle that boasted nothing but testicular fortitude while he played the part of the turtle to her hare.

But slow and steady wins the race.

For Tim it was just another thing he enjoyed about her. She had a stoic strength but with an appetite for adventure. He was feeling light and happy and the power of his own positivity propelled him the rest of the way on his journey through the fluffy flakes, right up until he hit the brake harder than he should've and slid to a stop before turning into her driveway.

He sat that way, in the deserted road, the yellow light of his turn signal blinking on and off reflecting off the trees in the silence.

The snow that covered the driveway was pristine.

It was still coming down steady, blanketing all that it touched. The fresh snowfall would've begun filling in the tracks her tires would have made as Lisa pulled in, but wouldn't have covered them completely. The snow on the driveway was unblemished.

No vehicle had touched that driveway since before the snow had begun to fall.

5

An awful foreboding seeped into him as he forced his foot to release the brake, and he turned into the driveway, cutting his own swath through the unsullied snow. He pulled up in front of the garage door and stopped. He took a deep breath and tried to relax. She had definitely been ahead of him but maybe she had stopped for gas. He probably drove right by her and was so focused on the road he didn't even notice. He tried to recall passing any of the gas stations or convenience stores along the way but couldn't think of anything that he may have missed; no particular memories solidified themselves. Tim pulled out his phone and called her.

No answer.

It brought him back to the Wednesday before in an instant. All the turmoil had turned out to be nothing on Wednesday, just like it would turn out to be nothing tonight. That logic was reasonably sound but he had difficulty finding any solace in it. He got out of the car and stomped through the snow. He did have a key. They had made it past that particular milestone in their relationship, so he let himself into the house. Standing in the darkened foyer, the melting snow from his shoes forming puddles on the tiles, his anxiety deepened. He dialed her number again.

Again, there was no answer.

Removing his shoes, he fought down the beginnings of the onslaught of panic. Without turning on a light or removing his coat he went and sat down on the couch. He could wait at least ten minutes for her to arrive before allowing irrational fear loose to course through his veins and taint his focus. He tried to convince himself he'd be able to wait ten minutes anyway. The absolute quiet of her living room provided no aid in bringing his running emotions to heel. He took a deep breath. He would see her headlights splash across the house as she pulled into the driveway any minute now.

Ten minutes later he called her again.

Still there was no answer.

He took another deep breath and made a slow five-count on the exhale. He did it again. He continued to repeat.

When another five minutes had passed, he tried her again. This time after a couple of rings an unknown man answered.

"Who is this? Where's Lisa?" he nearly shouted into the phone.

"Whoa," said the stranger who had just answered Lisa's phone. "My name's Bill, I'm the bartender at the Double Shot Tavern. This phone was left here earlier tonight. I only answered because you kept calling. I thought you might be the owner trying to find it."

"I'm sorry." Tim was trying to contain his emotions.

She didn't even have her phone.

She'd left it at the bar.

And now she was nowhere to be found. He shook off that last thought with a shiver. "The owner of that phone is Lisa Lathrop. I was there with her tonight. I was just starting to get worried about her but maybe she realized she had left it there and went back to get it."

Tim thought he would have noticed if she had passed him heading back towards town or that she would've alerted him somehow as she drove by, but maybe not. Now negativity and doubt were trying to worm their way into him. He recalled that she had the phone in her hand when he had gone to the bathroom. *How could she have forgotten it?*

"Could be," the guy said pulling Tim back. His tone made it apparent that he couldn't really care less about the circumstances regarding the phone, he'd already moved on.

"Listen, could you do me a favor?" Tim asked. "My name is Tim Boyd. Could you ask her to call me when she gets there to pick it up?"

"Sure will. She'll probably figure to give you a call, though, once she sees all your missed calls."

Tim could have done without Bill the bartender's flippant attitude in stating the obvious. "Thanks," he said and signed off the call. Tim walked around the house turning on some lights expelling the darkness then he sat back down and waited to hear from her.

Ten minutes later he stood up again and started pacing.

Five minutes after that, now a full half hour after he'd arrived at her house, Tim had had enough of waiting. He put his shoes back on and walked back outside. Small flakes were still drifting down from the blackened sky but the amount of snow that continued to fall had tapered off drastically. The temperature seemed to be making a slow ascent as well. The cutting chill had gone out of the air and the wind had died. He dropped into the seat of his car, looked at his phone and hit Lisa's number again.

After three rings Bill at the Double Shot answered again. He was less snide and a little more sympathetic this time.

"She hasn't picked it up?" Tim asked

"I'm afraid not."

"Okay. I'm going to drive back that way, maybe something happened to her car and somehow I didn't notice it as I drove by."

"Maybe, man, good luck, and you drive safe yourself."

"Thanks," Tim said but he was mentally far away. He dropped the phone onto the seat next to him at an utter loss. Could she have been pulled over on the side of the road and he was so absorbed with his own tense traveling that he drove right past her? He didn't think so, but nothing else really made any sense. He dropped the Honda into drive, swung around, and carved his second set of tracks into Lisa's driveway heading back out to the street.

He took it slow even though the weather no longer really required it. There was still a fair amount of snow on the highway but the center of the lanes, where the bulk of the traffic traversed, was clear, melted down to the asphalt. He could see plenty of spots where people had slid off the road but nothing that looked too serious. There were no cars still stranded in the ditches or anything.

As he closed in on Red Wing, well past the point where he had originally lost sight of her, he actually began to hope to see vehicles in the ditch. It would at least make some kind of sense. A fear of the unknown was beginning to grow and curdle deep in his guts. He rolled into town proper and began to feel dizzy. He couldn't find ways to process his thoughts; rationality seemed to have eluded him entirely.

He let the Honda ease to a stop in front of the bar but that unnamed fear gripped and held him. It squeezed him tight and wouldn't allow him to get out of the car. As if going in and retrieving her phone would somehow solidify the reality of whatever it was that was happening. That it would be the final nail in the proverbial coffin. That little turn of phrase bouncing around his head did nothing to alleviate his rising apprehension.

He reached for the door handle of the car, laid his hand upon it but still found it difficult to trip the latch. He looked up and down the street, willing her headlights to appear in front of him or in the rearview mirror. The street was silent. He looked at the clock on his dash and saw it was now approaching midnight. He forced himself to engage. He opened the car door and stepped out into the night. He walked to the entrance of the bar but faltered. Again, he looked up and down the street but the only visible light was golden pools cast onto the wet lacquered-looking road by the lampposts. No headlights; in fact, nothing moved. His throat felt thick, as if it were swelling toward shut. That cold fear continued to settle into his bones.

He struggled through the paralysis and opened the door to the Double Shot Tavern.

The number of revelers in the bar had dwindled. The feel of the place would've been different from when they had left regardless, but current circumstances gave the now-deserted dance floor a somehow vibrant lifelessness. He looked across the room at the man behind the bar. Tim could read the recognition in the barkeep's gaze as he glanced up and their eyes met. Tim must have been manifesting physical symptoms of his inner turmoil and it seemed Bill the Bartender could tell who he was in a glance. Tim walked to the bar and the guy grabbed Lisa's phone from a shelf behind him. Tim's heart lurched.

"She never showed up?" Tim was unable to keep the tremor out of his voice.

"I'm afraid not, man, I'm sorry," he handed the phone over to Tim. "The battery died since the last time you called. I don't have a charger that'll work for it here but maybe she's tried to call it?" He was trying to help, to inject a bit of optimism, but it fell flat.

"Yeah, maybe…" Tim's voice was distant, his thoughts far away. He thanked the bartender and walked back outside with the dead phone.

He slumped into the driver's seat of his Honda and wondered. Wondered about where she could be and what should be his next course of action. At what point do you call the police? He knew they wouldn't consider an adult who got into her own car and drove away into the night to be a missing person, not for at least twenty-four hours. No matter how vehemently he opined on her state of mind and the absurdity of her deciding to just up and drive away, protocol was protocol.

He dropped the car into drive and headed back for Lisa's house. He couldn't think of anything else to do. Once he was on the highway, every set of headlights he came upon renewed his hopes for a moment only to dash them seconds later as Lisa's vehicle never materialized behind those stabbing beams of light. Moments after the most recent car had passed, and to no avail, the fear began to mix and meld with anger and frustration.

He smacked the palm of his hand against the steering wheel, hard.

It didn't alleviate any of his angst or agony but in some primal way he felt that it helped, so he tried it again.

And then again.

And again.

And then repeatedly.

For a moment it did seem to actually make him feel a little better but then the steering wheel slipped amid the flurry of his flailing palm.

The Honda pulled to the right, out of the nice clean lane lines running down the center of the road and into the small drift of snow on the shoulder. His tires gave way their traction and the car began to slide. Instinct kicked in and he released the gas, he held the wheel steady resisting the urge to start wildly cranking it in an attempt to turn the vehicle. Until he felt the tires take purchase again it would be folly to attempt to direct them. He hadn't been driving overly fast and the slide didn't take him all the way into the ditch. But it did begin to turn the car sideways with a wretched slowness. Nice and easy he depressed the brake. It bucked but then took effect and he slid to a stop on the shoulder perpendicular to the road, the beams of his headlights now playing off of the trees along the side of the highway.

He took a few deep breaths to calm himself. His heart was racing, elevated by the sudden assault on the steering wheel and exacerbated the subsequent loss of control of his vehicle. He shut his eyes and fought back tears of frustration. He had exhausted any options he could think of as to what might have happened to Lisa tonight. With no further rational avenues to follow it was perhaps time to turn to the more unorthodox.

He contained, if not controlled, his emotions and pulled his own phone out of his pocket. He scrolled through his recent calls trying not to look too long at Lisa's name as it slid past under his finger. He found the number he wanted and hit send. As the phone began to ring in his ear, he put the car in reverse to back out onto the highway. At first the tires only spun in the fluffy snow still lining the shoulder but then they caught and pulled him back onto the clean asphalt. He palmed the steering wheel in a circle to the left turning the car back in the direction of town.

"Answer dammit," Tim said under his breath as the phone continued to ring. After an eternity it connected and his heart rate spiked, only to slow a second later when he realized that the voice on the other end was a recording, a voicemail.

He listened to the outgoing message and when it finished, he did, indeed, know what to do after the beep. What he might say though was another matter entirely. Struggling, he managed to speak.

"Stas, this is Tim Boyd... I need you to call me."

<u>6</u>

Ten minutes later Tim rolled to a stop in front of the Goodhue Municipal Building. He sat rooted to his seat once more. It was different though from the moment in front of the bar when he couldn't seem to bring himself to open the door. At that point he was being driven by an irrational panic. There was a rational finality in the fear that held him now as he sat alone outside the police station in what had become the wee hours of Saturday morning. He mustered his little remaining fortitude and again opened his car door.

The Goodhue Municipal Building housed both the Red Wing Police Department and the Goodhue County Sheriff's Department. At this point Tim would take either of them, anyone who would be willing to listen to him. The stark fluorescent lighting in the building was a huge contrast to the soft-edged fantastical aura of the now dissipating wintery scene outside. It was an added dose of unwanted reality this evening. Except that it was no longer evening, it had become morning.

The first person that Tim saw was a sleepy looking desk sergeant behind the automatic sliding glass doors of the police station so he veered in that direction. Before the doors slid open to allow him to pass, he caught a glimpse of himself reflected in the glass. He was looking a bit haggard and he took a moment to straighten his clothing and his hair, then walked through the doors having no idea what he was going to say.

The desk sergeant looked up and eyed him warily. After whatever assessment of him being made by the officer had been completed, the man spoke.

"How can I help you?" The cop's tone emphasised that being helpful was perhaps of the least amount of interest to him.

"I…I need to report a missing person."

"Male or Female?"

"Female."

"Age?"

"Thirty-nine."

"How long has she been missing?"

Tim checked his watch. It had only been a few hours but it felt so much longer. Civilizations could have risen and been felled in the time since she had pulled out of view in front of him fading into the snowy landscape. "A couple of hours," he said.

The desk sergeant stopped typing and looked at him. "Do you have any reason to expect foul play?"

"No. At least I don't think so." Tim's fingers were fidgeting and he forced them to stop. "We were in town here, seeing a show. We had driven separately and on our way home, somewhere between here and her house, south on 61 fifteen or twenty miles, she disappeared."

"Disappeared?"

"Yes." Tim knew the cop thought he was being dramatic but that was exactly what had happened. Somehow, between here and there Lisa had vanished.

"Okay, I'll take your information and prepare a report, but you realize that without any reason to expect foul play she won't officially be considered a missing person for at least twenty-four hours, okay?"

Tim nodded but was unable to manage any words.

Twenty minutes later, after providing the desk sergeant any and all of the pertinent information available to him, Tim was sitting in an uncomfortable chair on the other side of the room. Exhaustion had overtaken him. He wasn't sleeping but was starting to doze. His waking fears began to tangle with nightmares as he walked a tightrope along the line of sleep.

Another ten minutes passed before he was shaken back to reality by the ringing of a phone. Tim's eyes shot to the desk sergeant as he clicked his mouse and answered into his headset. Seconds later, still on the line, the cop looked up and right at him. Tim was out of his chair and crossing to the desk like a shot. The cop said something indiscernible and signed off of the phone call.

"What is it?" Tim did his best to resist the urge to shout at the officer.

"Okay Mr. Boyd, I need you to remain calm. That was a report from a State Trooper, and technically doesn't change anything for the moment, but I do have an update."

Tim's knees felt weak. He put his hands out on the desk to help support his weight.

"Are you alright?"

Tim nodded but it was a lie. He wasn't even in the same stratosphere as 'alright.' His face was hot and his hands shook where he had placed them on the desktop. He willed the sergeant to go on, hoping to heaven on high that he wasn't about to regret doing so.

Time dragged and Tim Boyd could hear every slight sound in the station as though it were amplified, the hammer of every key on every keyboard, the hum of an idle copier. Finally the desk sergeant spoke.

"Approximately five minutes ago Ms. Lathrop's SUV was located by a State Trooper. It was pulled off onto the shoulder of County Road 22, but there was no one present with the vehicle. It appears to have been abandoned."

Minneapolis...
Spring, 2017

1

The weathered bar-top gleamed. It was well cared for, just as it was well worn. There were faded sections here and there where elbows, his or others, had rested for hours and occasionally days at a time, but still it held a shine. Dusty's bar was a dive but not without its charm. And charm was achieved, generally, with at least some care, even if said care came in the upkeep of an establishment that was often reserved for the downtrodden.

He swallowed and then lowered his glass to the bar. The suds slid in lazy rivulets down the sides and pooled at the bottom. He checked the old-fashioned lighted clock behind the bar where the Hamm's Beer Bear pointed out the time. The clock was a relic from a time long ago. Its raised plastic face was lit from behind by a small fluorescent bulb. Dusty's was full of these little nods to the 1970s but they weren't affectation. The clock and most of the other pieces of signage had probably held those coveted spots on the wall since Carter trod the Oval Office. The giant vintage cash registers that sat beneath those old beer signs had likely seen presidential administrations stretching even further back.

"You want another, Stas?" Melissa called down to him,

returning from the small kitchen at the end of the bar. One bartender handled the whole place, including the kitchen. He loved this place.

"Nah, I gotta hit the bricks in a minute," he replied.

"If you say so." She nodded to the guy three stools down from him. The guy, Ed was his name, nodded back. She pulled the tap and let the beer flow.

"Where do you gotta get?" Ed asked as Melissa set the fresh draught in front of him.

"Gotta pick Shelly up."

"What time?"

"Eleven-thirty."

"It's only five after."

Melissa had watched this whole exchange with an air of boredom but now cocked an eyebrow in Stas' direction. It would take all of five minutes to get to B.J.'s where Shelly worked. Twenty minutes wasn't a lot of time to knock back a beer but then again, he was practically a professional. He gave the nod and Melissa poured.

"Dumbass snow is gonna keep coming for awhile," Ed, no literary lion, noted.

"At least it won't last," Stas said, picking up his part of this script with ease. Discussions on the weather, it was an insipid topic but they were barflies, made for such arts as that of idle chatter. They pontificated on a few of the other standard topics. Sports, and the way the old neighborhood was going to hell. Of course, 'going to hell' to the two of them really meant the gentrification of the blue-collar stomping grounds of their youth. The condo movement had already crept across the river from downtown and into Southeast Minneapolis which had always had a touch of uppity to it, but now it was creeping into Northeast. That the neighborhood was now generally referred to as 'Northeast' instead of the 'Nordeast' title passed down by their Polish forefathers was a topic they could speak to for hours if one would let them. Tonight, though, Stas was on the clock.

At twenty after eleven he hit the remote start on his

truck. It wasn't that cold but if the snow was collecting, this time of night it could freeze on the windshield. It was too late in the season to have to use a scraper, he'd let the defroster do its thing. Five minutes later he drained the remaining third of his beer, laid his money on the bar and called a goodbye to Melissa in the kitchen. He gave Ed the customary head nod and stepped out into the falling snow.

The truck was already nice and toasty warm, and the wipers cleaned the heated windshield of the evening's current accumulation with ease. His truck was big and shiny and new. It was about the only thing in his life that could boast any of those three things. He was a minimalist in most ways but he also lived in Minnesota and believed that a vehicle that started every time and could traverse any amount of snow was an absolute imperative.

He dropped the truck into drive and left Dusty's behind. He crossed the Broadway Bridge over the Mississippi River and moments later pulled into the parking lot of one of his least favorite places.

He found a spot to park close to the door and the red of the neon signage bathed the cab of the truck. He could feel it coloring his face and it made him feel low. A couple of tough-looking characters were darkening the door, grabbing a smoke. He didn't like that Shelly would have to walk past guys like these but he wouldn't go inside and get her. He'd seen her without her clothes before, a couple times. But those times were on their terms, in small magical moments when two stumbling souls needed each other. Not some manufactured moment that involved her swinging on some pole.

Stas wondered whose clever idea it had been to name a second-rate strip club B.J.'s. It wasn't so much that the place was sleazy as it was no-frills. It may have held a certain charm over the glitzy places downtown to a man who preferred a darkened neighborhood bar to just about anything, but he didn't have much use for strip clubs any which way and he hated this one. If his feet were held to the fire, though, the main reason for his distaste was because she worked there. Not that what he thought mattered a lick, they weren't in any sort of real relationship. They were friends, and on a few rare occasions something a little more than that, but only when it suited them both.

She appeared in the doorway and a small, unrealized smile turned the corner of his mouth. The smoking guys gave her a cursory glance as she walked by but it was nothing that got his ire up. She ran through the fresh snow and climbed into the truck.

"Hey," she said.

"Hey back."

"Thanks for the lift. Jody's not off for another hour and I didn't want to hang around tonight."

Don't know why you'd want to hang around ever, he thought, but said nothing of the sort. "No problem," was what did come out of his mouth. "Good night?" he asked, dropping the gear-shift into drive and putting the lighted neon of B.J.'s in his rearview mirror.

"It was fine, I guess…" She was staring out the window at the snow slipping from the sky. It seemed to him the sort of answer that probably meant she had more to say but he knew better than to push. "The snow is pretty though," she said after a stretching silence.

"At least it won't last long," he said repeating his lines from an earlier script. "Am I just running you home?"

"I could maybe use a drink if you're up for it." Her gaze never left the falling world of white outside of the window.

"As far as I know I'm still me, so yeah, I guess I'm up for a drink."

"No work tomorrow?"

"Nope." He freelanced on construction jobs. The season would be picking up soon but he had a couple weeks still before his next gig. He had thought about trying to catch on with one of the big companies throwing up condos in the neighborhood but knew he'd never be able to stomach it long term.

"Where do you want to go?" she asked.

"Let's just see where the road takes us." That it would take them somewhere there was no doubt. In this part of town there was, almost literally, a bar on every other block. And usually a church on the blocks in between.

He crossed back over onto their side of the bridge and headed north along the river. He passed Dusty's and thought about stopping, but Dusty's was his spot. There were plenty of other places to grab a beer up Nordeast. As if to exemplify this point, they passed Psycho Suzi's, the epitome of the neighborhood change. It had originally opened in the old Malt Shop as a Tiki bar with a killer patio that they called 'Poor Man's Paradise,' and it was. But it became very popular, and popularity led to expansion. Now they occupied a five-thousand-square-foot building with a kitschy patio stretching the entire length of the building out on the river. On a Friday or Saturday night you couldn't park within half a mile of the place and most of the clientele did not hail from the neighborhood. He drove right past.

He hung a right on Lowry at the north end of the neighborhood. A few blocks up they stopped at a light by the bar that bore his name. 'Stanley's,' which was indeed his given name, was a nice bar and restaurant. The building had been renovated and it was now a pleasant neighborhood place, the kind of spot that you could bring the kids in for dinner. He had preferred the old place though, before the renovation, the one without windows that bore his true moniker. It had been called Stasiu's, which was Stanley in Polish and shortened nicely to 'Stas.'

The light changed, he drove through the intersection and then pulled over in front of a bar called The Palace, exactly one block up. It was as good a place as any, and definitely more his speed.

They got out of the truck and walked up to the door. They could hear thumping music from within. Stas held the door for Shelly and the music smacked them. It was live and it was funky, emanating from a small band jammed in the back corner of the little bar. The Palace had the vibe tonight. He hadn't gone out planning to get drunk but sometimes, plans changed. Shelly had already walked halfway down the bar and was talking to someone she knew. He took in the collection of miscreants populating the bar and liked what he saw.

He was about to join Shelly when a large strong hand clamped down on his shoulder.

"You got ID?" the owner of the hand asked as the iron grip turned Stas to face the speaker. Stas was not a small man but he found himself looking up into the cool gaze of a guy that had at least six inches on him.

"Not on me," Stas replied, measured.

"No ID, No Par-Tee if ya know what I mean."

"You didn't ask her," Stas said throwing his thumb toward Shelly.

"She doesn't look like trouble."

"Are you saying that I look like trouble?"

"I'm saying that I need to see your damn ID."

"Well I'll run and grab it if you give me the key to your apartment. I think I left it on your bedside table last night."

For a moment that last statement just hung there and the two men stared each other down. Then the big man's face changed. A large grin broke across it.

"Stas, you're dreamin' if you think I'd let your punk-ass near my bed." Then the large man folded him into a bear-hug and lifted him off the floor.

"Jesus, Louis, put me down. You're gonna crush me."

"It'd be easy, too," Louis Jones said as he lowered Stas back to earth. "You're a fragile little man," he said expelling a chuckle.

"Just my heart, just my heart."

"Go grab a beer, softy." And with that he turned back to the door and asked the next schmuck crossing the threshold for his ID.

Stas had plenty of barroom pals but Louis Jones was one of the few people he considered a friend. He could probably count those true friends on one hand. He could only assume Louis held him in a similar regard as the man answered to the name that his mother gave him from the mouths of few. To most of the vagrants and vagabonds that populated his work space Louis Jones was known simply as Big Lou.

Stas left Big Lou to the work he was made for and sidled down to the section of the bar where Shelly had made a home. There he found a beer and two shots of a dark amber liquid waiting for him. One for shooting, and one for sipping along with his beer. So this was how it was going to be tonight.

Shelly held up her shot.

He held up his own.

Outside, in the center console of his truck, his forgotten phone began to ring.

Inside, the shot glass tapped the bar, went to his lips, then back down on the bar, empty.

In the truck the ringing phone fell silent.

At the bar Stas grabbed his beer and drained a quarter of it in a single pull and it tasted great. A few short moments later the beer had met its maker. Not long after that the other shot was gone too. His cheeks were nice and warm and the world felt blissfully blunt when his next beer arrived. Their little group expanded as acquaintances, old and new, joined them. By the time his second beer was gone and a fresh one had taken its place they had moved over to the dart boards for a game.

And his forgotten phone, all alone in the truck, had rung through to voicemail another four times.

2

An indeterminate amount of time later Stas peeled his eyelids apart but not without a hefty bit of effort. For a second, he didn't know where he was, all he knew was that his lower back was reading him the riot act. The southern section of his spine being in revolt was not the only mutinous party either. His head was in an unbearable state of duress. He came to realize he was on Shelly's couch. Well, part of him was on the couch anyway, much of his body was dangling off of various edges. It was not a couch made to sleep a man his size.

A vague memory of Shelly leaving her door open when she made her way to bed surfaced. Was that an invitation, perhaps? Maybe. Whatever it was, he was glad he hadn't acted upon it. Based on the state they were in by the time they got back here it could have only ended in regret, be it for him, her, or both.

He managed to sit up but it did very little to help his well being. The thudding in his head amplified and his gorge rose. He sat as still as he could and waited, patient but not hopeful, for his various ailments to recede. He considered lying back down but knew if he went in that direction, he might not make it back up to a sitting position much less standing, so he stayed put awhile longer. He rested his head in his hands but couldn't ignore the bright sunlight that was peeking in at him from beneath the curtains.

What time is it? he wondered.

He sat very still for a few long minutes. When he thought he could move again without his head exploding he dug through his pockets for his phone to check the time and came up empty. He must have left it out in the truck. He should go and find it. He hadn't even looked at the thing since some time yesterday afternoon. The phone would have to wait though until at least one, if not multiple, glasses of water had been consumed. Unfortunately, water would also have to wait until he could get up off the couch without passing out. He closed his eyes and waited for the furor between his ears to subside. He blamed the shots. No good ever came of that stuff.

A not exactly calculable amount of time later, ready or not, it was time to move. He stood, weathered the onslaught loosed inside his skull, and made it to the kitchen for that glass of water. He sipped his way through the first glass and then chugged the second. It didn't bring him back to anywhere near normal but this wasn't his first rodeo, and it refreshed him enough to at least get moving. He walked past Shelly's open bedroom door. She was sleeping and hard based on the snores emanating from where she was sprawled; he was envious. He'd check in with her later, no need to wake her now. He left

Shelly's apartment and tromped down the stairs to the street.

It had snowed a fair amount but the sun was already shining and the temperature had taken a delightful turn. It would take most of the day if not longer to melt all of the new-fallen snow but the streets were already clear and the snowmelt was running along the curbs toward the storm drains.

He walked the three blocks back to the bar and his truck. He climbed in and his head spiked again. He shut his eyes and waited for the newest round of agony to pass. When the waves of pain had finally receded, he reached into the center console and pulled out his phone. The display showed that he only had ten percent of his battery left but at least it wasn't dead.

It also showed he had five missed calls and a voicemail from a number he didn't recognize.

Or did he?

The number associated with the missed calls did seem familiar, but at first he wasn't sure why. Then a realization started to dawn on him elevating his heart rate, which did nothing but exacerbate his many current physical maladies. He had called that number before, sometime earlier in the week, when Lisa had dropped off the grid.

It was Tim Boyd's phone number. The fact that Lisa's boyfriend had called him five times in the middle of the night did not leave him brimming with optimistic feelings. He hit 'play' on his voicemail, put the phone to his ear and seconds later, the scant color that had managed to return to his face since he woke had drained away again.

<u>3</u>

A sound like church bells rang out in the belfry that was his head and he squinted his eyes against the ensuing result of the thunderous sound. Stas made it the rest of the way across the threshold into the cafe and turned back to look at the little jangling bell above the door as it slowed and settled into a prone position. The cacophony that was emitted by that little hunk of silver was ludicrous. The momentary spike of pain he had been made to endure ebbed and he turned his attention back to the interior of the cafe.

The overwhelming fragrance of eggs and frying bacon permeating the air were both mouth-watering and stomach-turning. Eating something was definitely a good idea, he only hoped his stomach would hold up its end of the bargain and not reject whatever he decided to offer up to it. He glanced around the little cafe and his eyes settled on Tim Boyd sitting alone in one of the booths. Tim's hands fidgeted along the handle of the coffee mug on the table in front of him and Stas wondered how many of those cups he had already downed. He made his way over and slid into the booth. Stas initiated the conversation.

"You're Tim, right?"

Tim Boyd nodded. For all they knew of each other, they'd never actually met.

"Thanks for coming," Tim said after a moment.

Now it was his turn to nod and Stas did so. He then looked out the window and squinted, again combating the sun that was stabbing at him though the glass. He leaned over and turned the blinds into a position that reflected its brutal rays in a different direction. "Is that cool?" he asked. Again, Tim nodded. "Thanks, I'm not a hundred percent this morning." Stas paused for a moment then said, "I hope you don't take this the wrong way, I don't even really know you, but you're not looking so great either."

"It was a long night last night." Tim removed his shaky hands from the coffee cup and laid them out flat on the table in an attempt to steady them.

"Yeah, for both of us…" Stas mumbled as the waitress stopped by. He proceeded to order a coffee, as well as eggs, bacon, hash browns, a side of sausage patties, and pancakes. Tim gave him a sideways look and he returned it. "I'm not sure what's gonna work for me this morning so I'm gonna try it all."

Tim made a sound somewhere between a sigh and a little humorless laugh. He picked up his coffee cup and sipped at it and Stas caught a glimpse as to how bad his shakes really were. Whether it was due to the coffee or not, this guy was in rough shape, rougher than he was, maybe even. He found it difficult to see how that could be possible, yet it seemed to be so. He collected himself as much as he could and attempted to begin some manner of dialogue.

"Okay, man. Tell me what you know." And then Stas drank his own coffee and he listened.

Tim started slow but he began to fill in the details that had been missed or glossed over in the crazed message he had left overnight and the hasty conversation they had once Stas had finally called him back this morning. Tim told Stas about how he and Lisa had been out, seeing a show. That they had gone out and had drinks after, and on the way home she had pulled away and left him behind, but then never showed up back at her house.

If it was any other situation Stas would have enjoyed a little laugh at Tim's expense whether he knew him or not. But Lisa's disappearance had removed any levity from the situation. Tim told him that Lisa had left her phone at the bar and that he had it now. He told Stas about the police station and the report of the abandoned vehicle.

"What did the cops have to say about the car?" Stas asked. His food had arrived and he sampled a few of the many options just to see what his stomach could handle.

"I don't think they're taking it seriously. The car was on the side of the road, there was nothing wrong with it. It was just parked there. The keys weren't in it and it was locked. The cops are saying that maybe someone picked her up but there was no sign that another car pulled over or anything. I don't know what the hell could have happened."

Tim let his head droop and pinched the bridge of his nose possibly fighting back tears. Stas grabbed a piece of bacon and turned his attention to the small slit still left between the blinds giving way to the outside world. He gazed off into the parking lot, giving Tim some time to think.

It was definitely strange.

Stas knew her pretty well and Lisa definitely had her quirks. He knew some things about her that Tim probably didn't. There were reasons he had started checking up on her and had called Tim in the first place last week when he hadn't heard from her for a couple days. But he didn't know Tim well enough yet to start passing off any of that information to him. Still, Lisa's quirks and history aside, this sort of disappearing act, the car left on the side of the road, it was weird.

He tossed the last bite of his bacon into his mouth and turned his attention back to Tim. "You said you have her phone, right?"

Tim nodded and reached into his pocket. He pulled it out and set it on the table between them. They both stared at it for a long second. "That was strange too," Tim said. "Someone called her right before we were about to leave, I went to the bathroom and when I came back, she was all ready to go. But it turns out she had somehow left the phone on the table. I guess she could have set it down when she put her jacket on and forgot it, but it seems odd to me. I mean, she had just had it in her hand."

"I assume you checked to see who it was that called her right before you guys left?"

He nodded again. "Not until this morning. The phone was dead by the time I picked it up from the bar and I couldn't find her charger anywhere at her house, maybe she had it with her, I don't know. Anyway, as soon as stores opened this morning I went and bought one to check it."

Tim pushed the phone across the table to Stas. He picked it up and hit the home button. The lock-screen lit up and he saw a picture of Lisa with Tim and his kid. "Do you know her password?"

Tim relayed it to him. "27737."

Stas couldn't keep a little smirk from crossing his face. Her password spelled 'ASSES.'

"What?" Tim asked with a hesitant perplexed little smile.

"Nothing." The lock-screen disappeared allowing him

access and Stas opened her call-log.

"That last call was from a number with a 320-area code," Tim said. "No contact name. It doesn't mean anything to me but I scrolled through her history and there are a decent amount of calls from that number. I thought maybe it was a telemarketer or bill collector or something but I checked a few of them and she actually had a couple conversations of reasonable length with whoever it was. Another odd thing, I clearly remember a voicemail notification popping up when it rang last night, but there's no new voicemail now."

"She deleted it?"

"I guess so. Is the number familiar to you at all?"

Stas shook his head but there was a veiled hesitancy to the motion. He had scrolled through the call-log as well and although he didn't recognize the 320 number, there was another number without a contact name that had a suspicious familiarity to him. If that number was what he thought it was, it might provide a modicum of clarity. Again though, what he knew about it and how it might be tied to Lisa's disappearance was nothing he was willing to share with Tim right now. He handed the phone back across the table and settled into his thoughts.

The only sound between them was the clanging of dishes from other patrons and the distant babble of short-order cooks jawing at each other on the line. After a time, Stas spoke.

"Alright, you should go home. I'm gonna head back up to the Cities, think on this, and make some calls."

"I should go with you." Tim's voice was desperate.

"No, what you should do is go home. You've got a kid, right?" Tim nodded. "Well, go see him, get yourself some rest. You need it. I'll call you if I find anything." He didn't wait for a response. He dropped cash on the table, stood up, and he headed for the door. As he went, Stas could feel Tim's eyes on his back, crawling all over him in a frenzy, searching for something more to say. But the fact of the matter was that there was nothing more to say. Stas crossed the battered tile floor of the café without looking back and waited for that little silver bell to tear into his head again.

4

Stas went home and he went to sleep. And he slept hard. Four hours later he hesitantly lifted his head up from his pillow and found the result of such an action to be, for the most part, acceptable. He wasn't quite right yet, but compared to the last time he woke, it was progress by leaps and bounds.

Stas busied himself around his apartment for another hour and a half stalling on what he needed to do. Partially because he was avoiding his next course of action but also because it was pointless to take up such an endeavor until the clock had stretched a bit further into the evening. When it was finally late enough, he grabbed his phone and sat down on the couch.

He pulled out his wallet and ferreted around in it for a second before he found what he was looking for. The old business card was tucked behind the other rabble on the side of his wallet that was usually reserved for things he wouldn't look at again until it was time to throw them away, gift cards with small change left on them waiting to expire and the like.

A single word was printed on the front of the business card: DESOLATE. He flipped the card over. On the backside, in chicken-scratch handwriting, a phone number had been penned. The digits matched those that he had recognized from Lisa's phone. Stas let out a long slow breath and hesitated another moment before quickly punching in the series of numbers and pressing 'send.' He put the phone to his ear and listened to the empty ringing with a sense of foreboding.

It went on for quite some time, ringing much longer than most people would continue to wait for an answer. After an eternity, though, it connected. A loud beep drilled into his ear canal recalling his subsiding headache from the back of his brain to the front. After the beep there was nothing, only silence. His throat constricted for a second not allowing him to speak but then he found a semblance of his voice. Into the phone he spoke the single word that was printed on the card and then relayed his own phone number and hung up. He dropped the phone onto the coffee table as if it were hot, and then he waited. Nothing happened.

After staring at the dormant phone for twenty minutes he was contemplating grabbing a beer. At the very least it would finally relieve the few remaining traces of his hangover. He was about to get up and grab one when the phone began to buzz on the table in front of him. Now it was his turn to let it ring for a long time, not long enough for it to roll over into his voicemail though. He snatched it off of the coffee table and answered it.

"This is Stas."

A stretching moment of silence was the only response until a gruff voice said, "Go to Jimmy's Bar, tell the bartender you want an Iron Butterfly, Iron Curtain style," and that was it. The call was terminated from the other end.

Stas let the phone slip from his ear and he absently dropped it into his lap. He wasn't exactly up on the protocol of this particular situation. The card with the code-word and phone number on it was old. It was one of the few things from that forgotten side of his wallet that hadn't turned over through the years, one of the few items he had never been able to bring himself to throw away. It had been ages since he had acquired it in the first place, back when he had acquired it for Lisa, a lifetime ago.

<u>5</u>

Twenty-five minutes later Stas pulled open the door, walked into Jimmy's Bar, and immediately questioned the validity of his decision making.

The guy currently manning the bar was named Al Witkowski. He'd known Al for a long time. They'd come up as kids in the neighborhood together but it would be a hefty bit more than a stretch to say that they were friends. When the waters were calm and the sailing was smooth, they tolerated each other. When the conditions of their acquaintance were less desirable, the relationship could become a bit more tumultuous.

It had been months at least, if not more than a year, since they had last crossed paths. Stas struggled to recall the terms on which they parted after their last meeting. He was still working on it as he sidled up to the bar.

"Stas Mileski, to what great honor do I owe you gracing my bar tonight?" The humor that might normally accompany such a statement was absent.

"It's been awhile, huh, Al?"

"Yep, it has."

"Can I get a Grain Belt?"

"Premium or Nordeast?"

"Premo."

Al grabbed a glass and sauntered down the bar towards the taps. Stas took it as decent sign that whatever their last encounter, they had both come out of it reasonably unscathed. He breathed a sigh of relief. He had no idea what he was about to get himself into but starting events off by trading barbs with an old school-yard adversary did not seem as if it would fall into the category of positive omens. Al returned but stopped short of placing the beer in front of Stas.

Holding it at a teasing distance he said, "You aren't gonna cause me any hassle tonight, are you?"

Stas shook his head. "The last thing I'm looking for tonight is trouble, man." The beer landed before him and he took a long sip before returning it to its place atop the bar. Al didn't seem interested in sparing Stas any more of his time and had moved back down to the other end of the bar. Stas was just fine with that.

Eighteen minutes later the last few sips of his beer awaited him in the bottom of the glass and he knew it was time. He drained it and waited for Al to make his way back down to him.

"You want another?" Al asked.

"Yeah." He hesitated for a long second then dove in. "I'll take an Iron Butterfly, Iron Curtain style."

Al Witkowski stared at him for an even longer second. He looked back down towards the other end of the bar then to Stas again.

"So, you're the one. I damn well should've known."

Stas said nothing.

"What have you gotten yourself mixed up in, Mileski?"

"Not really sure myself yet."

Al looked away again and then back at Stas. He shook his head, dropped his gaze, and spoke. "At the end of the bar there's a door. It leads to the basement. At the bottom of the stairs the cooler will be on your left and across from the cooler is a door. Behind that door is a short hallway. Go to the end of the hallway and knock on the last door on the right."

Stas nodded and pulled some cash out of his pocket.

Al shook his head and said, "Nope, this one is on me." Stas gave him a wary look. "Stas, you know there's never really been any love lost between us, right?" Stas said nothing and Al went on. "In general, I couldn't give half a shit about your well-being. But hear me when I tell you this. You need to be careful down there." And with that he grabbed the empty glass with the remaining suds of the Grain Belt Premium settling at the bottom and walked away. Stas stood up and looked down the bar-top that now seemed to stretch on forever.

Slowly he took the interminable stroll behind the backs of those bellied safely to the bar. When he reached the door, he glanced back but received no affirmation or encouragement from Al Witkowski. Al was cleaning glasses, focused on anything but the end of the bar. Stas looked back to the door leading down into the basement and opened it.

Minneapolis...
Fall, 1999

1

The rain splattered on the windshield of the parked car and then sluiced off as the wipers cleared it. It wasn't pouring but it had been coming down in a steady stream for at least the last half hour. It was heavy enough to keep visibility low even as the rubberized blades cleared the intermittent moisture collecting on the windshield between strokes. The falling rain gave the world around him a hazy, lacquered feel. Stas focused on the ethereal halos encircling the floodlights illuminating the main double doors of the Amtrak station and waited for her to appear.

She had called yesterday to see if he would pick her up.

He was twenty years old and had not heard one word from her since he was ten, a full decade ago. Then, as suddenly as their friendship had been severed as kids, it was reborn. Out of the blue she called him last night and asked him if he would pick her up from the train station. She had also asked that he not ask her any questions up front. She said she would explain when she got there. The tone of her voice, or more accurately the fear in her voice, made it easy to say yes to the request regardless of how much time had lapsed since they'd last been in contact.

She needed him. And he wouldn't even be here to help her tonight if she hadn't been there for him ten years ago. He would've died in the cool water of a wretched little pond in a time so lost in the past that it almost felt like it had happened to someone else.

Her name was Anne, but it wouldn't be for long. With his help she would soon become Lisa Lathrop and do her damndest to forget who she had been before. But Stas didn't know that yet. All he knew as he sat in his old beat-up Chevy, waiting in the rain, was that she needed him. And so he was there waiting, and would continue to be until she appeared.

The quiet filling the car, coupled with pelt of the rain and the squeegee sound that the wipers made every few seconds, added to the anxiousness he was feeling. He was a little nervous to see her after all this time. Ten years isn't a long time in the grand scheme of things but to him it was literally half a lifetime. And he'd have been a liar were he to say that he didn't find the nature of their reacquainting somewhat unsettling as well. He clicked on the radio and let the shouting guitars of some classic rock dispel the eerie quiet.

Twenty minutes later a trickle of weary travelers began to appear exiting the building and he turned the radio down. Three more minutes passed and he saw her. She looked different but the same, she was all grown up and yet in many ways she hadn't changed at all. She was standing below the awning dodging as much of the rain as possible as she had no umbrella; in fact the only thing she did have with her was a small backpack slung over her shoulder. He watched her squint into the darkness of the lot looking for him. She didn't see him right away through the deluge and he watched her turn quickly and look back the way she'd come. She continued to monitor her flank for a long moment. She made a slow turn back to the parking lot, casually tossing suspicious looks up and down the apron of the pickup area.

He could see from where he sat that she was nervous and Stas dropped the car into gear pulling out of his parking spot and into the pickup lane. Her bit of nerves did not seem to generate from the same source as his did. Surely it was going to be weird for her to see him as well, but she seemed to be preoccupied for other reasons. He pulled up alongside the curb where she was standing and pushed the passenger door open. A cautious and guarded stare turned into a still cautious but warming smile that turned back the time by ten years.

"Hey," she said.

"Hey yourself," he replied and returned the smile.

She slid into the seat next to him and pulled the door shut. But then she looked back out the window toward the glass doors of the train station. He moved to drop the Chevy back into gear but she stopped him, reaching out and staying his hand with hers even though her eyes never left the window and the world beyond it.

"What are ya looking for?" he asked.

"Anything..."

"Anything?"

"Anything weird."

"Are you expecting to see something weird?"

"I don't know," she replied. "And that's what worries me."

He had no idea what that cryptic sentence was supposed to mean and she didn't elaborate. She was going to take her time easing into conversation and he was fine with that. He was not an effusive man as those things went anyway. She kept her eyes riveted to the doors of the train station for another thirty seconds then she patted his hand, faced forward, and put her hand back in her lap as she spoke.

"Let's go."

He followed the command she had given and pulled out into the departing traffic.

2

Stas was sitting on his couch and waiting for her again. From the bathroom he heard the distant sounds of the shower shutting off. Any anxiousness he had felt while he had been sitting in the Amtrak parking lot had not diminished but rather had amplified based on the little bit of information she had provided to him since.

She hadn't talked much on the ride home but the little that she had said made an impact. She was on the run and whoever it was she was fleeing from was unlikely to have just let her go quietly into the night.

In the car she hadn't elaborated on who these potential pursuers might be, nor had she felt compelled to provide any further information as to what could have caused them to do so. He had barraged her with questions but she had told him she needed time; that he would get the whole story once they were back at the apartment. Then she had laid her head back and shut her eyes, perhaps she had nodded off but he hadn't thought so. He had left her to her thoughts and driven her back to his apartment.

From his vantage point where he sat now on the couch, he heard the latch on the bathroom door disengage. She walked back into the room still drying her hair with a towel. She was wearing a pair of sweatpants and a T-shirt provided by Stas as she had literally rolled into town with nothing more than the clothes on her back. And the backpack that had been slung there carried only one change of clothes and some clean underwear.

He was anxious to know what had brought her here under such circumstances but at the same time was not sure the knowledge would bring with it anything resembling relief.

"Can I get you a beer?" Stas asked as she settled in on his old tattered couch and kicked her feet up on the makeshift coffee table. He had at least removed the old pizza boxes from the wooden slats that comprised the little table as he had been on his way out the door to go get her.

"Got anything stronger?"

"Cheap whiskey."

"That's a start." Her voice was wistful and distant. He got up and rummaged around in the kitchen. It had not received the once-over that the coffee table had and still reflected the young men in their early twenties that lived there. "You live here alone?" she asked, almost on cue.

"No, got a roommate that goes to the U. He's got a long weekend, though, so he's back home, visiting his folks. He's the messy one," Stas added, indicating the state of the kitchen. Clarification was important even if it bore little resemblance to the truth.

"Uh-huh," she said through a chuckle as he returned and put the whiskey down in front of her. The single ice cube smacked against the sides of the cup.

"Sorry about the lack of ice. Hope you didn't want it on the rocks, the roomie must have forgotten to refill the ice trays before he left too." A sheepish grin was set in place on his face.

She laughed, "No, this is perfect. The less it's watered down tonight the better, I think. Thanks." The humor slipped from her features and the moment drew out. They both stared into similar points of empty space without the necessity of words for the moment. Then she spoke again. "And thanks for coming for me tonight. I know we haven't even talked in ten years but I didn't know who else to call. Or, I guess, the real truth of the matter is…there was no one else to call."

"Think nothing of it. Cheers." He raised his drink, she clunked hers against it. The plastic cups Stas had rustled up lacked the satisfying clink provided by glass, but they were clean, for the most part anyway. They both took healthy swigs before replacing them on the wooden slats of the table.

"Are you even twenty-one yet?" she asked him.

"Nope," he replied with a sly smile, "but I have a killer fake ID."

"Is that so?"

"It is decidedly so, and it wasn't cheap either, but it works every time."

She smiled at his little quip and he watched it hang there on her features for several seconds before it drifted away turning into pursed lips that seemed to be veiling some kind of sorrow.

"I guess you're probably wondering what the hell I'm

doing here," she said into the strung-out silence.

"I'd be a liar if I said it hadn't crossed my mind. The whole 'I'm on the run and there might be people chasing me' is a damn good attention-grabber."

She attempted a laugh but it petered out, unsatisfied. Her eyes were on the floor in front of her but her focus was elsewhere, somewhere beyond the walls of the shabby little apartment that Stas shared with his college buddy. She said, "Where do I start, though?"

The question seemed to be rhetorical, so Stas said nothing.

"Do you remember my parents?" she asked.

"Vaguely. I don't have many memories from those days but yeah, I think I remember them."

"Well, my parents died the year I turned sixteen."

Stas made a small choking sound on the sip of whiskey he had just taken. "Whoa," was the only weak rejoinder he could muster as he cleared his throat.

"Their dying wasn't the worst thing that happened to me that year, believe it or not, but that part of the story is for another time." Stas had no idea what that was supposed to mean but cryptic ambiguity seemed to be how she conveyed most information now. She went on. "They were killed in a car accident, the details of which were pretty suspect but slipped my attention at first because of grief, and then continued to elude me thanks to the trauma that I was subjected to later. A year or so ago though, after I had mostly rehabilitated my own mental state, I started to have questions about how they died."

She paused. Her hand found its way to her whiskey on its own, without the help of her eyes which remained planted on the floor. Stas couldn't even manage the nebulous commentary of a low whistle. He just sat, dumbfounded. She was dropping some pretty heavy stuff but all he could think of was how adult she sounded. She was only two years older than him, twenty-two, but somehow, she had aged. Losing her parents and whatever it was that came after had taken its toll on her.

She sipped at her whiskey and then raised her head, leveling him with her gaze. "I believe my parents were murdered and I'm pretty sure I know who did it, or who was responsible for making it happen at least."

The air in his little apartment seemed heavier and had become harder to breathe. After ten years of no contact she was now back in his life, sitting on his couch and talking about the possibility of her parents having been murdered. The ability to process such details was evading him. It made him feel slow and stupid to have no response but he was at a loss. He forced his mouth to move, still unsure of what might come out of it.

"Have you gone to the cops?" he managed after what felt to him to be an eternity.

Her hard gaze softened and a small, sad smile curled the edges of her lips. "No, Stas. It took every ounce of courage I had to get here tonight and a lot of courage from some others as well." The last came out under her breath. "And it was one or the other. If I'd gone to the cops and nothing had come of it, and believe me when I say that nothing would have come of it, I never would have been able to pull off my... I never would have made it here tonight."

Stas could clearly tell she had intended to use the word escape and then changed her mind. He had little doubt that that was how she viewed it, though, an escape. "Who are you running from?" His voice had slipped to almost a whisper.

"I'll explain it all, but before I do, I have to know if you can help me." As she spoke, she again lifted her whiskey to her lips and he could see that she was shaking.

"Anything, name it."

"You say you've got a pretty good fake ID, right?"

He managed a confused nod and sputtered, "Yeah."

"I need one too, one that's better than yours, not just a fake ID but a real one for a person that doesn't actually exist, at least not yet. I need you to help me disappear."

She bore into him with her gaze.

For a long time two old friends that hadn't spoken in a decade looked at each other and nothing else, a vast world of space and time between them even though they sat mere feet from each other.

With no small amount of effort Stas broke from her stare. He was already running through the list of miscreants at his disposal that might be able to make someone vanish.

Minneapolis…
Spring, 2017

1

And Stas had been able to make it happen, and disappear she had. Not from him, but from the rest of the world. She became Lisa Lathrop and left her entire life behind, with the exception of Stas Mileski.

Now he realized that wasn't exactly true, though; he had not been the sole exception.

The stairwell was dark.

Slow and steady he made his descent into the basement of Jimmy's Bar. At the bottom he stepped off the final stair and looked to his left at the big steel door to the cooler. There would be kegs in there and that sounded way more appetizing than whatever it was that he was about to get into. He turned his attention to the door on his right.

He took one deep breath and opened it, revealing the hallway beyond. The small corridor was lit by a single bare bulb and the throw of its light was impeded by copious amounts of dust. There were two doors on each side of the short hallway. His apparent destination was the second one on the right.

He crossed the length of the hall in a few quick strides. Just as he reached the door the one across from it opened. A guy with full sleeves tattooed on his arms walked out into the hall and met him. Stas shot a glance past the guy back into the room and caught a glimpse of a very scared looking young man seated at a table. The guy with the tattooed sleeves pulled the door shut behind him and directed Stas back to his original destination across the hall. He stepped past Stas and opened the door.

It opened into a small little office, with the only real piece of furniture being an old metal utilitarian desk. Sitting behind that desk was a short, squat man. There was nothing exceptional about him and yet instinctively he demanded respect.

The man behind the desk was named Viktor Sokolov and Stas had known that eventually that old card and the number scratched on it would lead to him.

Stas had known who Sokolov was for a long time, had heard stories about him from his dad. His dad had known him when they were kids and you couldn't have grown up in this neighborhood without having heard whispered rumors about the guy. Viktor Sokolov was a man who could help you acquire things, the kind of things that those who were confined to working within the restrictions of the law might not be able to procure. Stas had been in search of just that sort of thing for Lisa eighteen years ago.

"Well, well, well, if it isn't Stas Mileski. How's this for a convenient surprise?" Viktor said from behind the desk. Stas had no idea what he was talking about. "Wes, why don't you grab a chair and put it right there in front of my desk where I can get a goddamn good look at this kid," he said to the guy with the tattoos. Wes retrieved a chair from the corner and set it in front of the desk. Stas sat down but was unable to decide what to make of Viktor's obviously false affability.

"Hey, Vik, how are ya?"

"Better now, Stas, better now."

He didn't know what that was supposed to mean but Stas didn't like it. "Look, Viktor, I need some information."

"Oh, you need some information? You hear that, Wes? Stas here needs some information."

Wes said nothing from the corner of the room to which

he had retreated. Stas was still at a loss but was tiring of whatever this game was being played at his expense.

"Viktor, I just need to—"

"Shut up, Stas."

Sokolov had put no real malice behind the previous statement but he didn't have to. Stas stopped talking.

"What the fuck are you trying to pull here, Stas?"

"What do you mean?"

Viktor was aggravated. "I mean I'm just not sure what your agenda is. Are you trying to get me arrested, maybe killed? Or are you just being a good old-fashioned idiot?"

"I literally have no idea what you are talking about."

"I was just about to send Wes here out to find your dumb ass and then, what do ya know? Your old code pops up again and now you want to see me."

"Wait, you were gonna come find me? What the hell for?"

Viktor Sokolov gave him a long assessing look before speaking. "Your friend, that lady you brought to me all those years ago, a couple weeks ago she used that same old code just like you did tonight. I don't like doing business that way but I agreed to meet. She came to see me, but it seems now that she didn't come alone. Maybe she didn't know it, but she brought some trouble with her and then she left it behind for me to deal with."

"What?" Stas asked, incredulous. "Why did she contact you? What did she want?"

"The same thing people always want from me, Stas. The same thing you guys wanted when you brought her to me in the first place. New papers, a new identity, the ability to shrug an old life off and start a new one." He gave a small shrug as if to accentuate his point.

"And you did that for her, again?" Stas was tempering a slow, fiery anger that was beginning to catch and kindle deep in his guts. "And you didn't tell me?"

"Why the hell would I tell you, Stas? As far as I'm concerned, it's none of your business. I knew your dad, I liked your dad, and that fondness may have provided a modicum of leeway when it came to you but don't you go and make the mistake of thinking that it goes any further than that. Discussing the situations of my clients with others would be antithetical to the purpose of my business. My clients want to disappear." He paused. "Not to mention, she paid extra to make sure I'd leave you out of it."

"She did what?"

The embers of his anger were still smoldering but were beginning to be stifled by confusion. Stas had brought Lisa to Viktor a long time ago in order to help her escape a life that had become a living hell. Now it appeared she had sought him out again on her own, leaving him out of the loop and in the dark.

While he could derive some solace from the fact that this turn of events lessened the likelihood that she had fallen victim to some sort of foul play, he could make no sense of why she would ditch the life she had been building. Things had seemed to be on an upward trajectory for her with Tim and his kid. Stas was still casting about in his head for answers when something else Sokolov had said caught his attention.

"She paid you extra to leave me out of it, but you just said you were about to come find me, why?"

Viktor Sokolov fixed him with a hard stare. "Like I said before, whatever mess she has gotten herself mixed up in, it's trying to find its way back to me. I've temporarily had to move my business into this damn basement. That ain't going to work for me, Stas."

Viktor nodded in the direction of his guy, Wes, with the tattooed sleeves, and Wes left the room. "Go stand over there by the wall," Sokolov told him, "and don't say a damn word." It did not seem as though the request was negotiable so Stas did as he was told.

2

Wes returned, leading the kid Stas had seen sitting in

the room across the hall into the little office. The kid's eyes flitted towards where Stas was standing but quickly returned to his own feet. Wes led him to the chair in front of the desk that Stas had occupied just a few moments earlier. In the brief glance they shared, Stas could see that the kid was terrified. It made him wonder if he maybe shouldn't elevate his own level of concern regarding this strange interaction.

"Sit down," Sokolov told the kid. The kid, who was probably somewhere in his middle twenties, followed the directive and put his butt in the seat. Wes retreated to the corner and stood next to Stas while his boss went on. "You know why you're here?" he asked the kid.

"I think so, Mr. Sokolov."

"How long have you worked for me, Tommy?"

"About four years," the kid replied.

"And nothing like what went down yesterday has ever happened before, has it?" The kid, Tommy, shook his head in the negative. "You did the right thing, coming to me first thing," Viktor went on. "I know you told Wes, but I want you to tell me again exactly what happened. You give it to me straight and you've got nothing to worry about, okay?" Now Tommy nodded. "Good, go ahead."

Tommy took another brief glance around the room but didn't let his gaze linger long on either Stas or Wes. He dropped his eyes to his hands which were fidgeting in his lap and then, slowly, he began to speak.

"I got the call about two o'clock that the drop was going down. I came here and picked up the package, the papers, from you. Then I drove over to Sentryz Market. I parked on the north side of the building and went inside."

The kid stopped talking but kept fidgeting. Viktor gave him a gentle prod. "You're doing good, kid. What happened next?"

"I bought three baguettes. The long kind that would be obvious sticking up out of my bag. I left the market but walked south out of the building, away from my car."

He stopped talking again and shot a nervous glance

toward Stas standing in the corner.

"It's alright," Viktor said. "You can explain the drop in front of him."

Tommy nodded and started again, slowly. "I took a right on 15th and started walking, holding the sack with the baguettes in it out where it could be seen. A car pulled up and asked for directions to the Armory, which was how I knew it was them. I get in the car, hand over the papers, they drive me at least five miles away and drop me off. Then I catch an Uber back to my car at Sentryz Market."

"So, the drop went just as planned?" Sokolov asked, even though he knew the answer. The kid nodded. "What happened then?"

"As I'm walking to my car in the parking lot, this big, black sedan with tinted windows, like a Chrysler 300 or something, comes flying up and stops next to me. This tough-looking dude in a suit gets out of the driver's side and opens the back door like I'm supposed to get in."

"And did you?"

"Yeah, he didn't seem like a cop exactly but his what-do-you-call-it, his authority was obvious. He didn't show me any sort of ID so I knew it wasn't any kind of official visit. I was pretty scared. I didn't know if they were the law, or someone who worked for you, or…whatever. I just didn't have any idea."

"So, you get in the back of the car. What happened then?"

"There was another man in a suit sitting in the back, an older dude. He looked like a lawyer or something, definitely different from the other guy. The driver was obviously muscle, you could tell just looking at him. This guy had a snootier air about him. I noticed his briefcase on the floor in front of him. There was, like, a lanyard with a pass card or something on it. I couldn't read the whole thing but on the bottom, it said City Hall." At that point Tommy actually cracked a small hesitant smile. "I didn't know whether to shit or laugh when I saw that. I knew I was probably in some serious trouble but at that point

I figured at least they weren't gonna kill me."

Viktor Sokolov returned young Tommy's little smile but Stas had a hard time believing much in the way of its authenticity. "What did the guy ask you about, Tommy?"

The remnants of the smile slipped from the young man's face. "He started asking me questions. Most of 'em were softballs about me, what I do for work, that sort of thing. He knew my name which freaked me out a little. I asked him a couple of times who he was but he dodged the question, or just straight up ignored it, I guess. He was bugging me about where I went from Sentryz, but when I wouldn't give him a straight answer, he started asking me about the woman."

"What woman?" Viktor asked as if he were leading a witness.

"The Lathrop lady, the one that you had me run the papers for."

That got Stas' attention.

"This is the important part, Tommy," Sokolov told him, "be clear about the details, the little things count."

"He said he knew I was running new papers for a woman named Lisa Lathrop. He asked if I knew that I could be charged with a felony for my part in this. I told him I didn't know what he was talking about. He wanted to know what the new identity was, what her name would be. Like I would know, but still I stuck to my story. Then he launched into a diatribe about jail time and I relaxed. I knew they weren't gonna strong arm me during this interrogation. I asked him if I was under arrest, and told him that if I wasn't, I was leaving. And then he changed and it was a little freaky. He didn't get angry, he just dropped any act that he was trying to help me and he turned cold. He said 'I can't arrest you, Tommy, I'm not a cop. But maybe you'll wish I was. Sometimes it's just safer to be locked up.' Then he told me to get out of his car. I did and his goon, who'd been standing outside, just stared me down before he got back into the driver's seat and they pulled away."

"And that's when you called Wes?"

"Yeah."

"You did good, Tommy. I just have one more question for you." Viktor slid a photo across the desk to the kid. "Is this the guy that was in the car with you?" The color drained from Tommy's face and he nodded. Sokolov nodded as well and pulled the photo back. "Alright, Tommy, we're gonna have to take a few precautions. Wes will get you set up but we're gonna get you out of town for a little while. You cool with that?"

"Of course, Mr. Sokolov. Thanks."

"Go back across the hall and wait for Wes. He'll be over in a minute to take care of the arrangements."

Tommy stood, gave a slight nod, and left the room. Stas had a million questions but no idea where to start. He needn't have worried though. Viktor Sokolov continued to dictate the direction of the conversation.

"Sit down, Stas."

Again, he did as directed and now Sokolov slid the photo he had shown Tommy across to him.

"You know who that is?" Sokolov asked.

"No idea."

"His name is Ted Logan, he's the goddamn chief of staff to the Mayor of Minneapolis. Why is the Mayor's chief of staff trying to shake down my guy?"

For one of the few times in his life, Stas was speechless. He had no answer to the question and Sokolov didn't wait long for any weak nuggets of wisdom he might try and effuse.

"Because I knew and liked your dad, I did not go straight to breaking your legs. I'm going to give you an opportunity to find your friend, figure out what the hell is going on and to get the heat off of me. If you can't manage that in a timely fashion then I may have to resort to some less pleasant means of encouragement. You understand me?"

Wes had just stepped back into the room. No doubt he would be the one carrying out those less pleasant means of encouragement. Stas managed a nod.

"Good. Find your friend and put this shit to bed. Now get out of my office."

Stas stood slowly and walked to the door on unstable

legs. Wes gave him an unpleasant smile as he opened the door. Stas made his way out into the little hall and then back to the stairs. The climb to the top was laborious. When he finally made it back upstairs the world felt surreal. Al Witkowski was behind the bar but didn't even look at him.

Stas walked the length of the place and out of Jimmy's into the night.

3

The late evening air was crisp but downright balmy compared to what it had been twenty-four hours earlier. The air smelled of the coming spring and it was all but impossible to believe it could have been snowing just last night. Last night, for so many reasons, seemed as if it had happened a lifetime ago.

Stas wanted a beer, but he needed to think. He decided to just start walking. In this neighborhood a bar would find him just as easily as he would find it, whether he was looking for one or not. Making sense of Lisa's actions leading up to her sudden disappearing act was paramount, but getting into that woman's head would be no small feat. Stas had never known anyone who played things as close to the vest as she did. Part of the mystery was that, other than the fact that she was having occasional conversations with someone whom she didn't want identified by a contact name in her phone, he didn't have any idea what she'd been up to. Tim didn't seem to know either. And throw in the fact that the mayor's chief of staff had taken an interest in her, Stas was stumped. With these few facts spinning around in his head, he struck off, heading north on Fourth Street from Jimmy's Bar.

He did not notice the headlights that popped on from the darkness behind him. Stas walked on, oblivious. He turned his thoughts to Viktor Sokolov. Stas wasn't exactly scared of the guy but he knew better than to take his threats lightly.

Stas had always known who Sokolov was. He was the kind of shadowy figure that enamored the neighborhood kids when they were growing up. The kind of man who inspired their mouths to run whether they knew what they were talking about or not. When Stas had found himself in need of Viktor's services it only took a little bit of hustling to come up with the appropriate way to make contact with him. Once a few things had been arranged and the proper wheels greased, Stas had received that old business card with that one word, DESOLATE, printed on it. He was to call the number on the back, leave his code word and number, and then dispose of the card. He had followed the directions, right up until that last part.

The fact that Lisa had the number and his old password even though he had kept the card meant that she had known something like this was possible right from the start. She must have taken precautions and copied them down way back then, just in case, and it looked like 'just in case' had just become a reality. The leafless tree branches swayed along the boulevard in the slightest of breezes. Stas continued to stroll, lost in rumination, and his feet just continued to carry him on.

Behind him the headlights pulled slowly away from the curb.

Without the aid of any conscious decision making on his part, at some point his legs had apparently decided of their own volition that his destination would be The Palace. That was just fine, he needed to talk this out and Louis Jones, Big Lou, was one of the few people he could trust as a sounding board. He put his hands deep in his pockets, waited for a handful of cars to pass, and crossed the busier thoroughfare of Lowry Avenue into the pool of light tossed upon the sidewalk from the signage on the side of the bar.

Stas released a long exhale and walked into The Palace. He looked around the establishment but didn't see Louis anywhere. Stas checked the time and realized that Big Lou would probably not be taking up his post for another half hour or so. He sidled over to a bar stool to wait.

Outside of the bar, a gunmetal-gray sport coupe turned from Fourth onto Lowry Avenue. It crawled slowly past the front door of The Palace and came to a stop along the curb just up the street from the entrance. The headlights were extinguished.

Time passed, as did another light contingent of traffic. Then the street fell to a momentary quiet and nothing moved, an action echoed in the interior of the vehicle at the curb.

4

Stas checked the digital readout on the clock behind the bar. Big Lou would hopefully be showing up soon. While he was waiting, he wrangled up a pen from the bartender and grabbed a cocktail napkin. He needed to take some notes, if for no other reason than to at least keep a running tally of anything he knew before he went ahead and forgot it.

He wrote down 'Lisa's disappeared' then in parentheses he added 'again.' Below that he put Sokolov's name. He added the name of the man from the photo, 'Ted Logan.' He sat back and tapped the pen absently on the bar top. After a moment of contemplation, along the side of the napkin he scrawled the number 320 indicating the area code for the strange phone number from Lisa's call log. He circled it and drew an arrow pointing at Logan's name. He punctuated that latest notation with a giant question mark.

He sat back and looked over his very short list of clues. He took a swig of beer and another name floated into his mind. It was not one that had cropped up in connection with any of the events of the last day regarding Lisa's most recent disappearing act, but Stas thought it could be a tentacle that might need some pondering.

Cortland Whittier.

Whittier had been a major catalyst to why she had sought him out and needed a new identity in the first place. Stas had almost forgotten about the guy. He and Lisa never even discussed him anymore. Not for years, since he'd perished in a fire. But in the early days Cortland Whittier had been the terror that robbed his friend of sleep and haunted her waking hours

77

as well. In the early days he had been the topic of conversations between them often.

At that moment the door to the bar opened and the large silhouette of Louis Jones filled the entryway. Stas let Cortland Whittier, and the complicated history he'd created for Lisa, slip from his mind.

After ditching his jacket and punching the clock, Big Lou made his way down to where Stas was seated.

"Stas, what's up? You getting an early start tonight?"

"I wish. Unfortunately I'm only here for the pleasure of your conversation, so maybe I should have another beer, make it palatable."

"Aren't you a funny little man? What do ya wanna talk about?"

"I need a favor."

"Shoot."

"I need you to talk to your brother for me." The stare he received didn't bode well for the favor being granted.

"I don't think so. He's still pissed that you invoked his name after that barroom tussle you found yourself in last month."

"I wasn't gonna go downtown over those uptown A-holes. They come across the river and start shit, I was defending the neighborhood."

"Yeah, well, Terrell didn't see it that way. He saw it as your dumb ass using the name of the only cop you know to get out of trouble at closing time."

"I know other cops." Stas couldn't quite fight down an impish grin as he spoke.

"Just because other cops know you, that doesn't mean you know other cops," Louis said, but he was smiling too and Stas thought there was a decent chance he still might get the help he was looking for.

"Will you talk to him?"

"You tell me what you want to know and *then* I'll decide if I'm gonna talk to him."

"I've got a phone number. It's been disconnected but

I'm trying to track it. I think it might belong to a guy named Ted Logan. He works for the mayor. I think he knew Lisa somehow and I need to know how they might be connected."

"How would Terrell know that?"

"I wouldn't expect him to know, but maybe he could ask around or something?" Stas was trying not to sound like he was pleading, at least not yet.

"He's a patrolman, not a detective."

"Yeah, but the fact that he's a cop at all makes him a hell of a lot closer to being a detective than I am."

"Alright, Columbo, why don't you just ask Lisa how she's knows this Logan character?"

"Because she's disappeared."

That gave Louis Jones pause. "How do you mean disappeared?"

"I mean like the first time. When we were in our twenties, only this time she didn't tell me it was happening and I don't have any idea where she's gone, or why, or whether or not she had a choice in the matter."

Louis continued to fix Stas with that unflinching stare. He ran his big hand over his face and his gaze softened. "Alright, man, I'll ask him. I wouldn't expect too much though."

"Any help is more help than I've got now. Thanks, Lou."

"What are friends for, right? Give me that number and I'll pass it along. Anything else?"

"Nope, that's it." He wrote down the phone number on another bar napkin and handed it to Louis.

"Stay out of trouble, Stas," Big Lou said as he turned and walked back to his post at the door. Stas drained the rest of his beer and followed him towards the exit. He pantomimed slapping Big Lou on the butt as he passed him and received a glare that would have caused any regular patron of The Palace to crumble. But Stas had seen that look before and lived to tell about it so he walked on by and out the door, back out into the night. He crossed Lowry and headed back up Fourth Street to where his truck was parked in front of Jimmy's Bar.

As soon as Stas had crossed the busier intersection at Lowry Avenue and disappeared down into the more residential part of Fourth Street, the headlights of the gunmetal-gray sport coupe parked up the street popped into life again and the car pulled away from the curb.

<u>5</u>

Stas peeled his eyelids apart. This time it was not the previous night's debauchery that had sealed them shut but rather the opposite, he had slept the sleep of the dead. Arriving at his apartment last night, Stas had lain down in bed and pulled out the cocktail napkin containing his few notes. The next thing he knew he was struggling to get his eyes open and the sun was streaming through the windows.

He searched around him on the bed for the napkin he had dropped when sleep had taken him and found it crumpled beneath his body. Stas dragged himself out of bed, put some coffee on, and spread the napkin out the best he could on the counter.

He did little more than stare at it for the few minutes it took for the coffee to brew. The beeping from the coffeemaker alerted him that the next stage of waking up was now ready to commence. He poured a cup and took it, along with the napkin, to the couch where some real thinking could be done.

When he had originally scribbled down the information, Stas had thought the 320 area code number might possibly be connected to Ted Logan, the Mayor's mysterious Chief of Staff. Tim Boyd had told him that Lisa had actually had some calls of lengths that would constitute a conversation with whoever had once resided at the other end of that number. Logan obviously knew who Lisa was but did she know him? And were they having occasional conversations on the phone?

He grabbed his beat-up laptop and moved it to the coffee table to do some research. It was a tough reliable machine that he'd put through its paces over the years and it bore the scars, the dings and dents, of heavy use. As he sat and flipped open the computer a smoldering ember of long-forgotten initiative caught deep in his gut and flamed into tentative life.

Last night Stas had told his good friend Louis Jones that he was no detective, but that did not mean he didn't have an investigative knack. His senior year of high school Stas had been on the verge of failing an English class that would have kept him from graduating. A dedicated teacher determined not to let a kid like Stas slip through the cracks had assigned him a side project enabling him to pass the class and graduate.

She told him he could write a paper for extra credit on a book called *All the President's Men*. Stas hadn't previously read a book cover to cover during the entirety of his high school career, but from the first chapter he had been hooked by Woodward and Bernstein's dogged investigative reportage. He took to it so well that for a while he'd given real consideration to pursuing a career in journalism, even interning for a summer at the Star Tribune, the Minneapolis daily paper.

Life got in the way and eventually he strayed from his journalistic pursuits to a trajectory more in line with those of his peers from the neighborhood. But in quiet moments he still sometimes felt the pull to dig in and tear up the intricacies of a good mystery, to reacquaint himself with those skills he had started to develop in his youth. And today that mystery was Ted Logan.

A quick search gave him a rough outline of who Logan was, at least as a public figure. He seemed to be a man who liked to be near power or at the very least, prominence. Logan had had his hand in all sorts of small-time elections and candidacies in his younger days. His career had continued to ascend over the subsequent years. He'd even worked his way up to being on staff for several Governors in the past. In fact, he'd been a high-ranking member of the current Governor's cabinet until two years ago when he'd left to attach himself to rising political star Sammy Douglas and his bid for the Minneapolis Mayor's office. Being the Mayor of Minneapolis was not often considered a stepping stone position but Mayor Douglas seemed destined for a bigger and brighter stage and Ted Logan was well aligned to be by his side for the ride.

While Logan's resume was interesting background information and might be important later, it didn't advance the pursuit that he was on at the moment. Stas took a sip of his coffee and found it had cooled beyond what he could stomach. He went to the kitchen to dump it and get a, if not fresh, at least hotter refill. Returning to the couch and computer he decided to see if he could find out a little bit about where Logan was from. If it turned out he was from the St. Cloud area or anywhere out near Stearns County that would be a pretty solid connection to a number with a 320 area code.

His fingers flitted across the keys. Several minutes later he was beginning to become disheartened. Not only was he unable to pin down where Ted Logan hailed from, anything he did find seemed to lead him well toward the northern part of the state which wouldn't land his guy in the geographical area he was shooting for. The 320 area code ran like a belt across the middle of the state. It excluded the metro area which had its own area codes, and anything more than seventy-five miles north of the city was out as well. Not that where he was from would preclude Logan from being the owner of the phone number, but with no confirmed connections, it remained nothing more than a guess.

Stas decided to dig into the one story that at least helped him place Logan up north. A little more hunting and pecking and he was able to establish that Mr. Ted Logan, chief of staff to Mayor Sammy Douglas, had been born and raised in McGregor, Minnesota. A quaint small town whose population swelled during the summer as visitors descended upon the many lakes in the surrounding area.

Stas was not exactly unfamiliar with that area of the state and his stomach did a little somersault leaving him queasy for just a second, like he'd hit a moderate, but unexpected, drop on a roller coaster. The town of McGregor lay just down the highway apiece from a lake called Minnewawa.

And located on Lake Minnewawa was a little resort where Stas had spent a couple summers as a kid, up until he almost drowned in a fishing pond. An old friend of his had spent more than a couple summers there, quite a few actually, back when her name had been Anne Callahan, before she had shed that skin and become Lisa Lathrop.

Technically all that Stas had really discovered with the location of Logan's home town was a coincidental proximity, but it felt like more than that. It felt like a connection.

He pulled up Ted Logan's Wikipedia page and began scouring the reference section. He missed it on his first pass but as he looked over the page again, he found something promising. It was an article from The Voyageur Press, the local paper that served McGregor and surrounding areas, written a couple of years ago when Logan had joined the campaign for Sammy Douglas. It looked to be a 'local kid made good' kind of story.

Stas clicked the link and grabbed his coffee to sip on as he skimmed the article. It started with a small retrospective on Logan's early life, but when he got to the second paragraph Stas nearly dropped his coffee. A small portion sloshed over the lip of his mug and onto the floor by his feet but he paid it no mind.

A smile curled at the edge of his lip. He was no longer speculating on coincidental proximity. He had just established a firm connection between Lisa Lathrop and Ted Logan.

He popped into the kitchen to grab a towel to clean up the spilled coffee. The towel was hanging, draped from the handle of the refrigerator. As it pulled free from the handle in his hand, Stas stopped.

He stared at the fridge.

Something Lisa used to say to him, the way she would sign-off of their phone calls, flitted across his mind. For years she had been saying the same thing every time. She claimed it was from some movie, and she had said it so often, he'd basically stopped hearing it. It wasn't the whole puzzle, but it might be a piece. Maybe not the one that pulls the whole picture into focus, but one piece could lead to another and that's how a puzzle gets solved.

<u>6</u>

Stas stepped out into the sunshine with his keys in hand and a spring in his step. When Viktor Sokolov had tasked him with the daunting endeavor of uncovering what sort of interest the Mayor's office might have in his oldest friend, Stas could see no path to the completion of the directive. Even with the clear message that failure would result in great peril to his own personal well-being. Now, less than twenty-four hours later, while he was still just nibbling around the edges, he had something to go on. A thread he could pull and see what it might unravel in regard to Logan, as well as a possible lead when it came to Lisa's whereabouts.

He unlocked the truck and climbed in. It was a beautiful day for a drive and Stas was going to make a day trip to Red Wing to have a look around Lisa's place, to see if there was anything to the memory that had just surfaced. The peculiar phrase she would use to close out their calls. It came back to him looking at his own little refrigerator and now he wanted to have a look at hers.

Tim Boyd hadn't found anything he thought useful at Lisa's house, but Stas had a feeling the two of them probably said their goodbyes in a different manner, and Tim hadn't had any idea what he might be looking for.

Once he had cleared out of the Twin Cities Metro area and was cruising south on Highway 61 running along the Mississippi River, Stas had time and allowed his mind the freedom to wander. He began to dissect what he had learned from the Voyageur Press piece he had stumbled upon.

In the fall of 1980 golden boy Ted Logan left the sleepy, small-town, lake life of McGregor behind and headed off to the big city of Minneapolis and the University of Minnesota to pursue a degree in Political Science. But in the spring of 1982 when the hometown hero returned for the summer, he spent that summer, as well as the next few, working at the Minnewawa Resort.

Lisa's parents had worked there from the time it opened in 1980 right up until their deaths. Lisa had been around it her entire childhood, had lived nearby her whole life until that rainy night in the fall of 1999 when he'd picked her up at the Amtrak station. She would have only been about five years old in 1982 but she would have been around for the couple of summers that Logan worked there. The resort was a decent size but not huge by any stretch of the imagination. There had only been so many employees; Logan would've known who she was. A precocious kid like her would not have gone unnoticed.

So Logan would've known Lisa when she was a kid, but how that connected to his interest in finding her now was information Stas was still lacking. He was hoping to find something at Lisa's house that might flush out any further connection.

According to the Voyageur Press article, after graduating from college Logan had spent one final summer at the resort then moved full time to the Cities to continue the pursuit of his chosen career. He would have been in his early twenties and Lisa would have been about eight years old when his employment at the resort ended. Since Logan had worked at the resort, not only would he have known Lisa, he would have known her parents as well. They would have been roughly the same age, contemporaries at least.

And if Logan had known Lisa's parents back then, could it have been possible that he had known Cortland Whittier as well? If there had been any connection between those two there could be some dark roads that would need to be travelled before he might be able to parse with any clarity what sort of mess Lisa had found herself in.

He was getting way ahead of himself. Much like he had earlier with the 320 phone number, Stas was speculating, and speculation without corroboration would only lead to trouble. With little reluctance he shifted his mental gears as he physically pressed the brake and slowed to turn off of Highway 61 and onto the smaller county road that led to Lisa's house. Minutes later he slowed again and turned in, passing her mailbox.

He pulled up to the end of her long driveway in front of the attached garage and shut off the engine, listening to it tick and cool. He listened to the world around him. It was full of sounds, the call of birds, the hum of insects, but to Stas it was still so quiet without the messy thrum of city sounds. He got out of the truck and looked at the house.

It had been a long time since he'd been out here. She'd done a lot. The landscaping looked great. The house itself looked nice too except that it had a definite empty, or maybe abandoned, feel that gave him the creeps. He turned and looked back down the driveway. In another week or two the road would be out of view, covered by the incoming dense foliage of the many trees adorning the front yard.

But this early in the spring the branches were only just beginning to push out their nascent buds and he could see the end of the driveway quite well, providing him an excellent view of the road.

It also provided an excellent view of a gunmetal gray sport coupe as it drove past the end of the driveway and continued up the road. His heart jumped without warning from its rightful place in his chest to somewhere in his throat.

It struck him right then that he'd been seeing a lot of that little gray car lately. It had been parked across the street this morning when he'd left his apartment.

Had there been someone inside?

He couldn't be sure but he thought that maybe there had been. And he thought he'd seen it last night too, a couple of times.

Now, standing stock-still in Lisa's front yard, he cocked his head as he did his best to follow the receding sound of the engine. He didn't have to track it for long. The engine cut out seconds later and not so very far from the spot he stood. He looked straight out through the woods toward where he thought he had last heard the sound of the engine. Even without the adornment of leaves the trees were thick enough in that direction, to the south of the house, that he could gain no good visual advantage. He did a quick scan of his entire surroundings attempting to determine the best course of action. After finishing his assessment, he made a hasty but calculated decision.

He whirled around and sprinted for the far corner of the garage, in the opposite direction of where he had last heard the hum of the car's engine.

He cleared the corner and slowed, walking with quick strides to the back of the garage. He stopped at the far corner and peered around into the backyard where not so long ago Danny Boyd would have been working on adding a curveball to his pitch selection. Now the yard was empty and it shouldered an ominous quiet in the still morning air. He could hear nothing from the far side of the house, just the call of nature that, so subtle when he had first arrived, seemed to be everywhere now.

From there he skirted the perimeter of the yard staying within the cover of the trees lining it, his eyes remaining riveted on the far side of the house watching for any movement. He was attempting to maintain silence but was all too aware of the clamor he was causing with every step. The bird calls were more present; the cracking of twigs beneath his feet seemed deafening. All sound had taken on an amplified quality except for the path trod by whoever had been driving that sporty gray car. That newcomer seemed to be the epitome of silence and stealth.

Slow but steady he made his way around the wooded edge of the yard moving from the relative cover of one tree to the next. He'd come to a position where he had pretty good visual coverage of the south side of the house and the forestry beyond. He posted up and waited, eyes trained in the direction of where he'd last heard the engine before it cut out.

Crouched between two trees that were growing right next to each other Stas thought he was well camouflaged but the longer he sat with no sign of his stalker, the more an anxious edge began to infiltrate. Like an itch he couldn't scratch, it wouldn't allow him to remain still for long. Some course of action was required. He readied himself to move but then stopped just in time.

The sound that halted him was slight but it stayed his movement and at least for a moment it kept him from surrendering his position. A second later he caught a glimpse of something, the fabric of a shirtsleeve perhaps, from behind a tree that was no further than five feet from where he crouched still hidden by those two trees. He held his breath. Birdsong lilted through the air from tree to tree, but nothing moved.

<u>7</u>

The shirtsleeve, if that was what it was, had slipped back behind the tree that was mere feet from him. Stas now knew his adversary's position while his own remained concealed. He potentially had the upper hand but his knees were beginning to voice their displeasure with the crouching position he'd found himself in. He didn't dare move, though. Another soft shuffling sound drew his attention and the shirtsleeve materialized into a man as the guy stepped out from behind the tree.

Stas let the breath he'd been holding out at such a low slow meter that it seemed to defy time itself. The man started to move, away from him, showing Stas his back. Stas could reach him in two or three strides if he went now, if his aching knees would still allow him to spring. It was time. Another second and the man would be far enough away that he might hear Stas coming before he'd be able to close the distance between them. It had to be now. He took one deep breath and then shot up like a piston. His knees held up their end of the bargain and he was able to launch himself but they cracked as he did so, popping like a gunshot. The man heard it and started turning in his direction a second before Stas hit him with a flying tackle.

He got a very good look at his mysterious stalker just a

second too late to slow his momentum, and Stas drove Tim Boyd into the ground, finishing the tackle in a way that would have made his high school football coach proud. He heard Tim gasp as the wind ran out of him. Stas rolled off him and stood, a little short of breath himself. Tim writhed on the ground struggling to pull any of the fresh spring air into his lungs.

"Shit, man! I'm sorry," Stas managed between his own halting breaths. Tim could muster no more of a response than a terrible wheezing sound. It went on for a minute or two and then mellowed as Tim slowly began to manage the function of breathing again. "You scared the crap out of me." Stas told him as he helped Tim to his feet and waited for him to recover to the point where he might be able to speak. "You've been following me since last night? I kept seeing that little gray car of yours. I thought I might have some real trouble on my tail."

"Sorry," Tim croaked.

"Seriously, man... I was ready to kick the crap out of you."

Tim straightened up and put his hands on his hips. His eyes narrowed to a squint and he put his face to the sky still trying to regulate his breathing. Stas waited for him.

"I know, it was stupid, but I was driving myself crazy. I couldn't just sit and wait anymore," Tim said once he could speak without wheezing. "Damn cops aren't doing anything and I have no idea where my girlfriend is..." Tim was still squinting but now it seemed to be because he was fighting back tears.

Stas released a long, heavy sigh. "Alright, man, I get it." They both took a second and at last fully caught their collective breath. "Let's make ourselves useful then. You have a key for the house?" Tim nodded. "Good, let's check it out."

"Did you find something?" A pleading excitement was tingeing Tim's voice.

"Yeah, I might have found something. Let's go inside."

"Is she safe?"

"I think so." Stas cut himself off before he could add 'for now.' He didn't think that sentiment would be helpful at the moment. "Let's go, I'll fill you in as best I can." Tim nodded and they walked back to the front of the house.

At the front door Tim used his key to open it and he walked in with Stas following behind him. There was still some detritus smeared across the tiles of the entryway from when Tim had tracked snow and muck in with him the night Lisa disappeared. Stas took it all in, in particular the way Tim tried to avoid looking at the signs that would remind him of the last time he was here.

Being in Lisa's house without her was weird enough for Stas; he couldn't imagine how it would be for Tim who had practically lived here up until a couple of days ago. While Tim's presence here might actually be helpful, Stas would have to finesse things with him around. He couldn't really just start digging through stuff with Tim hanging over his shoulder. Half the stuff in the house could be Tim's for all Stas knew. And he wasn't sure how much he was willing to share at this point.

Stas waited in the kitchen while Tim made a quick tour of the house opening shades. He eyed her refrigerator which had been the instigation for this little trip in the first place.

Lisa signed-off phone calls with him the same way every time. *'If anything ever happens to me, look behind the ice box.'* Maybe it was actually from a movie, maybe not, but he was getting the feeling that at the very least it wasn't just the nonsense he'd always assumed it to be. He longed to pull the fridge from the cabinet and check behind it, but he was still reticent to lay out all his cards on the table.

He turned his attention to the backyard, this time noticing Danny's pitch-back leaning up against the backside of the garage. For a second something that seemed like movement from deep in the woods caught his eye. He watched that spot intently for a couple of seconds until he was satisfied it was nothing. He was probably just a little jumpy after having been tailed by Tim for the better part of two days.

"So, what brought us out here?" Tim asked, walking back into the kitchen.

Stas debated giving him a hard time about the

implication of his question being that they had come together. Not that one of them had followed the other. But he decided Tim didn't need to be hassled any more than he had already been so instead he asked, "Do you know if Lisa knew a guy named Ted Logan?"

Tim shook his head. "Never heard of him, who is he?"

Stas sighed again. "Let's sit down. I think we've got some stuff we need to talk about." He could tell from the look that came over Tim's face that any conversation that required a sit-down was not where he was hoping this conversation would go.

For a second Stas thought Tim might balk, but he didn't. Instead he said, "I know it's early but if this is going to be a conversation that we're gonna have to sit down for, I think I might need a beer, you mind?"

Stas gave a little chuckle. "Nope, not as long as you have one in there for me too." Tim just stood there for a moment, a vacancy creeping over him, then he gave a slow nod and turned toward the fridge. Stas took a seat at Lisa's little breakfast nook and watched Tim open the door to the refrigerator. Beyond where Tim stood, Stas could see bottles of beer lined up on the bottom shelf like a marching band waiting to take the field.

Stas watched Tim's shoulders slump as he looked down at those bottles of beer, those bottles of beer that she had stocked up on for the rest of their weekend, a weekend that never was and now, may never be.

But in an unprecedented turn of events, Stas Mileski's thoughts now went beyond the beer, to what might possibly be hiding behind it.

8

"How do you know she's safe?" Tim asked. He was fidgeting with the label on his beer bottle where he now sat across the little table from Stas.

"I said I *think* she's safe."

"Okay…what makes you think so?"

"Because of what happened on Friday…" Stas was having trouble finding the right way to put it. "I don't think she was abducted or anything. Disappearing was a conscious choice that she made."

Tim seemed to resist the idea. He released the label on the bottle he'd been picking at and looked away, chewing on his lip. "Yeah?" Tim paused, "what makes you think that?"

"Because she's disappeared before, only the last time I helped her to make it happen." Tim shot him a look but Stas didn't allow it to deter him. "I didn't help her this time but I know who did." Tim's hand moved absently back to the bottle and started peeling the label again. Stas waited for him to say something. When Tim did not, he went on. "How much do you know about her past?"

Tim shook his head. "Not much at all," he finally managed. "She never talked about it, not her family, nothing."

Stas took a long draw from the neck of his bottle and set it back down on the table. He didn't really feel like it was his place to have this conversation with her boyfriend but saw no other real option at this point. "Well, I guess by not telling you anything, it kept her from having to tell you a bunch of lies."

"What do you mean?" Tim's voice cracked.

There was nothing to do but wade into it, and Stas did so. "Lisa grew up in a cult," he said as matter-of-fact as he could put it. That first revelation dropped and sat heavy between them in the quiet kitchen. "The name her parents gave her was Anne Callahan. The parents that gave her that name were religious nut-jobs." Tim's jaw started to move as if he meant to speak, but nothing came out. After a second his lips came together in a tight, grim line. Stas went on. "Her parents died under what she considered mysterious circumstances not long before she turned sixteen. For another six years she stayed with that cult, until a night in 1999 when she escaped, found me, and I helped her change her identity to Lisa Lathrop."

Tim was struggling to find coherence in the words that he was hearing. He lifted his beer to take a sip but then returned it to the table before it had actually made its way up to his mouth. It took a serious effort but after a time, he found his voice. "Her real name was Anne?"

"She didn't consider anything from that part of her life 'real.' She had been brainwashed and mistreated. That wasn't her. The woman you know, Lisa, that's who she really is."

For a long moment it looked like Tim would try to continue to speak but the words were eluding him just as all sanity seemed to be eluding this conversation.

Stas said, "I helped her find someone who could get her new papers, a new identity. Apparently, a week or so ago, she made contact with him again and established another new identity." Stas gave his story a break, allowing Tim a moment to soak it in. Stas could tell just by looking at him that it wasn't going well. "You doing okay, man?" Stas asked, but it wasn't a question that really required any response. The obvious answer was written all over his face.

Tim stood up from the table but still said nothing. He paced a few steps away across the kitchen floor running his hands through his hair. He let them come to rest on top of his head. Stas was hit by a sudden strong image of Tim snapping and screaming, trying to pull his hair out. But instead he just stood there, dumbfounded, his hands balled up gripping the hair on top of his head.

"I ask because now we're getting to the part pertaining to her safety that I'm less confident about. The guy I asked you about, Ted Logan, he's chief of staff to the Mayor of Minneapolis."

"What?" Tim managed to mutter. His hands relinquished their clutch on his hair but still rested, helpless, on top of his head.

"I know, man. On the surface it doesn't really make any sense."

Tim upheld his position, staring into nothing, trying to decipher connections that would make this information make any kind of sense. "What the hell would that have to do with Lisa?"

"I don't know, but the guy who ran the new papers for her was getting some heat from this Logan guy. We're not the only ones looking for her."

"I literally don't know what you're talking about. Why would some guy from the Mayor's office be looking for her?"

Stas shook his head. "I don't know what his motivation might be now, but I think he knew her when she was a kid, which would mean this Logan guy knew her parents too. I'm thinking he might be the owner of the 320 area code phone number…possibly." Stas expected some sort of response from Tim but for a second received nothing. Then in a sudden quick movement Tim's hands popped up off his head; now he just held them suspended a couple of inches above his hair.

"What the…" Tim said trailing off. He was staring out the window into the backyard.

"What is it?" Stas asked standing as he spoke. He was struck by a sudden distant pang. A scant memory surfacing from when he'd first walked into the kitchen and thought he'd seen something out in the yard. Seconds later Tim affirmed that thought process.

"I think there's someone out there, in the woods." Tim's voice came out low almost in a raspy whisper.

"Where?" Stas asked, his voice dropping as well because the situation seemed to dictate it.

Tim pointed out the window and Stas tried to follow the line designated by his finger and at first saw nothing. But maybe there was something out there, fifty or so yards into the tree line? It was nothing discernible, just an oddity, an incongruity amongst the trees. But then that incongruity solidified and a man broke from his wooded cover racing deeper into the forestry. Seconds later Lisa's back door was slamming shut behind Stas as he and Tim gave chase across the yard.

9

They hit the woods in unison, crunching brush and old

94

dead leaves beneath their pounding feet. Stas saw no sign of their adversary and didn't think Tim, who had fallen slightly behind him, could either. They were running hard and, for the most part, blind. All they had to go on was the direction the guy had been running in the first place. Since that initial glimpse neither of them had seen their quarry and they were moving too fast to really survey their surroundings. Stas was about to pull up and take stock when he hit the hill that Danny Boyd had slipped on all those months ago while searching for his baseball.

Much like Danny last fall, Stas was unable to keep his feet. His knee buckled at the sudden change of elevation and he hit the ground hard, rolling a few feet further down the hill. He popped up hopping on one leg, reticent to put the one with the knee that had failed him back down for a second. He tested it and found with some amazement that it held and that the pain was not as bad as he would've expected. Tim slowed up and stopped, standing next to him.

"You alright?" Tim asked, somewhat out of breath.

"Fine. You hear anything?"

Tim listened for a moment then shook his head. They both scanned the forest floor around them looking for anything out of the norm that may indicate the direction that the man may have taken. There was nothing and Stas was about to say so when, not so far from the spot they stood, an engine roared to life.

"Boat!" Tim exclaimed. "He's on the river." Then he took off running in that direction. Stas followed but was falling behind. His knee was not causing him any great aggravation but he couldn't bring himself to trust it bearing the weight of an all-out sprint yet. Tim had distanced himself by a good ten feet or so when they heard the throttle open up and a powerful engine begin to put distance between them. Stas couldn't favor the knee any longer. He put his trust in the fact that it would hold and began to run hard.

Tim broke through the tree line and stopped short just as Stas had almost covered the gap that had opened up between them. Stas reached him and tried to slow but didn't make it quite in time and he ran into Tim. They didn't go down but stumbled a few steps closer to the embankment that Tim had pulled up in an effort to avoid. They shuffled toward the decline holding each other in an awkward embrace but didn't fall.

When they had their feet settled beneath them, they separated and turned their attention to the speedboat that was cruising away up the river and the lone man on board at the helm. He was dressed in a drab green-colored shirt, not quite camouflage but it didn't stick out either. The only discerning thing about him was the stocking cap he wore despite the moderate temperature. It made him look like a longshoreman. Stas supposed it was appropriate seeing as he had just made his escape on a boat, on a river.

At that moment the man turned and looked back at them. He was far enough away that it was difficult to make out the sly smile on his face, but the sarcastic salute he tossed up in their direction was impossible to miss. Then he reached down and grabbed a bundle of something off of the floor of the boat and stowed it under the captain's chair.

"Screw you!" Stas called out, his voice echoing around between the trees lining the Mississippi but still not loud enough to get past the now receding sound of the boat's large motor. The man straightened up, retaking control of the boat just as the river veered to the left. He opened up the throttle and seconds later he was gone, out of sight. Tim made a quick turn as if to run back up toward the house. "Whoa, where are you going?" Stas asked.

"After him, the highway follows the river at least for a little while."

"Do you have any idea how many tributaries he will have hit by the time you get a mile up the road? He's not gonna stay right out in the open on the river now that we've seen him."

"So, what do you suggest? You think we should just let the only potential lead we have so far just vanish?"

Stas knew Tim was upset but still found it difficult to bite his tongue and stymie the smart-ass retort that wanted to sneak out. Instead he took a measured breath and said, "Since we're never going to catch him, I suggest we focus on what the hell he might have been doing here."

He watched Tim struggle with this reasonable and rational logic then after a long moment of inner turmoil, accept it. Tim nodded and they both began to walk back the way they'd come.

"What do you think he was doing here?" Tim asked.

"No idea. But the fact that he was here at all means we might be onto something."

The distant rush of the river and the whistling tune of the birds was the only sound as they walked until Tim broke the silence. "Do you think he's working for that guy, this Logan you were talking about."

"Could be." The response from Stas was an answer that was no answer at all.

After another short silence Tim made a frustrated scoffing sound. "People sneaking around Lisa's yard, cults, and strange ties to the Mayor's office? This is ridiculous…" Tim trailed off.

Stas didn't respond but came to a halt without warning. "What's that?" he asked, pointing off to his left at a little rickety looking shed.

Tim looked at the structure for a long moment with confusion slipping across his features. "I don't know, I've never noticed it before." He turned as if to head off in the direction of the shed but Stas put his arm out to stop him.

"Wait, do you see the padlock?"

Stas watched Tim nod but there was little fervor in the action. "That lock looks awful new to be on an old piece of crap like that shed, doesn't it?" Again Tim nodded but the motion was even slower and more methodical than the movement had been a second before. "And you have no idea what she keeps in there?"

"None." Tim's voice was distant.

Without another word they both started with slow measured strides over toward the little shed. When they reached it Stas examined the padlock. There was not even a trace of rust on it. He then put his hand up on the door as if the little structure might give off some sort of vibration that would provide some clarity. When, of course, that didn't happen, he grabbed the latch. It was two pieces that were clasped by the padlock. He gave it a quick hard shake and was surprised by how sturdy the doors seemed in spite of their decrepit appearance. He looked at the hinges and realized they were also new and, upon further examination, the 2x4's that made up the door frame were as well. This little dump had been well fortified.

Stas couldn't help a slight smile creeping across his face as his hand returned to the lock and another realization came to him. The little slit where the key would be inserted gaped at him, mocking, as the phrase Lisa would end their calls with wafted across his consciousness. Without looking at Tim he said, "Go look behind the refrigerator, I think you might find something there, maybe a key." Tim stood idle for a moment then ran for the house.

The newest realization was that he had become so used to hearing Lisa say '*If anything happens to me, look behind the ice box.*' that the fact that she would occasionally change it up, just a little, had slipped past him. Sometimes she would say '*the key is behind the ice box*' instead. Stas had no doubt that Tim would find a key and that this was the lock it was meant to open.

"What did you have going on out here, lady?" he asked the empty air but received no answers from the trees, or Lisa, or anyone else.

Tim returned a few minutes later and tossed a little black case towards Stas. It was a magnetic Hide-A-Key case, Stas had been right on that front, but the case was empty. In Tim's other hand he had a set of bolt cutters. Stas put his hand out for the tool but his confidence was wavering.

If she'd meant for him to find the key and this shed if anything had happened to her, then why wasn't it there now?

And even worse, if she *had* left it in hopes that he'd find it, then who found it first? Could it have been the guy on the boat?

The two men shared a long glance. Tim nodded and Stas returned the gesture. Stas stepped up to the lock again, placed the sharpened edges of the cutter on either side of the U-bolt that was hooked through the latch. Then he squeezed the handle and snapped the lock and watched it fall away to the ground.

10

The lock hit the ground at their feet and they almost smacked their heads together looking down at it. It landed face down amidst the crab grass clearly displaying its 'Master' brand name stamped across the back. In unison they lifted their heads returning their focus to the no longer impeded doors of the shed.

Stas reached his hand out towards the latch.

"Wait." Tim stopped him short, then asked, "What do you think we're gonna find in there?"

Stas just shook his head. He had no idea. "Only one way to find out, I suppose." And now he did grab the latch, sliding it free of its other half. He pulled the section of the latch, he was holding. For a moment the door was stubborn, clinging tight to its fit in the jamb, but then it came loose and swung open in a lazy arc.

The interior of the shed remained dark and shaded. He pulled the other door free, widening the opening, and the light poured in. Both Stas and Tim stared upon the contents in a stupefied silence. There were so many things that could have been occupying the little space. From the terrible, to wonderful, to the mundane, but what they were actually staring at somehow still defied all logic.

Lisa's shed was a small, well kept, tidy little living space. A bedroll was laid out along the back wall. A small table with a battery-powered lantern set upon it sat in the corner.

"What the…" Stas heard Tim say and trail off behind

him. He thought Tim's unfinished question summed up the situation quite well. Or did it?

His head was suddenly thumping. Not with the angry furor he had endured the day before but like something was banging around in there, running wild. Set loose but unable to find a clear pathway to freedom. It was a thought, an idea, that he couldn't quite grasp, that wouldn't solidify.

He was chasing around inside his head for the flitting idea. And then it was there, far away, as if it had just appeared at the end of a tunnel. Without warning he was whooshed up, speeding along towards the light as if he were being propelled. The maw of the tunnel grew larger as he hurtled toward it. Then he was launched out into the light and clarity was there, everywhere, blinding him like a sudden sun.

He recalled the man on the boat.

Stas had seen him reach down for something and stow it under the captain's chair. Now that the adrenaline had run its course and was no longer pounding inside of him, he realized what it was the man had been stowing. It was something pink, a girl's backpack.

Stas came back to himself and looked all the way around the little room in the shed, soaking it up, the bedroll, the little table. There was a shelf with a few supplies, batteries, a small case of bottled water.

He didn't know who, he didn't know why. But his old friend, who it now seemed had a penchant for disappearing herself, might have been causing others to do the same.

Minneapolis…
Fall, 1999

1

The rain had stopped.

Last night at the train station it had been pounding but at some point during the small hours it had slowed to a drizzle then ceased altogether. Whether that occurred during their little cups of whiskey and the bit of story time she had dropped on him or after, Stas had no idea. He had been consumed by the yarn she had spun. When she had finished talking and the words had all been spent, there had been nothing left to do but sleep.

While there was no precipitation this morning, the sky remained heavy and overcast. A fine mist was drifting up the banks of the river, which was where Stas found himself perched on some large rocks with a woman he'd known forever, and yet barely knew at all. The city skyline, a little further downriver, was just a ghost of an idea in the fog. They sat and watched as the river ran and the mist crept and the silence reigned.

They'd come to the river to get out of the house. There would be a fair amount of waiting to be done today and doing it cooped up in his little apartment didn't seem like it would be helpful to the general state of their collective sanity. After they had woken up he'd made some calls on Lisa's behalf. (He had asked her what she would want to be called if she got to choose. She liked Lisa, so he was already making the mental shift). And now, if they were lucky, a 'friend of a friend' of an old neighborhood acquaintance would be getting in touch with instructions.

But first, they'd have to wait.

So, without the necessity of words they watched the water and killed some time. Stas was trying to work out in his head the right way to get more information out of her. Last night the tale had been mostly focused on her escape from what sounded like a life of imprisonment. And it was one hell of a story. It was not without some great peril that she had been able to break away from the people, the cult, that she had once considered family. Her faith had been shaken, and in more ways than one. After all that she had been through it would probably be a while before she could find much to believe in when it came to her fellow humans. And on top of that she still didn't entirely believe she was free of them. She knew in her head that she wouldn't have ever made it out of the train station last night if they had any idea where she was, but her body was still tuned to an acute fear of being followed.

As if to accentuate this point, there was a rustling of foliage and a few twigs cracked somewhere in the trees behind them and she whirled around. It was just some critter but she was still on edge, scanning the trees for longer than would have seemed necessary before turning her attention back to the river and losing herself again in the muddy waters. After another long but not necessarily uncomfortable silence she spoke.

"You could get all the way here, right to this point, from up there," she mused. He wasn't quite sure what she was talking about.

"How do you mean?" Stas asked.

"The place we lived, it was not far from the resort where you and I met. From Big Sandy Lake, which was right across the highway from Minnewawa, you could get to the river and take it all the way down here, to Minneapolis."

Stas nodded. "Further even, I suppose, if you wanted to." Their conversation was not pertaining to anything of substance but if he could keep her talking maybe they'd work their way into something.

"Maybe that's what I'll do. Go down the river. Once I'm officially a Lisa and Anne Callahan is nothing but a sad memory."

To this he could find nothing to say in spite of his urge to keep her going. It brought the whole thing home in a way that was all too real. She would be an entirely new person in a day or two, assuming Stas was able to find the people that could make it happen, and he was confident he could. Growing up a neighborhood delinquent had at least a few perks.

Stas struggled for something to say and got there eventually. "A new name, moving further down the river, you must really want to get away from these people."

She let out a long sigh then upheld the silence for another second or two before saying, "They weren't all bad… Most of them were good, if only misguided." Another pause. "But some of them were awful people. One in particular."

He waited, but when she did not go on, he pressed. "And who was that?" He wasn't certain he would get a response but he did.

"An asshole of the highest order named Cortland Whittier."

<u>2</u>

The name drifted into the air and dissolved into the mist that was still blanketing the trees on both banks of the river. Her face, after speaking Whittier's name aloud, bore a bitter resignation and he hoped not to have to see her look like that often. But at the same time his curiosity was gnawing at him.

"Do you want to talk about him?" he asked in a low, hesitant voice.

"Nope." The response was pointed, but then she went on, "but I think maybe I'd better."

He waited and still the river ran, powerful but quiet, and then she began to speak.

"My parents were young when my mom got pregnant with me. My dad was eighteen and my mom was sixteen. My mom's parents, who were just this side of zealots themselves, were livid. They wanted to send my mom away until I was born and could be put up for adoption. But my parents were young, and in love, and weren't having it. Eventually, after a lot of bitter fights, my parents left. Whether they ran away or were ostracized by their own families, I never knew. But they struck out on their own.

"They had both been raised in crazy religious families and had nowhere to turn. I guess it's not surprising that they did what they did. They joined a commune. It was faith-based but inclusive and not as stringent as either of the homes they had just left. The commune was where I was born and where my parents first met Cortland Whittier."

She paused and watched the current pull the river past them, then went on.

"Whittier was a charismatic man and he was drawn toward leadership roles amongst the group. My parents were not alone in being taken with him nor were they alone in siding with him when things went bad. Whittier began having power struggles with some of the other leaders of the commune who didn't share in some of his more unorthodox beliefs. In 1980, when I was three years old, they kicked him out and about half of the people, including my parents, went with him. Joining him as he took them on his self proclaimed New Faith Journey."

She paused again and the bitterness filling her countenance not only remained but seemed to have deepened. Stas didn't like it any more than he had before. He also did not like the sound of this guy's 'New Faith Journey' or whatever his 'unorthodox beliefs' might have been. It only promised to get worse, and it did.

"Whittier is the scum of the earth," she said after having taken a second to regroup. "He brainwashed his followers and they all, my parents, all of them, bought into his madness. And that's where I grew up, in the middle of that insanity. My family worked at the resort but we all lived in a closed little hell run by Cortland Whittier just up the road apiece. He called the place we lived Norumbega, after some lost city.

"I suppose I started to figure out that things weren't exactly normal in Whittier's world the fall after you guys stopped coming up to the resort. That was actually the last summer I spent much time there too. When a kid turned twelve they sort of graduated, I guess, from youth programs to young adult, which was where they really started working on your head. When you were a kid there was nothing really out of the ordinary that happened to you but when you moved up to the next level things started to intensify. At first, I would ask my parents about some of the stuff that I didn't understand but the answers were always insufficient.

"Until I was fifteen. Then my parents started to change. I think they were starting to rethink their life choices, particularly as to how it would affect their only daughter. You see, being fifteen in that world was weird enough, but being a sixteen-year-old girl under Cortland Whittier's reign was an absolute nightmare."

Now Stas could barely recognize his old friend, it was almost as if the bitterness had consumed her whole. Before he could think better of it, a question slipped out. "Why?" he asked, and immediately regretted it. He didn't want to know. She turned a hard, hateful gaze upon him and, even though the malice it bore was not intended for him, it made him feel cold from the inside out.

"Because when a girl turns sixteen the 'honor' is bestowed upon her of becoming Cortland Whittier's wife." She physically put the air quotes on the word 'honor' but didn't need to, the ugly emphasis she made with her voice drove her point home with unflinching clarity. "And she would remain so until some other unlucky lady turned sixteen and took her place." She seemed to be spitting out her words now as opposed to speaking them. "I think my parents were going to leave the group in order to spare me my turn in Whittier's bed... And he orchestrated a car accident that killed them to keep them from doing so."

3

Whatever Stas thought he had wanted to know, now that it was too late, he had definitely changed his mind. It was all way more than he could process. And if he couldn't handle the wretched truth of her situation, it was impossible to imagine how she must feel. After another long silence she stood. Her tale hadn't been long but it had wiped her out.

"Can we go back to your place now?"

Stas nodded, no longer trusting his own voice, and they climbed down off the rocks they had perched on. They walked back toward the apartment leaving the river and its latent mist behind. With the exhaustion of any dialogue, they trod on in silence.

Once they reached his building and were in the stairwell climbing up to his floor an inexplicable anxiety overcame Stas. Would the light on the answering machine be blinking when they got to the apartment and if so, what would that mean? What would come next?

They stood shoulder to shoulder in front of his door. Not a word had been passed on the whole walk home and that did not change now. If the light was blinking and there was a message then they would begin the next step in erasing her past. Removing Anne from history and launching Lisa's story. The weight of the moment was not lost on either of them as he slid the key home in the lock on his door.

He turned it and then the handle, one right after the other, and the door popped open. From where they stood in the hallway, they both had an excellent sightline of the answering machine sitting on the counter by the phone in the kitchen. The light on its face was a solid red, not blinking.

No messages.

But there was something on the floor.

Stas stepped over the threshold and one by one they walked into the apartment. The thing lying on the floor was an envelope. Stas crouched to get a better look at it. There was nothing exceptional about it, just a blank envelope. He grabbed it and stood. He felt her step in close behind him to get a look over his shoulder. The envelope was sealed, sealed but blank, no postage. Someone must have slipped it under the door. His heart quickened its pace as he ripped it open and slid out the contents, a single business card. There was a phone number written on one side. He flipped it over and was met by a single word printed on the face of the card: DESOLATE.

Lisa closed the door behind them.

Minneapolis…
Spring, 2017

1

Back in the comfortable confines of his own neighborhood Stas pulled into the parking lot of Stanley's Northeast Barroom and checked the time. It was ten minutes before six in the evening. He was even slightly ahead of schedule. Stas took a deep breath and opened the car door.

As he and Tim had been walking back up to the house, both of them quietly processing the discovery and possible implications of Lisa's shed, Stas had received a text from his buddy Louis Jones. Big Lou's brother, Officer Terrell Jones of the Minneapolis Police Department, wanted to see him back in the city.

He did not know whether to be optimistic or reticent about the fact that Terrell wanted to see him in person. But like he had said to Tim standing outside the shed doors, there really was only one way to find out. So, he had left the shed and the questions it raised to Tim and hit the road back up to Minneapolis. Now he walked into Stanley's, formerly Stasius, his namesake, at the time that had been appointed to him by Big Lou's brother.

He saw Terrell sitting at one of the big radiator tables that ran down the middle of the bar with a couple of other people. Officer Jones did not quite share the sheer formidable size that his little brother had been born with. He was not quite as tall or thick but he was, nonetheless, intimidating. He was compact and muscular, he looked coiled and always ready to strike. He looked like a cop. Many of these traits were echoed in the men and women sitting around the table with him.

Stas made eye contact and Terrell acknowledged him with a nod then scooped up his drink. Stas grabbed a spot at the bar and flagged down the bartender. He had no interest in sitting and shooting the bull with a bunch of cops, a sentiment he was pretty sure those officers would have shared in regard to him. Terrell pulled out a barstool and sat down next to him.

"What's up, Stas?"

"Another day in paradise, how bout you, Terrell?"

"I was better until my brother started asking me for favors…and for your dumb ass nonetheless."

"Yeah, I didn't think you'd be too excited about it but I didn't know what else to do. I'm kind of grasping at straws here."

"Your friend Lisa is in some kind of trouble, huh?"

"Guess I don't know that for sure, but it kind of seems that way." The bartender, who looked like a Nordic Viking with his long blonde hair and goatee, had delivered his beer and Stas took a healthy, refreshing swig.

Terrell tasted his own beverage before speaking. "Yeah…it does kind of seem that way."

Stas shot him a look. Terrell just stared back at him, revealing nothing about the context of his last statement. "Did you come up with something?" Stas asked.

Officer Jones looked away, took another swig of his beer, replaced it on the bar and then turned his attention back to Stas. "Did I come up with something, as in, like, answers? Nope."

Without realizing it Stas sagged slightly against the bar; he'd allowed himself to get his hopes up.

Terrell wasn't finished, though. "But what I did find out is that simply asking questions about Ted Logan can start trouble."

"What do you mean?"

Terrell said, "I've got a buddy, an actual detective, who I trust. He's also pretty tight with our Chief which puts him one step away from the Mayor. I asked him to see what he could do. It didn't take any time at all for him to figure out that your phone number wasn't Logan's actual number. No surprise there. So, my buddy goes to his partner. Now my buddy's partner, she has a friend that does some sort of admin job in Logan's office. He gets her to prod her friend a little bit, see if she can't find out if Logan's got an off-the-radar phone, a burner so to speak. Most of those scumbag politicians up on the fourth floor do."

Stas knew from some unpleasant past experience that downtown at City Hall, the county lock-up was in the basement, the cops were on the floors above that, and above them, all the way upstairs, were the so-called elites. Stas could not have agreed any more with Terrell's description of the not-so-civil servants at the top of the food chain but he said nothing. Terrell seemed as if he still had more to say and the fact that he'd actually been able to tap into somebody in Logan's office was way more than Stas had dared to hope for. He just continued to sip his beer and listen as Terrell went on.

"Angela, that's my buddy's partner, she asks her friend that works for Logan about the possibility of a second phone and lets her know that she's really trying to find any connection to a woman named Lisa Lathrop. The friend gets back to her right away and says it's highly unlikely that Logan's up to any funny business with the phone, he's not married so there's nothing to hide from a wife or anything like that. Again, no big deal, not like we really expected to find anything here, right?"

"Like I said, I was grasping at straws," Stas said taking another slug off of his beer. Terrell took the opportunity to sneak a sip as well before continuing.

"Right, right…but here's where it gets weird, Stas. An hour and a half after she talked to her friend, Angela gets another call from her. She tells Angela that she found herself alone in Logan's office and his date book was sitting on the desk so she just took a quick glance at it. Lisa went missing on Friday, right?"

"Yep."

"This lady tells Angela she saw Lisa's name written in on Saturday, the day after she'd disappeared. There was a note that said 'exit interview' and then an address. She found it weird that there would be an exit interview for someone who didn't even work there. She also thought the address connected to it was odd, because it was in Red Wing."

Stas did not like anything about the sound of an 'exit interview,' and the fact that Logan had coupled it with a Red Wing address only furthered his unease. "Did you get the address, by any chance?" he asked.

Terrell nodded. "She took a picture and sent it to Angela." He passed a post-it over to Stas with a street number.

Stas read it and smiled. It was Lisa's official address but it wasn't her house. Her legal street address was that of the local post office, with a PO Box acting as an apartment number.

Stas found some solace in the fact that Logan's ominous sounding 'exit interview' might have hit a dead-end thanks to the address. It hadn't stopped him, though. He'd still somehow made the connection to Viktor Sokolov. Stas could only hope that, whatever had actually gone down, Lisa had continued to stay a step ahead of Logan. But hope was a flimsy frame on which to hold up any confidence. He was lost in thought until Terrell spoke again.

"Angela's friend asked around the office a little but no one would own up to knowing Lisa," he said. "But it turns out, someone must have."

Stas gave him a questioning look.

"I don't know how much you know about the Mayor's Office, but the biggest piece of power he actually has is that he appoints the Chief of Police. And wouldn't you know it, not two hours after tossing out some feelers about Lisa, my buddy and his partner are in the Chief's office getting read the riot act about their priorities and sticking to their caseload and minding their own damn business."

Stas fiddled with his glass. Lisa had been up to something. What they found in her shed left little question in that regard. But the interest taken in her and her whereabouts by power players down at the Minneapolis City Hall provided no connections, only further consternation.

"I don't know what you and your friend are mixed up in, Stas," Terrell said. "And I don't want to. Maybe this information will be helpful, but if you need anything else, you're on your own. My buddy is tight with the Chief. He can sustain a bit of heat, but a beat cop like me? I don't know that I'd be so lucky if the boss came downstairs to find out about my interest in the Mayor's chief of staff."

Having said his piece, Terrell Jones collected his beer from the bar and stood up from the barstool to go rejoin his other pals. From the jocular nature of the sounds being emitted from that table it seemed a much more pleasant place to be but Terrell stopped, delaying his return to them to relay one final sentiment.

"Be careful, Stas."

Stas Mileski had been hearing a lot of that lately. It was probably good advice but he wasn't sure he'd be able to heed it. "I'll do my best," he told Terrell.

"Well, I hope your best is good enough." And then Officer Jones was gone, back to the backslapping being doled out by his brethren, and Stas was alone at the bar.

With wary eyes he gazed upon his half-full beer. He lifted it from the bar and drank a third of its contents. He set it down and regarded what remained. Not pleased with what he saw he flagged down the pillaging Swede manning the bar and ordered another.

McGregor…
Spring, 2017

1

In the early afternoon the next day Stas wheeled off a little two-lane highway onto a small access road that led to two buildings on the north side of a pocked and potholed stretch of asphalt. A slight, nearly indistinguishable pause came and went before he continued toward the building on his left, the convenience store, leaving the one on the right, Mark's Bar, and its undoubtedly delicious libations for other weary travelers.

Behind the two structures greater Minnesota stretched out into the distance as far as the eye could see. He was on the outskirts of the township of McGregor, although he thought the term outskirts to be a bit misleading as he was almost quite literally also a stone's throw from the city center. But McGregor and its city center or lack thereof was not his immediate destination or concern. Nor was the convenience store, it was only a pit stop before the final leg of his journey north which would end at the Minnewawa Resort.

He was returning to the scene of his near-death experience at the tender age of ten years but he was not returning to face down his own distant demons. He was in pursuit of one Ted Logan, or Mr. Logan's past to be more specific. He thought about asking the kid with the gauges stretching his earlobes behind the counter if he knew anything about McGregor's golden son but was dissuaded by the kid's bored indifference. The kid had very little interest in peeling himself away from his comic book long enough to sell a soft drink, much less to sit and answer some tourist's questions. So Stas paid for his pop, climbed back into his truck and continued north.

Why Logan had taken an interest in Lisa again recently was still beyond his grasp. But one of the few things Stas did know was that the intertwining of their stories had begun long ago at the Minnewawa Resort. He could only hope by stumbling around the geography of their youth he would find another thread on which he could tug.

A short time later he turned onto the main drive leading up to the resort and realized that he was holding his breath. Once he had decided that he would make the trip, Stas had booked a room at the Minnewawa. He wasn't sure himself if it was for the sake of nostalgia that he had opted to stay there instead of one of the cheaper motels, but whatever it was he had not expected it to cause such a reaction in him. With more effort than should have been necessary he was able to force a rough exhalation and tried to convince himself that it was natural to be nervous returning here after all this time. He had almost died on these grounds after all.

He drove up the long sprawling drive to the main lodge but didn't recognize it at all. The Minnewawa Resort was no longer a quaint little operation. The lodge still looked rustic but there was no question that a healthy bit of money had been pumped into it over the years. It had a certain country charm but that charm had been achieved at a cost. The upgrades perhaps explained why it had been plenty more expensive than some of the other hotels in the area. The grounds had changed as well, small hills sprawled out from behind the main lodge for a healthy distance before meeting a forested wall on all sides. There were a few large structures within his view that he assumed were guest cabins. There were also small paved pathways that ran back into the midst of the surrounding forestry almost certainly leading to other cabins.

He rolled to a stop in the car park in front of the main entrance. Stas got out of his truck as the front doors were opened for him and he was greeted by a young woman wearing khaki capri pants and a blue 'Minnewawa Resort' polo shirt. Judging from the short-sleeved shirt she was clearly enjoying the sudden turn in the temperature as well.

"Welcome to the Minnewawa, checking in?" she asked.

"I am," he said, removing his sunglasses and pocketing them.

"Front desk is right over there." Her outstretched arm indicated he should continue through the main doors and to his left. He thanked her and walked into the Minnewawa Resort Great Room for the first time in over twenty years.

Again, there was nothing familiar about it. It may have been totally renovated or the old one razed and a new one built in its place, he couldn't tell. What he did know was that it was all very nice. He stepped over to the front desk and was greeted by another friendly smile.

"Good afternoon. Checking in?" the desk clerk asked.

"I am. The name is Mileski."

After a moment of typing the clerk asked, "Stanley?"

Stas chuckled under his breath, "Yep, that's me."

"We've got you down for three nights, is that correct?"

"Yeah. If I need to stay another night or two would that be possible?" Stas asked.

"Since we are now in season the weekends are generally booked, although because you're already staying with us you would receive priority on the waiting list. Shall I put you on the list just in case? And if a room becomes available but you don't need it, we can just take you off?"

"Alright, that sounds good, let's do it."

The clerk punched a few more keys. "Very well, Mr. Mileski, you're all set. We have you staying in the Carver House Cabins. Our grounds are enclosed but you can park in the lot just up from the car park and Carrie will pick you up in a cart and give you a ride to your accommodations." The clerk was indicating the woman in the blue polo that had held the door for him. "There are bikes located at stations around the grounds as well that you are free to use."

"Sounds good," Stas said again and headed back out to park his truck. He started it, drove up to the lot, and parked. Carrie pulled up in a golf cart before he was barely out of the truck. She grabbed his suitcase as soon as he opened the little rear door of the cab and she stowed it in the back of the cart.

"Hop in," she said with a tilt of her head toward the passenger seat of her little buggy.

"You guys are pretty efficient, huh?"

"It's the Minnewawa way," she said, a charming smile gracing her face. As soon as he was seated, she pulled the cart out onto a little asphalt path that ran around the main lodge. Again, he was struck by how different everything was. It was as if he'd never been here at all, like he had never nearly died in the small fishing pond. He looked around but couldn't be sure of which direction the lake and pond lay.

"Where's the lake?" he asked.

Carrie with the blue polo answered, "Carver House, where you're staying, is just over this next hill here. When you walk out from the cabin there will be a path to your right and that runs down to the lake."

A little sound that fell somewhere between a grunt and a laugh escaped from Stas and he shook his head. "I used to come here when I was a kid. The place has certainly changed."

"Oh, yes, it sure has."

Stas looked at her, his only new acquaintance so far here at the resort. She was probably in her early twenties, too young to know anything about the people he was interested in. "How long have you worked here?" he asked.

Her features clouded a little, as she thought about it. It was the first time since he met her all those minutes ago that she hadn't been smiling. It left her looking almost sad. "Since I was eighteen, four years or so, I guess." The smile returned and any perceived melancholy vanished.

"What brought you to work at the Minnewawa Resort? Did you grow up around here?" he asked.

"I guess you could say that," she said as the little cart crested the small hill. My parents worked here for many summers when I was young. It was a pretty natural fit for me."

"Your parents worked here, huh?" Carrie nodded and they began the descent down the slight slope that led to Carver House where he was staying. "Did you spend a lot of time here, then?" Again, she nodded and shot him her charming smile as she pulled the cart to a stop in front of the cabin. Although the term 'cabin' did not really do the structure justice, like the main lodge, the money spent on it was obvious.

"Feels like my whole life, practically," Carrie said as she grabbed his suitcase from the back of the cart and walked up the front porch of Carver House. She held the front door open for him and he walked past her into the communal area of the cabin. It was a hybrid, somewhere between a lobby and a living room. "Your cabin is to the right over there. This room is shared space with the other three cabins in the house."

"Thanks," he said, taking the suitcase from her. He handed her a tip all the while debating whether or not to start asking questions. If she'd been around since she was a kid, she might at least remember Lisa's family. He decided to slow roll it and just keep talking for a second. "This place is a lot nicer than it was when I used to come here as a boy."

"It was sold back around 2003. The new owner spent a lot of money on renovations."

Stas was trying to do some quick math in his head. She would have been too young regardless but he decided to take a stab anyway. Maybe she'd heard rumors when she was younger about a suspicious car accident that had orphaned one teen-aged girl. "When I was here as a kid there was a family that worked here, since you spent time here when you were young too, I was wondering if you might have ever heard of them. Their name was Callahan?"

She gave it a second or two of thought before shaking her head. "Nope. Sorry, the name doesn't ring a bell," she said then added, "thanks," indicating the tip. "You enjoy your stay." She gave him another one of what he was beginning to think of as her patented smiles and then Carrie was off, headed back out to the golf cart.

He stepped over to the door to his cabin and slid the passkey into the lock. Carrie's patented smile was warm and genuine. There was nothing about it that seemed false or as if it bore any pretence, certainly nothing about it that would lead someone to believe she was lying.

But that was exactly what Stas did think, his new friend Carrie was lying.

He pulled the key back out of the lock, watched the light turn green, and opened the door to his temporary quarters.

2

His new home for the next few days was a suite, not a cabin. He walked through the sitting room and stowed his suitcase in the bedroom. He kicked his shoes off and sat down on the bed wondering what it was that made him think Carrie had lied to him. He couldn't put his finger on it. She hadn't displayed any of the normal triggers he was used to seeing when people lied. And Stas was pretty well versed when it came to liars, both the very bad and the very, very good. The fact that he could pinpoint nothing did not deter him from the gnawing feeling that she was lying, though. He dropped from his sitting position backwards onto the bed to really give it some thought and promptly fell asleep.

Some time later, someone knocked on the outer door of his rooms and he woke with a start. He could have been asleep for three minutes or three hours, he had no idea. Whoever had knocked had said something as well but Stas hadn't caught it in his momentary stupor of waking.

"Excuse me?" he called out, walking back into the sitting room rubbing sleep from his eyes.

"Room service," the voice returned the call from the

other side of the wall.

"I think there's been a mistake," Stas said, opening the door. "I didn't order anything."

Standing on the other side of the threshold carrying a silver room service tray was another woman wearing a blue Minnewawa polo shirt but she was probably thirty years his new friend Carrie's senior. "No?" Her brow furrowed for a moment then smoothed into a pleasant grin. "Oh well, guess you'll get a free sandwich, then," she said and walked past him into the room without invitation to set the tray on the table. "Go ahead and shut the door, son," she said even though she was probably only ten or fifteen years older than him. "This'll take me a second to set up for ya. Hope you'll be on board for the best club sandwich north of the Cities, even if you didn't order it."

"Sure," Stas managed. He was still out of sorts from waking up and not sure what to make of this intrusion, but this lady had a strong command of her duties and seemed fully invested in executing them. She began setting out a napkin and silverware for him and he released the door which began to swing shut on its own.

The last clutches of the sleep that had taken him were clearing. Depending on how long the woman setting out his unexpected lunch had worked here, based on her age, she would probably be a better source of information than young Carrie. He began to articulate a question but then choked on it, stopping short.

The door clicked shut behind him and in a moment that seemed simultaneous to him the woman dropped any pretense of setting up his lunch and leveled him with a hard gaze.

"You need to stop asking questions."

"What?" he managed, taken aback by the sudden change in her demeanor.

"Whatever it is you think you need to know, you need to keep your mouth shut about it around here." She was still staring daggers into him but Stas began to regain some of his composure.

"You talked to Carrie?"

"She talked to me." The woman's disposition did not soften a bit.

"So, she did know who the Callahans were?"

"She doesn't know anything. Nobody around here knows anything, at least if they know what's good for 'em. You catch my meaning, son?"

There she went calling him son again. "I'm not sure that I do, Ma'am."

"Well you better hip to it quick. Stay away from Carrie and the rest of my staff while you're here. Enjoy your stay," she finished, dropping the rest of his silverware to clatter on the table.

She had said her piece and was done with him. That much was clear as she walked to the door. He had hit a nerve within minutes of his arrival and it seemed to run deeper than he dared imagine possible. He tried to assimilate his thoughts and find a way to keep her a minute longer. He tried to keep the tone of his voice calm. Behaving frantic or aggressive would get him nowhere.

"You've worked here awhile then? Did you know the Callahans?"

She turned back and the hard nature of her gaze never wavered. "We're done. Enjoy your sandwich."

Before she could make her move to open the door and leave Stas to sort through his sudden confusion alone he managed to spit out one last question. "What about Ted Logan, did you know him?"

That last query seemed to slip past her guard and crack the tough veneer she had put up. The intense gaze she had used to pin him to the spot he stood slid away from her face. For the first time since she had barged into his room, he sensed a hint of uncertainty. She recovered quickly and tossed him a last stern glance before looking down and digging into one of the pockets of her khaki capri pants. She pulled out a small pad of paper and a pen and scribbled something on the top sheet. She ripped the paper off and handed it to him but her eyes met his and again the ferocity he saw in them held him before he could look down at whatever she had written.

"There's a bait shop out of town on Highway 65, north of town four or five miles. Go talk to the guy that owns it. He might be able to help you." Her gaze intensified even further and her tone carried a desperate bitterness as she continued. "Talk to him and maybe you'll get somewhere but don't you ask another one of your questions around here. It's dangerous, and not just for you. You're putting people at risk." And with that she brushed past him and out of the suite.

He watched the door close and latch behind her. He looked down at the piece of paper she had pushed into his hand. It had an address and the name of the bait shop she had told him about. The cozy small-town sensibility of the name was almost too much for him.

He looked around his room but there was nothing else to learn here. He checked the time. It was four o'clock in the afternoon. The bait shop would hopefully be open for another hour or so. He grabbed half of the sandwich that his strange, surprise visitor had left for him and headed for the door. It closed behind him and he was off to see how the proprietor of something called Bob's Beer & Bait Shop might possibly be able to help him.

3

Stas pulled his truck into the lot past a seven-foot plywood Muskie with the word BAIT painted along the fading scales of the fish's back. He rolled across the gravel parking pad and the truck came to a rest to the right of the little store. The wooden lap-siding was painted a faded peeling white but the sign above the drooping screen door had been painted or at least touched up recently. The sign informed him that he had managed to find his way to Bob's Beer & Bait. He wondered if this Bob was actually the owner of this little roadside shack and the man he was sent to find, or if it had been sold at some point and he would be looking for someone else entirely.

Stas climbed out of the truck, stowed his sunglasses and looked across the highway to the west. The early April sun was just beginning its descent, starting its slow slip down towards the horizon. The spring season was still in its infancy but without a cloud in the sky to deter it, the sun was pumping the mercury up and the snowfall of a few days ago seemed little more than a distant dream. He turned back to the little store and walked through the screen door into a darkened gloam permeated by the fishy smell of bait.

"Help ya?" a silver-haired gentleman called from behind the counter in the back.

"I hope so," Stas replied, not really sure what he was going to say to the guy, assuming this was even the man he had come to find.

"Well I hope you're not looking to fish," the guy behind the counter said. "All the houses came off the ice a month ago. Don't think you'd want to try your luck on any of the ice that might be left now anyway, what with the weather lately. I suspect ya might find yourself wetter than a fella might want to be," he said with a chuckle.

"Nah, no fishing for me." Stas was stalling a bit. Now that he was here, he wished he'd given a little thought to how he was going to broach the subject of the reason for his visit. Should he just come out and say that he'd practically been assaulted for asking questions about a family involved with a car crash twenty-five years ago? And that that car crash may or may not have actually been murder? Or should he start with the fact that the stern woman who'd initiated that assault had then sent him here as soon as he brought up Ted Logan, the Mayor of Minneapolis' Chief of Staff. He decided the best place to start would be to find out whether or not this silver-haired guy was really the man he had come out here to see. "You own this place?"

The man behind the counter held Stas with his gaze for a long moment. His face was lined, but looking at him now, Stas thought he was perhaps a bit younger than the weathered face and silver hair had originally led him to believe; on the back side of his fifties but maybe not into his sixties quite yet.

The look he was leveling at Stas was not necessarily suspicious but was definitely an assessment. The man's eyes were shrewd, sizing him up. Before the moment could grow awkward, though, the weathered face shifted back to a smile and the man spoke. "Yep, this is my little kingdom, welcome," he said, spreading his arms to indicate the rest of the store. Coolers filled with beer lined one wall and live bait tanks the other.

"Are you the aforementioned Bob, then?" Stas asked.

"The one and only, how can I help you?"

"I'm staying at the Minnewawa Resort."

"Nice place."

"Yeah, it is. I met a woman that works there who told me you might be able to help me with something."

"Is that so?" The man's smile never wavered but that shrewdness behind his eyes seemed to intensify somehow. Stas caught it and was determined not to overlook it.

"I'm looking for some information about some folks." Stas paused for a second trying to read the reaction of the other man as he spoke. "A family called Callahan and a guy named Ted Logan."

The response was minimal but it was there. The smile was still in place but the corners of the man's mouth tightened and his eyes narrowed by the smallest of percentages. "Can't say that I'm familiar with anyone named Callahan," he said, "but I sure as hell have heard of Logan."

At that moment the screen door gave a ratcheting whine as it was pulled open and two guys that looked barely old enough to drink walked into the little store. They strode over to the coolers along the wall where the beer part of the Beer & Bait equation was housed here in Bob's kingdom.

"You have any idea why the woman at the resort might've sent me to see you?"

"I might have an inkling, I suppose." His eyes shifted to the guys at the cooler for a second then back to Stas. After a beat he looked to his watch. "Tell you what, I'm getting pretty close to shutting her down for the day. Did you see Mark's Bar on your way into town?" Stas nodded. "You up for a beer once I close this place down?"

Stas gave him a single nod. "Can't remember the last time I wasn't."

Bob chuckled, "Why don't you head down there. I'll meet ya shortly and we can chat about Logan." He'd lowered his voice a tiny bit and glanced again at the guys sorting out their beer choice at the cooler. Stas didn't have any idea if he'd dropped his tone because Logan was a taboo topic to other locals, or if he just didn't want to be overheard talking about him to some out-of-towner.

"What's your name, son?" the older guy, Bob, asked.

"Stas Mileski," Stas replied offering his hand.

The silver-haired gentleman accepted the proffered greeting. His hand was calloused and his grip was firm as they shook. "Bob Gurley, I'll see you at the bar," he said as he released Stas' hand, dismissing him as the two guys walked toward the counter, their beer finally selected.

Stas relinquished his spot at the counter turning it over to the young men and walked back outside letting the screen door slap against the jamb as he exited.

4

Mark's Bar was everything Stas dared hope for. The wooden paneling was anything but affectation. It was small-town through and through. The old-fashioned jukebox in the corner by the small dance floor was dark but Stas could imagine it wound up on a Saturday night when the place came alive. He assumed the bar would be cranked up for the weekend as it was one of the few places for miles where someone could soak up the week's troubles, and, in some cases, probably a healthy amount of the week's wages as well. There were tables set with vinyl red-and-white checked tablecloths and had black, padded, metal-framed chairs pushed in around them. Mark's Bar also probably doubled as the spot for a family to grab a burger and fries on a night out.

There was a handful of patrons in the bar when Stas arrived. He imagined it would probably fill up a little more once five o'clock hit and whatever businesses propped up the local economy had called it a day. He popped himself up on a bar stool, giving himself plenty of space from the few other guys holding up the other end of the bar, and commenced waiting for Bob. The bartender made his way over.

"What can I get for ya?"

"Do you guys have Grain Belt Nordeast?"

"Not on tap but I have tall-boy cans."

"Good enough," Stas replied with a smile. Even all the way up here they carried the beer of his people, the beer named for Northeast Minneapolis. It might not be his favorite but he liked to see who carried it whenever he was out of the neighborhood. The bartender cracked the tab on the can, set it in front of him, and walked back to the other end of the bar. Another five minutes or so and the door swung open, letting some light slip into the bar and along with it Bob Gurley.

"How we doin' today, Earl?" Bob called to the guy tending bar as he made his way over to Stas.

"Another day, another dollar," Earl replied, walking back down the bar toward them. "You want the usual, Bob?"

"Sure do, thanks."

Earl nodded, grabbed a glass and stepped over to the taps.

"How's the beer and bait business?" Stas asked, trying to break the ice.

"Beer's better than bait these days but come May the bait will give the beer a run for its money, or try to at least." He chuckled as he settled onto the stool. "But I got the impression you're not here for an in-depth discussion on the plight of the local small businessman."

Stas uttered a little laugh. "That, sir, is the truth."

Bob put up his hand to keep him from going on though. "Just a sec," he muttered as Earl returned and dropped off Bob's beer. It was light enough that Stas could see right through it. Earl made his way back down to his post at the far end of the bar hanging out with some of the other locals.

"Sorry to cut you off," Bob said, "not that Earl's a bad guy but whispered rumors are their own kind of currency around here. And people's ears perk up when the subject of the talk is Logan."

"Why's that?"

Bob gave him another one of those long assessing looks. "He's the closest thing we have to a celebrity, I suppose," he said as he turned back to his beer. "What's your interest in him?"

Stas' first impression was that Bob Gurley could be trusted, that he was a straight-shooter, but he still wasn't quite sure he could just spill his guts based on first impressions.

"I think he might have known an old friend of mine."

Bob gave him a look and it was clear to Stas that the man had expected more of an answer than that. "Is that so?" Bob asked, palming his beer and pulling it across the bar toward him.

"My friend lived up here when she was a kid, her parents worked at the Minnewawa Resort. That was right about the same time that Logan was working summers there too and I'm coming to think there may have been some connection between her family and Logan."

"I assume this friend of yours, and her family, are the Callahans you were asking me about earlier?"

"That's right, detective."

"I'm no detective," Bob said, but he did so through a small chuckle and a gruff smile.

Stas said, "I think that Logan had come back into my friend's life in some fashion recently, and it might not have been expected."

"And since you're here asking questions about the guy, I'm gonna assume Logan's unexpected reappearance might not have involved the best of intentions?"

"Sure seems that way." Stas grabbed his can of beer

from the bar and took a healthy swig.

"So, what's the business between them?" Bob asked.

"That's part of the problem, I don't know."

Bob toyed with the coaster his beer was sitting on for a second before speaking. "I guess I'll go ahead and ask the obvious question. Why haven't you asked her about it?"

"I wish I could." Stas had tried to keep his voice neutral but something in his tone pulled Bob's gaze from the coaster he was working at to look up at him again. "She disappeared a couple days ago," Stas finished.

Bob's shrewd eyes narrowed, "Disappeared?" Stas nodded and Bob returned his gaze to his beer. "Now that's interesting," he said and raised the glass to his lips.

They both took a moment to regard their beverages. At some point during their conversation some other patron had taken it upon themselves to plug in the jukebox and now the haunting strains of Bobbie Gentry's "Ode to Billie Joe" spilled through the bar, providing a background track to all that transpired within.

"How about you?" Stas asked after another sip of his own beer. "Why is it that some very intense lady from the resort I'm staying at sent me to see you as soon as I mentioned Logan?"

Bob didn't look up from the bar. "I suppose it was Jane up to the Minnewawa that put you onto me, then?"

"Could be, I caught a fair amount of her angst but never got her name."

"Yep, that sounds about right," Bob said through another little chortle. "Her name is Jane Devorak, she plays cards with my wife, Norma. They get together with a couple other ladies up there at the Minnewawa every other week. Apparently, at one of their recent games it came up that I don't necessarily carry a high opinion of Mr. Logan. I guess, because of what I used to do for work, Jane took an interest in that."

"You haven't always been the beer and bait guy?"

"Nope, that's pretty new for me, bought the shop when we retired over here a year or so back. Before that we lived over in Castle Danger and I had spent twenty plus years as the Sheriff of Castle County."

That got Stas' attention. "And is Jane Devorak onto something, do ya think? Does the sheriff in you—"

"Former sheriff," Bob said cutting him off.

"Does the former sheriff in you have thoughts about Ted Logan?" Stas amended.

Bob took another swallow of beer before addressing that last question. He dragged his sleeve across his upper lip clearing a small bit of froth that had collected there and he settled back onto his barstool. It creaked and moaned, not necessarily because of his size but more likely due to its age and the hard years of service it had already put in anchoring other troubled souls to the bar. "Yeah," he said finally, "I've got thoughts about Logan." Bob let the statement sit there. In the background Ms. Gentry was singing about throwing something off the Tallahatchie Bridge.

Stas had no immediate rebuttal so he helped himself to another taste of his Grain Belt Nordeast. As he swallowed a thought occurred to him. "She said something funny to me," Stas said, "that asking questions about Logan was dangerous and not just for me."

"Dangerous?"

"That's what the lady said."

"Interesting." Bob sipped at his beer. "I don't know what would lead her to believe that," he paused again. "But the thing of it is, I don't think she's wrong." The two of them shared a thoughtful glance before Bob changed the subject. "Let's come back to Jane Devorak in a minute, tell me more about your friend."

Stas weighed his options with a quick efficiency. He didn't know where to start or how much information to hand up, but at some point during this conversation he had decided he could, and would, put his trust in Bob Gurley. So he just started talking. He started at the end and worked backward.

"She went missing last Friday night, just drove off into the night. The cops found her vehicle abandoned on the side of the road early the next morning. I'd never heard of Logan, she'd never mentioned him over the years, but he had some sort of appointment with her written down in his date book for just after she vanished, her name and address."

"You've got access to Ted Logan's date book?"

A slight but wicked smile crept across Stas' face. "I guess you could say I have a connection or two, myself."

"And pretty damn good ones from the sound of it." Bob took another swig of his beer. "And this friend of yours, her family worked at the Minnewawa? And her name's Callahan?"

Stas paused but the hesitation was instinctual, he already knew he was all in on this conversation. "She did grow up not far from here, and her name *was* Callahan, but she changed it when she moved away."

Bob was still picking at his tattered coaster but now he stopped. "Changed it? Legally?" he asked.

"Not exactly… Legally, I mean."

Bob soaked up the information. "She was on the run, then?" he asked after giving it some thought.

"In a sense…"

"Was she running from her family?"

"She was an only child and her parents were dead, killed in a car crash. She lived in a commune, a religious thing that was really more of a cult. She stayed there until she was in her early twenties. Then she got out. The people in the cult, that's who she was running from."

Bob released a heavy sigh. "And did they come after her?"

"Maybe, she thought so, but I never knew for sure. I helped her find someone that could get her new papers, an actual new identity, and for all intents and purposes she disappeared."

The corner of Bob's mouth turned up in slight smile. "So, she's got a bit of an M.O. when it comes to this sort of thing."

"I guess," Stas said, matching the little grin. "She got in

touch with the same guy not long ago to get another set of new papers. Logan struck out with her address, it was just her local post office, but then he somehow managed to track down the kid that was delivering the new papers for her. That's how I came to know about Logan. The guy that the kid worked for was less than pleased about Logan's sudden interest in his business."

The smiles drifted from their faces and they both tasted the beers sitting before them. The front door of the bar opened and closed but neither of them noticed.

Bob set his glass down and looked like he was about to say something but didn't. Earl the bartender had just walked back to near where they were sitting to grab a bottle of Jack Daniels and mix a drink. Both Bob and Stas let the silence linger for the duration of his time spent in their vicinity.

"You guys need anything?" Earl asked, finishing the drink he was making and turning toward them. Stas checked the weight of his can, found it acceptable and shook him off. Bob did the same and Earl walked away to deliver the drink.

Bob watched him walk the length of the bar and set the drink in front of a shaggy-haired rail of a man that looked to be in his early forties wearing a battered Anthrax concert t-shirt and a light flannel. The guy had entered unseen by either of them but now the scruffy, tough-looking figure caught and held Bob's attention.

His eyes never left the guy but to Stas, Bob said, "So now you're trying to backtrack her history with Logan, eh?" After a quick exchange with Earl, the guy wearing the Anthrax T-shirt looked down to where they were seated and his eyes happened to meet Bob's.

"I came up here on a wing and a prayer," Stas said, "but it looks like I got lucky right off the bat." His own attention remained on his beer can which he was absently turning in endless circles upon its own coaster. He wasn't aware that Bob's concentration was no longer concentrated on him.

The scruffy looking guy with the shaggy hair broke his gaze from Bob's and did his best to make their connecting glance seem inadvertent but his attempt wasn't very convincing. Bob knew who the guy was and, even though there was no real cause for it, something about crossing paths with this particular local troublemaker in this particular moment was causing him some concern.

When the guy took no more than two quick sips of his freshly delivered drink and then left it behind to head for the door, Bob felt vindicated in his sudden consternation. On his way to the door the guy seemed to be looking anywhere except back towards the end of the bar where Bob and Stas were seated. Then he was out the door.

"I think maybe we should get out of here." Bob did not let his eyes stray from the recently closed door as he spoke. Stas turned his attention from his can of Nordeast to Bob and then followed the focus of his gaze to the empty doorway.

"What is it?"

"Not exactly sure," Bob replied, "but I don't like it."

Stas picked up his can of Nordeast and finished what was left in a single swallow. Bob did the same but took it down in two. Stas reached for his wallet but Bob stopped him and tossed some cash down on the bar. "Let's go." Bob was already up and moving and with some haste. "Can you meet me at the bait shop tonight, about nine-thirty?" he asked over his shoulder.

Stas nodded as he tried to keep up with Bob who was hustling toward the door. Bob walked out into the afternoon sunlight and Stas followed behind him, still mostly confused by the sudden shift in his companion's demeanor. Stas watched Bob scan the parking lot with no idea what he might be looking for. He investigated the surroundings for himself but found nothing that would equate to any sort of answer.

The parking lot was empty.

<u>5</u>

Three and a half hours later the darkness had crept out across the sky from the east and taken the land. The painted plywood Muskie that stood tall on the side of Highway 65 in front of Bob's Beer & Bait jumped from the shadows as it was bathed in the soft, cool, blue luminescence of LED headlights. The throw of light grew larger as the vehicle approached, widening out and spilling onto the structure behind it. Then the whole building and parking lot lit up as Stas turned his truck in just past the plywood fish. The lot was empty as he expected; he pulled around to the back of the building and parked next to Bob's Ford Ranger pickup.

He cut the engine of his own truck and the quiet dropped like a stone. Earlier, standing in the parking lot of Mark's Bar, Bob had given him a reason for their quick exit. The guy wearing the Anthrax T-shirt, even though Stas had never even seen him, was named Willy Gustafson. A guy, Bob had explained to Stas, who split most of his time between a busted up old trailer on a plot of land on the east side of Big Sandy Lake, and doing stints of various lengths in the county lock-up. Bob had no concrete reasons why the presence of this Willy Gustafson character had gotten his hackles up, but Stas thought he'd trust Bob's judgment in that regard. They had confirmed their later rendezvous and then had parted ways.

Stas got out of the truck and walked up the couple of aged steps to a small landing at the bait shop's backdoor. He rapped on the battered wooden door and waited. Seconds later the deadbolt rattled and then Bob opened the door for him. He ushered Stas into a small stockroom at the back of the store, then Bob headed down a creaky set of stairs to the basement and Stas trailed behind him.

They walked into a little basement office that gave Stas an idea as to how Bob was handling his retirement. Photos and note cards posted on various cork boards, red twine tacked up connecting certain pieces of information, and a white board filled with dates, times, and locations led him to believe that perhaps a cold case or two was still eating at former Sheriff Bob Gurley.

A desk piled high with papers and what looked like old case files sat in the middle of the room. Bob signaled to Stas to pull up a seat. Stas grabbed an old wooden chair from along the wall and dragged it over in front of the desk. Bob walked around the desk to a file cabinet situated behind it. He rifled through one of the drawers for a second until he located what he was looking for. He removed a manila file folder that was about three quarters of an inch thick, leafed through it giving the contents a quick once-over, and then handed it across the desk to Stas.

Stas gave the file his own quick assessment and found newspaper clippings and notes, for the most part related to Logan. "You have a file on him?" Stas asked. He looked up and found himself, once again, under the shrewd, assessing gaze of the former sheriff.

"That's right," Bob said after an extended period of evaluation. "Something about the guy has always rubbed me the wrong way, ever since I came to know who he was. But then about six months ago something happened that made me officially suspicious, hence the file." A ghost of a thin smile slipped across his face for a second.

"Yeah, what was that?"

"Norma and I have dinner up at the Minnewawa every now and again. They've got a pretty nice restaurant up there. You tried it yet?"

"Haven't been to the restaurant but I know they make a pretty damn good club sandwich," Stas said through a sardonic smile.

"It was last fall," Bob said. "I remember because we finished our supper but they had the baseball game on in the bar. It was the night Jack Mavis threw the what-do-ya-call-it? Three outs on nine pitches?"

"An immaculate inning," Stas answered, recalling the game himself.

"Yeah, that's right. Anyway, I sent Norma home and I hung around to catch the end of the ballgame. I was alone in the bar bellied up at the far end. There's this big booth in the restaurant, I would think of it as an Executive Booth, I guess. It's away from most of the other tables giving you some semblance of privacy for a meeting, that sort of thing. As I discovered though, not a lot of privacy if someone happens to be sitting where I was. The booth is on the restaurant side but it's exactly opposite of a partition situated at the end of the bar."

"And ya heard something interesting, did ya?"

"Yep. Interesting enough that I wrote it down, as best I could remember it anyway."

Bob paused to lean down and pull open his bottom desk drawer. From it he removed a bottle of Maker's Mark and two glasses. He set them on the desk and eyed Stas. Stas nodded and Bob poured a finger full in each then passed one over to Stas.

"Don't worry," Bob said, "I don't wash the glasses out in the bait tanks or anything."

"Hadn't really worried about it until you brought it up." Stas gave the glass a healthy dose of scrutiny, found it acceptable, and took a sip.

Bob grinned. "Hand me back that file for a second."

Stas did as he was bid and Bob rifled through it as he continued.

"I wasn't exactly eavesdropping, not at first. There were two guys in the booth kind of yucking it up, laughing back and forth. It had the feel of a camaraderie fueled by alcohol, like they weren't initially paying much mind to their surroundings."

"And one of them was Logan?" Stas asked.

"That's right. Their conversation dipped but I heard the other guy call him by name. That's when I really tried to start listening in but they'd dropped their volume and I couldn't really hear anything." Bob pulled a sheet of paper from the file but kept talking. "I only had one eye on the baseball game at that point, hardly even realized that Jack Mavis was making history right in front of me. Then Mavis closed the game out and there was a bit of a reaction from the few folks still left in the bar and restaurant, seemed like everyone but Logan and his friend were at least tracking the game on some level. Anyway, the little bit of cheering that went up seemed to alleviate the quiet of the whole place for a couple minutes and the slight din that followed allowed Logan's conversation to gain a bit of volume."

Bob handed the sheet of paper over to Stas, who looked it over and raised an eyebrow in Bob's direction. "What is this?"

"I took down their conversation as best I could and typed it up later."

"This is everything they said?"

"Well, not exactly. It wouldn't hold up in court but I think I got it mostly right, at least the bits that seem like they might be important. Not that they make a lick a sense to me, though."

Stas returned his attention to the sheet of paper and began to read.

Oct 3:

> **Man 1: If Randall opens his mouth about the Devil's Paddle we are going to have serious problems.**
>
> **Logan: If Randall opens his mouth he'll be in more trouble than either of us.**
>
> **Man 1: That's not true and you know it. If the true nature of the Paddle came to light, it could wreak havoc for Randall. But if he runs his mouth, no one will fall harder than you and I.**
>
> **Logan: You're right, but it would still be the end of him professionally and he's more scared of that than any pressures of morality.**
>
> **Man 1: You'd better be right.**
>
> **Logan: We've had a scare or two before but in the**

end no one resists the Devil's Paddle, don't worry about Randall.

Stas handed the sheet of paper back to Bob and took another sip of his whiskey. "I guess that could grab a guy's attention," he said as he swallowed.

"Certainly grabbed mine," Bob said. "You ever hear of a guy named Joseph Randall?"

Stas shook his head.

"You'll find some information about him in that file. I can't be certain that's the guy Logan was talking about but I'd be willing to place a reasonably sized wager on it. Joseph Randall was a former prosecutor up here in Bolton County. With Logan's backing he became a state senator. The only interesting thing about him, besides Logan and this other guy feeling like they needed to keep his mouth shut about this Devil's Paddle, is that he's a potential candidate to run for the U.S. Senate in the next election." Bob picked up his glass and settled back in his chair, resting his other hand atop the slight paunch of his belly.

"You have any idea what the hell the 'Devil's Paddle' is?" Stas asked.

"No idea, couldn't find any reference to it anywhere. I guess Logan succeeded in keeping Randall's mouth shut on that count."

Stas sighed, "It sounds suspicious but it could just be some dumb crap that politicians would get bent out of shape about."

"Yep, that definitely is a possibility."

"Any idea who the other guy, this 'Man 1,' might be?"

"Maybe." A sly smile crept across Bob's face as he spoke, "There's another thing that's not in that file but only because it's brand new information and I haven't had a chance to update it yet. Two nights ago my wife Norma and I celebrated our anniversary—"

"Congratulations."

"Thanks, anyway, Jane Devorak got us set up with

dinner reservations at the Minnewawa. It also just so happened that the guy that owns the resort, the one that dumped all that money into it, was on site that night. I'm not sure what Jane's motivation was, I haven't had a chance to talk with her yet, but she had the resort owner stop by our table and wish us well."

Bob stopped to take another sip from his glass and Stas took the opportunity to do the same. He had only known the man across the desk from him for a few hours but he could tell that now Bob was coming to the point. He enjoyed the inner warmth being provided by the amber liquid and he waited for Bob.

He didn't have to wait long.

"I think she wanted me to meet him for a reason, and I still don't know exactly why, but she definitely could not have known the significance that meeting him would have for me. He delivered us a complimentary bottle of wine for our anniversary. When he offered his congratulations, I recognized his voice immediately. The man that owns the resort is the very same man that Logan had been sitting with in that booth that night."

Stas released a long, metered breath. He tasted his whiskey, felt the welcomed warm burn, and then set the glass back on Bob's desk. "So, the guy that owns the Minnewawa is involved with Logan. And they are having quiet conversations late at night in bars about keeping some guy's mouth shut and something called the Devil's Paddle."

Bob gave an assenting nod to each statement, sipped his own whiskey, and then spoke. "And Logan was trying to track down your friend right before she disappeared. So, I guess it's no wonder that Jane Devorak might think questions regarding Logan at the Minnewawa could be dangerous."

6

Stas pulled into the resort parking lot a few minutes before eleven p.m. and parked. He locked his truck and walked toward the main lodge instead of the path that led around the building back into the grounds and to the cabin he was staying in. He'd decided to see if the restaurant or bar was still open and if there might be anyone in it worth striking up a conversation with.

The bar was practically empty and after a quick tour around it he decided to just head back to his rooms. He walked out the double doors at the back of the lodge onto the patio. To his left he found one of the racks that contained the bikes for complimentary use on the grounds. He grabbed one and pedaled across the quiet grounds to Carver House.

He walked into the shared living space of the cabin but he had it all to himself. Stas thought, it being the middle of the week still, that he might have the whole of Carver House to himself. He pulled out his phone as he walked to the door of his own quarters to check his messages. Tim Boyd had been calling and texting for much of the evening looking for information. Stas felt bad but he didn't really have anything for him, nothing that made any sense yet anyway. Stas used his key card to open the door and stopped short after walking into the suite.

Someone had been in his room.

The sandwich tray had been removed. That was what caught his attention right out of the gate. He was able to rationalize that, though; housekeeping could have been by to clean it up.

The mess on the desk was more than he could just move on from, though.

The resort's informational literature, originally stored neatly in a little display placard, was now strewn willy-nilly across the desk. He made a quick inventory of the room and found nothing else out of place. But the adjoining door to the bedroom was closed.

He had definitely left it open when he had departed for Bob's Beer and Bait Shop. Stas stood still in the sitting room of his cabin and listened for any sign of movement on the other side of the portal to his bedroom. He heard nothing. He took another glance around the room again, this time looking for anything that might be used as a weapon. His gaze fell upon the fireplace. It was gas fueled, operated by simply flipping a switch on the wall to turn it on or off, but sitting on the hearth was an ornamental set of fireplace tools.

He took three quick steps to the hearth treading lightly on the balls of his feet to keep any noise he made to a minimum. The fireplace tools looked real and the poker should do just fine were he to find himself in need of an apparatus with some heft to swing at an intruder. He grabbed it and in doing so almost yanked the whole set over. The resulting clamor would have put a quick end to any stealth he might have managed to achieve. He looked the set of implements over and realized that each tool, being unnecessary for its intended purpose and strictly for aesthetic, had been soldered to the stand. He applied a small bit of force to the joint connecting the poker. The slight metal bond was thin and shouldn't be hard to break. When his initial effort met with some resistance, he applied more pressure and, after a long moment, the poker snapped free.

The resounding crack seemed to echo through the room louder than it possibly could've actually been. Stas froze for a moment and listened for any change from the direction of the bedroom. There was still nothing and the silence was supreme. He lifted the recently liberated poker and found the heft of the thing to be to his satisfaction. He readjusted his grip and took a few cautious strides over to the door. Stas set his left hand, the one that was not squeezed tight on the grip of the poker, onto the handle of the door and listened. There was not even the slight noise caused by the HVAC system. There was nothing. He raised his right hand poised to strike.

In a single motion he pressed down on the handle disengaging the lock and pushed the door open. The door was light and swung open fast, giving him a full view of the bedroom. He watched for any movement but the room was empty. From his vantage point, still standing in the living room, he could not see the master bathroom. With hesitant cautious strides he crossed the threshold and moved far enough into the bedroom to where he could see the bathroom and its door standing open.

There was no one in the little lavatory but the shower curtain was pulled shut. He had no idea if he had left it that way or not. He lowered the angle of the poker so that its tip was now pointed towards the shower like a sword. He stepped from the carpet to the tile floor of the bathroom. Still leveling the poker he reached his left hand out towards the curtain, the screeching strings of the *Psycho* theme echoing throughout his head. In a single motion he clutched and pulled the dangling curtain.

The rings holding the curtain to the rod made a jangly ratcheting sound as they slid along it at an awkward angle. In spite of the racket that it caused, the opening of the curtain revealed nothing more than an empty tub. Stas released his breath and it ran out of him leaving him feeling deflated and weak. Collecting himself he left the bathroom and stepped back into the bedroom.

He saw a pamphlet propped up on his pillow.

Stas walked over to the bed, sat down, and grabbed it. It was a map of the grounds and must have come from the desk with the rest of the resort's info which might explain why it had all been tossed about on the desk. Stuck to the map was a post-it note with nothing but a time scrawled across it: six o'clock a.m. The little note wasn't signed but Stas thought he recognized the handwriting. It was similar enough to the scribbled wording on the little piece of paper that had sent him in the direction of Bob Gurley to deduce who wrote it. He unfolded the map and saw that a particular spot had been highlighted.

The little spot of yellow wavered in his vision and he felt light-headed. Stas had never put much stock in serendipity or coincidence, but his eyes remained riveted to the little section of the map that glowed from the rough strokes of the highlighter. Demarked was a little fishing pond a short distance off of the main lake. It was the little pool of water where Stas had almost departed this world at the age of ten.

7

The hours leading up to six a.m. were long and filled for Stas by a dragging fitful sleep. His dreams were many and haunted, rooted in old memories that had been for the most part forgotten. He was continually returned to that little pond, sometimes as an adult, sometimes as the child he had been, and others as a not-entirely-impartial observer. He would come up from sleep like he was coming out of the pond, gasping, seeming to alternate between coughing and choking, then he'd slip back into an uneasy slumber and back down into those foreboding waters.

He had committed himself to putting that day, and that place, in his past. And, it being so long ago, had for the most part succeeded. The jumbled memories that surfaced now with the dreams seemed to be of some import but he had difficulty determining which aspects were real and which were just figments of his sleeping mind set loose to ramble through the darkened halls of his subconscious.

Sometimes he stood on the dock, sometimes on the shore watching his own hand crack and slap at the surface of the water, and sometimes he was actually in the pond. The latter he experienced both as a drowning boy and as an outsider, floating in the murky depths and watching the weeds that covered the floor of the pond as they unnaturally wrapped themselves about the legs of the boy he'd been. He saw his childhood self open his mouth to scream and freeze in terror as the water filled his lungs. Watching from afar Stas could still feel the crush in his chest even as he watched the pockets of air, his younger version's last breath, bubbling up to the surface. Then he would wake or the dream would change again.

Occasionally he imagined a warm lighted presence approaching. Perhaps it was his mind's interpretation of Lisa coming to save him, but those safe moments were few and far between. More often there were shadows, darkened figures blurred at the edges, standing along the shore of the pond. These shadowy onlookers carried with them an air of

141

malevolence and seemed only to revel in his pain and terror.

A few minutes past five in the morning, after stumbling back from the depths of the most recent incarnation of the nightmare, Stas gave up on the charade of sleep and took a shower. After doing his best to wash away the residue of the dreams, he stared at the television without actually watching it for another half hour or so. A little before six he punched the power button on the remote, dropped it on the bed, and left the room. He stepped out onto the front porch of Carver House as the darkness was still draped across the land. Sunrise wouldn't commence for another half-hour or forty-five minutes so this anonymous meeting would transpire without the aid of any daylight. He had debated bringing the fireplace poker along on this morning rendezvous but he didn't think he'd need it as he was fairly certain whom he would be meeting.

The spring morning air carried a chill and he was glad he had donned a sweatshirt. He struck off down the path to the right of the cabin that Carrie had told him about the afternoon before when he had arrived at the resort. He walked about a quarter mile passing another couple of the large structures that the Minnewawa so humbly referred to as cabins. Up to that point the surroundings struck no chord, but soon thereafter the density of the trees began to soften and he started to feel the slight tug of familiarity. A few moments later the path broke from the trees.

The beach and the entirety of Lake Minnewawa spread out before him. While so much else had changed and to drastic degrees, the lake remained much the same as he remembered it. Stas was slapped by an immediate nostalgia, its onslaught so visceral that his cheek tingled slightly as if an open hand had actually just connected with it. The hanging half-moon glistened, both in the sky and in its wavering reflection on the shimmering surface of the lake.

Stas took a deep breath and walked down the beach to his left, attempting to put cascading memories to the side for the time being. He continued toward the small path that would lead indelibly to the fishing pond where he had once nearly expired. He found the break in the trees and hit the small trail without a moment's hesitation. His conviction did not remain so stalwart when he reached the far end of the path. He stopped and took in the lay of the land.

The pond lay at the center of a small clearing in the trees, ringed by a small shoreline. The fishing dock had been replaced, upgraded at some point but otherwise it could have been yesterday that he last stood before this pond. He forced his feet into motion and they carried him out a few feet onto the dock on legs that he no longer felt he could confidently claim as his own. He stopped. The air felt thin and his chest felt heavy. The surface of the pond was pristine, like glass, and he had to fight down the images his mind was trying to cultivate of his own little hand rupturing its serenity and smacking angry ripples into the unblemished smoothness. If he'd had to combat these visions for long, quite likely the battle would have been lost, but to his great relief he was distracted by the soft padding of cautious footsteps approaching.

He turned and watched as, clad in black, Jane Devorak materialized from the depths of the forestry. She beckoned him to her and with very little reluctance he stepped back off the dock and walked up the small bank to where she stood at the edge of the trees.

"You have a pretty amazing sense for the dramatic, even if it was unintended," he told her.

"How's that?"

"I almost drowned in this little pond once upon a time."

"Is that right?" She seemed curious but not necessarily concerned. Stas nodded and she said, "Well, let's hope it's just coincidence and not some kind of omen. Did you meet Bob?"

"Yep, he seems quite the character. Full of interesting information, too." Jane Devorak offered him a questioning glance. "He thinks Ted Logan and the guy that owns this place might be mixed up in something that might not be exactly above board. Is that why you didn't want me asking questions around the resort?"

She sighed, "It's only the tip of the iceberg but yeah, I guess so. Do you have any idea what this place is?"

"How do you mean?" he asked, confused.

She shook her head instead of answering but then surprised him by changing the subject, coming to the point with a sudden stinging sharpness. "I knew your friend, when she was a teen-ager. I knew Anne Callahan."

His prior confusion was in no way alleviated, in fact it was compounded. "What?" he managed to sputter.

"You showing up here and asking a bunch of questions particularly about those two people was, and is, dangerous. Logan, because he might catch wind of it, and the Callahan girl..." She trailed off. "You're friends with her, even to this day?"

"That's right."

A slight smile flit across Devorak's face then she nodded as if affirming something to herself. "Would she trust you?"

"You could say that." Stas did his best to temper the sarcasm in his tone.

"Did she ever tell you about Norumbega?"

That caught him off guard. Norumbega was the name of the compound where Lisa had grown up, where she'd been imprisoned in a sense, and it had been not so far from where they stood now. The name came from Norse mythology tied to a lost city somewhere supposedly up in New England. To Stas it was just the kind of pretentious crap that a cuckoo religious nut would find and align himself with in an attempt to lend credence to his zealous, lunatic ideals.

Jane was still talking, "I ended up there when I was in my twenties. I was so lost, struggling for any sort of an identity. I thought I'd found it there."

The admission that she had known Lisa when Lisa was still Anne had stunned him. The realization of the ramifications of the fact now hit him like a strong right hook. Jane Devorak had lived with her, had been one of them.

"When I first arrived at Norumbega I thought she was

like a queen," Devorak went on. "Your friend, she was at the right hand of our exalted leader. An inspiration, I aspired to be her, but of course what I didn't realize then was that I would never be her. I could never hold that position. It was reserved for younger women and those selected would never have any choice in the matter. It was no honor, it was a sentencing. That young lady that I so ignorantly admired was living an absolute nightmare."

Bitterness had made a haggard mask of her face. Stas had seen it before, when Lisa had originally explained her past to him. It was born of anger and regret, cultivated at the hands of a master manipulator.

"You got out, though, right?" Stas tried to redirect the sour turn they had taken. "All of you did, when Norumbega burned." He and Lisa had watched it on the news. About three and a half years after she had made her escape, her former home had burned to the ground. The networks didn't get any of the details right, none of the nuance of what was actually happening in that compound. All they had was their aerial shots of the fire and weak stories in the aftermath of the 'religious group' that was disbanded when their home went up in flames. It was the happiest he'd ever seen Lisa.

Now, on the opposite end of the spectrum from where Lisa had been that night, Jane Devorak loosed a short bark of humorless laughter into the quiet night, "Got out?" She was shaking her head again.

"Yeah, that was the end of the whole thing, right? The cult died in that fire." But Stas had an uneasy feeling about the validity of that sentence even as he spoke it.

Her eyes gleamed with barely veiled anger. "Do you know anything about prairie restoration?"

Stas had no idea what that question was supposed to mean and shook his head.

"Have you ever heard of a prescribed burn?" she asked.

"I guess," which he had, "but I can't say I really know what it means," which he didn't.

"Prairie plants have deep roots. They can survive and

grow again starting anew from their roots beneath the ground. A prescribed burn, a fire set intentionally, eliminates non-native plants and clears the land so the true plants can thrive again."

That previous feeling of a heaviness sitting in his chest had returned, weighing Stas down. Goosebumps were standing out all over his flesh in spite of his sweatshirt. "What are you saying?" His voice was thin, little more than a whisper.

"Norumbega burned so that it could live again. It still exists, it just has a different name."

Stas was shaking his head as if he thought by negating he could strangle out the truth of her words. "That can't be…"

"It can be, and it is. And you're standing in the middle of it."

Stas had never felt so stupid and infantile.

"The new ownership, all the renovations here at the Minnewawa, all of it came to pass not so long after Norumbega fell to ashes." There was no denying the truth as she spoke it. "There's a road on the north end of the grounds marked for staff vehicles only. At the end of it is a large gate, heavily secured. On the other side of that gate is a community that houses all of the employees that work here at the Minnewawa. We live there. We work here. Norumbega is alive and well and it's just up the road."

Nothing moved and yet the world shook beneath his feet, his legs wavered on him. Norumbega hadn't died. The implications of that were staggering.

Stas struggled to find his voice, "The guy Logan was sitting with—" Even though he was adrift he realized she wouldn't know what he was talking about. He rephrased. "The guy who owns this place…?" He still couldn't manage to finish the sentence but she didn't need him too.

"He is called many things by many different people but I believe the one you're struggling for is his real name."

"No…" His voice was a paper-thin whisper.

"Cortland Whittier."

Stas shook his head, "He's dead. He died in the fire."

"Deep roots, evil has deep, deep roots and it grows

from the ashes."

Stas was spared the absurdity of any response he might have mustered by the buzzing sound of her phone vibrating against the keys in her pocket. She pulled it out and he caught a glimpse of the display and the contact information for the incoming call.

His pulse quickened.

No name, just a number. And while it was not a number he recognized, it was awful close to one he'd come to know just lately. The number bore a 320 area code and only the final two digits differed from the one that they had found in Lisa's call log. Too close to be coincidence.

"Who's calling you?"

Jane Devorak silenced the call but before she could answer him, she whipped her head around in the direction of the path leading from the beach to the pond. He followed her gaze but it did nothing to clarify the motivation of her glance. She turned back to him her eyes suddenly brimming with a desperate urgency.

"I've got to go."

"Are you still in contact with her?" Stas' was harried but she seemed confused.

"Who?"

"Lisa… Anne, I mean."

"I haven't talked to her since the day she disappeared from Norumbega." Her eyes cut toward the path again and now he heard what had drawn her attention. The sound was still distant, maybe just coming upon the trail back on the beach side of the path that led through the wood to the pond. It was a small battery-powered motor. It was one of the golf carts used by the staff.

Her voice now matched the urgency in her eyes. "I have to go now. Get with Bob, find out about a woman named Debbie Keller."

"What—"

"Debbie Keller, can you remember the name?" She was speaking in a harsh, rushed whisper. Stas managed a nod.

"There is some kind of connection between her and Whittier. You and Bob need to find it."

Before Stas could manage another word, she was gone, disappeared into the trees.

"Wait—" but he was speaking to nothing but the morning air and surrounding forestry.

Stas tried to pull himself together. He repeated the name she'd given him, Debbie Keller, in his head a couple of times to commit it to memory as he turned and made a hasty scramble back down the small bank to the pond.

Whoever was approaching, he thought it would be less odd and awkward to be discovered on the dock then lurking at the edge of the small woods. As he hustled onto the wooden slats stretching out over the water, he realized the sky had lightened. He wasn't sure how long he'd been out here, sunrise had not been achieved but the darkness had softened and daylight was coming.

He had stepped back onto the dock only seconds before the golf cart appeared on the path, a guy driving. He was wearing the typical blue shirt, the uniform of the resort, only his was a sweatshirt, appropriate for the chilly morning. He waved in Stas' direction and pulled the cart to a stop near the spot where the dock met the shoreline. Stas waved back and took a few more steps further out over the water putting more distance between them.

"Morning," the guy called out, still sitting in the cart.

"Morning." Stas returned the greeting.

"Getting an early stroll in, eh?"

"Yep, couldn't sleep."

The guy got out of the golf cart. He was stocky, thick. "Sorry to hear it." He spoke with a hearty jocular nature. "Don't tell me our beds aren't comfortable enough for ya?"

"No, nothing like that."

"Well, that's good to hear at least." The man smiled as he walked over and was now standing at the foot of the dock. The smile seemed genuine but Stas was reticent to trust it. The guy put his arms behind him, at the small of his back, and stretched looking around at the tree line surrounding the pond. Neither of them spoke for a couple of seconds.

"You're out pretty early yourself," Stas said to fill the space, trying to maintain a friendly tone, and keep any underlying nervousness out of his voice.

"Indeed. The name's Jason Tolbert. I'm head of security here at the resort." In the recesses of his mind Stas felt a slight tug, something about the guy's last name. "I like to make a quick tour of the grounds in the morning each day," Tolbert went on, "make sure everything around here stays fit as a fiddle."

"Sure," Stas said, turning away. He took a few more steps further out onto the dock hoping that the pre-dawn light was still shadowy enough to hide his clouding countenance. After the conversation he'd just had with Jane Devorak he was getting a bad feeling about the level of coincidence involved in being interrupted by the head of security. "How's the fishing out here?" Stas asked, attempting to keep the mood light.

"Not too bad, the pond is stocked with lots of Sunnies for the kids to catch. You got to be careful with your lines in these waters though, they can get tangled, the weeds at the bottom can be wicked."

Stas made a slow turn back toward the shore and saw that the man had walked out a few steps joining him on the dock, no more than twenty feet from where he was standing.

Jason Tolbert, head of Minnewawa security, stood with his stocky muscular frame between Stas and the relative safety of the shore. Stas realized that if Tolbert was in charge of security at the resort, then his orders most likely came directly from Cortland Whittier.

And the guy had just cut off his only course of retreat. Stas faced Tolbert while, spreading out around him on all sides, the cool waters that had already tried to take his life once sat placidly. The surface of the pond reflected like glass in the soft morning light.

Red Wing...
Spring, 2017

1

The sounds of baseball on the radio drifted down to him from up by the house. Danny was throwing at the pitch-back and listening to the first getaway-day game of the regular season. Tim Boyd was sitting on a small stump further out in the woods. He was sitting alone and staring at Lisa's shed.

The doors stood open giving him a full view of the little makeshift living space. The defunct lock still lay in the grass where he and Stas had left it. Tim's thoughts churned and toiled in search of answers but continued to fall short of finding any purchase. Whatever the purpose of the shed, there was a correlation between it and Lisa's disappearance, Tim was sure of it.

When Stas had skipped town, and in his heart of hearts Tim did believe it was for good reason (even if he had wanted to strangle the guy), Tim had taken the rest of the week off and brought Danny down here, down to Lisa's house. If there was nothing to do but wait, this was where they'd do it. Here, at her house, where the proximity to her stuff made it feel as if she was close by, even without the facts to back such a theory.

Since they'd arrived at her house though, an obsession

with the shed had been infiltrating him. He had gone through it countless times in the short period that he'd been back. The small bedroll was little more than blankets and a foam mattress topper; then there was the table and lantern, and the shelf holding a couple of plastic totes with supplies. The contents of the bins consisted of granola bars, a flashlight, bottled water, some batteries and various other household supplies. The purpose of the shed was clear, the reasoning behind that purpose was less so.

He thought about opening the totes on the shelf again to look through them once more, but how many times was he going to do that? The three tours of the contents that he had already made had not revealed any new information. On the fourth inspection would some new piece of the puzzle magically appear, or the fifth? It seemed unlikely.

As despair dug its way deeper into him - it was an emotion he had become so familiar with he barely realized that he now carried it with him always - his attention was diverted. He heard a resounding 'YES!' drift down from where Danny was pitching and listening to the game. The local nine must have pulled off the victory.

Tears welled in his eyes. Danny, his boy, was getting short shrift these days. Tim was so caught up in his own anguished emotions that he wasn't giving proper consideration to how Danny was handling it. For the most part Danny seemed to be holding up but since they'd been back in Red Wing he'd taken to sleeping with Tim in Lisa's bed instead of his room, the one that had become his own when they were here.

As he was thinking about their current sleeping arrangement a memory struck him that twisted the knife of nostalgia further bringing forth more tears. He'd been thinking about Danny's favorite book as a boy, the one they had to read every night before bed.

The little girl in the book was scared because she had a monster residing under her bed. But as the story went on, she realized that it was a friendly monster and it only acted scary to keep other people away. It was actually protecting the things under her bed because that was where the little girl hid her treasures, the things most important to her.

Tim steadied himself as he stood up from the little stump. He walked the few steps to the shed and stood in front of it, then he stepped inside onto the wooden plank flooring. He crouched down in front of the little makeshift bunk. The little girl in the book hid her treasures under the bed. The makeshift mattress was laid out right on the floor but that didn't mean there couldn't be something beneath it. With an unsteady hand he reached out for the little foam mattress topper. He pulled it aside bracing for whatever monster might be lurking to protect Lisa's secrets, but there was nothing. Beneath the bedding was nothing more than the continuation of the wooden plank flooring.

Tim released a long sigh and started to slide the bedding back into place but then stopped. There was nothing but flooring beneath it, but upon closer inspection one of the planks was a little odd. It was shorter than the rest. And while the floor was old and battered this one plank was not quite as worn. It also didn't meet flush with the other adjacent boards on the longer ends. There was just enough room between the planks to get a slight fingertip grip on it. Tim worked his fingers into the space between until he had enough of a hold to manage some leverage and he lifted. The board resisted, but only for a moment. After a brief hesitation it popped up revealing a small space beneath it.

In the little hiding space was a heavy-duty black plastic case. Tim lifted it up and it had a certain heft to it. Even though he didn't have much experience with such a case or the contents it might keep, he knew instinctively what it was. He popped the latch and looked down at the gleaming, black metal from the barrel of a hand-gun. His breathing was becoming labored, tougher to come by. He closed the case and latched it, setting it aside to continue his inspection of the little hidey-hole. The gun case had been sitting on top of a box of ammunition. He lifted the box and heard the bullets rattle inside. They had room to move; the box wasn't full. He slid it open.

Bullets filled the box about halfway but sitting on top of them was a key. A small singular key attached to a little plastic keychain. He lifted the key out of the box for a closer look.

2

Danny sat in the passenger seat of Tim's Honda clutching the little key. Tim kept glancing over at him. The plastic keychain had come from a place called Wurzer's Marina. It was about five miles north of Lisa's place right on the river. He had asked Danny if he wanted to go look at some boats. Tim didn't think Danny actually cared a lick about looking at boats when he could be throwing baseballs, but he acquiesced after an ice cream bribe was thrown in to sweeten the pot.

They pulled into the marina's parking lot and Tim put his hand out for the key. Danny set it on his palm without looking at him. His attention had been drawn to the banks of the river. Perhaps the kid had more interest in maritime affairs than either of them might have thought. Tim was equally surprised by the fleet docked at the banks of the river.

Wurzer's Marina was no run-of-the-mill boat rental. The facilities alone boasted a certain level of elegance, and the giant houseboats moored in immediate view of those arriving were no exception. On either side of the houseboats were docks holding speedboats and fishing boats that, from what Tim could see, seemed very well maintained and of a superior echelon. Wurzer's seemed to cater to a certain type of clientele.

Tim parked in front of the office. It was a large white building up on a little hill with a porch that faced the parking lot. The porch wrapped around the far corner, overlooking the river. They walked up the steps and into the office. The desk was just to their left and beyond it were large windows that gave a stunning view of the river as it went rushing by. There were a handful of other patrons lingering about in front of the desk waiting their turn to speak with a Wurzer's staff member. Tim looked around before deciding if he would join the queue and saw that to his right a small open area hooked around the other end of the building, opposite the river, and seemed to spill out into another room. He headed in that direction to investigate and Danny followed. They came around the corner and Tim found exactly what he had been hoping for. The small vestibule did open out into another room and one of the walls was covered with a bank of lockers.

The room was long and narrow with the lockers stretching out across one wall and windows adorning the one opposite them. On this side of the building, though, the windows faced the woods as opposed to the river. Danny stopped as he would anytime that he found himself in a space that might possibly represent the depth between home plate and a pitching mound. He began to work through his motion even without a ball in his hand.

Tim looked at the key in his hand. The number on the keychain was twenty-three. He began a slow walk along the bank of lockers looking for the one with a corresponding number. He found it and came to a stop standing before it. The pace of his breathing quickened but felt shallow. He slid the key into the lock. Over his shoulder, from a few feet away he could hear Danny muttering, doing his own play-by-play. Goose-bumps rippled into life, tingling up and down Tim's arms as he turned the key. He heard the latch disengage and the locker swung open.

The locker was small but felt vast when contrasted by its contents. It was empty but for a woman's wallet.

With a hand that showed the slightest of tremors he reached in and retrieved it. He tried to stay his hand as he released the catch that held the wallet shut. The two sides parted. On one half, in the billfold, was a stash of cash. At a quick glance, Tim guessed around five hundred dollars. He turned it around so he could see the clear plastic slots for the ID and credit cards. The credit cards were registered to a Sarah Anderson. He checked the driver's license and it brought a lump up into his throat. The name matched the credit cards, Sarah Anderson, but the face looking back at him was Lisa's.

An uncomfortable curdling feeling rippled through his innards. Whatever had happened to her, wherever she was, Lisa did not have her new ID. The fact that she had attained the driver's license and credit cards hurt Tim in an unquantifiable way, but that she was without them now scared the hell out of him. He snapped the wallet shut with enough force to draw Danny's attention.

"What is it, Dad?"

To that question, Tim had no response. "It's nothing, a wallet," he managed after a long pause. "And it's not mine so I'm just gonna put it back."

"Is it Lisa's?"

"No…" The image of Lisa's picture next to that other name filled his head. "Not exactly, buddy." It was not a sufficient answer and yet it managed to pacify the ten-year-old brain for the time being. That particular brain had larger, more extravagant concerns at the moment.

"Can we go look at the boats now?"

"You bet. You go take a look, I'll be right there." Danny was off like a shot. "Stay off the docks 'til I get there though," he called out and Danny tossed a thumbs-up above his head to acknowledge the message received. Tim turned back to the open locker and with a heavy heart he set the wallet back into the otherwise gaping empty space. He took one long look at it then closed the door, listening to the latch snap home and lock.

Tim's mind felt untethered as he stepped back out onto the porch that ran around the building. Danny was already down looking at the gigantic houseboats. Tim walked over to him trying to come up with a legitimate reason that the wallet might still be in the locker but nothing viable would surface.

Tim stepped up next to Danny and put his hand on his son's shoulder. Danny's gaze didn't waver from the luxurious home afloat before him. Tim looked at it as well but with unfocused eyes.

"Think we could see the inside?" Danny asked.

"I don't know. I guess we could check with…" Tim's response trailed off. He had absently turned away from the houseboat and toward the speedboats docked directly in front of the Wurzer's Marina office.

Danny was saying something else but Tim didn't hear a word of it. It was like his muffled voice was coming from far away, as if it were nothing more than a distant radio signal. Danny wasn't far away, he was standing right behind him, but Tim's focus had been stolen from his son, and completely.

It had been whisked away without consent by a beautiful Criss-Craft, a powerful speedboat, up on a lift on the second dock over. Tim had seen that boat before. Much like now, he had been in a state of confusion when last he saw it, yet he would never forget it. It was the very same boat that had sped away up the river right before he and Stas had found the shed.

McGregor…
Spring, 2017

1

Head of security Jason Tolbert brought his golf cart to a halt in front of a large gate at the end of a road marked 'staff vehicles only.' He waved his keycard in front of a sensor and the metal gate slid open, running smooth and silent on its track. He drove through and it closed behind him.

Within the walls of the compound the morning was well under way; people moved about and a bus was being loaded to take staff members into the resort for their morning shifts. Tolbert put on a cheery smile and gave the bus a wave as he passed by even though his outer demeanor did not jibe with his inner unrest.

He'd left the man he'd met this morning standing on the dock. That the guy had been out so early was not all that abnormal but his actions had seemed nervous which in turn made Tolbert nervous. Jason Tolbert's job was to get to the bottom of things that made him nervous.

Just through the gate were various buildings that comprised the Minnewawa staff housing. Beyond the housing was a park area abutted on the far side by the Wellness Building. The Wellness Building was a large structure for worship, exercise, classes and faith gatherings. Behind it another small road cut back further into the woods. Tolbert made his way to this road and followed it until it came to an end in front of a small squat utilitarian building. It was all brick with no windows and a single metal door for an entrance.

He exited the golf cart. There was a battered laptop sitting on the passenger seat of the cart that he grabbed and brought along with him.

Tolbert passed his keycard in front of another sensor and heard the latch on the metal door disengage. The exterior door opened into a claustrophobic concrete room that contained only another metal door and a window looking into a security office. In the office an intense-looking young man was sitting behind a control desk. His left hand rested on the desk, his right was just below it. The weapon it held was hidden from view just like he'd been taught. The young man gave Tolbert a nod and pressed a button on his console. A loud buzz emanated from the door. Jason opened it and stepped through. To his left was an access door to the office and in front of him was a set of metal stairs leading down into the nerve center of Minnewawa's security building.

The room at the foot of the stairs consisted of ten workstations and each station was made up of a desk with four monitors. Tolbert walked to one a third of the way back.

"Roll number two back to a few minutes before six this morning," Tolbert told the guy monitoring that particular bank of screens. The guy made some quick keystrokes and the screen jumped to an image of the dock on the little fishing pond. "Run it forward for me." The clock counter on the screen sped forward but for a moment nothing changed. Then the man he had met that morning zipped onto the screen. "Stop, roll from here," Tolbert ordered, and the video slowed to real time. The man stood at the edge of the fishing dock for a moment then walked back up toward the tree line and disappeared from the frame. "Is that all the coverage we have over there?" But Tolbert already knew the answer. He knew every inch of camera coverage on the grounds.

"I'm afraid so, sir."

"He's talking to someone," Tolbert mused aloud. The guy manning the bank of monitors knew that no response was required of him. Jason Tolbert rarely elicited advice from those who worked for him. In silence the video continued to run without any action occurring. A few minutes passed and Tolbert had still not said a word; he was thinking. Eventually the guy walked back into the frame and happened to look in the direction of the camera.

"Freeze it."

The video operator did as he was told.

"Zoom in on his face as best you can." The charge was executed and the man's face filled the screen. Tolbert stood still and quiet for another long moment staring at the image then pulled his phone from his pocket. He went to the third contact on his favorites list and pressed it to call his younger brother. The phone rang in his ear.

"What's up?" Jason Tolbert's little brother, Aaron, said without the need for any further pleasantries.

"Have you picked him up yet?"

"He just got back from his morning jog, he's in the shower then I'll drive him into the office, why?"

Tolbert looked at Stas Mileski's face filling the screen in front of him. "I think we might have a problem. The second Logan gets out of the shower, tell him to call me."

2

Stas stopped on the porch of Carver House before entering the building. He stepped over to one of the windows and looked in on the common room. He still didn't know if he was sharing his quarters with anyone else or not, but the communal area remained empty as it had always been since his arrival.

After the Minnewawa head of security had left him standing on the dock he'd remained there for another ten minutes or so collecting his thoughts. Now he wondered if that had been such a good idea. He couldn't be certain that Jason Tolbert would be taking any further interest in him, but assuming that he wouldn't seemed like it very well might be a mistake. And if Tolbert wasn't finished with him then Stas had given him a healthy head start.

With cautious, measured movements he entered Carver House and stepped over to the door leading to his own cabin. Stas put his ear up to it and listened. He slid the keycard into the door and cringed at the resounding click. When he heard nothing from inside, he slid the key back out and opened the door.

He walked into his room and realized his fears had definitely been founded. For the second time in as many return trips the sanctity of his cabin had been breached. This time he didn't need to waste time worrying that anyone still might be lurking about. It appeared that whether it was Tolbert, or one of his underlings, they had found and taken what they had come for. His laptop was missing.

Stas didn't waste a breath deciding that it was time to cut his stay at the Minnewawa Resort short. He threw any of his personal belongings that had made their way out of his suitcase back into it in a furious, haphazard manner. Zipping it shut he made a quick inventory of the rooms to see if he had left anything or if anything else was missing. He hadn't and there wasn't. But they had his laptop and with it a browser history full of search queries into Ted Logan. And he now knew that Logan was involved with Cortland Whittier. It was definitely time to bug out of here.

He stepped back out onto the porch and stopped. There was not necessarily a flurry of morning activity but people were beginning to move about the grounds. Calling for a cart to pick him up was out of the question, that would draw way too much attention to his departure, but he might not go unnoticed walking across the grounds with his suitcase at this point either. He reversed his course back into the building.

Returning to his room he opened the suitcase again. He threw a pair of jeans and a sweatshirt out onto the bed. He pulled out another change of clothes but stuffed this set into his backpack. Leaving the suitcase open he took stock of the room. He grabbed his toothpaste and toothbrush and put them back in the bathroom. Now he was satisfied that whoever violated his privacy next could conceivably be sold on the idea that he still intended to return.

He left Carver House, grabbed one of the bikes, and pedaled up to the parking lot with his backpack slung over his shoulder. He smiled as naturally as possible at anyone he passed, guest or staff, but now the intention of any of those wearing one of those blue shirts could no longer be trusted. He tried to keep any eye contact to a minimum in hopes his passing would not stick long in anyone's memory. As he closed in on the parking lot an ominous feeling descended upon him. Jason Tolbert, or one of his minions, would appear, materializing out of thin air, and ask Stas to join them on a little ride leaving him no choice in the matter.

He was thirty yards from the lot, then fifteen. Stas scanned his perimeter attempting to get a lock on a likely position from which the intercept would come. But he was still only waiting for it when the tires of the bike hit the pavement of the lot, and his truck was right in front of him. He stowed the bike in the docking station, threw his pack into the back of the cab and got in swinging the door shut behind him.

Stas slid the key home but didn't turn it. His paranoia level was currently off the charts. For a second, he had actually imagined turning the key only to detonate some manner of explosive. Whatever Cortland Whittier and his people were up to here, blowing up a vehicle in their own parking lot would probably still be considered excessive. And yet he couldn't help but hold his breath as he cranked the ignition. The engine roared to life and he dropped it into gear. He attempted to remain calm and not peel out as he backed out of his spot. Stas cranked the wheel and hit the gas leaving the lot and the Minnewawa Resort behind.

<u>3</u>

Fifteen minutes after his perceived escape from the resort, Stas was parked at a curb in what passed for downtown McGregor. He had a few hours before Bob would be opening up the bait shop so he had some time to kill. From where he sat in the cab of the truck he had a reasonably good view of the interior of the only café the town could boast. It was like any other small-town diner, a lunch counter and a handful of booths. McGregor was a tiny community and anyone interested in his movements would probably be able to nail them down, but still he had to remind himself that the Minnewawa Resort was not the whole town and because of their insidious nature, they were probably more insular than less. A healthy dose of paranoia could be wise but letting it paralyze him might become detrimental. He climbed out of the truck, looked both ways for traffic that didn't exist, and crossed the empty street to the diner.

The tinkle of the bell on the door as he entered, while it was no longer exacerbating a hangover, did call him back to a morning just days ago. The morning he'd met Tim Boyd and learned that Lisa was missing. It was before he knew anything about Ted Logan, and Cortland Whittier was still dead. He checked out the counter but decided on a booth instead.

The waitress that approached his table looked to be about his age and she had a friendly smile. The tag pinned to her uniform told him her name was Tammy.

"Start you with something to drink?" she asked, handing him a menu.

"A coffee would be great."

She nodded. "You got it."

Tammy the waitress started to turn away but Stas stopped her. "Do you by any chance have a pen I could borrow?"

"Sure thing, Sugar." She pulled one from her apron and handed it over before heading off to retrieve his coffee. Stas grabbed a napkin from the carousel on the table. He scratched the name 'Debbie Keller,' the name Jane Devorak had implored him to remember, on the napkin. He sat back and pondered his options. He had a name and nothing more and without his laptop it was going to be difficult finding out why Jane had told him to find her. Locating a library that might have a few community computers was going to be a necessity. A few moments later Tammy the waitress returned with his coffee.

She set the cup in front of him and he thanked her. She didn't have her notepad out to take his order but she didn't move on from the table either. He realized she was giving him a questioning look. He had no idea why so he just returned it with a curious smile of his own.

"You some kind of a writer?" she asked.

"I can honestly say that I've never heard that one before," he said with a little laugh. "Why would you think that?"

She pointed at the napkin. Stas looked down at it, and the name scribbled across it, but neither provided any insight as to why anyone might think that he was a writer. The only thing he could be relatively certain of was that it wasn't his barely legible handwriting that had led her down that line of inquiry.

"Debbie Keller," she said. "When strangers show up interested in the Keller girl, they're always looking to write a book or an article or something."

"You know who she is?"

She gave him a long look like she was trying to decide if he was pulling her leg. After a moment she said, "Everybody does. Well, I should say everyone knows who she *was*." Stas gave her another questioning glance that she returned with a curt, grim nod.

"She's dead?" he asked.

Tammy the waitress continued to bob her head in a slow nod. "Murdered, in fact. Even if you're not from around here it's kind of surprising you never heard of her. It was big news, state-wide, got some national press even."

"Really?"

"Yep, she disappeared a few years back. There was a big manhunt. Cops and first responders from all over showed up, volunteers came out of the woodwork. The whole thing was like a *20/20* episode waiting to happen."

"How do you mean?"

"She was a pretty normal girl, a nurse over at the hospital in Bolton. She led a pretty stable life up until she disappeared. They searched for her for weeks and then from out of nowhere the Bolton County Sheriff's Department gets a tip and they find her body in the woods. The thing is the search parties had already been over that section of the woods a couple of times, so obviously someone had dumped her there later."

Tammy looked around the little diner, taking a quick inventory of her tables; satisfied with what she saw she slid down into the booth across from Stas clearly warming up to her role as a town news source.

From a few booths away a guy in a faded work shirt called down to her. "You on a break or something, Tammy? I need some coffee."

Tammy looked at the guy over Stas' shoulder and shot him a sly smile. "You know where it's at, Garrett. You can go get it yourself. I'm busy talking to my new friend here…"

She looked at Stas clearly waiting for his name. "Stas," he told her but immediately wondered if handing his real name out to anyone in this town was still such a good idea.

"Stas? That's an interesting name."

"It's Polish. Did they ever find out who did it?"

"They arrested a guy, convicted him too. It was a load a crap though, if you ask me."

"Why's that?"

"The kid," she paused, "well, he wasn't really a kid but kind of seemed like it, ya know? He was slow…upstairs." She tapped her finger against her temple to symbolize some sort of mental inadequacy. "Something about it didn't seem right, the things they said he did, it just didn't add up. And there were other things. Evidence that it seemed they just ignored once they had an easy target and could go ahead and close the case all nice and clean."

"How do you mean?"

"Like I said, she seemed like a pretty normal girl but then there was all this mysterious stuff that came out about the weeks before she disappeared."

"Like what?"

"I don't remember all the details now but there was some odd stuff having to do with the hospital where she worked and then she was being linked to some super rich guy and there were rumors that he maybe wasn't exactly, shall we say, above board."

Stas sat back in the booth and looked out the window at the street. He still had no idea why he'd been sent chasing after this dead woman but if her murder was as big of a story as Tammy the waitress was making it sound, there was a good chance Bob might have a little more information than what might be included in small-town gossip. As he was musing he realized that Tammy was looking at him. He turned his attention back to her.

"If you're not writing some book or article," she asked, "why *are* you looking for information about Debbie Keller?"

Stas measured his response. "I'm looking for someone and I thought there might be a connection between the two of them."

"Who are you looking for?"

"An old friend, but it doesn't look like Ms. Keller is going to be of any help to me."

"Not unless you have a Ouija Board." She shot him her sly smile and slid back out of the booth. "Nice to meet you Stas, you come on back if you need any more help with any of the deeper mysteries of McGregor, Minnesota." And with that she was off and back tending to her other tables.

4

Stas tipped his head in mock greeting as he pulled in

passing the plywood Muskie out in front of Bob's Beer & Bait Shop. It seemed as if he and that fish were becoming acquainted quite well as of late. He pulled his truck around to the back of the building and parked in the same spot that he had the night before. Bob's truck was not in the lot but it was only just after ten-thirty in the morning and the shop didn't open until eleven.

Stas pulled a scrap of paper out of his pocket with a name and phone number written on it. He grabbed his phone and punched in the number, then put the phone to his ear and steadied his breathing as it rang. He heard the click as the line was connected.

"Riverwood Healthcare Center Hospital, how may I direct your call?"

"Could I get the third-floor nurse's desk?"

"One moment please."

The receptionist put him on hold and the cause of soothing his soul was furthered by some soft jazz music. Then the music disappeared and the phone was ringing again.

"Third floor, this is Amy."

"Hi, Amy," Stas glanced down at the name on the paper, "is Heidi Finman available?"

"I'm sorry, Heidi is on her rounds right now, is there anything I can help you with?"

"Well, I think so, my dad was recently admitted there and I was wondering if I could—" Stas ended the call abruptly in hopes it would seem as though it had been accidentally dropped. He folded up the scrap of paper with the hospital's phone number and Heidi Finman's name written on it and jammed it into his pocket.

While there wasn't much in the little township of McGregor, there was a library. After wolfing down a couple eggs, finishing his coffee, and bidding adieu to Tammy the waitress, Stas had headed into the small heart of the city to find it. With very little difficulty, the library, and access to a computer, had been located.

As it turned out there was plenty of information

available to sort through when it came to the murder of Debbie Keller. Of the most importance to Stas though, was that some of the people involved in her case may have finally provided his first tangible connection to Lisa.

As Tammy from the diner had told him, a young man had been convicted of Debbie's murder; his name was Gordy Flesner. While Flesner had never officially been given a diagnosis of any manner of developmental disability, it did seem likely that the reason for that was only because nobody ever seemed to care enough to look into it. Not his parents. Not a teacher. Not even the lawyer that was charged with the task of keeping the guy out of prison for the rest of his life. Flesner seemed like an awfully convenient suspect for a town that was desperate to put a horrific incident behind them.

And Tammy had not misled him either about the existence of other intriguing facts that seemed to have been overlooked. A not insubstantial part of that intrigue was provided by the contradicting statements given by Heidi Finman, Debbie's friend and co-worker at the hospital.

Stas looked up as Bob Gurley's Ford Ranger pickup came around the back corner of the building and pulled in next to his own truck.

"Morning," Bob called as he climbed out of the cab. "Got your message about the Keller girl, sounds like you've been busy."

Stas gave a little exasperated laugh as he climbed out of his own truck. "It's been an adventure since I left your place last night, that's for sure. You know anything about Debbie Keller's case?"

"I'm familiar, peripherally. Come on in and let's see what we can put together."

Bob started the coffeemaker and left Stas occupying the seat he had the night before while he went up and put a sign on the door letting any potential morning beer buyers know that he wouldn't be opening to wet their whistles until noon. Bob walked back into the office, poured them both a cup of coffee, and took his own seat behind his desk.

"Alright," he said settling into his chair, "I'll tell ya what I can about the Debbie Keller case, but it's been awhile."

"I did a little research at the library this morning so maybe we can just fill in a few blanks for each other." Bob nodded and Stas went on. "It looks like Keller had a connection to Logan and in turn, the Minnewawa." Bob's chair had been squeaking as he settled into it but it silenced as his attention was grabbed. Stas continued. "And I think there might be some clues within her case that could help us figure out what happened to Lisa."

"Is that right?"

Stas nodded. "Are you familiar with the guy they convicted of the murder, Gordy Flesner?"

"A bit, Castle County is just one county over from Bolton. I was still sheriff when she went missing and I sent a lot of my guys over here for the search effort. Came over myself a time or two as well. So, yeah, I followed the case best I could once the body turned up."

"What'd you think of his conviction?"

Bob sipped his coffee and formulated his response. His former profession had conditioned him to not speak lightly on such matters. "If I recall correctly it seemed to be hasty and shoddy work by the public defender at best." He paused to sip at his coffee again then placed the cup on his desk.

"That sounds about right to me," Stas said. "Do you remember a girl named Heidi Finman?"

Bob gave him a slow thoughtful nod. "The name is familiar, refresh me on her involvement."

"She was a friend of Debbie's. They worked at the hospital together. She never testified but her statement was used in Flesner's trial."

"That's right," Bob said, the details starting to return to him. "What did you find on her?"

"She was interviewed several times by the police but there seem to be inconsistencies in her statements. Or at least the one she gave when Debbie went missing is different than what she said once the body was found."

"Yeah, I remember now. At the trial they used the Finman girl's statement to connect Flesner to the dead girl. But then later the guy that was Flesner's arraignment lawyer, who for some reason wasn't the public defender assigned to the trial, went to some reporter and started talking about how the kid had gotten jobbed. That there was some other potential suspect from Finman's original statement that had been ignored or something like that?"

"Exactly." Stas had been nervous when he arrived at the bait shop, and he still was, but now as he spilled what he had learned this morning to Bob, excitement was sneaking in as well. For the first time since he'd picked up his phone from the console in his truck and seen all those missed calls from Tim Boyd, it seemed like he was on to something. That lost feeling that Woodward and Bernstein had kindled in him so long ago had been sparked again and the flame was being fed.

"But nothing ever came of the arraignment lawyer talking to that reporter, right?" Bob asked.

"Nothing," Stas affirmed. "The reporter he had talked to was from the Cities. She was young, trying to make her mark by digging into unpopular angles of a mysterious murder, but her story was never finished. She never filed it."

Bob gave a slight tilt of the head and his eyes narrowed. "Why not?"

"Because she died before it was done, she perished in a single vehicle car accident, just like Lisa's parents."

"What about the arraignment lawyer, he never followed up with anyone else after Flesner was sent up?"

Stas shook his head with a slow deliberation. "Nope, in fact, within a month of the reporter's car accident, out of the blue, the lawyer decided that he needed a change of scenery and moved away to Colorado."

Bob leaned forward again, putting his elbows down on the desk between them. "Well, that certainly seems suspicious, and it creates a lot of questions for the Bolton County Attorney's Office and their Sheriff's Department, but how does it connect Keller to Logan?"

Stas smirked. "After high school I kicked around the idea of going into journalism for a little while. I managed to snag an internship at the local daily, the Star Tribune. It's the same paper that our dead reporter worked for."

Bob chuckled, "Journalism, eh?"

"What, you're not seeing it?"

"Just the opposite, I think maybe you gave up on it too soon."

Stas laughed. "Anyway, one of the guys I interned with still works there. We're still in touch, relatively. I called him up to see if there was anything he might be able to dig up for me." Stas paused and the slight grin returned.

"And?" Bob pressed.

"The reporter's story was never filed but her notes were archived and my buddy was able to find them for me."

Now Bob laughed out loud. "Forget reporting, maybe you're the one that should have been a detective. What'd her notes say?"

"Heidi Finman's original statement had been focused on a relative of a kid that she and Debbie had been treating at the hospital. The kid was there for an extended stay and apparently Debbie had possibly started dating a guy that was the kid's uncle or something. But something about the 'uncle' had made Heidi nervous. At least that's what she supposedly said initially. Then Debbie's body turns up, Heidi gives another statement, but the 'uncle' never comes up again. The only person of interest that comes out of that second statement is a guy she basically mentioned in passing, Gordy Flesner."

"Yeah, yeah," Bob said, leaning forward in his chair, "and that's all that the prosecutor needed to throw the book at him."

Stas leaned forward now himself, meeting the gaze of the man across the desk from him. "The girl that Debbie Keller was caring for at the hospital, her parents worked at the Minnewawa. And her 'uncle,' the guy Heidi Finman mentioned in her original statement, was named Aaron Tolbert."

Stas paused, letting the name sit there in the air between

them. After a moment Bob shook his head. He couldn't place the name, it meant nothing to him.

Stas enlightened him. "Aaron Tolbert is currently employed as the personal assistant and security for none other than Ted Logan."

The reason Jason Tolbert's name had seemed familiar to Stas when he met the man standing out on that dock was because he'd seen the name Tolbert in a story somewhere when he'd originally been researching Logan. Only it had been Aaron Tolbert, not Jason. The two of them had to be related, probably brothers. Now Stas connected the dots for Bob.

"This morning I had a chance run-in with another man named Tolbert, Jason Tolbert, who just so happens to be head of security at Minnewawa. One Tolbert works for Logan, the other works for the guy that owns the Minnewawa Resort."

Stas gave Bob a moment to let that sink in before going on. The only sound in the little office was the distant hum of the beer coolers above them kicking on and off.

Stas cut into the quiet, "And Jason Tolbert, and everybody else who works at the resort, they all live on the grounds. They work for, and follow, a man whose name is Cortland Whittier, the man that ran the cult that my friend Lisa escaped from all those years ago when she changed her name the first time."

Bob raised an eyebrow while settling back in his chair. Across from him Stas did the same. They both picked up their coffee cups and helped themselves to a taste. They sat in silence ruminating, but then a thought occurred to Bob.

"Wait, you're saying everyone who works at the Minnewawa is a follower of this guy, is still a part of their cult or whatever?" Stas nodded. Bob seemed disconcerted. "So that means Jane Devorak is probably in the middle of whatever is going on over there as well."

"That's right. In fact, she's the one who told me that Whittier is still running things and then put me onto the Keller girl."

"Jane told you that?" Bob's countenance clouded.

"When?" he demanded.

Stas couldn't make sense of the sudden shift in Bob's demeanor. He spoke with a slight hesitancy. "This morning. She set up a secret meeting with me in the middle of the woods, real cloak and dagger stuff."

"You saw her this morning? What time?"

Confusion was deconstructing Stas' confidence. "Six o'clock... Why?"

For a long moment Bob didn't move, and then he blinked slowly, letting out a deflated sigh. "My wife tried to call Jane this morning around nine about an upcoming card game. Whoever she talked to over there told her that Jane couldn't be contacted because she had left on a vacation, but they told my wife that she had left after work yesterday and they didn't know when she'd be back. My wife thought it was odd because she hadn't tried to reschedule the card game. Now you're telling me you talked to her at six this morning, but by nine or so Minnewawa's public position is that she's on vacation and can't be reached..."

Bob trailed off without finishing his sentence, but he didn't need to. Stas did it for him.

"Then where the hell is she?"

Above them the beer cooler kicked back in.

5

Jason Tolbert sat in a high-backed chair in a very elegant study. His chair faced a large, ornate mahogany desk that almost assuredly had been carved by hand. The walls were lined with bookshelves that stretched the full fifteen feet to the ceiling of the room. He'd sat in this chair many times before and sometimes under some uncomfortable circumstances, but never one like this. Tolbert's outward demeanor remained calm for the most part. The only tell to his inner unrest was the anxious way he was handling the folder in his lap.

He heard the large doors that led to the study open behind him and for a moment his breath caught. Seconds later

Cortland Whittier walked into his view. Whittier was in his fifties, tall and fit. He had a full head of jet-black hair that could only be dyed but Tolbert would never be caught dead postulating that theory aloud.

"Jason," Whittier acknowledged him as he took his own seat behind the beautiful desk.

"Sir," he returned the greeting.

"What do you have for me?" Whittier's voice remained calm and steady. Tolbert rarely heard him sound any other way though. Jason slid the folder across the desk to his boss.

Whittier thumbed through it for a second or two before selecting and removing a photo. "This is the guy you ran into at the fishing pond this morning?" Tolbert nodded his assent. "Who is he?"

"His name is Stanley Mileski. He's from Minneapolis, works doing freelance construction."

"And what is he to me, Jason?" Whittier was smiling but Tolbert found nothing about it pleasing or pleasant. "What is it about this fellow that has the unshakeable Mr. Tolbert up in arms first thing in the morning?"

"I talked to Logan earlier, as soon as I found out who the guy was. I had Logan find someone to pull Mileski's phone records…"

"And?"

"He knows Anne Callahan, well." Tolbert paused and gauged Whittier's reaction to her name. It was an intangible shift even as it seemed to change the molecular makeup of the air they breathed. He drew a tough breath and went on. "Now that Logan has uncovered the fact that she's been going by Lisa Lathrop, he's been able to obtain her phone records. Mileski called her often. They talked to each other on the phone all the time."

If Cortland Whittier's smile had reached his eyes at all before, it no longer did. That not-so-pleasant grin was still in place but his eyes could not hide the unbridled hate that was curdling there. It took every ounce of constitution that Tolbert had not to squirm beneath his gaze. Just when he thought he was going to lose the battle anyway, Whittier turned away and spoke.

"So, if he knows Anne so well, he must know she's dropped off the radar." Whittier gave his statement some thought then added, "And then he shows up here. That is not good."

"No, it is not. And it's not the end of the bad news either." Tolbert would have given anything to not have to finish this particular thought. "We have his laptop. As of a couple of days ago he's been doing a healthy bit of digging for information on Logan."

Whittier's eyes narrowed. "So, he's made a connection between Anne and Logan, and now both of them to us?" Tolbert knew better than to attempt any sort of answer to that question. Whittier's temper could take him in any number of different directions right now, none of which would be aided by anything Jason might add. The unnerving silence stretched. Whittier had looked away for a moment but now he returned his gaze to his head of security, and when it fell upon him, Tolbert was riveted by its intensity.

"Do we have any reason, whatsoever," Whittier paused to accentuate the importance of what he was about to ask, "to believe that The Devil's Paddle has been compromised in any way?"

"Absolutely not, sir." Tolbert spoke the words with an unerring conviction.

He knew why Whittier was asking. The smooth operation of the resort had recently endured a hiccup. They'd had a recent disappearance of their own. And it seemed possible that Anne Callahan may have had something to do with it.

He had no reason at all to think that their latest snafu could be linked to The Devil's Paddle, though, and he monitored very closely any potential problem in that regard. If anyone who wasn't supposed to became aware of its existence, or the events that transpired there, all the furies of hell would seem like a small vacation compared to what would befall him.

Whittier sat back and tented his hands in front of his chest, thinking. Tolbert took this to be a good sign. He needed his boss focused on the issues at hand and any immediate threat to the resort. If The Paddle were ever to be uncovered, it would most likely be because the Minnewawa had, for whatever reason, first come under the public's microscope.

Their lifestyle was one that was not often understood among the general populace and it was just that sort of misunderstanding that might cause someone to start digging. And an uninvited interest would be the best chance that someone might stumble onto some of Whittier's extra-curricular endeavors.

If some of the aspects of how Whittier was tending his flock became public it could be very troubling. But if anyone ever found out about The Devil's Paddle, and the true nature behind its machinations, it would be devastating. The resulting scandals would send shockwaves that would reverberate through much of the state, toppling many of its substantial pillars.

And right now, the immediate threat to the resort was Anne Callahan. They had been so close, for the first time in years. Then she vanished. Maybe she disappeared because some tragedy had befallen her and she was already dead, but that sort of happy accident would be too much to hope for. Unless he saw it with his own eyes, her dispatching would remain on Tolbert's to-do list.

Whittier spoke, bringing him back. "What do we know about this Mileski character and, more importantly, what does he know about us?"

"I'm still compiling a file on him…but it's more than he should, that's for sure. Once I had his laptop and saw the searches on Logan, I went back to his cabin to have a little discussion with him but he was gone. Most of his stuff was still there but I'm pretty sure he's high-tailed it."

"And what are we doing about locating him?"

"I've got Childress working on it." Michael Childress was one of Tolbert's best men. "He's got good sources on the outside and I don't think Mileski will leave town." Tolbert considered 'the outside' to be anyone or anything beyond the Minnewawa walls, beyond his control.

"Why don't you think he'll leave town?" Whittier asked.

"Because he might know who Logan is, but he still doesn't have any idea about what happened to his friend."

"Lisa Lathrop."

Tolbert's discomfort returned hearing Whittier speaking her assumed name. His boss' disdain for the woman bordered on obsession. Her escape from Norumbega had been the first, and a great embarrassment. Over the years, that embarrassment had become a severe nuisance, but now things were escalating and they had to perceive her as an actual threat.

After a pause Whittier spoke and his voice was tempered but authoritative. "Stay on top of what Childress finds. I want this Stan Mileski taken off the board before tomorrow's festivities." The command was measured but Tolbert wouldn't dare miss the nuanced urgency in the undertone.

"We'll take care of it."

"Good." Whittier checked his watch and Tolbert saw him smoothly change gears. It was how it had to be with great leaders. "I have lunch with my wife so I'll have to leave in a minute. There's just one more thing." He started flipping again through the file Tolbert had brought him.

Whittier's marital situation was the only thing about the man to whom he was so devoted that gave Jason cause for concern. It didn't have anything to do with any sort of a moral compass on his part. He was way too far down the road himself as those things went. His concern was that it could be a potential liability. To Whittier his wives were about power, both wielding and cultivating it. Many of them went on to do great things for them but others, Tolbert feared, could be dangerous to the bigger picture, in particular some of the things that transpired at The Devil's Paddle.

His attention was drawn back to his boss as Whittier selected a photo from the file and held it up. "What's this?"

Whittier asked.

"I'm convinced Mileski was talking to someone just before I came upon him this morning. He was beyond coverage of any of our cameras but I pieced some things together from other cameras from time periods shortly after. That's the only thing from any of them that popped. It was captured from one of the bunkhouses not long after I stumbled on Mileski."

Whittier looked back down at a photo of Jane Devorak stepping onto the porch of her residence. That unsettling smile that didn't quite reach his eyes returned to Cortland Whittier's face.

"Bring her to me," was all he said.

6

Bob Gurley sat behind his desk alone in his basement office. It was past noon but Bob's Beer & Bait Shop remained closed and would probably remain so for the rest of the day. Stas had left to pay a visit to Riverwood Healthcare Center Hospital to see if he could arrange a conversation with Heidi Finman.

Spread out across Bob's desk was an in-depth map of Bolton County that covered a handful of lakes. The larger two lakes were Big Sandy and Minnewawa, but also included on this particular map were two smaller ones called Round and Horseshoe. It was the area around Horseshoe Lake that was drawing Bob's interest at the moment. It sat a little northeast of Minnewawa and the two were connected by a small tributary.

The Minnewawa Resort was conveniently located in a remote area on that northeast side, nestled in between the two lakes. There was one small road that ran along the west side of Horseshoe that Bob assumed would also run along the section of land that Stas thought housed the resort employees. He couldn't be certain that something untoward had happened to Jane Devorak but all signs pointed to a likely probability that it had. He couldn't just sit on his hands and hope. At the very least he was going to have to get out there and have a look around.

His attention was pulled from the maps as the phone on his desk began to ring. Bob was not so old school as to avoid cell phones but he still liked having the real thing on his desk. It was a throwback to his days as sheriff. He liked to have a real handset just in case he needed the satisfaction of slamming it down to hang up on someone with a flourish. He grabbed the phone from its cradle mid-ring.

"Bob's Beer & Bait, this is Bob."

"Bob Gurley, how the hell are ya, you old cuss?" asked the voice on the other end of the line.

"Not too bad, Jim," Bob said through a broad smile, "how about yourself?" He and Jim Gutte went way back. Jim was one of the best investigators Bob had ever met. He had used him a number of times on cases back in Castle Danger. And it just so happened that Bob's old friend Jim had also worked for the prosecution in prepping for the Gordy Flesner trial, until he had been unceremoniously dismissed, that is. His termination alone was enough to make Bob's antennae go up. People didn't just fire Jim Gutte.

"Doing well, Bob, thanks," Jim replied. "I gather from your message you've got some questions about the Flesner case."

"I do. I'm looking into something for a friend and I feel like there may be some similarities between the two cases. What were your impressions on how things went for the kid?"

"How things went?" Jim Gutte let out an exasperated chuckle. "That whole trial was one of the biggest jokes I've ever been witness to."

"Yeah, that's kind of the impression I got as well. What makes you say that, though?" Bob asked.

"That prosecutor over there at the time, Randall, I think his name was, he was a piece of work. I know it was his job to get a conviction but the whole thing seemed rotten to me."

"Wait... Randall, as in Joseph Randall?"

"Yeah, that's him alright."

"Joseph Randall prosecuted the Flesner case?"

"Yeah, why do you ask?"

Bob took a long pause. "Nothing. I guess I forgot that it was him, that's all." Bob couldn't believe he hadn't put that together after overhearing Logan and Whittier's conversation about the man last fall. "Anyway, what made it seem rotten to ya?"

"First of all, when they hired me they specifically told me that they weren't interested in anything that didn't pertain to Gordy Flesner. They didn't want me spending any time pursuing anything that wasn't directly connecting Flesner and the Keller girl."

"And could you connect them?"

"In a manner, I guess you could say. They knew each other peripherally. Flesner had a job at the local hardware store cleaning, mopping floors, that sort of thing. Debbie Keller was a bit of a do-it-yourself kind of gal and she used the hardware store with some frequency. They would have been acquainted."

Bob was scribbling notes as fast as he could. "But you weren't buying that the kid was so in love with her that he killed her?"

"Hell no, I don't think he was capable. I'm fairly certain that at the very least Flesner had a pretty serious learning disability, probably more than that though. The reason everyone referred to him as a kid even though he was twenty-three at the time was because that's how he seemed."

"How come that never came up at his trial?"

"Beats me, I was absolutely shocked that his lawyer never had any sort of mental evaluation done. But that's the thing, Bob, Flesner's own lawyer didn't seem all that interested in getting him off the hook. It was almost as if the public defender was in the pocket of Mr. Prosecutor, Joseph Randall, from the get-go. And don't even get me started about the cops."

"What about the cops?"

"Every statement Gordy Flesner gave was so blatantly

and ham-handedly manipulated by the police it made me sick. I'm telling you, Bob, I can only hope it was incompetence and laziness that caused them to get so fixated on Flesner because if it wasn't that, a guy could get to thinking something criminal might have been going on." Jim Gutte paused and Bob scribbled on. "Anyway," Jim continued, "I'm pretty sure that's why they fired me."

"Come again?" Bob had finished scribbling his notes but hadn't fully caught Gutte's last statement.

"They would say they fired me because I didn't produce, which I guess is technically true. I wasn't able to dig anything up for them because I don't think there was anything to find. But the real reason they fired me is because I started to question the validity of the charges they were levying."

"So, if they didn't really have anything solid on him, did they convict Flesner based on the police statements?" He didn't say it but he was mainly talking about the one given by Heidi Finman. Bob heard Gutte loose a long, deep sigh on the other end of the line.

"They probably could have convicted him on those bull crap statements, Bob. But they didn't need to. They rustled themselves up a star witness who climbed up on that stand and then lied like a rug. Some local good-for-nothing named Willy Gustafson."

The phone slipped from where Bob had it pinned between his ear and shoulder. He juggled it for a second before regaining control and putting it back up to his ear.

He had wondered if he had given too much credence to the unease that he had felt yesterday when he looked up from the bar to find the very same Willy Gustafson staring down at him and Stas. And then the guy had high-tailed it out of the bar seconds later. That was, at the very least, suspicious.

"Willy Gustafson." Bob repeated the name aloud into the phone and let the hollow words travel down the line until they bounced to some cell phone tower to be delivered wirelessly to wherever Jim Gutte was at the moment.

7

Stas sat in a comfortable chair in the lobby of the Riverwood Healthcare Center Hospital. He watched the sliding glass doors slip open as an elderly gentleman rolled his wife out in a wheelchair to an awaiting vehicle. Slowly and methodically the guy helped her from the chair into the passenger seat of the car. A helpful passer-by stopped and offered to return the wheelchair back inside. The old guy thanked him and made his way around to the driver's side with small, tight, compact steps. Watching the nice elderly couple Stas couldn't help but wonder if he would ever find someone that he would want to spend the rest of his life with, let alone find someone that would ever put up with him.

The ding of an arriving elevator drew him back from any pointless pondering of future relations. He looked across the lobby and watched as a handful of people exited the elevator and split off in differing directions. He ticked their faces off on a mental checklist but the one he was looking for was not among them. They had found a photo of Heidi Finman on the hospital's website. Another call to the third-floor nurses' desk and a couple more white lies and Stas had nailed down a rough timeline for the next shift change.

He had just allowed his gaze to return to the hospital's exit and the comings and goings there when he heard the elevator ding again. He turned back and watched as the doors of the newly arrived lift slid apart, and there she was, standing right in front.

Heidi Finman walked out of the elevator and towards the front door. Stas prepared to do a bit of acting by slapping the biggest grin he could manage on his face. Then he called her name out across the lobby.

She turned and looked at him, returning his smile at first. As Stas made quick strides toward her across the lobby he watched the smile slip a little displaying a slight confusion. She recovered quickly, though, reinstating a grin in an attempt to cover the fact that she had no idea who this approaching stranger was. Nor why he was greeting her with such familiarity.

"How are you?" he asked, putting all the warmth he could manage into his voice as he closed the last of the distance between them. Stas was careful to stop before infringing on her personal space. He didn't want to make her skittish, at least not yet.

"I'm good, how are you?" Her smile was still in place but it was clear that as she spoke, she was running through a mental rolodex, trying to place him and coming up empty.

"I'm great," Stas said. He let the moment linger, keeping his own pleasant grin in place but saying nothing more. They stood that way, smiling awkwardly at each other for as long as she could handle it. Eventually it got the better of her and she broke down.

"I'm sorry, this is embarrassing, but I just can't seem to place how I know you."

"Oh," Stas said letting out a forced friendly chortle as he spoke, "we don't actually know each other, Heidi." He was still grinning but Heidi Finman's smile faltered and her countenance slipped, now tilting toward confusion.

"Okay…" She was uncertain but still didn't seem to be nervous.

He stuck his hand out, "Stas Mileski." She was hesitant but took the extended hand and shook it. Still shaking her hand Stas quickly changed his tack, "I need to know whatever you can tell me about Aaron Tolbert."

Heidi Finman's reaction to the name he'd just dropped was visceral. She yanked her hand back out of Stas' grip and took a step back, fear overtaking her features.

"Please, there's nothing to be afraid of," he tried to reassure her. She was off-kilter, which was his intention. He figured he'd need to take her by surprise if he was going to get her to talk. But he also hoped that being on her own turf, here in the hospital, would keep her level enough to not freak out on him and start screaming obscenities. Keeping her somewhere in between he thought he'd have the best chance of getting the information he wanted. "I don't mean you any harm," Stas said. "I'm not a cop or anything," he added a slight pleading tone to his voice. "I have a friend that's gone missing and I'm afraid that she might be connected to what happened to Debbie Keller."

Heidi recoiled further as if she'd been slapped. Debbie's name obviously held a certain gravitas for her, even more than Tolbert's. Again, she recovered and looked at Stas and their eyes locked. Stas was not an emotional man but he hoped she would still get a hint of desperation from him. He didn't know that Lisa was actually in the sort of danger that Debbie Keller had found herself in, but he couldn't technically rule it out either.

Heidi broke away from his gaze and glanced around the lobby. She seemed to be trying to make up her mind about something. After a long moment she looked at him again and spoke. "The hospital cafeteria is right over there," she pointed off to his left. "You want to buy me a cup of coffee?"

Stas smiled, relieved. He gave her a nod and then followed her across the lobby and into the cafeteria. Heidi found them a booth with as much privacy as the commissary could offer while Stas fetched them both a cup of coffee.

He slid into the booth and pushed one of the steaming cups across the table to her. It wasn't particularly good coffee but she took a moment to inhale the smell anyway, letting the steam bathe her face, then she sat back giving it a second to cool.

"So, I'm sorry to hear about your friend going missing, but what makes you think it might be connected to Debbie?" she asked.

"Honestly, I'm not really sure yet," Stas said. "But her name came up while I was poking around," he paused, "and then I came across the name Tolbert." More accurately, a guy named Tolbert had come across him standing on that dock but he wasn't looking to get into the subject of Jason Tolbert yet; this conversation was about Aaron. "And shortly after that I came across your original statement to the police."

He gave her a moment to process and he wanted to handle this next bit with some care. "In that first statement it seemed like you had some opinions on this Aaron Tolbert guy, but then he kind of fell off as a suspect or person of interest."

Heidi looked away, out the window of the cafeteria. Stas didn't get the sense she was seeing beyond the window, though. She was steeling herself, preparing. Turning back she grabbed her coffee and took a sip with little care as to whether it had cooled sufficiently or not. She blinked back the sudden presence of tears before they could make an attempt to fall.

"I can't tell you the guilt I feel about what happened to Gordy Flesner. Do you know who he is?"

Stas nodded. "Why did you change your statement and go away from Aaron Tolbert?"

Heidi Finman looked across the table at him and made no attempt to hide the shift to a burgeoning anger. "I didn't change my statement." Her voice was tinged with a tough conviction.

"What do you mean?"

"I told them the exact same thing every time I was interviewed. What they did with it was their prerogative."

"I don't understand…"

"The last statement I gave to the police was a hundred and eighty-three pages. The one that they used in court, the one that helped them implicate Gordy Flesner? That statement only consisted of forty-seven."

"Wait, are you saying the cops redacted parts of your statement?"

"Redacted, omitted, fabricated. I don't know what all they did to it. What I do know is that it was not the whole thing and the entire situation stunk."

Stas fidgeted with the cup on the table in front of him. "If the cops were negligent, or intentionally messing with your statement, why didn't you say anything?"

The sound that Heidi emitted would best be described as a scoff but even that didn't really encapsulate it. A distant melancholy came over her. "Because I was weak…but even more than that, I was just plain scared."

"Scared of what?"

"Aaron Tolbert, mostly."

And now they'd gotten to it, the crux of what he was looking for. "Will you tell me about him, about what you think he may have had to do with Debbie's death?"

She didn't speak. Heidi pulled her coffee cup from the table and raised it to her lips. After taking a sip she set it back down and took a long look around the cafeteria. Stas tensed a bit fearing he had lost her but then she nodded and looked down at her hands. Slowly she began to speak.

"I guess I should start with Brandy Redmond. She was the little girl that came to the hospital about three months before Debbie…before Debbie died."

She managed to spit out the word 'died' but it seemed the real word for what happened to Debbie, murder, was still beyond her. Stas said nothing and just continued to listen.

"Brandy was sweet and Debbie really liked kids. They hit it off right away. But Brandy had a strange familial situation."

"Tolbert?" Stas couldn't help the interjection.

"Yeah, but it was more than just him. Brandy was six years old and her mom couldn't have been more than twenty-one or twenty-two at the time which would have made her only fifteen or sixteen when Brandy was born. No father in the picture that we ever saw, just Aaron Tolbert. And he wasn't even her actual uncle, he was a family friend, I guess, but he was clearly in charge when it came to Brandy. The mother was about the meekest little thing I'd ever seen."

"Wait, what do you mean he was in charge?" Stas asked. Between the age of the mother, the fact that she worked at the resort, and what sounded like her deference to a man who wasn't the child's father, the situation had Cortland Whittier written all over it.

"As far as things with Brandy, Tolbert made all the decisions. The mom was really only there to give her consent to whatever he said."

"And did that seem odd to you?"

"Oh, it definitely was weird but then again, you work as a nurse long enough and weird starts to become the norm. Just when you think you've seen it all, you find out you haven't."

"So, what was the connection between Keller and Tolbert?"

Heidi shifted in her seat. It was a subconscious movement but exuded unease. "Debbie had a great relationship with Brandy and spent a lot of time with her. That proximity meant she was spending a lot of time with Aaron Tolbert."

"Were they involved, outside of the hospital?"

She shifted again, "That sort of thing is frowned upon but, yes, they started to date. When Brandy left the hospital, they continued to see each other."

"When did you start to become suspicious of him?"

"It seemed like Debbie was maybe drinking more than she used to. She was going to these lavish parties at some extremely wealthy friend of Tolbert's. That was the first thing, those subtle changes. Then she told me that he wanted her to start going to these meetings with him. She said they were about personal betterment, that sort of thing, but it sounded pretty cultish to me."

"Did she ever go to one of these meetings?" Stas tried to keep the urgency he was feeling at bay. He did not want to put undue pressure on her right now.

"She said she never did, but I think she was lying. She knew I didn't like the idea. So, she told me that she hadn't ever gone but she started to distance herself from me and the others at the hospital."

If Debbie had actually gotten involved with the so-called religious aspects of what was going on at Minnewawa that definitely escalated things. It was a deeper connection to Logan but still gave Stas nothing in regard to Lisa. "So, was it the fact that she had potentially gotten involved with this cult, for a lack of a better term, that you fingered Tolbert in your statement?"

She watched him intently from across the booth.

Around the hospital cafeteria those populating it went about the business of living their lives, but in the booth he shared with Heidi Finman everything else had ceased to exist. She was biting at her lip. She was working up to something, at least he hoped so. He maintained his patience as best he could. A decision was made. She inhaled deeply and leaned in towards him, compelling him to do the same. Stas acquiesced.

"I never fingered Tolbert as a suspect. All I did was mention his relationship with Debbie. As I said before, I was consistent about that when I spoke to the police after she… after her body was discovered, even if they didn't care to make that a part of the case going forward. But I never would have tried to implicate Aaron Tolbert directly because I was terrified."

"Why?"

She looked up and around the cafeteria. It was not a passing glance. She looked at every single person within her view to make sure no one was paying attention to them before she spoke. "I've never told anyone this before. I can't believe I'm about to tell a total stranger." She blinked back a tear.

"I won't sit here and tell you to trust me, but I'll tell you this. I don't know what happened to my friend, but the one thing I do know is that Ted Logan, the guy that Aaron Tolbert now works for, had something to do with it."

After another deep breath and another look around the cafeteria Heidi dropped her voice a notch and continued. "Debbie stopped here, at the hospital, in the early morning hours the day she disappeared. Nobody knows that she was here. She had been at that rich friend of Tolbert's house, the one that I mentioned before. Travis Olmstead is his name. Anyway, as far as the police are concerned, Olmstead's house was the last time she was seen by anyone before Gordy Flesner supposedly killed her. The prosecution's star witness found her car abandoned in the parking lot of the hardware store later that morning, that's how they were able to pin it on Gordy. He worked at the hardware store."

She wiped at her eyes again smearing fledgling tears

across her face. She pressed the bottom of her palms against her cheekbones in an attempt to absorb the wetness while Stas tried to get all this information straight in his head.

"They charged him with murder just because her car was found in the parking lot?" he asked.

"The low-life that found the car supposedly knew Flesner. On the stand he painted a pretty devastating picture of how Gordy was obsessed with Debbie, that's how they got the conviction."

"But you're not buying the witness's story?"

"He was a scum-bag. Gordy was a little slow but he wasn't trouble. Not like this guy. And the witness, the guy that found the car, I know he lied."

"How do you know that?"

"Like I said, I saw her, after she left Olmstead's party but before her car showed up in that parking lot. The last text Debbie ever sent was at about 3:45 that morning, and it was sent to me. The cops checked it out, obviously, but the text she sent me was just a bunch of random emoji's. I told the police that I had no idea why she sent it and once it had been established that she'd been at a party earlier in the night, it was chalked up to her being drunk."

Stas had finished his coffee and was now picking at the lip of the paper cup. "But let me guess, the emojis did mean something?"

Heidi gave a single, deliberate nod. "The hospital is a non-smoking campus but Debbie and I would sneak one every now and then while we were working, she would send me an emoji text: a cigarette, a bomb, and a winky-face. It meant that I should meet her at her car for a quick smoke. I was on an overnight and Debbie wasn't working. We'd been falling further and further apart at that point so I was a bit surprised when I got the text."

"Why'd you lie to the cops about the text?"

"For the same reason I never told them that I was probably actually the last person to see her alive… Aaron Tolbert."

These Tolbert boys were shaping up to be quite the pair. Put them in conjunction with a monster like Cortland Whittier and Stas was not a fan of what it might mean for Lisa. Logan with his political clout looking for her had been scary enough, put them all together and it spelled real trouble. He tried to stay focused on the present, on Heidi Finman.

"What happened after you got the text?" he asked her.

"It was a quiet overnight at the hospital so I went outside to see if she was actually here. She was parked in her regular spot. She looked rough, like she'd had a long night, but she didn't seem drunk. Travis Olmstead later testified that he had been entertaining, just a small cocktail party. He said Debbie stopped by looking for Aaron Tolbert. He said she stayed for a drink and then left because Tolbert wasn't there."

"But she told you something different when she showed up here at the hospital, that she had actually been with Tolbert at the party." It was more statement than question.

"Not only that, but it's also how I know that the guy who found the car and ultimately got Gordy Flesner sent to jail was full of it too."

"What do you mean?"

"Debbie was parked in her usual spot when I came out but she wasn't in her car, she was driving Aaron Tolbert's. So, someone else put her car in the hardware store parking lot to be discovered later."

"Did she say anything about what happened at the party, about why she was there in the middle of the night and driving Tolbert's car?" He received another slow nod from Heidi then she looked all the way around the cafeteria again.

"She said they went to Olmstead's place, but not for a party. Aaron needed to drop something off. When they got there though, there was a party of sorts going on. Tolbert told her to stay in the car and he grabbed a briefcase from the back seat. She said he was in the house for what seemed like forever. She turned off the car and grabbed the keys intending to go find him but as she walked toward the house a woman came out of a door on the side of the house that led to a little veranda. The woman lit a cigarette and, in the flare from the lighter, Debbie recognized her. It was Brandy Redmond's mom but she apparently didn't look so meek now, she was dressed very seductively. Debbie veered over to the veranda and called out to her. As soon as she saw Debbie though she dropped her cigarette and hurried back into the house. Debbie followed her, walking up to the big glass doors that led into the house. The doors led to a study and in there she saw Aaron Tolbert and another man talking. Brandy's mom said something to Aaron and he looked up and saw her on the veranda. Tolbert said something back to Brandy's mom, then she left the room and Tolbert let Debbie in."

"She told you all of this, with such detail?" Stas interrupted.

"Yes. I didn't realize it at the time because she hid it well, but she was scared. I think she wanted someone to know everything, every detail, just in case."

"Okay, what did she say happened then?"

"Tolbert opened the door and invited her in, apologizing for taking so long. He introduced the other man as his brother. His brother greeted her and handed her a drink then he started cleaning up papers on the desk behind him, putting them back into the briefcase that Aaron had brought with him from the car."

"Did she see what any of the papers were?"

"She didn't get a good look but said that a few of them were photos, surveillance photos or something, of two men. They were both wearing expensive suits."

"Did she recognize either of them?" Stas asked.

Heidi shook her head, "but she thought there was something familiar about them. Anyway, she was feeling nervous and she said that she sucked down her drink pretty fast and suddenly felt dizzy."

Heidi paused and Stas took the opportunity to interject. This was a story he'd unfortunately heard before, the darker realities of a barroom lifestyle. "But it was more than just the drink hitting her wasn't it... Tolbert's brother had drugged her with something?"

"That's what Debbie thought and I agreed, it explained why she looked like she'd had a rough night but wasn't drunk."

"What happened then?"

"They got her sitting on a chaise lounge in the study. Whatever they gave her worked fast. In matter of minutes she was drifting. Debbie had generally been gullible when it came to Aaron Tolbert but she was overall a smart girl, she knew she was in trouble, she started intentionally letting her head loll pretending she was more out of it than she was. Tolbert got her laid out on the lounge then he and his brother left the room. When they opened the door, she caught a momentary glimpse of the great hall. Standing out there was Brandy Redmond's mom and another woman who was dressed similarly. They were arm-in-arm with the two men from the photos. Then the door closed and she did actually pass out."

"And she never found out who the men were or what they were doing there?"

"No," Heidi said, "Debbie came around and was alone in the study. She said she cracked the door that led out to the great hall of the house but it was empty. She said the house was quiet, it seemed like whatever had been going on, that the party was over. She heard a few muffled voices across the hall but just a few of them. She thought it was probably just Tolbert and his brother and Olmstead. She shut the door quietly and stayed in the study. Then she remembered she still had Tolbert's keys. She let herself out the way she had come in, by way of the veranda, took Tolbert's car, drove to the hospital and texted me."

Heidi Finman looked as if she could use one of those cigarettes that she and Debbie used to sneak. Stas had been picking at the lip of his cup but Heidi had finished her coffee and crumpled hers into a nervous little ball.

"And that was the last time you ever saw her?" Stas asked. Heidi averted her eyes but nodded. His next question was an obvious one but he didn't want to put it to her indelicately. "Can I ask why you never told the police any of this?"

Modest tears tracked their way down her cheeks but now she made no effort to remove them. "The police seemed more than happy to overlook Aaron Tolbert either way, but I had a reason for the choices I made." She shut her eyes for a moment and with a slow, deliberate effort she dragged her sleeve under both eyes removing the tears that had settled there. "For as long as I live, however long that may be, I will harbor a terrible guilt for what happened to Gordy Flesner. If I believed for a second that I could have spared him I would have talked. But Gordy was going to jail either way, the only thing that would have changed if I had opened my mouth...is that he would be serving an extra life sentence for my murder as well."

She put her head in her hands and sat that way for a very long time. Stas wanted to leave her to her grief but there was more he needed to know. He would tread as gently as possible.

"I'm sorry to have to ask this," he said, "but why do you say that?"

Heidi collected herself but didn't say anything. She picked up her phone and scrolled through it for a minute. She found what she was looking for and handed the phone across the table to Stas. It was a picture of a Zippo lighter that had a peace sign engraved on it, sitting on the seat of a car.

"What's this?" Stas asked.

"The day after I last saw Debbie, before her car had even been found at the hardware store, I received a text from a blocked number with that photo. That's the Zippo I used to light our cigarettes that night. I must have dropped it because in that picture it's sitting on Aaron Tolbert's car seat. I'm not always the most perceptive person in the world, but once Debbie turned up missing a few hours later, I knew that text for the threat it was meant to be."

The silence stretched for a moment as Stas had no idea how to respond. Before anything appropriate came to his mind, she went on.

"Look, I'm sorry, but I have to go. I hope this is helpful to you somehow. That you can find your friend and that you find her alive, but please...please, leave me out of it from here on out."

He blinked and nodded. This interview was over. She had told him a ton and was scared for her life. Heidi Finman lived with plenty of grief and Stas would not heap anymore upon her if it could be helped. They both stood and he walked her out of the cafeteria and to the front entrance of the hospital.

The sliding glass doors split apart and they stepped outside. Standing on the sidewalk they shared one last glance. She gave him a small sad smile but said nothing. Then she turned and headed off on her way.

Stas lingered a moment watching her go. She'd been through a lot but he feared it was only the tip of the iceberg. The Tolbert brothers, Ted Logan, and Cortland Whittier were involved in things that went well beyond some cultish brainwashing and he intended to find out what exactly that might be. He hoped he'd be able to keep his word and leave her out of it, but his true loyalty began and ended with Lisa. Stas would do whatever necessary to find her.

He watched as Heidi walked around a corner and into the parking ramp out of his view. He turned to head across the street to the open-air lot where he had parked his truck. He was lost in his thoughts and smacked into a guy that he didn't see until it was too late. Stas tossed a quick apology over his shoulder as the guy passed by him and through the sliding glass doors into the hospital. He crossed the street to the lot trying to compartmentalize the information he just received to make sure he wouldn't miss anything when he was relaying it back to Bob. He climbed into his truck and pulled out of the lot heading back toward the bait shop.

A moment later the sliding glass doors of the hospital slid open again and the man Stas had just bumped into walked back out onto the sidewalk. He looked off toward the ramp where Heidi had been heading then to Stas in his truck as it drove away.

Willy Gustafson, the man who had allegedly found Debbie Keller's car and whose testimony got Gordy Flesner convicted of her murder, pulled his phone from his pocket and placed a call.

Red Wing…
Spring, 2017

1

The reflection of the moon broke and shimmered then reformed as the river ran, whisking along on its way past Wurzer's Marina. The weather had continued to warm and it was feeling more and more like summer but it was still early April and in spite of Daylight Saving Time being in effect, the darkness still fell at a relatively early hour. A development Tim Boyd could find no fault with at the moment.

It had been a long day since he and Danny had stood by the houseboats and he had seen the Criss-Craft docked at the Marina. The same Criss-Craft that had been used by whoever had been skulking around Lisa's land before he and Stas had run him off.

He had dropped Danny at his parent's house. He hated to leave him again but he hadn't heard from Stas in over twenty-four hours and now he had the only thing resembling a lead that he'd been able to stumble upon since Lisa had disappeared. His desperation was beginning to get the better of him. After dropping Danny off, he spent some time researching online and making phone calls until he found an electronics store just outside of the Cities that supplied the specific type of device that he was looking for.

Now, sitting in his car in a darkened corner of the Wurzer's parking lot, Tim looked down at the little piece of equipment sitting on his passenger seat. He'd already synced it to his phone and tested it. It was a GPS device meant to track a vehicle in case of theft but Tim hoped to put it to use in a different manner.

Right around dusk he'd watched a couple of young guys walk the docks making sure all the boats that were in their slips had been secured. They'd disappeared into the building and he hadn't seen them since. During his short reconnaissance at the marina that afternoon he'd come to realize that a few of the houseboats were actually occupied even while they were docked. He'd have to be wary of them as he attempted to plant the device. The one closest to the Criss-Craft seemed to currently be empty and Tim was thankful for small favors.

Once he had satisfied himself that the Wurzer guys were not going to be making any further security rounds Tim switched his dome light to the off position, grabbed the tracking device, and exited his vehicle. He went around the building, skirting it but sticking to the cover of the trees that surrounded it. He passed the windows of the lighted vestibule where the lockers were located and went around the back. From there he moved down to the river, coming upon the docks, and the Criss-Craft, from the far side.

He assessed the situation from the corner of the building closest to the river. Looking up he could see the windows by the registration desk that had a view of the river. He had to assume that any employees still at the desk would be able to see him once he was out on the dock if they happened to look in that direction. Security lighting poured down over the boat lifts making discretion difficult to achieve. He'd have to just walk out on the dock and find out the hard way if his cover was blown. He steeled himself, checked the houseboats and saw nothing to deter him, then stood and started to stroll in the direction of the boats.

Halfway out onto the dock he hazarded a glance back at the illuminated windows. He could see one of the guys who had done the short security check a few minutes ago but he could only see the back of the kid's head, turned away talking to someone Tim couldn't see. Tim picked up his tempo.

He hustled over and dropped to a knee in front of the Criss-Craft. He unclasped five of the snaps that were tethering the boat cover at the stern of the boat. Previously he may have been able to guess that the back of the boat was called the stern, but he'd solidified that information doing some research earlier on this particular model. From that research he had learned that there was a storage compartment under the seat at the back of the boat, which was what he'd really been digging for. He lifted the padded seat cover and dropped the GPS tracker into the storage space. He replaced the seat and reattached the snaps on the boat cover. He stood and checked the windows up by the desk. The kid up there was still engaged in his conversation and there was no sign he'd been detected. He made his way down the dock but as soon as he stepped onto the shore he was brought to a halt, frozen in his tracks.

"What do you think you're doing?" someone hollered out from the houseboat two over from where he stood.

Tim made a slow petrified turn, churning through every lie that might adequately explain his actions. His knees almost buckled when he saw the man on the deck of the houseboat. The guy who had asked the question might've seen Tim on the dock, if he were to have turned around that is. He hadn't and at the moment the entirety of his attention, and the mock-frustration of the demand he had loosed, was directed at his dog. The guy was just out playing with the pup and had no idea Tim was even there. Tim wasted no further time in hustling himself around the backside of the building and out of the line of sight.

He made his way back around the building and over to his car parked in that darkened corner of the lot and there commenced the waiting.

<u>2</u>

Tim had never been on a stakeout before and for the first half hour he was giddy with excitement. An hour later when Wurzer's officially closed, he was less so; another two hours after that, when the last of the lights glowing in the few occupied houseboats were extinguished, he was downright bored.

When he first got back to Red Wing that afternoon he'd gone to the marina and checked into the possibility of renting a particular Criss-Craft. That was how he had come to learn that the specific boat he was interested in was already committed to a long-term rental. Of course, Wurzer's Marina couldn't supply him any information about the renter, but they were more than happy to offer him another boat, an offer he readily accepted. With the rental of his own boat Tim learned that although the Marina closed at night, long-term renters did have twenty-four-hour access to their boats. A security code punched in on the lift would unlock it and disarm the alarm for that particular boat. And the same code worked for the main gate which was locked at closing. So Tim had paid the hefty deposit on his boat rental and now he waited for the opportunity to use it.

He was starting to doze when headlights splashed across the parking lot. He sunk down in his seat but it was just instinct. The light from the approaching vehicle hadn't come close to illuminating his cozy corner of the parking lot. The beams from the headlamps cut through the dark from the entrance where the vehicle had stopped on the far side of the main gate. For a moment nothing moved but puffs of flitting dust in the beams of the new arrival's headlights. Then Tim heard a deep mechanical grumble as the main gate rumbled open. The car drove through and the gate closed behind it. At a comfortable distance, the car crossed Tim's field of vision and headed to the far end of the lot, closest to the river. It pulled into a parking spot and the headlights were doused.

The distance between Tim and the man that climbed out of the vehicle was not that great but Tim was no longer a young man and it was dark. A few sodium arc flood lights were lit to provide safety for the lot but the shadows were still abundant. He reached behind him and dug through his bag in the back seat. He'd packed a few things that he thought might come in handy on his little stakeout. His hands found the case he was looking for. Some Christmas long ago Danny had received, from one grandparent or another, a set of binoculars. Tim opened the case and raised the miniature set to his eyes.

He didn't know for sure that he'd be able to recognize the man that he and Stas had seen from the shore that day but it didn't matter. The longshoreman's cap that the guy was wearing was a dead giveaway; it was the same man. Tim watched him walk down to the Criss-Craft and go through the process of getting the boat off the lift and into the water. Tim grabbed his phone and opened the app for the GPS tracker. The signal he was getting was nice and strong.

Slow and quiet, the boat started to slip downriver. Tim would track its progress but he thought he could probably get a head start. Lisa's house was downriver of the marina and a likely destination. When the boat was out of sight Tim started his car and dropped it into gear.

3

Tim pulled up in front of Lisa's garage and the GPS told him the Criss-Craft was still about half a mile upriver. He watched the little blip on the screen as it slowly drifted closer to his location. Doubt started sniffing around his resolve. He wasn't exactly sure what the heck he thought he was doing. The man approaching on the boat could be a violent criminal, he knew nothing. He'd have to take his chances, though. This guy might not know what happened to Lisa or where she was but he knew something. And Tim intended with every fiber of his body to come to possess whatever information this man had.

He returned his attention to his phone and saw the GPS tracker slowing as it closed in on Lisa's property. Tim exited the vehicle and ran around to the back of the house. No longer enjoying the luxury of time, he also no longer bore the burden of over-thinking. He made a snap decision to find a place to post up somewhere near the shed.

He ran through the darkened wood giving heed to the small hill that had taken Stas out and (unbeknown to him) Danny as well. He found a little nook in a fall of tree branches that provided cover from the direction of the river but also gave him a clear sightline to the shed from about twenty-five yards away. He checked his phone and saw that the blip had stopped. The orange dot representing the tracker was so close to the blue one demarking his phone that they were practically touching. He silenced his phone, slipped it into his pocket, and listened.

It wasn't long before Tim heard him. The approach was cautious but not silent. The guy didn't expect any trouble, not in the middle of the night. Tim hunkered down as best he could in an attempt to maximize the coverage provided by his hiding spot. A few seconds later the man in the longshoreman's cap walked into his view. Tim steadied his breath. The man walked right to the shed as if he'd been there before. But he stopped short when he saw the shed doors.

"Shit!" the man barked in a harsh whisper that drifted off into the night. He looked in the direction of the house and then quickly all around him. Tim resisted the urge to shrink further into his crouch. He was well hidden this far away in the dark. The only thing that might betray his presence would be any sudden movement.

Seeing nothing the man returned his attention to the shed. He walked over and examined the latch that was no longer clasped by the padlock. He looked around at his feet and then kneeled, retrieving the busted lock from the grass where Tim and Stas had left it. He handled it thoughtfully as he returned his gaze toward where the house sat somewhere off in the darkness.

Tim felt a wave of thankful relief that he had taken Danny back up to the Cities. He was scared enough for himself. The presence of his son on the property in this moment would've upped the stakes to a level he wasn't comfortable contemplating.

Mr. Longshoreman Cap dropped the lock back into the crabgrass at his feet and stood. He opened the shed doors and stepped inside. Tim couldn't see him in the deep, heavy shadows blanketing the shed's interior but could hear the muffled sounds of the man moving around; then they stopped and there was nothing but the distant drifting sounds of the night. Seconds later the man stepped back into view with his phone in hand. He fiddled with the phone and then put it to his ear.

He looked right at where Tim was crouching in his little barricade. For what felt like an eternity Tim watched the man looking right at him. There was no way the guy should be able to see Tim in his hiding spot but still the man stared right at him. One of the hardest things Tim had ever done in his life was to trust what he knew to be true, not his instinct, and stay put. Finally, he was rewarded. The man's call connected and he turned his blank stare away from Tim as he spoke.

"Someone has been here."

Tim waited out the silence while whoever was on the other end of the line responded. After what felt like another whole eternity, the man resumed his end of the conversation.

"I don't know, but there's no sign of her here now."

There was another pause and Tim's heart skipped a beat at the thought of Lisa and her whereabouts being the subject of the call.

"Well, as long as Logan feels the same, we should still be alright."

The guy knew who Logan was. That caught Tim off guard and he rocked back in his crouch the tiniest bit. The sound was infinitesimal, just the softest rustling of dead leaves.

But the man on the phone heard it and again looked in his direction.

4

The eternities that Tim Boyd had previously thought he had endured now seemed like nothing. Space and time had ceased to exist. The man in the longshoreman's cap stood silent with the phone to his ear looking towards the little deadfall of branches where Tim had concealed himself and neither of them moved.

Tim held his breath and still the other man's eyes did not stray, remaining riveted in his direction. The time stretched and pain began to bloom in his chest. He pursed his lips and released his breath as slow and quiet as possible, never removing his own eyes from the man in the cap either.

Finally, the man turned away resuming his conversation. "No, thought I heard something. I found the gun but that's it." He paused again, listening. "I'm heading back, there's nothing left to find here."

He terminated the call and disappeared back into the dark toward the river. Tim's strength failed him and he slumped in relief against the tree next to him. He took a few long deep breaths trying to bring his heartrate back under control and continued to do so until he heard the engine of the boat spark into life in the distance. The sound receded and Tim stumbled to his feet, then made his way back to his car up at the house.

A few minutes later he was at the gate of Wurzer's Marina again. He was about to punch in the code to open the gate when he checked his phone. The guy must have been flying as the orange dot was almost upon him again. Tim put the car in park and quickly cut the headlights of his vehicle. He rolled down his window and listened.

He heard the approaching boat right away and turned his attention to the water. Moments later he saw the small red and green of the port and starboard light at the bow of the boat and another set at the stern. No other lights were lit on the watercraft. Tim readied himself to reverse out of the marina entrance if the boat looked like it would dock but didn't need to. He watched as the little port and starboard lights, which were all he could see of the boat, passed. The guy had stayed well toward the other bank of the river to avoid the spill of light from the marina.

Tim punched in the code on the keypad and dropped his Honda back in gear as the gate rumbled open. He parked and made his way down to the dock where his own rental awaited. He punched the code in again on the lift and lowered the boat into the water. Three minutes later he motored off into the darkness following that orange blip on his phone as it drifted further up river.

It was not the first time that Tim had been at the helm of a speedboat but he was far from a pro and was far more used to the generally placid conditions of a lake on a sultry summer afternoon. It took a moment to get the hang of cutting against the current of a powerful river in the dark.

A cloud cover had drifted in obscuring what moonlight there had been earlier in the night. The rushing waters lapped and slapped against the fiberglass hull as he moved along keeping pace but at a healthy distance. The map on his phone, which showed the progress of both him and his quarry, was some help with navigation, but twists and turns that the river took were all but invisible until he was right on top of them. He was receiving a nice, strong signal from the GPS tracker so he was satisfied to take it slow and easy.

Some time later he watched the orange blip slow and slip into a tributary just north of the Treasure Island Casino. Tim was still about two miles south of the casino himself. The blip moved a short way into the tributary and stopped. Now there was nothing but the emanating pulse from the orange dot. An anxious excitement began a slow creep and Tim could physically feel it start to squeeze.

Another few minutes and some of the darkness began to dissipate as the lights from the casino pushed the night back. Tim opened up the throttle to make use of the light while it lasted. He slowed again once he had passed through the long throw of illumination from the casino, partly because of the dark but also because he was now approaching the tributary where the boat he was following had come to rest.

He found the offshoot from the river and throttled down as he entered the mouth of the small waterway trying to eliminate as much noise as possible. The engine purred quietly as he drifted along.

The cloud cover was breaking up now and the light of a half moon started to return, casting a slight glow. He saw the Criss-Craft tied off at a makeshift dock that was floating on big blue plastic barrels about a hundred yards from his current position. Tim scanned the shoreline for any movement and saw nothing, at least no movement. He couldn't quite tell but it looked like there may have been some sort of light source coming from the woods a little way up from the dock.

He probably should have found somewhere else to beach his boat but now he was at the dock and he'd come too far. He kept his eyes riveted to the shoreline as he let the boat slide in next to the dock opposite the Criss-Craft. Using a loose slip-knot he secured the boat, sliding it over one of the pylons. He'd be able to pull it loose quickly if a hasty retreat became necessary. Tim stepped from his boat onto the wobbly dock.

At the shoreline some old rotting wooden stairs went up a short incline to a trail that cut back into the woods. His earlier assessment had been correct; there was some sort of light spilling onto the trail, but its source was still out of his sight. Keeping up a constant surveillance of his surroundings he climbed the deteriorating steps then moved off the trail into the cover of the trees.

From the safety of the woods Tim followed along, moving parallel to the path, and discovered the light source was coming from a small cabin. He slowed and took in the structure.

The cabin was two levels. The entrance was on the ground floor and looked to be some sort of garage or storage space. Above it was the living space. Light poured through a window on the second floor where a young, probably teenaged, girl stood staring out into the darkness. Tim held his position for a long moment before he decided that the girl wasn't on the lookout for anything but just staring out the window into the night. Tim wondered if that young girl might not be the owner of the pink backpack that the man he was stalking had stowed on the boat that day. And in turn what that man's intentions toward her might be.

He was about to sneak to the other side of the path to see if he could get a better view through the window into the cabin when he froze, all of his senses locking up on him.

Behind the girl, from a section of the room that was cut off from Tim's view, a woman walked into his sightline and put her arm around the teenaged girl. Tim struggled to draw a breath. It had been a while, what felt like forever, but it was a face Tim Boyd would never forget. The woman said something to the girl and a hesitant smile broke on her innocent face. Tears rimmed Tim's eyes as he prepared to race to the cabin heedless of repercussions.

He never got the chance.

Pain alit, exploding through his head starting at the back of his skull. The woman in the window filled his vision but the image of her shimmered, wavered, and then disappeared completely as the world fell to black.

Tim Boyd's limp body slumped to the ground in the soft moonlight, twenty yards away from the cabin and Lisa Lathrop.

Minneapolis…
Spring, 2017

1

Al Witkowski was feeling delighted by his acumen so he tipped a tap and poured himself a beer. He'd just checked the clock. It was two-fifteen a.m. bar time, five after in actual time, and he had Jimmy's Bar all to his lonesome. He'd run off the last of the lingering vagrants with little difficulty which wasn't always the case at closing time. The transition could be far from smooth on any given night. He took a nice long draw off his beer, savoring the taste, well deserved after a long shift. And right then, when he couldn't have been happier, some idiot started pounding on the door to the side entrance.

"We're closed," he hollered without getting off of the stool he was sitting on.

He heard some garbled nonsense that didn't make it through the closed door. A second later, more pounding. Al set his beer down with an aggravated sigh and walked over to the door.

"I said, we're closed! Go the hell home!"

This time, closer to the door, he could make more sense of the garbled and slightly slurred response, "I left my keys in there, man, please, can I just grab 'em?"

"I didn't see any keys." This guy was starting to get on Al's nerves.

"I was in one of the booths, maybe they slipped down and into the cushion…"

Al gave it a second to let his anger simmer. He wanted to be properly surly before further engaging this yahoo. "Alright, you dumbass," he said, flipping the lock, "I'm gonna give you two minutes and if you don't find 'em, I don't give a shit, you're outta here."

Al Witkowski opened the door and Aaron Tolbert hit him in the face hard, breaking his nose with a sickening crack. Al reeled back into one of the tables, knocking it over as he went to the floor himself.

Tolbert came through the door with a lithe speed for a man his size. He swung it shut behind him and flipped the lock again before turning his attention back to the bartender. Al was trying to get back to his feet but he was woozy, swaying and staggering. Tolbert hit him a second time and Al went to the ground again, skidding across the sticky barroom floor.

Aaron Tolbert pulled two sets of zip-tie handcuffs from the backpack he was wearing. He zip-tied Al's hands at the wrist and used the second set on his ankles.

"What the hell, man…?" Al asked, but his words were mushy and slow.

Tolbert didn't respond. He got up and looked over the top of the bar. He found a bar rag and stuffed it into Al's mouth. The bartender started to squirm but in a lethargic, lazy motion. He did not have full control of his faculties, probably had sustained a concussion. Tolbert didn't give a damn as long as he was incapacitated. Satisfied that was the case Tolbert returned to the door and unlocked it.

He stuck his head out, looked up and down the empty sidewalk, and gave a nod to the car parked at the curb. The rear door opened and Ted Logan stepped out onto the sidewalk. He walked past Tolbert who was holding the side door open and into the bar.

Logan paid the hog-tied barkeep no mind and continued directly to the door in the corner at the end of the bar. He opened it and went down the steps to the basement with Tolbert close behind him. At the foot of the stairs he turned right and entered the small hallway. Again, he walked straight to the last door on the right.

Ted Logan tried the door and found it locked. There were two deadbolts above the knob and the top one looked new. He was definitely in the right spot. The directions he'd received had been impeccable. Young Tommy, who once had worked for Viktor Sokolov, had learned the hard way that Ted Logan was a man who got what he wanted. They had lost the kid the day he went to drop Lisa Lathrop's new papers, but Logan didn't lose people twice.

He had learned with little difficulty that Sokolov had moved his operation to Jimmy's Bar. They set up surveillance on the place and waited for the kid to turn up. He had been pleased when young Tommy had appeared with the tough-guy sporting the tattooed sleeves. When the two of them again left the bar a few hours later, Tolbert followed them and did what was necessary to secure a conversation with young Tommy. The kid had not needed much convincing after seeing what happened to the guy with the tattoos. He'd told Logan and Tolbert exactly how to get to Sokolov's office, and once there, where they would probably find what they were looking for.

Logan stepped aside from the door leading to Viktor Sokolov's office and let Tolbert take over. Removing a bump key from his backpack Aaron Tolbert went to work bumping the pins on the top-most deadbolt.

As Tolbert worked, Logan thought about the one thing that was rankling him concerning the night they had set up that surveillance of Jimmy's Bar. At that point he had no idea who Stanley 'Stas' Mileski was but when Aaron's brother had sent the still image from the Minnewawa security camera, Logan had recognized him immediately. That guy had also been at Jimmy's that night and Logan could only assume Mr. Mileski's business had also concerned Sokolov.

Tolbert relieved him of having to give Stas Mileski any further thought at the moment by bumping the final lock and swinging the door open. Tolbert went straight to a file cabinet behind the desk in the center of the room and started working on the lock with a more old-fashioned lock-pick set. Logan settled himself behind Sokolov's desk with his palms out on the desktop and waited.

Logan heard Tolbert pop the lock and slide the drawer open. He listened as Tolbert rifled through the files, his lips pressed together in a tight line, equal parts smile and sneer.

2

It took some time but eventually Aaron Tolbert passed a file folder off to Logan. Tolbert continued to sift through the cabinet behind him and Logan examined the file he'd just been handed. There was no name on the heading of the file, just a single word printed in block letters: DESOLATE.

It was a good thing that the kid doing Sokolov's grunt-work, Tommy, valued his fingers enough to be very specific in his directions, all the way down to the exact file cabinet and drawer that he thought he'd seen Sokolov pull the file from. Otherwise they could have been digging through these nameless files for hours. Logan flipped the jacket open and chuckled.

The first thing in the file was a photo of Logan himself. The next few documents contained the latest identity of a woman he had known since she had been a young girl, Anne Callahan. She had disappeared from Norumbega long ago and it had taken years for him to track her down. Now her name was Lisa Lathrop and she'd slipped through his fingers again.

Tolbert had finished digging through the file cabinet without finding anything else of interest. He went back around in front of the desk and sat in the same chair Stas had sat in the day he was in this office.

Logan continued to comb through the file in his hand. He flipped past a few pages then stopped. That tight-lipped sneer tipped, sliding closer to becoming a wicked grin.

He lifted an envelope and held it in both hands staring at it. There was a paper inside of it but the content of the correspondence was of no interest to Logan. What was of some importance though was where it had come from, the return address. Lisa Lathrop had mailed it from her home, an address that thus far had eluded him. He was very interested in having a look around her current residence to see what, or who, she may have been keeping there.

Anne Callahan had embarrassed Cortland Whittier when she disappeared. Once she became Lisa Lathrop, the things she had done went well beyond that. Other girls had disappeared and Whittier felt she had a hand in helping them, but most of the girls that had gotten out were scared and meek. They just wanted a different life and didn't know anything that could be destructive. But Brandy Redmond, the girl that turned up missing from Minnewawa last week, she might be a different story.

She *shouldn't* know anything, but *shouldn't* wasn't good enough. Brandy's mother was familiar with The Devil's Paddle and if she had breathed so much as a word about it to her daughter, the girl could destroy everything they had built.

Having found what he needed, Logan glanced quickly through the rest of the contents of the file. He stopped at the very last item. Apparently Sokolov had started keeping tabs on Stas Mileski as well. Logan slipped a photo with a post-it-note stuck to it from the file. It was a photo that looked like it was taken from a distance, the subject being a woman walking out of a little club called B.J.'s. Scribbled on the post-it was a question: *Mileski's girlfriend?*

Collecting a little insurance never hurt. As his wicked grin grew wider Logan handed the photo across the desk to Aaron Tolbert.

McGregor...
Spring, 2017

Bob Gurley cruised along a dirt road that ran down the east side of Horseshoe Lake. To his left the lake shimmered in the afternoon sunlight. To his right stretched a wall of wooded forestry so dense it seemed impenetrable. Bob was certain that was the attraction of this stretch of land to the likes of Cortland Whittier and Jason Tolbert.

A mile or two east of his current location was Minnewawa Lake and the resort of the same name. A resort that had somehow managed to operate as a luxurious summer spot for the public while being run by a megalomaniac cult leader who employed his flock, both legitimately and otherwise, and also kept them housed close by. In fact, if Stas had been correct in his estimation, they lived somewhere in the small wood that Bob Gurley was gazing upon at that very moment. He pulled his truck over on the side of the road and got out.

He stood on what passed as the shoulder looking into the gloom cast by the canopy of trees despite the bright sunlit day. It was not difficult to imagine untoward acts taking place somewhere out in the depths of the isolated quiet.

Bob had still received no word at all from Jane Devorak. Coupled with how Stas had described their early morning rendezvous, and how it had ended, he didn't have a very good feeling about her sudden absence. She had been part of the insular community being lorded over by Whittier. And the more Bob learned about Whittier and his reach, be it Logan or former prosecutor Joseph Randall, it didn't bode well for Jane.

He waded into the woods. If she was being held somewhere in that compound, Bob was going to have to try to liberate her. If that were to happen though, he needed to know what he might be walking into. And it was literally walking that almost became his undoing.

A single ray of sunlight that had fought its way through the dense foliage saved him. An infinitesimal reflection of light in front of him brought Bob to a halt just before he stepped into some serious trouble. The little glimmer that had caught his eye was at about shin height. He crouched down and then looked up trying to locate the slim beam of sunlight. He found it and followed it back toward the ground. There was no repeat of the small reflection. He relaxed his eyes and let them drift one way and then the other, from side to side. He saw it again and this time was able to focus on the little glimmer.

The thing that had caused the reflection materialized, suddenly appearing in its entirety. A trip-wire stretched off in both directions. They had alarms rigged on the perimeter of the property. He could step over it but he feared there might be further triggers, maybe some that he wouldn't catch.

His phone started buzzing. He wrestled it out of his pocket, not the easiest maneuver from his crouched position. The display told him it was Stas.

"Gurley, here," Bob said, accepting the call.

"Bob, its Stas. Where are you?"

"I'm at the woods east of Minnewawa, out where you thought maybe Whittier's compound was located." The whole time Bob was replying his eyes did not waver from the ominous trip-wire.

"And?" Stas asked.

"There's definitely something out here. They have

security in the woods, a trip-wire alarm." There was a pause as the information sunk in.

"Could we get around it, do ya think?"

More and more Bob Gurley was coming to the realization that he really did like this kid. "Now that I know where it is, we could step right over it. I barely saw it before I walked right through it though. Makes me nervous about what else might be out there that we'd never see until it's too late."

"Okay…"

"How bout you, you find anything?" Bob asked.

"Oh yeah, Heidi Finman was a fount of useful information."

"Is that right?" Bob said as he stood, his knees creaking and aching in uniform displeasure.

"Yep, you ever hear of a guy named Travis Olmstead, really wealthy guy? He's got a big mansion on the Sandy River just off of Big Sandy Lake."

"I think I've heard of him," Bob said. "But there's nothing about him I can recall specifically."

"I'm pretty sure he's mixed up with Whittier and Logan by way of Aaron and Jason Tolbert. I don't know if it's connected to Lisa but it looks like Debbie Keller stumbled onto whatever it is that they are up to, and was killed because of it."

"Damn," Bob muttered.

"I want to go have a little chat with this Olmstead guy. Can you meet me out at Big Sandy? I'll fill ya in and we can go talk to Olmstead together. I'm heading that way now."

"Okay," Bob said. "There's a lodge on the south side of the lake, I'll meet you in the parking lot. I should be able to be there in five or ten minutes."

"Sounds good, you'll probably even beat me there."

Then Stas was gone and Bob was alone in the woods again. He made sure that he still had a visual on the trip-wire and spent a few minutes making some mental notes of landmarks so that he could hopefully find the wire again if need be. Then slow and steady, keeping his eyes peeled, he made his way back to his truck. Once in the truck he wheeled it around, kicking up dust and gravel, and headed back up the dirt road on his way to meet Stas.

Bob Gurley had done a fine bit of detective work ferreting out that little trip-wire alarm, but he'd also been right to worry about other trappings that he may not have had the good fortune to uncover.

Jason Tolbert liked to be able to observe as much of the Minnewawa campus as humanly possible. Having a camera focused on the little dirt road that ran along the backside of the compound was no exception.

<u>2</u>

Twelve minutes after disconnecting his phone call with Bob, Stas pulled into the Big Sandy Lodge parking lot. He would have thought that Bob would already be there waiting for him, but Stas didn't see the Ford Ranger anywhere in the lot. He found a conspicuous spot to park where his own truck would be easily noticed as soon as Bob arrived.

Ten minutes later when there was still no sign of Bob, Stas picked up his phone to call him. The call rang through to his voicemail. Stas hesitated then disconnected without leaving a message. Something didn't feel right. Bob should have been here by now. Stas gave it a few more minutes then called again but got the same result.

After a moment of tense deliberation he jammed the truck into gear, cranked the steering wheel, and the tires peeled as he tore across the asphalt toward the exit. He didn't want to think about what might have happened, but if some sort of trouble had befallen Bob before he got clear of Minnewawa then Stas needed get out to Olmstead's before there was any chance that Olmstead could be alerted and already awaiting his arrival.

Stas had been back at the library when he'd first contacted Bob to tell him about his conversation with Heidi Finman. He had made a pit stop to see if he could figure out where this Travis Olmstead character lived. It took a bit of digging but he had located Olmstead's address. The guy lived on a sprawling chunk of land on the northernmost bend of the Sandy River, a small winding waterway that connected Big Sandy Lake to the Mississippi River.

Stas found the house with relative ease but slowed and took the long, wooded driveway with as much caution as he could muster. He saw nothing that gave him the sense of any impending danger, no sign of Jason Tolbert or anyone else waiting to welcome him. Eventually the forest-lined drive opened up to a large circular parking pad in front of the massive house. There were no vehicles currently parked there but on the right side of the parking pad stood a six-bay garage. An enclosed stone-walled walkway led from the garage to the house.

He parked his truck and it looked out of place as the lone vehicle in front of Olmstead's vast dwelling. He walked past a fountain and some manicured landscaping along the entryway leading to the large front doors of Travis Olmstead's riverside mansion.

Stas rang the bell and heard its chime echoing through the place. No one answered the resonating ringing of the doorbell. Stas decided to make a quick tour of the grounds. He walked around the house to his left. On the side of the house was a veranda; he could see a lavish study on the other side of glass French doors that led into the house from the patio as he passed. He realized that this must have been the spot that Debbie Keller had entered Olmstead's house on the night she died. A small shiver ran down his spine and Stas continued around to the back where the opulent yard unfurled down to the small river.

A large structure that could only be a lavish boat house stretched along roughly fifty yards of the shoreline. Other than two porthole windows on either side, a large arch in the center of the building was the only opening, giving a view of the river beyond it from the yard. He strolled across the lawn and entered through the arch. A deck ran along the entirety of the interior of the boathouse on the near wall. There was no back wall on the river side, just pillars stretching up and out of the water that held up the angled roof covering the boats. Otherwise it was open to the river. From the deck a couple of docks stuck out into the water. The two on his right housed a pontoon and a speedboat respectively. To his left there was only one dock and it ran out the length of a thirty-five-foot, beautiful, recreational trawler yacht.

Stas walked out the length of the trawler on the dock, taking in the luxurious cabin and pilot deck as he passed. When he reached the back end of the impressive vessel Stas came to a halt. He was taking in the name adorning the stern of the boat.

The Devil's Delivery.

It was not The Devil's Paddle that Logan and Whittier had discussed in Bob's little dossier, but Stas was having trouble convincing himself that the similarity in names had anything to do with coincidence. He pulled out his phone and snapped a quick picture of the beautiful lettering spelling out the name of the craft. Stas was still holding the phone in his hand as he walked back toward the bow of the boat and caught some movement through one of the boathouse windows.

He stepped quickly over to the side of the little window where he could sneak a look into the backyard without being seen himself. Walking across the lawn toward the boathouse was a man incongruent with his surroundings. The lush rolling turf and mansion rising behind him as a backdrop didn't jibe with the scraggly-looking, tattered flannel-wearing man that was rambling toward him.

As Stas pulled his head back from the window, a couple things snapped into place. He'd seen this guy before. It was the same man he'd bumped into outside of the hospital. When Stas smacked into him he'd been distracted, his mind still on his conversation with Heidi Finman. He'd noticed the guy's flannel but not the shirt beneath it.

The guy walking across Olmstead's yard, who had conveniently showed up at the hospital as Stas was leaving, was wearing an Anthrax concert T-shirt. It was the same guy that had spooked Bob at the bar that first day they'd met.

Willy Gustafson.

The very same Willy Gustafson who had lied for the Bolton County Prosecutor's Office and gotten Gordy Flesner convicted of Debbie Keller's murder.

Stas made a frantic search of his surroundings for anything resembling a weapon. There was a boat hook hanging on the wall, an aluminum pole with a hook on the end to pull a boat in to the pier. It would have to do. Stas set his phone on a ledge next to it and grabbed the pole. He turned, brandishing it like a baseball bat, and waited for Willy Gustafson to walk through the arch into the boathouse.

3

Bob Gurley reached the end of the dirt road that was abutting the Minnewawa Resort and knew he was in trouble. Two SUVs, bearing the title 'Property of Minnewawa Resort' on their respective doors, were parked nose to nose blocking the road, cutting off his only path back to the highway. He knew from the maps that he had studied before commencing this little adventure that there was no outlet in other direction, it was a dead end.

Bob slowed his own truck and angled a little to his right so that his driver's side window slightly faced the makeshift roadblock. At the same time, he pushed his phone down as far as he could in the seam where his seatback met the seat. He rolled down the window as a stocky, muscular man popped out of one of the other vehicles. Bob recognized Jason Tolbert from Stas' description of the man.

"There some sort of problem?" Bob asked, keeping his voice as pleasant as possible. Since the day he'd retired Bob had never had a single regret about no longer carrying a firearm. That was a stance that now ceased to carry merit.

"I'm afraid I'm going to have to ask you to come with us," Tolbert said. His tone remained even and pleasant but Bob knew better than to put any trust in it. Two more gentlemen in blue Minnewawa shirts had stepped out of the vehicles to join

217

Tolbert.

"Not sure I'm really interested in that," Bob replied, sizing up any possible escape route. Nothing of any substance presented itself.

"I can't imagine you would be, Mr. Gurley, but unfortunately, I'm going to have to insist."

They knew who he was. That didn't bode well. Bob sized up the moment, compartmentalizing as much information as he could soak in. He saw the right hands of the two men that had joined Tolbert creeping around their hips toward the small of their backs. Bob had to assume they had weapons holstered there. He did not like this one bit.

Tolbert, it seemed, was sizing him up at the same time. "I wouldn't do anything stupid. This doesn't have to get ugly unless you decide to make it so. I just want you to come back with me and have a little chat."

Bob thought that sounded most unpleasant.

"Leave your keys in the ignition," Tolbert said.

Bob reached with his right hand across his body to grab the door handle. It was not a natural movement but it allowed him to leave his left arm, the one closest to the door, to dangle next to it. As he grabbed the handle his body shifted and his dangling left arm dipped into the little storage area on the door where he had a little multi-tool pen stowed.

With the sudden seasonable spring temps a lot of the youngsters were already running around in shirt-sleeves, but Bob was still prone to a bit of a chill now and then and was wearing a light flannel. He thanked his lucky stars for those long sleeves as he managed to slip the little tool up past his cuff as the door opened. He stepped out and closed the door behind him.

"Pat him down," Tolbert ordered and one of his men stepped forward.

Bob did his best to steady his breathing as he put his arms out accepting the pat-down. He felt the multi-tool pen fall into the part of his sleeve that was dangling from his arm and could only hope it would be good enough to remain unnoticed.

The guy did a decent job hitting around his waist, and then getting his legs. But the attention given to his arms was cursory and Tolbert's henchman never came close to feeling the tool.

"Put him in my vehicle," Tolbert said to the guy that had patted him down. Then Tolbert turned to the other man that was with him. The guy hadn't said a word so far. "Childress, you ride with me, in the back, and keep an eye on Mr. Gurley, here."

Tolbert then walked around to the driver's side and got in. The guy that had patted him down hopped into his SUV. Tolbert's other man, Childress, ushered Bob into Tolbert's vehicle and climbed into the backseat with him. His eyes were shrewd and locked onto Bob.

The engine of the other SUV, which was still parked nose-to-nose with Tolbert's, fired and then pulled out back onto the highway heading in the direction of the resort. Tolbert made a U-turn and followed behind.

Bob watched the trees lining the highway slip by out his window. He could feel the eyes of the man next to him still watching him. He wasn't going to give the guy, Childress, the satisfaction of looking at him, nor would he squirm under his gaze.

Bob was surprised when both SUV's slowed about a mile before they would have reached the resort. They followed the vehicle in front of them across the center line and parked behind it on the opposite shoulder. He watched the guy that had patted him down hop out and unlock a gate that was blocking a hardly noticeable non-descript access road. Tolbert drove around the other SUV and onto the little road. They passed through the gate and left the other vehicle behind. Clearly this was a back entrance that allowed them to bypass the public section of the resort.

Still Bob wouldn't look at Childress; he kept his eyes focused on Tolbert's in the rearview mirror. "So, what are we gonna be chatting about if you don't mind my asking?"

Tolbert raised his eyes from the road to meet Bob's in the mirror. "You're going to tell me what you've been up to with your new friend, Stanley Mileski. And your old friend Jane Devorak is going to help us fill in any blanks."

4

A small bead of sweat slipped from his forehead as Stas waited for Willy Gustafson to appear in the arch of the boathouse. He had the boat pole raised and ready to strike. A shadow fell across the opening from the far side and Stas tensed. A second later Gustafson appeared.

From the porthole window he'd watched Gustafson walking across the yard. At that point Willy's hands had been in his pockets. They were no longer, and in his right hand he held a snub-nosed .38 revolver.

If Stas had struck as soon as Gustafson had rounded the corner he might have successfully disarmed him. But Stas had suffered a momentary hesitation at the sight of the gun and now Willy had recovered and raised the weapon, taking aim at him.

Stas received a lopsided grin that he thought was perhaps short a tooth or two. The two men stood silent and still on the deck in Travis Olmstead's boathouse. The various beautiful watercraft docked there bobbed as the river lapped against them. Stas didn't think this guy would shoot him, not here on Olmstead's land, but something in Willy Gustafson's eyes looked wild and unshackled making rational motivations untrustworthy. Another bead of sweat rolled from his forehead. His eyes bounced back and forth from Willy's down to the man's trigger finger waiting for the devastating twitch.

The longer the moment stretched the more Stas became certain that he was going to be shot. A small buzzing started from his right, interrupting the tension and stealing Gustafson's focus for a second. It was Stas' phone sitting on the ledge of the wall receiving an incoming text. That second was all he needed and the pole whistled through the air. It snapped in half at the force of impact when it hit Gustafson's wrist, but it did the job and he dropped the gun. It clanged off the decking and over into the river.

A moment later Stas smacked into Gustafson with the full force of his weight. Gustafson grabbed him and they pitched and listed, both struggling to find their footing. Then the solid ground of the deck disappeared and, tangled up together, they slipped through the air and splashed heavily down into the Sandy River.

The River…
Spring, 2017

1

Tim Boyd's eyelids fluttered as he came awake. He was lying on a bed that was relatively comfortable but his hands and ankles were bound. The back of his head was thudding and the pain brought with it some recall of how he came to be here. He'd seen the girl in the window and then Lisa stepping up behind her. And then he'd been blindsided. The most likely culprit in that blindsiding and his current headache being the man seated at his bedside.

The guy no longer sported the longshoreman's cap, but Tim still knew who he was. Rage and fury blossomed and Tim began to struggle against his bonds.

"Stop," the guy said.

"What did you do to Lisa?"

"Nothing, Lisa is fine."

"Bullshit, I want to see her." Tim put as much authority into the statement as he could muster still tied-up and lying on his side.

"That's not going to happen. But you need to trust me, she's fine."

"Trust you? I don't think so. I know who you're working for."

A slight haughty grin slipped across the man's features. "Is that so?"

"I heard you on the phone." Tim did his best from his position of disadvantage to return the smug smile. "You work for Ted Logan."

The man was still smiling but it shifted and now actually seemed somewhat genuine and a slight warmth crept into it as well. He paused for a long moment before replying, "Tim, I don't work for Logan, I work for Lisa."

Those words should have sounded false, like lies, but they didn't and they rocked Tim. The bed now felt like a small dinghy on a vast and angry ocean, rolling and pitching and ready to capsize. If he hadn't already been lying down, Tim probably would have fallen.

The man moved his chair closer to the bed. "My name is Dylan. Do you want me to free those hands?"

Tim nodded through his confusion and struggled his way into a sitting position, offering out the rope at his wrist.

Dylan produced a knife and slit the rope that bound Tim's hands. "I'll get your ankles in a minute."

"I want to see her."

"I'm afraid that's not going to be possible for a little while."

"Why not?!" Tim spat in frustration as he tried to stand. It was a difficult maneuver with his ankles still tied together. Dylan put a gentle but firm hand on his chest and directed Tim back to a sitting position with a little shove.

Dylan took his time before speaking. "Look, there's something Lisa needs to do, that we have to do, and you can't be a part of it."

"What are you talking about?" Tim was crumbling, utterly overwhelmed.

"Lisa cares for you, a great deal," Dylan paused. "What we have to do is dangerous, and if you had the details you wouldn't want her to do it. But unfortunately, what you want is of little consequence. In a couple of days, if she and I are successful, we can all go back to our regular lives. But right now things have been set in motion. Things that can't be stopped. That's why she had to disappear the way she did."

"It was you." Tim was starting to put some of the pieces together. "You were the one that called her. You're the one with the 320 phone number."

"That's right. I called her while you were at that bar. Logan had been looking for her and was getting too close for comfort. I picked her up after she'd lost you and she disappeared for her own safety," Dylan paused. "And for yours."

Tim felt untethered, his emotions swinging from one extreme to the other. He did his best to rein them in and, although it was not whole-hearted, he began to accept what Dylan was saying.

"So, what happens now?" Tim asked.

"We need your help. There's a girl out in the living room."

Tim was nodding. "I saw her in the window, a teen-ager?"

"She's fifteen."

"Is that who Lisa was hiding in the shed?"

Dylan gave him a long look. "So, it was you and Mileski that found the shed? Did you find it that day, the day I saw you?" Again, Tim nodded. "That's good, better it was you than someone else." He paused again. "That's where you heard me on the phone. You were in the woods, weren't you?"

Tim didn't answer the question but asked another of his own, "Why were you keeping her in that shed?"

Dylan looked away, biting at the inside of his lip before responding. "How much do you know about Lisa's past?"

"Not much, only the little bit Stas told me after she disappeared. That she grew up in a cult."

Now it was Dylan's turn to nod. "That's right, I did too. That's how I know her. We both escaped a long time ago. And now we help others to do the same, if we can…and if they want to be rescued."

"Some of them don't want out?"

"Nope. Most are content and happy. They're completely brainwashed, of course, and think Cortland Whittier is the be-all end-all. But we might be able to change that, to end the whole thing and bring Whittier down."

"How's that?"

"That girl in the other room is named Brandy Redmond and she knows some things that could destroy not only Whittier, but a lot of other powerful people as well."

2

The woman who was now called Lisa Lathrop, formerly Anne Callahan, and if everything went as planned would never need to be called Sarah Anderson, sat in the Criss-Craft as the dawn broke around her. In forty-eight hours the issue of her identity would be settled one way or the other.

She and Dylan would be successful in the coming endeavor and she would return to her life as Lisa Lathrop. Or they would fail and she'd become Sarah Anderson, assuming that in failing she didn't also get killed. If it came to the point that she had to take up the Sarah Anderson identity, Lisa would disappear forever and she would never see Tim Boyd or his wonderful little boy, Danny, again.

The sky lightened and the boat in which she sat rocked slowly in the early morning mist that was floating just above the little tributary leading out to the Mighty Mississippi. It was still about twelve hours until Stas Mileski would meet Willy Gustafson while standing on Travis Olmstead's dock, but she didn't know that. And she didn't know anything about a man named Bob Gurley who, sometime later today, would be taken by Jason Tolbert.

She did know Jane Devorak.

For all intents and purposes Devorak worked for Lisa, even if Jane was unaware of that fact. Her only contact was with Dylan. Nor was Lisa privy to the fact that Jane Devorak had been compromised as well and was currently being held by Minnewawa security. Known or not, the dominos were falling and at a pace that was beginning to quicken.

Her thoughts were on known commodities, in particular the young lady they currently had in their care, Brandy Redmond. Brandy Redmond was going to be a gigantic asset. She knew things about Whittier's operation, things she shouldn't have known, things that Lisa could use to tear down the blocks that upheld his empire.

During the despicable time in her life that she had spent as Whittier's wife Lisa had learned a few things. She came to realize that, while Whittier was a complete scumbag who absolutely took advantage of, and abused, young women, he had ulterior motives as well.

He was screening them for a higher purpose and Lisa had not made the cut.

She had endured him, but some of the other girls revered him. Of those girls that lavished him with their attentions and relished their position in his court, Whittier would select a few of them to join an elite group within the cult. He called them his 'Council.' These women lived like queens and while she knew they had certain duties in their service to Whittier, Lisa hadn't known all of what that entailed.

Brandy Redmond's mother was one of those women. And before Brandy had realized what it took to join Whittier's 'Council' and decided she wanted nothing to do with it, before Jane Devorak had made contact and Brandy had learned that there might be a way out, Brandy's mother had told her things. Not the least of which was the existence, and intended purpose, of something called The Devil's Paddle.

3

From where she sat in the Criss-Craft floating in the morning mist, Lisa heard the sound of a closing door echo down through the woods from the cabin. Assuming he was able to handle everything with Tim, it would be Dylan coming to join her.

She'd known Dylan most of her life. He and his family

had come to Norumbega shortly after Stas had stopped coming to the resort. Stas had actually met him once, sort of, but that was a long time ago. Dylan was a couple years younger than she was but they'd become very good friends. When she had escaped, the only bread crumbs she'd left behind had been for Dylan.

She had left a note for him in a spot that only he would find. It was three lines long. The first said that he could find her if ever he needed to. The second was a jumbled list of numbers. And the third line, after the numbers, was nothing more than a simple instruction:

Memorize and burn.

Using a code that they had played with as kids Dylan would have been able to parse a phone number from the second line of jumbled digits, Stas Mileski's phone number.

Two years later Dylan made that call. Shortly after making her own escape Lisa had told Stas that he might be contacted, but being a conduit was the extent of his involvement. He'd done enough as it was. After finding out Dylan had made the call Lisa took over, and the first people she helped liberate from Cortland Whittier were Dylan and his little sister.

Since then she and Dylan, with the help of Jane Devorak, had helped a handful of others to their freedom, the most recent being Brandy Redmond. With any luck, based on the information Brandy had provided them, no one else would need her help. Whittier was going down, and not in some false fire, some prescribed burn, like what had happened at Norumbega. This time she would be there and she would watch as Whittier, and all he'd built, burned to the ground.

Dylan appeared and came down the rickety steps to the dock. He climbed into the boat and sat in the captain's chair.

"How is he?" she asked.

"He's confused and upset, but I think he understands. He'll take care of Brandy." Dylan turned the key and the engine purred. Lisa removed the ropes that were securing the boat to the little dock.

"He'll take better care of her than I ever could." Lisa's voice was distant as she spoke.

Dylan turned the wheel and the sleek watercraft slipped away towards the mouth of the little tributary and the Mississippi River beyond.

"He had the key," Dylan said, tossing the Wurzer's key and chain over to her. "He said the wallet and all the ID were still there, he locked it back up and left it."

"Let's just hope to all that's holy I don't ever need to use it."

They fell to silence as they reached the river and headed south. The last of the lingering night had dissipated yet the light but dense mist gave the morning an eerie, ethereal feel. It lay across the river like a blanket but seemed to lift as they passed, closing again behind them as they rolled further down the river. Lisa turned her thoughts to what would come.

Tomorrow night Cortland Whittier and Ted Logan would be hosting one of their 'events.' The Devil's Paddle would be put into service. Many people with power throughout the state would be there, most of them because they'd been tempted into transgressions and now there was no going back. That was the real power behind Whittier and Logan. They manipulated and blackmailed and grew their reach, building their secret brand.

They had started small, on the county level. They infiltrated quiet rural municipalities, corrupting and subverting from within. The wealthier the area the better but they were not all that selective. Money and power could be drained even from those who didn't technically have a lot. Some people could be driven to great lengths to have their secrets kept and their positions remain intact and unblemished. It was how they had arranged for the conviction of Gordy Flesner, Debbie Keller's supposed killer. They owned the souls of a select few who held the power in the prosecutor's office and the Sheriff's Department of Bolton County.

But now they were growing.

Lisa wondered if Whittier was aware of how much

Brandy Redmond actually knew. It would all depend on Brandy's mother. Once her daughter had turned up missing from the compound would she betray her and tell Whittier everything she had told her daughter? Even if she was willing to betray Brandy, was she willing to risk the repercussions that the transgression of running her mouth would levy upon her own head?

Either way, Lisa was confident that Whittier would go forward with his plans for tomorrow night. He'd have put too much into it, pulled too many strings to pull the plug at this late date. But if the disappearance of Brandy Redmond was enough to put him on alert, the loss of the potential element of surprise could be detrimental enough to their plan to foil it.

Dylan spoke, pulling her back from her thoughts.

"Tim mentioned that he thought Stas was still in McGregor."

"That'll be good for us. Assuming he hasn't gotten himself into trouble sticking his nose where some people don't want it. We'll contact him tonight, once we're on our way."

"You're sure he'll help us?"

"I've never been so sure of anything in my entire life."

Another comfortable quiet descended; conversely, the mist was lifting. It drifted away, ceding its hold on the beautiful spring morning. They closed in on Wurzer's Marina where they would leave the Criss-Craft and switch to another boat they had on rental. A larger vessel more suited for a longer trek up the river.

1

Dreams of drowning came rushing back to Stas Mileski as the water rushed into his throat. For a split second he was trapped between the nightmares of a night ago and the flitting memories of the time he had actually almost drowned in a little fishing pond. Then his head breached the surface, he choked for a second on the fresh air, and he spit the muddy river water from his mouth with an ugly retch.

His hands were still clutching the shirt being worn by Willy Gustafson who was currently struggling to get his own head up out of the water. The river wasn't deep at the spot they had tumbled off of Travis Olmstead's dock, maybe three feet, but both men were having difficulties getting their legs back under them. Stas used what little leverage he had and thrust the man in his grasp further down in the shallow water.

Stas struggled to hold him down as Gustafson kicked and flailed. Stas found his footing in the murky river bed and now had the position of advantage. He was above Gustafson who still hadn't gotten his legs under him. Stas let go of the shirt with his right hand so he only had a grip on the thrashing maniac with his left. Willy was able to struggle against his hold and get his head out of the water.

That was fine with Stas. As soon as Gustafson's head

broke the surface it was his turn to start retching. As Willy tried to suck air from any possible source, Stas' right arm rocketed back down. His fist connected with Gustafson's face with a sickening dull thud and his head flopped below the water again.

Stas strained pulling him up from river then hit him again, very hard.

The satisfying way his head snapped back was pure motivation. Stas repeated this process and then felt the fight slip out of Willy Gustafson. The guy's feet were still moving trying to find purchase but the frenetic energy was gone. He continued to thrash but in languid, slow movements. Stas looked at his fist covered in blood from Gustafson's face. He released his grip on the other man's shirt. Gustafson slumped and Stas turned away, sloshing his way back to the deck of the boathouse.

He pulled himself up and scrambled over to where his phone sat on the little ledge. He pressed the home button and the display lit up. There on his lock screen was the text message he'd received that had distracted Gustafson just enough for Stas to knock the gun out of his hand. It was one word, DESOLATE, and a phone number. Stas didn't know what it meant but didn't feel like it was going to turn out to be anything good.

He spared a single glance behind him. Willy had pushed his head up above the water for a second before slumping back down under. He might be unconscious. Stas didn't care.

Maybe he'd come around when the water filled his lungs and started to choke him, and maybe he wouldn't. Stas didn't care.

Stas mustered his strength. With his adrenaline waning his soaked clothes were starting to bear a weight that was more than he thought he could manage. He would have to, though. He released a long deep breath and with everything he had he ran across Travis Olmstead's manicured lawn toward the house and his truck.

2

Stas peeled off his wet shirt as he ran across the yard. Upon reaching the truck he threw the shirt on the passenger seat, started the truck and cranked the heat. Moderate spring temps or not, that river had been cold. Once he was off of Olmstead's property and back on a public county highway, his breathing began to slow and regulate.

He'd deal with the text message but he needed a second to process what had just happened to him. And to deal with the boat. Olmstead's yacht had been called The Devil's Delivery and, as he had been thinking just before Willy Gustafson had interrupted him, the similarity in the name to The Devil's Paddle was too much to chalk up to simple coincidence.

The heat was pumping out from the dash and warming his shirtless upper body nicely but he was still shivering. The soaking wet pants he was sitting in would have to go as well. He turned off the highway the first time a smaller, less traveled, county road presented itself. Once on a quieter little thoroughfare he found another access road and turned off. He grabbed a pair of jeans out of his backpack and hopped out of the truck. He stripped off the wet ones without a thought about standing naked on the side of this little road. From where he stood, he could still sort of see the main highway. Not enough to actually make out any vehicles but he could get a sense of the traffic as it passed. His focus remained there.

Stas got his pants on, grabbed a fresh T-shirt from his backpack, and kept a watch on what he could see, or sense, of the highway for five minutes or so. There was nothing in the way of commotion that he thought might be related to him. No vehicles speeding by, either away from or toward Olmstead's place. No sirens. He decided he was safe for a moment and grabbed his phone. He punched in the number from the text message and waited for it to connect.

"Stas," a familiar voice said in his ear as the call was picked up. But it was not a voice he had expected to hear.

"Viktor?" he responded hesitantly. He assumed because

of the word used in the text that it would have something to do with Sokolov but had not expected the call to go directly to the man.

"That's right, Stas."

"Look, if you're calling because you've decided my time's up and you're going to go ahead with breaking my legs... I think you're gonna have to wait in line."

"If only breaking your legs was still on my agenda." Sokolov's voice carried a wistful resignation. Stas had no idea what that was about. "You in town?" Sokolov asked.

"I'm up in McGregor, chasing down some leads."

"Have you seen the news?"

"Not lately, why?"

"The cops found a guy with tattooed sleeves shot to death in some heroin deal gone bad down here. It was my guy, Wes."

"Shit, I'm sorry, Viktor."

"Not nearly as sorry as I am. We don't mess with heroin. The whole thing stinks, it's a set-up. Somebody got to him and that kid that worked for me, Tommy, before we could get him out of town. I'm assuming it was the meathead that was with Logan the day they shook Tommy down about Lisa's papers."

"What makes you think Logan had something to do with it?"

"I haven't seen or heard a word from Tommy, and then last night at bar close Al Witkowski got jumped. The guys he described sounded like Logan and his muscle. They went right downstairs and rifled my files."

Stas felt for Sokolov but his mind was whirling, trying to make sense of what this might mean to him. "They find anything?"

"They found Lisa's file. I don't think she's been using the new papers yet but they know the identity now." Sokolov paused but Stas could tell he wasn't done talking. The moment drew out and that made him nervous. "There's something else, Stas."

"Yeah?"

"I was keeping tabs on you, too. What I had compiled was in that file as well."

Stas did not like where this was going, not even a little bit. "What are you saying, Viktor?"

"I had a picture of your friend, the gal that works at the strip club, Shelly." Stas had removed his wet clothing but now those cold shivers returned. "They took the picture, so I can only assume by now they may have taken an interest in her."

"You bastard," Stas muttered.

"You jacked up my business, Stas. That sort of thing would usually buy a guy a trip to the hospital at least, if not much, much worse. But I might have compromised your friend. That's as close to even as we're ever gonna get."

Stas couldn't speak. He was fuming.

"I'm clearing my stuff out of Jimmy's, then I'm gonna disappear for awhile. If I ever see you again, Mileski, it will be far too soon."

Then he was gone and Stas was alone, standing on a little turn-off in the middle of nowhere, stunned. All at once his motor function returned, crashing back into his body. He jumped in the truck and peeled out back towards the highway, already flicking through his contacts on his phone.

He found Shelly's name and pressed send. "Come on, pick up the phone," he said under his breath. She did not. The call went right to her voicemail. It was pushing five o'clock so hopefully she was just at work already. He couldn't hold to hope, though, not at this point. He punched up another number.

Again, the call went right to voicemail. This time he heard his old pal Louis Jones' voice say in a cheery voice: *Like Dark Star says, if it's good news or money...leave a message.* Then he was greeted by the familiar beep.

"Lou, call me back, man, I need you. As soon as you get this, haul your ass over to B.J.'s and get Shelly the hell out of there. I'll explain later. I'm still up north but I'm on my way."

He ended the call, dropped his phone on the seat beside him, and pushed the gas pedal toward the floor.

3

The SUV being driven by Jason Tolbert was headed toward a short, squat, brick building. Bob Gurley sat in the backseat with the other security guy, Childress, next to him. The vehicle continued past the building and onto another smaller dirt track that ran back off further into the woods. A few minutes later they came to a stop in front of a second brick building. It was short as well, one story and no windows, but it was much longer than the one they had passed before.

Childress got out and came around to where Bob was seated. He opened the door and indicated that Bob should get out. He did as he was bid, being careful to keep the multi-tool pen that was hidden in the sleeve of his flannel from showing or slipping out. Childress shut the door once Bob was out and Tolbert drove off, back in the direction they had come.

"Stand right there, and don't move," Childress said without any hint of emotion.

Bob wasn't sure what help his little tool would be, or what would be the right time to make use of it, but he was sure this wasn't it. He was alone with Childress and could utilize the element of surprise, but he feared by the time he got the thing out of his sleeve Childress would already have his handgun out of the little holster at the center of his back. Bob decided he'd follow directions, for now anyway.

Childress removed a keychain and selected one that he used to open several locks on the outer metal security door. He pulled it open and then ushered Bob through. The interior of the building was dank. It was nothing more than a long hallway on one side, lined on the opposite side with small rooms. Each of these rooms had a door comprised of tightly spaced steel bars.

The Minnewawa security force had its own jail.

Childress led Bob toward a cell halfway down the row

and Bob continued to go along without resistance. Childress unlocked the barred door.

"Where's Jane?" Bob asked.

"I believe she's being debriefed," Childress replied evenly. But Bob didn't care a lick for the potential implications of the word 'debriefed.' "Make yourself comfortable, I'm sure we'll get this misunderstanding all sorted out once she gets back." His tone was flat-lined.

"A misunderstanding, is that what we're having?" Bob asked. "Don't believe I've said enough to be misunderstood, and on the flip-side, I think I understand you just fine." As Bob was speaking, he walked into the little cell of his own volition then turned and faced his captor.

The door was swung shut by Childress who was still watching Bob with his emotionless eyes through the bars. His keys rattled and the tumbler on the lock fell, and at last the stoic mask Childress wore slipped away. His lips parted in an ugly sneer and Bob Gurley got his first tangible sense of the evil he was up against.

4

Jason Tolbert pulled to the end of a road deep amidst the forestry that led to the most remote corner of the Minnewawa grounds. At the end of the road lay Cortland Whittier's expansive residence. Whittier's home was well away from both the resort and the employee compound; he required his privacy. Tolbert pulled in behind the only other vehicle in the driveway, parking behind a sleek burgundy late-model Jaguar.

Tolbert walked toward the entrance which was opened by an elegant looking woman, one of Whittier's former wives that now sat on the Council. She led Tolbert toward the study and opened the door. Whittier was expecting him.

"Come in, Jason," Cortland Whittier called from behind his desk. Another man, the owner of the Jaguar, was seated across from him. He stood to greet Tolbert. The man was dressed casually but his clothes smacked of affluence. He was short and trending toward balding but he was lean and fit, very well kept.

Travis Olmstead shook Tolbert's hand.

"Jason," Travis said, acknowledging him before taking his seat again.

Tolbert returned the greeting and took the other chair in front of Whittier's desk.

Cortland addressed Jason directly. "Travis and I are just going over some of the details for tomorrow. I'd like you to sign off on a few things from a security standpoint." Whittier passed a folder across to him.

Jason looked through the folder as Whittier continued to summarize its contents.

"Logan will arrive mid-day at your house, Travis, as will Joseph Randall who will have with him a few up-and-coming political players that we will be welcoming into The Devil's Paddle covenant." Whittier turned up the corner of his mouth in an impish grin. "For lack of a better term," he finished. Religion and government were intended to be separate, Church and State were not to intertwine. But Cortland Whittier had managed to find a loophole or two and was reaping the rewards. Whittier continued.

"The newcomers will be acclimated at Olmstead's. Assuming Randall can get them to take the bait, they will board The Devil's Delivery and Travis will handle their transport out to The Devil's Paddle."

"They'll arrive at your place staggered, correct?" Tolbert asked Olmstead. He nodded.

"Half-hour intervals," Travis responded. "Then I'll bring them out and return for the guest of honor."

"He's not coming with the others?" Tolbert asked.

Whittier handled the question. "He and his people will join later. Logan thinks it's better that way, more pomp and circumstance."

"And Logan always knows best," Jason Tolbert said with a grin. The other two men laughed as well.

237

"It's not our first rodeo, gentlemen," Whittier said, bringing the conversation back with a serious tone. "We've done this before and we'll do it again. But we do need to be very careful this time. I don't believe we've been compromised but there is more heat surrounding this excursion. It is absolutely imperative that our guests do not feel the slightest inkling of danger."

"We should have the majority of our problem spots immobilized shortly," Tolbert said. They had detained Jane Devorak and Bob Gurley and he had received word that an outside source used by Childress had eyes on Stanley Mileski. They should be bringing him in soon.

"Good," Whittier said. "I assume we'll have the usual help from the Sheriff's Department in keeping that section of the river closed?"

Tolbert nodded. "The Sheriff will have two boats like always, one upriver and one down, effectively closing fifteen miles of the Mississippi. They'll handle any stray traffic that we might not be expecting."

One of the first coups their little collective had managed was involving key players in the Bolton County Sheriff's Department. The current Sheriff had enjoyed a good long run in the job with very little pushback come election times. And there was a very good reason for that.

Whittier's great strength was that he understood how the people he meant to manipulate operated. He understood it with his followers, and he understood it with the political power players that he would eventually convert into his pawns. The hammer of blackmail was a powerful tool in converting them to the cause. Then, when combined with the velvet glove, it made the decisions very easy for those people.

When the choice they faced was to have their careers burned to the ground in a very embarrassing public display or to further join the elitist debauchery that Whittier offered, only asking for certain well-placed favors in return, there was really no choice at all.

"Very good," Whittier said as he stood. "Travis,

someone will see you out and we'll be in touch before our guests begin arriving tomorrow. I have a few things to discuss with Jason that we don't need to bore you with." He shook Travis Olmstead's hand. Travis bid goodbye to Tolbert and left the room. Whittier returned to his seat and awaited a more detailed report.

"Bob Gurley is in the pen. I don't suspect he'll crack easily, but maybe we don't even need him to as long as we keep him out of circulation. We've been having discussions with Devorak. She's a tough customer but I think we've got what we need. She definitely helped Brandy Redmond get out but I don't think it has anything to do with what's transpiring tomorrow. It's not connected to The Devil's Paddle. The timing is just coincidence."

"You know I'm not much of a fan of coincidence, Jason. Coincidence will burn you more often than not."

"I know, but Brandy doesn't know anything."

Whittier didn't seem overwhelmed by Tolbert's attempt to placate his concerns but he moved on. "Is Devorak working for Anne Callahan or Lisa Lathrop or whatever the hell her name is now?"

"I believe she is, but I don't think Jane knows it. She only had contact with a guy called Dylan, but that's not his real name. You remember a kid named Ben Henderson?" Tolbert knew full well that Whittier knew Henderson, Whittier knew the name of every single person that had ever dared to escape his flock. There were only a handful of them that had managed it successfully. With so many eyes and ears about, usually any potential runner would be ferreted out well before they mustered the courage or conviction to actually attempt it. And they were dealt with appropriately and publicly. It helped deter others from choosing the same path.

"Henderson was the first to get out after Anne, and probably with her help," Whittier said, answering the question. His lips had tightened to a thin line. This was, of course, not new information to either man.

Tolbert took the measure of his boss. Whittier's anger

at the exodus of any of his people was prodigious. But Anne Callahan had been the first, and so she bore a special place, a level of unbridled angst that wouldn't be rivaled.

Tolbert did his best to keep the conversation focused. "Both Ben Henderson and Anne Callahan were long gone by the time we put The Devil's Paddle into use, and Devorak was never close enough to anyone on the Council to have heard about it."

Tolbert was right about one thing. None of the former wives of Cortland Whittier that made up his Council would ever have spoken to Jane Devorak of The Devil's Paddle or what went on there. The women on the Council were utterly devoted and would never do anything to knowingly compromise Cortland's work.

What neither of these men knew was that it was actually this same sense of devotion that had caused Brandy Redmond's mother to tell her daughter about The Devil's Paddle, even if to speak of it was forbidden. Brandy had told her mother of her growing disillusionment with their lifestyle. Her mom thought hearing the stories of The Paddle would inspire her daughter to want to welcome her part in what they were building.

It inspired the young woman, alright, but not to devote her life to some sadist like her mother had. It inspired Brandy Redmond to rebel.

.

Minneapolis…
Spring, 2017

1

Stiletto heels clacked on the thick molded plastic that made up the stage of the hole-in-the-wall strip club called B.J.'s. What was transpiring on that little stage was of no interest to Aaron Tolbert. His concern here was with one dancer and one dancer only, and she had yet to make an appearance.

Aaron had dropped Logan back downtown at the office to handle some last-minute business before they left town for Olmstead's place and, ultimately, The Devil's Paddle. Every time that The Paddle was utilized was special but tomorrow carried specific weight.

To many, it had seemed a lateral move when Logan left the Governor's mansion to work with then mayoral candidate Sammy Douglas. Anyone that thought so though was naïve to the motivations of Ted Logan. The now mayor of Minneapolis, Sammy Douglas, would be joining them tomorrow. And if he could be tilted by The Devil's Paddle, as so many before him had been, then they would hold sway with the Minneapolis Police Department when the next Minneapolis Chief of Police was named. Having the Bolton County Sheriff's Department in your pocket was one thing. Having the entirety of the state's largest police force would be a whole other ballgame.

After leaving Logan at the office Tolbert had posted up at the bar inside of B.J.'s to wait for Shelly Langford, who might or might not be Stan Mileski's girlfriend. Whether she was or not, she would serve their purpose just fine. They needed to get Mileski's attention, distract him from whatever the hell he thought he was doing poking around in McGregor.

Tolbert sipped his beer slow and kept tabs on pretty much everything happening in the little club with the exception of the dancing. He tracked who came and went. He watched particularly for girls coming on, or going off, of their shifts.

While he waited, he gave thought to another matter. Word had come down from his brother that Mileski had met and had a long conversation with Heidi Finman that afternoon.

Aaron Tolbert had been quite clear about what would happen to her if Heidi were to start telling people anything she knew about Debbie Keller or anything that Debbie might have heard while spending time with Aaron. All this time Heidi had kept her mouth shut. Had she gone and done something stupid now? If so, she'd have to be dealt with. The rest of the night and tomorrow were going to be very busy for Aaron Tolbert.

He checked his watch. He'd been at the bar for a couple of hours and seen nothing of interest. Most of the clientele were of the blue-collar sort that he would've expected in this kind of joint. Guys just getting off of their shift work looking to grab a beer and an eyeful. None of them actively seeking out any trouble, at least not yet, but it was early. Twice Tolbert had needed to dodge and duck out of conversations with the bartender. He hoped not to leave much of an impression, just another sex-starved low-life spending a couple hours staring at women without their clothes on.

If he was able to locate the girl, Shelly, he would persuade her to join him (by whatever means necessary) and take her north tonight to his brother. While Logan wielded all sorts of power and clout, the only place to safely hold a person illegally and against their will was at the compound. He hoped she would show her face soon. He was beginning to tire of B.J.'s.

Tolbert's beer was running low and he saw the bartender making his way down the bar toward him. He was saved from another insipid attempt at conversation as the phone behind the bar began to ring and the bartender changed course to answer the call.

Behind him the door opened and a modicum of light slipped into the dank bar.

Aaron Tolbert turned and watched Shelly Langford walk in past the pool tables. She had a bag slung over her shoulder as she came down the steps into the main room. The stage stretched the length of the back wall. He watched as she went past the end of the bar and disappeared into a little hallway just to the left of the stage. The bartender was on the phone and paying him no mind. Tolbert got up and followed her.

He walked into the little hallway. The restrooms were to his left, and straight ahead was an old wooden door marked 'Private.' Tolbert gave the sign no credence. He pushed it open and walked through.

2

Louis Jones pulled his phone away from his ear and called out across the room to the guy manning the bar at The Palace. "Tony, I gotta roll for a minute, I'll be back as quick as I can."

"What the hell are you talking about, Lou?" the bartender hollered back.

"No time to explain, man. I'll be back." And then Louis Jones was out the door and running through the warm spring evening across the street to where his prize possession, his sparkling Dodge Charger, was parked in the lot. Stas had been frazzled on the phone but Lou got the point. He needed to get his butt across the river to B.J.'s and get Shelly out of there.

He drove as fast as traffic would allow down toward the river. Just before the Lowry Bridge that spanned the Mississippi, Lou hit a red light. He took the opportunity to dial another number. He waited, anxious, as the phone rang. The light changed and Lou gunned it across the bridge. Finally, the line connected.

"B.J.'s, this is Mike," the voice on the other end said.

"Mike, this is Lou from over at the Palace."

"Big Lou, what is going on, man?"

"All sorts of shit, is Shelly there yet?"

"Yeah, she just walked in a second ago."

Louis Jones breathed a sigh of relief. He hung a left on Washington Avenue; he was about thirteen blocks away. He'd be there in minutes. "I need you to do me a favor, Mike. Don't let her get on stage. Have one of your guys stay with her and I'll be there in about two minutes."

"What the hell is going on, Lou?"

"I'm not exactly sure, man. Have you noticed any weird dudes hanging about the joint this afternoon?"

"What kind of a question is that, Lou? The *only* dudes hanging around this place are weird dudes."

"You know what I mean, someone out of place, that doesn't quite seem like they belong?"

"Matter of fact I got a guy at the bar right now that I got a strange feeling about."

Lou's heartbeat quickened and he applied a little more pressure with his right foot. He flew through a traffic light that was closer to red than yellow. "He's there now?" Lou asked.

"Yeah, he's right— Shit." It was as if Lou could see through Mike's eyes as he turned around. He would be looking down the length of the bar for the creep and seeing nothing but an empty barstool. "He's gone," Mike finished, telling Lou what he already knew.

"Get downstairs and check on Shelly, Mike, right now." Lou terminated the call. He blew past the car in front of him by passing on the left, in the lane for oncoming traffic, and then through a light that was totally red. Around him the cross traffic shrieked as tires locked up and cars skidded off to the side of the intersection. Louis Jones didn't even spare them a glance.

3

Mike Delborn slammed the phone down and hollered at his bouncer who was sitting by the door chatting up one of the cocktail waitresses.

"Cody, downstairs, now!" Mike yelled at him and lumbered toward the door to the stairs himself. Cody was right behind him by the time he hit the stairs. Mike was not a small man and he was huffing when he reached the bottom of the steps.

"Find Shelly," Mike instructed between labored breaths. At the foot of the stairs there were dressing rooms on either side of a short hall. Cody went one way and Mike the other.

"Where's Shelly?" Mike asked the smattering of women in the dressing room. Clearly, she wasn't in the room.

"She left with Stas' friend," one of the girls said.

"What?" Mike demanded, incredulous.

"A guy came down here, said Stas was in trouble and wanted her to go with him, called him Stan though, that was silly…"

Cody came across the hall from the other room shaking his head. "She's not in the other room either."

Before Mike could respond, a wailing siren began to screech from every speaker in the place. Mike looked down the short hallway to where another set of stairs went back up to the main level. Through the door at the top of that staircase was a little vestibule from which you could do one of two things. Either reenter the bar, or go the other way, through the fire exit, which would set off the fire alarm, the fire alarm that was now blaring.

Mike Delborn could lumber his way down the hall and up those stairs, and he would, but it wasn't going to do any good. He was slow and they were already gone.

4

Visible smoke filled and billowed for a second from the

wheel-well of Big Lou's Charger. It appeared accompanied by a terrifying shriek as he locked up the brakes. There was too much traffic in the intersection he'd just reached to run the red light without regard.

He was now sitting where the two major thoroughfares of Washington and Broadway Avenues crossed. To his left, kitty-corner across the intersection, sat the squat little building that was known as B.J.'s. The building was right on the corner and the parking lot was at the rear a little further up the street.

Something wasn't right. From where he was sitting at the light, he could only see a part of the lot just past the back corner of the building. The parking lot was filling up with people walking out of the little run-down club and milling around. Big Lou's stomach dropped. In the matter of minutes since he talked to Mike Delborn something had gone amiss.

At the first potential break in the cross traffic passing in front of him, Lou crushed the gas pedal to the floor. The big, powerful engine responded and he shot out, turning left into the flow of traffic. The driver behind him hit his brakes and, apparently feeling as if he had been wrongfully cut off, shot a single digit salute in Lou's direction. He didn't even see it.

The entirety of Lou's focus was on a vehicle that had just nosed through the milling crowd behind B.J's to the exit of the lot. He recognized neither the driver nor the vehicle but the frightened, wide-eyed woman in the front seat he knew quite well. The look on Shelly's face gave him nothing to believe that she was in that car of her own volition.

The car was waiting to take a left out of the lot so it would come right across Lou's field of vision as it pulled out and turned. Lou was still a good hundred feet or so away and there was no oncoming traffic. The man that had just taken Shelly against her will took the opportunity and pulled into the street crossing just perpendicular to Lou.

Louis Jones loved his car. That Dodge Charger was his baby. If asked he probably would have said the only person who could usurp his love for his car was his mother. Apparently though, Stas, or Shelly, or some combination of the two, made that list as well. He hammered on the gas again, and again, the engine responded.

He closed that last hundred feet in seconds and drilled the other vehicle right at the rear wheel and quarter-panel as it crossed the street. The tire that Lou had struck blew immediately and the car spun wildly out into the street before coming to a rest.

Lou saw none of that though. On impact his left arm was hit with a searing heat and the world went white as the airbag exploded into his face.

5

From the darkness came a flicker; it became a flutter before solidifying and a very woozy Louis Jones came back to himself. He wasn't sure if he'd actually lost consciousness or not, but his sense of time had abandoned him. Lou pushed himself back from the deflating airbag as best he could, trying to give some care to his left arm that had been burned by the bag as it fired out from the steering wheel on impact. He managed to get the driver's side door wrenched open and he lurched out of the car.

The first person he saw was Mike Delborn coming around his wrecked Charger toward him and it immediately brought the situation back into focus. Lou looked back into the street at the car he'd smashed into. It was sitting in the middle of the road angled awkwardly across the flow of traffic. He'd crunched the quarter-panel quite nicely and blew the rear tire out. It looked as if it had been struck on the other side by the oncoming traffic as well. None of that mattered, though. What mattered were the two front seats of the vehicle, both of which were currently empty.

Lou turned and stumbled toward Mike, favoring one leg. "Shelly?" he managed to mutter as the two met on the sidewalk.

"She's fine. Cody has her right over there." He pointed to the lot and sure enough, she was standing there with the

247

bouncer. "We lost the other guy, though. Someone saw him get out of the car and run off that way."

Lou looked in the direction Mike had pointed, thought about trying to chase him, and scrapped it. In the distance he could hear the approaching sound of sirens. He'd have some questions to answer and he wasn't going to catch him on a bad leg. And the important thing was that Shelly was safe.

Big Lou limped around the destroyed front end of his prized vehicle without looking at it and followed after Shelly who was being helped back inside the club.

<u>6</u>

Two hours later the statements had all been given and at least a half-hearted search was underway for the man that had attempted to abduct Shelly Langford. The car had been registered to some mid-level staffer down at city hall that upon hearing his car had been involved in an incident, immediately proclaimed it stolen. The cops would look for the other driver, but with limited information, they'd never find him.

Louis Jones didn't know who the guy was but had a pretty good idea who he might be working for: Ted Logan, the guy Stas had been trying to dig up information on. The car, and who it had been 'stolen' from, only further solidified that theory. Lou hadn't made any mention of that, though, to any of the officers on the scene.

His phone had rung no more than three minutes after the crash. The Charger's plate had been called in and went out with the call over the scanner and his brother, Terrell, being a Minneapolis cop, had heard it. Terrell had called him, and after a cursory inquiry into Lou's well being, he had wanted to know if this had anything to do with Stas. When he learned it did, he had told Lou specifically not to mention Ted Logan. When Lou asked him why not, all Terrell had told him was that it was more trouble than Lou needed to involve himself with, and then told him to ask Stas.

So that's what Lou planned to do. He and Shelly were

now camped out at Stanley's Northeast Barroom. They were sitting on the bar side at one of the high-top tables that had been built on an old radiator salvaged from the bar when it was known as Stasiu's.

Now they sat sipping beverages at Stanley's, formerly Stasiu's, and waited on their old friend Stas.

They didn't have to wait long. A few minutes later a road weary Stas walked in and scanned the restaurant side of Stanley's, then the bar. When he located them, a broad smile broke across his face. The three of them convened and doled out hugs for a couple minutes, assuring each other that they all were relatively unharmed.

While Stas' initial concern had been with Shelly, he had a harder time believing Lou was fine. There was a bandage on the big man's arm where the airbag had seared him and he was moving with a noticeable limp. Lou was not a man that searched out sympathy or accepted it with ease, so Stas let it go, but it was concerning nonetheless.

They moved back to their table and, once a fresh round of beverages had been delivered, they began to fill each other in.

"I got the rest of the night off from the Palace," Lou said. "I can hang with Shelly if you need me too."

"Thanks, Lou. I'm afraid I'm gonna have to get back up to McGregor as soon as possible."

"Are you going to tell me why someone has to watch over me?" Shelly asked. "Why some asshole dropped your name and then tried to kidnap me from work?"

She was pissed but Stas was pleased to see it. Shelly was back to herself and not showing any lingering signs of shock from the ordeal that she'd just been through. Before he could respond, though, Lou jumped back in.

"He works for that guy, Ted Logan, doesn't he? The guy you had Terrell checking out?"

Stas nodded. "Logan is mixed up with some pretty bad dudes. I think they're up to something and it ain't legal, something secret that Lisa stumbled onto. I'm still not sure what happened to her, but I think the reason she disappeared was because they were onto her. They grabbed you to get me away from McGregor, away from whatever it is they're doing."

"You shouldn't go back up there, Stas," Shelly said. "Call the cops or something, this is out of control."

"I wish it was that easy. I think the cops up there might not be entirely trustworthy, either. Logan and the guys he's involved with are connected to powerful people. They seem to hold a lot of sway that they shouldn't necessarily have."

"Sounds like maybe you shouldn't be taking off on your own then, Mr. Lone Ranger. It could be dangerous," Lou said.

"I've got a guy up there helping me. He's a former sheriff." Stas failed to mention that former Sheriff Bob Gurley, was currently incommunicado. He had tried calling him a number of times during the drive back to the Cities and had still gotten no answer.

Lou looked like he was about to say something else, probably to continue to protest the idea of Stas returning up north alone, but he was interrupted. Stas had left his phone sitting out on the table and now it started buzzing as a call came in.

Stas picked it up off the table to check who was calling. He looked at the display and a slight sizzle ran through his nerve-endings. There was no contact name but it was coming in from a number he recognized, a number with a 320 area code.

It wasn't the phone number they had gotten off of Lisa's phone. It was close, but not quite. The last two digits were different. It was, however, the exact same number that Jane Devorak had received a call from just seconds before she took off into the woods not to have been seen by Stas since.

For a moment the phone just buzzed in his hand.

Stas took a deep breath and tapped the icon to accept the call. He put the phone to his ear. "Hello?" His voice was cautious.

For a long moment there was no response and then it came, a single word, not a question but a simple statement of acknowledgement.

"Stas."

He didn't know who he expected to hear on the other end of the line but any guess he might have attempted would have been inaccurate. It was a woman's voice, a familiar voice.

He smiled as he responded, "It has been awhile, Lis."

McGregor...
Spring, 2017

<u>1</u>

For almost thirty years Bob Gurley had spent his life on the opposite side of the bars he now found himself staring through. He wasn't finding the experience much to his liking. It had been about a half-hour since Jason Tolbert's man, Childress, had locked him up. No one had come or gone since.

In that time, he'd done as much reconnaissance on his current dwelling as he possibly could. The cells had a single cot, a toilet and a roll of toilet paper, nothing more. He didn't see any cameras or a monitoring system but if he had learned anything about the Minnewawa, it was to always expect you were being watched.

Bob lay down on the uncomfortable cot facing the wall. If there were any hidden cameras monitoring the cells, he hoped his body would block them as he checked the little multi-tool pen that he had been able to smuggle in. It was a pen that unscrewed into three separate pieces. He could put the pieces back together in various arrangements that also made it a screwdriver or a nail file. The small compartments also housed various other little goodies such as a thin razor-blade and a tiny little hacksaw as well. If he had been sentenced to ten years Bob thought maybe he would have had time to saw through the bars. For better or worse, he didn't feel as if he would be here for that amount of time.

Bob heard keys rattling in the outer door of the little jail and quickly put the pen back together and stowed it. The door opened but the throw of light that came with it was minimal. The sun must have started its slide to the horizon and, this deep in the woods, was not allowing much light in through the dense forestry surrounding the building.

A security officer he didn't recognize marched a woman in that he did. Jane Devorak. She seemed to have her head held high but her right hand was wound in bandages.

They've been working her over, Bob thought as he watched the guy walk her down and unlock the cell next to his. She was unceremoniously shoved in and the cell door slammed shut behind her. The guy locked it and left without ever saying a word. They heard the tumblers fall in the outer locks, and then they were alone.

"Are you alright?" Bob asked as he approached the barred door of his cell on the side closest to Jane's.

"I'll live," she said from just on the other side of the wall. He couldn't see into her cell but she was waving an arm through the bars, out where he could see it, trying to get his attention.

Bob leaned his head up against the bars attempting to get even the slightest view of Jane. He could just barely see part of her head, which was also up against the bars of her own cell. He saw her grab her ear and tug at it. Then with the same hand that she had used to tug her ear, she pointed up at the ceiling. Bob put two and two together.

There may not be any cameras in this little jail, but they were listening. The lack of any visual surveillance was most likely intentional. It would give whoever they locked up in here the perception that they weren't being monitored and they would be more likely to speak freely. It was crafty. If the powers that be at Minnewawa suspected anything of any of their people, they could throw them in here and just listen to whatever they talked about.

Bob was not at all pleased about his captivity but part of him wished that if it had to happen it had happened sooner. Maybe they would have laid off of Jane and just hoped that two of them would have handed up the information they had tried to extract from her by other means.

Not much he could do about it now.

Instead he grabbed a piece of toilet paper and his multi-tool. It turned out the pen might come in handier than the tools. He scribbled something on the little piece of tissue.

Aloud he said, "I'm sorry we have to meet like this." He passed Jane the scrap of toilet paper between the cell doors.

How's your hand?

She said, "Yeah, me too, Bob. Me too." But she put her hand out between the bars asking for the pen. He handed it over and seconds later she passed a note on her own piece of toilet paper back.

It's not comfortable but I'll live. (Also, I guess it was a stroke of luck that they didn't know I was left handed.) She stuck her bandaged right hand through the bars as Bob was reading and he had to bite down on a little laugh before it could escape. She passed another square over to him and this time the pen came back with it.

Did you boys have any luck on the Debbie Keller angle?

Stas made some connections. He was on his way to a guy named Travis Olmstead's place when they nabbed me. You ever hear of him?

Oh yeah. Olmstead is a liaison of sorts for the bastard that runs this place. They're planning something for tomorrow night...

Any idea what?

No, not exactly.

Jane passed the note to Bob but again kept the pen. Aloud she said, "My hand is killing me, I'm afraid I need to lie down for a few minutes." But a few seconds later she passed another scrap of T.P. back to Bob.

I don't know all the details. They bring important people in for some kind of event or party and then somehow blackmail them. That's how they're able to run this place, how they get their money.

"Okay, take care of yourself," he said aloud and then the silence drew out. There was not even a hint of ambient noise. The little cell block was a dead space, all the better for listening ears, Bob supposed. Jane still had the pen. A moment later she passed it back with another scrap of tissue.

The good news is that I'm guessing we'll be left alone and locked up until they're done. Their resources will be depleted while the security forces are allocated elsewhere.

A short pause, and then came another note.

But as long as their plan is to deal with us after their shenanigans tomorrow, we might still have a chance. I've got someone else on the inside.

She had sent the pen along with the last note. He wanted to ask about her insider but there was something else that had started gnawing at him.

What happens if they do decide to deal with us before tomorrow?

He sent the correspondence and the pen over and awaited a response. Her good hand popped back out between the bars with another note.

Well... that would be unfortunate since 'dealing with us' almost certainly translates to killing us... I'm flushing these notes down the toilet. Give it twenty minutes and then flush yours.

Minneapolis…
Spring, 2017

1

The lights of the Minneapolis skyline twinkled at their backs and reflected off the river behind them. Lisa Lathrop and the man she called Dylan had just passed under the Hennepin Avenue Bridge and the giant lighted Grain Belt Beer sign shone down on them as they churned upriver.

They had stopped and spent much of the day in the town of Hastings, a medium-sized river city between Red Wing and Minneapolis. They spent the day shopping. Lisa had a list of items that could be purchased at various home goods and home improvement stores. Separately there was nothing of particular note about these items, but combined with the contents of another bag that she had stowed in the cabin of the boat, that could be quite a different story.

By late afternoon their shopping was finished. They had resumed their trek heading north up the river and night had fallen by the time they were cruising through the city of Minneapolis.

They left the lights of downtown behind them but could see the colorful arches of the new Lowry Avenue Bridge lit up ahead of them. To their left, on the west bank of the

Mississippi, the gleaming buildings of the heart of the city had given way to industrial shipping yards and scrap-metal processing plants. To their right, the side of the river where Northeast Minneapolis lay, it was dark. As they continued a flicker of light began to appear in the darkness. A few minutes later those flickers solidified into flames as they came upon a stretch of burning torches. It was the Psycho Suzi's tiki patio, and it was in full swing on this beautiful spring evening. The revelry was not for them but it meant they were close.

Lisa checked their location by the GPS on her phone. She compared it to the pin that was denoting their destination. The two were practically on top of each other. She pointed Dylan, who was captaining their trawler, toward the spot on the east bank. Behind a restaurant called the Sample Room there was a small communal dock on the river that could handle a few boats.

They veered in toward it. The dock came into view and so did the man standing on it. Lisa wasn't smiling much these days but she did now. Dylan angled the boat in, next to the dock as close as possible so that Stas Mileski could board.

<u>2</u>

The city slipped away behind them. They cleared the Anoka County line and left the urban landscape of the metro area in their wake. They were alone, quietly pushing up the dark muddy waters of the Mississippi River. Dylan continued to captain the ship. Stas and Lisa sat at the galley table below the bridge for a long overdue conversation.

The pleasantries had been handled quickly. They'd known each other for a very long time, had been through much together. They didn't need to revel long in their reuniting. They were mired deep in some uncharted muck and dove right into the handling of their business.

"So, you told me so much about your past over all these years, but failed to mention that the whole time you've actually been smuggling people out?" Stas asked.

With a small smile, Lisa nodded. "He was the first." She pointed toward Dylan up at the helm sitting in the captain's chair. "You remember the name Ben Henderson?"

Stas turned to look over at Dylan. "That's Ben Henderson?" Stas had received a phone call from him once, a long time ago.

"*Was* Ben Henderson, now his name is Dylan."

"Were you using Sokolov for their identities?"

She shook her head. "No, I get them fake papers, they're good, but not like the real ones that Sokolov did for me." After a pause she said, "I didn't trust that Sokolov wouldn't tell you." She didn't look at him as she spoke that last.

It did ignite a small flare of anger but he let it go. "How often were you," Stas paused, "extracting people?"

"Not as often as I would've liked to," she said wistfully. "Most of Whittier's people are too brainwashed to even want to leave. And the ones that aren't are mostly too scared to try. People that cause problems for him have a tendency to disappear and not to the safety of a new life, like I try to provide."

"That seems accurate." Stas wasn't even really talking about Whittier's followers though. He was thinking about Debbie Keller. And Gordy Flesner, who disappeared to prison, as well as two thirds of Heidi Finman's statement to the police that disappeared to God knows where.

"If they were to try, it was usually the parents, like mine," an old bitterness tinged her voice. Stas recognized it from conversations of years gone by. "They'd realize they didn't want their kids growing up there and try to figure out a way to save them."

"That day that we watched the news, and the original Norumbega was burning, you really thought it was over then?" She nodded but didn't speak. "When did you know Whittier had started things back up?" he asked.

"It was a year or two later, the first time someone made contact trying to get out."

"How would you get them out? How did they know to

find you?"

"Jane Devorak. She had been like a mom to Dylan and his sister at Norumbega, their real mother being all too dedicated to Whittier's cause. Jane had known that Dylan wanted to get out and when she realized there was a possible way of making it happen, she helped him and his sister then continued to help others. She was still embroiled with Whittier's people when the Minnewawa was established. She stayed, selflessly dedicating herself to helping others. She'd watch for anyone that showed signs of discontent and then would start to vet them. If they panned out, she would offer them the option of escape."

"How would you get them out?"

"Dylan smuggled in a phone to Jane so they could be in contact. She never knew I was involved. They'd set an appointed date and time. I don't know how Jane facilitated things on the inside."

Stas chuckled to himself. From the little he knew of the woman he had no trouble imagining Jane Devorak handling things on her end. Before long he would have to bring up the troubling situation of her current whereabouts, but he'd wait until Lisa had finished.

"Jane was able to get them into an underground drain pipe that she had found access to. Its outlet was at Horseshoe Lake right across from Minnewawa."

Unbeknown to both of them, that drainage pipe ran right under the road Bob Gurley had been investigating when he ran into Jason Tolbert and his men.

"Jane would take them to the end of the drainage pipe," Lisa went on. "From there the person escaping would have to swim about a hundred yards across the lake. Dylan has a guy that would pick them up from one of the docks. He'd drive them over to Big Sandy Lake where Dylan would be waiting with a boat. Dylan would take them from the lake to the Mississippi and they'd make the long journey down to my place in Red Wing."

Stas didn't interrupt but he wondered if they even knew

how dangerous that escape route was. The only way to get from Big Sandy Lake to the Mississippi was the tributary river that ran right past Travis Olmstead's backyard.

"When they got to my house," Lisa said, "they'd stay in my shed, which I heard you found." Stas nodded. "We'd keep them there for a week or so while we made sure the extraction was clean and then we'd move them to a safe house."

Stas shook his head. "I can't believe you never told me."

Her sly smile returned. "A girl has got to have some secrets." Then the coy grin slipped. "And I never wanted you to be involved. I didn't want to put you at risk."

Now it was Stas' turn to don a devilish smile. "And yet here we are."

"Yeah, here we are… Sorry."

"It's nothing," he shrugged it off. "In fact, I was getting kind of bored, I needed a little excitement." Stas' countenance clouded as he changed the subject. "We should talk about Jane Devorak though," he said loud enough that Dylan could hear him up on the little bridge of the boat.

Dylan turned away from the river unfurling in front of them to look at Stas. "What about her?"

"When was the last time you talked to her?" Stas asked.

"This morning, right after she talked to you."

"Bob, the guy I've been working with, his wife tried to contact her later this morning. At the resort they're saying she's on vacation but they're lying. Something's happened to her."

Stas let that sink into the quiet night air. Dylan turned back to look out over the bow of the boat, navigating the river, but Stas knew he was still listening.

"Bob went to check out the compound," Stas said. "He was supposed to meet me right after but never showed up. I can only assume Whittier and Jason Tolbert have them both. It was my intention to try and locate them but then Sokolov called me and told me that Logan might be going after Shelley and I had to haul my ass back down here. They're doing a pretty damn good job of keeping our focus split."

"We've got to find them," Dylan said without as much as a glance in their direction. Stas felt the tiniest sensation as the trawler picked up a little speed.

Stas turned his attention to Lisa. He watched as she processed the information. She had a detached manner that he knew well. It could be maddening at times but it was a defense mechanism she had developed at a very young age and it had served her well.

"What's our ETA in McGregor?" she asked Dylan.

He checked a few of his instruments and looked at his watch, "I think I can get us there shortly after day break."

"We'll have time during the day to see what we can find, but we'll have to be careful. We can't do anything that might compromise the real reason we're going up there. Our focus still has to be on The Devil's Paddle."

She might as well have slapped Stas in the face. A slight tremor ran through him almost as if she had. "What did you just say?"

"I'm sorry," Lisa said, not understanding the reason for his dismay. "We'll do our best to help them but the thing that matters most is taking care of Whittier and what he's doing with The Devil's Paddle."

Stas was finding the words difficult to come by. "The Devil's Paddle…? You know what it is?"

Lisa nodded slowly but her eyes were shrewd. "What do you know about it?"

"Bob overheard a snippet of a conversation between Logan and Whittier at the Minnewawa one night. They mentioned The Devil's Paddle and that they were trying to keep someone's mouth shut about it. But neither of us had any idea what it was."

"I'm sure they did want to keep people's mouths shut about it. It's the crux, the center piece, of everything that they've been able to build."

"So, what is it?"

"It's a replica of a nineteenth century paddle steamer."

Of all the ruminating Stas had done on the topic, the

truth was an option he'd never considered. "Wait... The Devil's Paddle is a boat?"

"According to Brandy Redmond and her mom, that's exactly what it is."

Stas shook his head in semi-disbelief.

"Brandy told us that on very special occasions, with some *very* special guests on board, The Devil's Paddle embarks upon the Mississippi. It sounds like it's a club, I guess, illegal riverboat gambling, women, drugs and booze. They get these luminaries, powerful public figures, out 'enjoying' themselves and they document various illicit and illegal stages of it. And then they blackmail them, give them a choice. Be exposed and have their careers ruined or join the club for the small price of a few favors. Cops looking the other way in certain instances, pieces of legislation that are important to Whittier getting passed, that sort of thing. And in the meantime those conferring these favors continue to take part in all of the debauchery that The Devil's Paddle can provide."

"I'll be damned," Stas muttered. And then another puzzle piece clicked into place. Olmstead's boat. The name was definitely no coincidence. The Devil's Delivery was probably being used to deliver some of these powerful people to her sister ship, The Devil's Paddle. Stas was about to try and vocalize that connection when Dylan's phone began to ring.

Dylan scooped the phone off the console where it sat next to him. He looked down at the display and then his eyes shot up to Lisa.

"It's coming from the Minnewawa. It's Jane's phone."

Lisa was out of her seat in a second and up on the bridge with Dylan. Stas remained down in the galley and watched as they both stared at the display. The phone continued to ring. Their eyes met and Lisa gave a curt nod. Dylan put the phone up to his ear.

"Jane?" he asked.

But it wasn't Jane. Jane was still locked away in a cell. It wasn't Jane Devorak at all.

McGregor…
Spring, 2017

1

Carrie (she of the patented smile) had the day off from her duties at the Minnewawa resort. She would not be schlepping guests back and forth from their cabins in her little golf cart today.

Instead she sat in the lobby of the Wellness Building pretending to read a book. The big glass walls would allow the lobby to be bathed in sunlight if the conditions were right but today had broken overcast. Carrie didn't mind, she kind of enjoyed a gloomy day. But more important, the lobby of the Wellness Building had an excellent view of the grounds.

It wasn't abnormal for her, or any of the other Minnewawa residents, to spend an afternoon reading in the lobby on a day off. In fact, several people had joined her already. The longer she spent waiting there, though, the more anxious and conspicuous she felt. She wasn't actually there to read a book, she had another agenda. Finally, she saw what she'd been waiting for.

Four black Suburbans came around the corner of the building from the back and turned left onto an access road that ran out into the woods. Carrie knew that the road they had turned onto led back out to the highway. No one ever left by that route but the upper echelon members of the compound and rarely in such numbers; one vehicle maybe, occasionally two. But not usually more than that, except under particularly special circumstances. Today's circumstance undoubtedly fell under that category.

Whittier had his Council, former wives that held prominent positions and aided in executing the true work that their spiritual leader aspired to. Jason Tolbert had a different selection process for his staff, but he had an assembled group of young men that served to keep the Minnewawa resort secure.

There was no crossover in jobs between the men and the women. Whittier was a misogynist through and through. Carrie, like so many other young women here, had no place in either party. But unlike a lot of the other women, Carrie wanted more from her life and intended to have it.

She knew those Suburbans were carrying Tolbert's men. She didn't know exactly what they were up to. She didn't know what The Devil's Paddle was. She did know though that at least eighty percent of the heavy hitters on the security end of things had just left the compound.

Carrie put her book down and walked outside. She turned left toward the corner of the building where the vehicles had just passed by and walked around heading toward the back of the Wellness Building. Halfway between the front and the back she stopped, checked her surroundings, and then dashed across the little road and into the woods. She had learned there was a dead spot there. A place the cameras couldn't cover.

Once safely within the confines of the trees she pulled out a phone. A phone she wasn't supposed to have. It had been given to her hastily early yesterday morning by the same person who taught her about the camera dead spots on the property, Jane Devorak.

Last night Carrie had called the number that Jane had told her to use. The number she was to use if Jane didn't show up for her next shift, which she hadn't. This time Carrie didn't call, she just sent a text. Simple and to the point: *Security detail has departed.*

Then Carrie struck off to the east through the woods. She walked with her head up, scanning the trees high up on their trunks. She stopped when she saw one with a green plastic prism attached to it. The kind used to trap and kill the emerald ash borer insects that were decimating ash trees. She looked both directions until she located another of the green panels on a different tree. Slowly she walked toward the trees as if to pass between them.

Now her eyes were on the ground. When she was almost in line with both of the trees she stopped, did a quick bit of surveillance, and then stepped over the trip-wire running between the two. That was another trick Jane had taught her.

She repeated the process several times. There were multiple perimeters of alarms waiting to be tripped but they were all denoted by the green ash borer prisms and relatively easy to avoid since Carrie knew what she was looking for.

At an absolutely indistinct spot in the dense forestry Carrie came to a stop. She looked around for a moment and then dropped to a knee and felt about in the foliage and dead leaves on the ground. After a moment her hands found pay-dirt.

It was heavy but still manageable for one person. She wrestled the manhole cover back and forth until she had moved it aside. She stared down a rickety ladder that dropped off into a drainage pipe that ran out to Horseshoe Lake.

2

Lisa Lathrop was a woman of many talents. After having known her for so long, he didn't think she would still be capable of surprising him. But that wasn't the case.

After the call from Carrie at the Minnewawa last night, and learning that Jane Devorak was almost certainly being held captive, Dylan had become singularly focused on getting them up the river as fast as possible. Exhaustion had been nipping at

Stas and he went down to one of the bunks in the cabin of the boat to get a bit of rest.

When he woke an hour or so later, he had found Lisa sitting at the galley table where they had conversed earlier. The surface of the tabletop was covered with the supplies she and Dylan had purchased during their pit-stop in Hastings. When he asked what she was doing, Lisa had calmly explained that she was constructing home-made timers and detonators for explosives. When Stas shot her a questioning glance she slid a bag out from under the table. She flipped back the cover to reveal a bunch of little compact packages of C-4 explosive.

It was her intention to find a way to board The Devil's Paddle, to blow it up, and to make certain the proverbial captain, Cortland Whittier, went down with the ship.

And now that they had to make a stop at the Minnewawa compound, she thought perhaps they could kill a few birds with the same proverbial stones. Stas felt the construction of improvised explosive devices was beyond him and had opted to go back to bed.

This time when he woke, Lisa was snoozing in one of the other bunks. Watching her sleep brought him back with a striking clarity to the morning he'd woken to her sleeping on his couch after she'd first escaped Whittier and Norumbega. There had been a lot of recovery and late-night phone calls since then. It seemed surreal that they were now returning to exact some kind of vengeance for those bygone wounds. Stas went up to the galley and bridge to check on their captain.

Dawn was on the horizon and Lisa's handiwork of the night before had been packed up and stowed. He was sure she hadn't attached the detonators to the C-4 yet, and he understood that the stuff was supposed to be very stable, but the proximity still made him uncomfortable. He found Dylan still piloting the ship but he was looking a little bleary-eyed.

"How's it going, man?" Stas asked dropping into the seat next to him.

"Chugging along," Dylan responded but it was clear that he was losing steam.

"Where are we?"

"We came through Brainerd about-" Dylan checked his watch- "half-hour or so ago. Probably another couple of hours until we get to Big Sandy and Minnewawa."

"Is this thing hard to drive?"

"Not as long as you keep her in the middle of the river and away from either bank."

"How about you let me drive for a minute and you can grab a little shut-eye."

Dylan didn't take much convincing. He talked Stas through a couple of the particulars of the boat and went down below. Stas heard him snoring in a matter of minutes.

<u>3</u>

Sunrise came masked in gray and the day was dark. Heavy clouds hung lazy in the sky above the river as Stas watched the landscape slip by. He checked the GPS and saw that they were now in Bolton County and would be coming to the mouth of the Sandy River within the next fifteen minutes or so.

He was about to holler down into the cabin when he heard movement from below. A few seconds later, Lisa appeared and hauled herself up into the seat next to the captain's chair.

"Are we getting close?" she asked, rubbing the sleep from her eyes.

"Yeah, I was just about to wake you. We'll be to the Sandy River soon, then on to Big Sandy Lake," Stas paused, "but I'm nervous about taking that river. We'll have to go right past Travis Olmstead's place. If you're right about The Devil's Paddle, and I'm right about Olmstead being their conduit to it, boating right by his house this morning might not be the best idea."

She thought about it for a second. "I don't think we have any choice. We'll have to risk it. And it will give us a chance to have a look at the place. No one knows this boat, we should be fine."

Stas nodded but he wasn't so sure. He didn't have a lot of time to dwell on it, though. He checked the GPS and they were now ten minutes from where the Sandy River broke off from the Mississippi.

He looked at Lisa. "We better get Dylan up."

She nodded and went below.

Fifteen minutes later Dylan was at the helm again. Stas and Lisa were back down in the galley which was enclosed and gave them cover. They could see out the windows but no one on shore would be able to see in. Stas watched with multiple emotions striking him as they closed in on the section of the little river where Travis Olmstead's boathouse lay.

Even from some distance they could see people moving about in the boathouse. Stas was sure it wasn't Olmstead, just his lackeys preparing for the evening's events, but he slunk down in his seat a little nonetheless. There was no sign of the struggle between him and Willy Gustafson. He wondered vaguely at Willy's fate but didn't really care. If he hadn't sealed it, Stas got the feeling someone else probably had.

Up on the bridge of the boat the windows were larger, giving more of a view to the interior, and Dylan tossed the customary wave at the people working on Olmstead's dock as they passed. They waved back but otherwise didn't seem all that interested in the boat that was just cruising by on its way to Big Sandy Lake.

Stas breathed a sigh of relief as Olmstead's place disappeared behind the bend at the northernmost point of the river and they headed back down toward the lake. Once it was out of sight, they joined Dylan on the bridge.

"I found us a marina where we can dock close to the lodge on Big Sandy," Dylan said. "But since we hadn't planned on a trip over to Minnewawa we're going to need a course of action."

Lisa nodded. "It's only a mile or so tops between Big Sandy and the Minnewawa Resort but if we're going to go in through the drainage pipe, get Bob and Jane out, and plant a few of these little treats," she said, pointing to the duffel bag under the table, "I don't think walking it will be our best option."

The trio sat in silence, all lost in their own plotting thoughts. Then a slow smile crept across Stas' face.

"I think I might know who could help us," he said.

4

Stas found himself waiting in the parking lot of the Big Sandy Lake Lodge yet again. Yesterday when he'd been here, he'd been expecting to see Bob Gurley pulling in at any second. Instead he hadn't seen him since.

Thanks to Carrie from the Minnewawa (it felt like a hundred years ago that she'd helped him to his cabin), they now knew that both Bob and Jane were being held in Tolbert's stockade. And with a little luck they very soon would be conducting a jailbreak.

Stas watched as a blue Camry pulled into the lot and towards the entrance. It was the one he'd been told to look for. He turned and nodded to Dylan and Lisa seated on one of the benches behind him. They each had a backpack under their legs. One for the detonators and one for the explosives.

The blue Camry pulled up to the front entrance and Stas waved. It slowed and came to a stop then the passenger window slid down. Tammy, the waitress from the café who had originally informed Stas about Debbie Keller, leaned across her passenger seat and greeted him.

"I can honestly say that this is probably the quickest I've ever had someone call in a favor after having just met them," she said.

"I guess I'm probably gonna owe you one, huh?" Stas said through his most charming smile.

"You can buy me dinner someday," Tammy said through her own grin. "But not at Mark's Bar or any crap like that. You can take me somewhere nice, like the Minnewawa."

Stas laughed. "We'll see about that." With any luck the

Minnewawa would be closing shortly, at least until new ownership could be established.

"Oh, yes, we will," Tammy said. "Climb in."

"Thanks." He turned and saw Lisa and Dylan walking over toward the car. Each of them had a pack slung over their shoulder. He turned back to Tammy. "You mind opening the trunk?"

A few minutes later, with the backpacks stowed in the relative safety of the trunk, they were rolling down a rural country highway on their way toward Horseshoe Lake. They would have to pass by the Minnewawa and Stas was beginning to wonder how long their luck would hold if they were going to continue to run around right under the noses of those that were most certainly on the lookout for them.

Tammy continued to pay dividends, though. She actually had a girlfriend that lived on Horseshoe Lake. Her friend was out of town but a quick call to her and they had permission to use her canoe. Swimming out of the culvert to escape Minnewawa under the cover of darkness was one thing. Trying to enter in broad daylight was another.

They drove by the entrance to the Minnewawa Resort and all eyes but the driver's tracked it as they passed. The resort fell away behind them and they all relaxed. A few minutes later Tammy pulled into her friend's driveway and popped the trunk.

Lisa got out quickly and went around the rear of the car. She opened one of the backpacks and pulled out a smaller one from inside. She opened it and removed a black case, handing it to Dylan. Then she opened the other two packs and took several of the contents from each, putting them in the third bag. With the trunk up blocking Tammy's view of them Stas saw Dylan remove a handgun from the case, check the clip, and put it in his belt. Stas closed the trunk as Tammy was getting out of the car.

They had decided Stas would stay back while Lisa and Dylan tried to enter the Minnewawa compound. If anything were to happen to them while inside, Lisa had given Stas very specific instructions about what he was supposed to do. The

Devil's Paddle was not to survive the night, no matter the cost.

They walked through the backyard to the storage rack where the canoe was stowed. They got it in the water and loaded on the backpack.

"You have the radio?" Lisa asked Stas. He held up one of the walkie-talkies that she had purchased on their shopping excursion in Hastings and nodded.

She returned the tip of the head and she and Dylan climbed into the canoe. They pushed off and started to paddle across the water toward where the drainage pipe supposedly emptied into Horseshoe Lake. They slipped away leaving Stas and Tammy standing on the shore.

Tammy turned to Stas. "Any chance you're gonna tell me what you all are up to?"

Stas was silent for a long moment before speaking. "Not until it's done. Once it is though I'll tell you the whole thing." He turned to her with a tired smile, "And then maybe you'll be the one that's going to be writing a book."

5

From deep in the dank darkness of the drainage pipe Carrie watched the canoe slip across Horseshoe Lake toward her. She'd never met the woman paddling across the lake but certainly knew of her; she was a folk-hero of sorts.

As the canoe got close Carrie stepped from the shadows to the edge of the pipe where they could see her. She watched as they located her and adjusted their course toward the culvert. They navigated in abreast of the opening and Carrie helped them out and into the drain pipe.

Once they were out, Carrie stepped back while Lisa and Dylan rotated the canoe and then pulled it as far into the pipe as they could to get it out of view. Three quarters of the way in would have to do. They set it down and Lisa turned to Carrie.

They handled the introductions with a quick efficiency and Carrie explained the situation at the Minnewawa as best she could. Jane and Bob were being held in the little jail which was on the other side of the grounds. They could get there through the woods but would have to be careful as there were alarms and cameras everywhere. Once they were back on the surface Carrie would point them in the right direction and show them how to locate the trip-wire alarms but then she would have to show her face in the compound again. She'd been off the grid too long and someone might notice.

The drainpipe was tall enough that they could stand upright but just barely. With Carrie taking the lead they moved deeper into the pipe towards the ladder that would take them above ground.

"When Jane didn't show up for work yesterday, I knew they'd taken her," Carrie said as they walked. "If they're holding someone, they'll usually feed them around three in the afternoon. That's about fifteen minutes from now, I think that will be your best chance to gain access to the cells."

"Will the person delivering the food be armed?" Lisa asked.

"None of the security people carry openly, but I wouldn't believe for a second that means that they're not, I believe they all have handguns."

They had reached the ladder that led back up to the surface within the confines of the Minnewawa compound. Carrie continued to lead and one by one they climbed up and out, back into the overcast afternoon. Carrie slid the cover into place but didn't camouflage it with foliage.

"I'll leave it uncovered in case you have to try and find it without my help on your way out."

"Thanks," Lisa replied.

"Will you be able to find it again?"

Both Lisa and Dylan looked around, taking in their surroundings. "I think so," Lisa said at last.

"And you're clear on the green prisms denoting the trip-wires?" Lisa nodded. "Good. If you head that way," Carrie pointed north through the woods, "you'll run into the cell block. First you'll pass the security building but that place is a bunker, no windows, so if you stay away from the road and skirt the building to the rear, staying in the woods, you should be fine."

They parted ways imploring each other to stay safe. Carrie headed back towards the heart of the compound, and Lisa and Dylan headed off through the woods. They were new friends, well met, but it was a good thing Lisa had taken a second to make sure she would be able to locate the entrance to the drain pipe again. They were going to have to find it on their own.

6

The building was quiet as a large majority of the men that usually staffed it were elsewhere attending to the evening's business. Michael Childress, the last bastion of Minnewawa Security, sat behind his desk looking over reports.

The phone began to ring and a slight chill tightened the skin on his arms. It could just be Tolbert checking on some last-minute detail. But it could be something else, and any extraneous distractions on the day The Devil's Paddle was set to sail were unwelcome, to say the least.

Childress grabbed the phone, grunting in way of a greeting, and waited for the incoming information.

"Sir," one of the young men from the monitoring room said, "I think you should come have a look at this."

"On my way." Childress hung up the phone. He pushed back from his desk and stood as a creeping unease began its infiltration. He walked down the hall and into the main monitoring room. The kid who had called him already had his hand in the air hailing his boss. "What do you have?" Childress asked, walking across the room to him.

The kid typed in a few commands and two of his monitors jumped to new images. "Don't know that I would have caught it, but my live feed happened to cycle through multiple cameras trained on the Wellness Building at the same time. I'll run them from the same spot in real time so you can watch them both."

He started the video and Childress watched. The first monitor showed the back of the Wellness Building and there was nothing of interest on the screen. The second showed the front corner on the same side and for a moment nothing of interest happened there either. Then a young woman appeared walking towards the front of the building from the back, but she had never been caught by the first camera. Watching both screens at the same time it was as if she had just materialized from thin air.

"Damn," Childress muttered. He tugged at his lip for a moment before slapping the young man on the back. "Good work, son. I guess I'd better go have a chat with that young lady." The jovial act that he had put on for the kid evaporated as he walked toward the stairs. His consternation, on the other hand, was swelling at an alarming speed.

7

Lisa and Dylan slowed as the small brick security building that Carrie had warned them about appeared ahead of them peeking out through the dense forestry. They moved to their right to skirt the building within the safety of the woods along its backside.

As they were veering off a loud buzz emanated from the front of the building. In unison they dropped to a knee, getting low. Lisa made eye contact with Dylan then looked back to the building.

The outer metal door slammed open and working off pure instinct they both dropped again, now down to their stomachs, lying on the forest floor. A man exited the squat brick structure and made a quick glance around his perimeter. It seemed cursory. He climbed into a golf cart that was parked in front of the building, wheeled it around, and sped back down the road out of sight.

Lisa released her breath and shared another glance with Dylan. It had only been a matter of minutes since they had parted ways with Carrie and the hurried exodus of the man from the security headquarters felt like an ill omen. She could afford it little thought. Turning her mind to the matter at hand, she got to her feet. Dylan followed suit and they struck off behind the building with a raised level of caution.

Another five minutes and they began to see the outline of what had to be the cellblock building. They slowed and moved back to their left to get to a position with a view of the entrance.

Lisa checked her watch. Carrie had said that someone would be delivering food to the wards of the cellblock in about fifteen minutes. That was thirteen minutes ago.

8

Carrie made it back to her bunkhouse without incident. She had seen a few people, put on a few forced smiles, and hoped her presence had now been registered and that her absence had not.

Inside she took quick, concise strides down the hall to her own room and shut the door. As the latch snapped into place her resolution slipped. Carrie slumped down onto her bed with her heart beating fast in her chest.

She had always been proud of the small part she played helping Jane get young women out of this place. But the key was that it had been small. Carrie didn't feel she had the courage or strength that Jane did. And now that she was compelled to take on a bigger role in Jane's absence, she was no further convinced of, or confident in, her ability to execute the job.

She was just getting her breath and heartbeat regulated when something outside drew her attention, people talking in the yard. Carrie stepped to her window and moved the shade aside the slightest bit. Her breathing was back under control, but now it stopped altogether, at least for a moment.

One of the other girls from the bunkhouse was exchanging greetings with the man who'd just arrived, Michael Childress. Their voices were muffled but Carrie clearly heard

Childress mention her name and then the girl nodded and pointed toward the bunkhouse entrance.

Panic was upon her in an instant but she fought it with all she had. Carrie grabbed the phone Jane had given her and fired off another quick text. Then she dropped to the floor reaching under her bed. She felt around with a furious abandon until her hand found the little rip in the backing of the box spring.

She slipped the phone into the space behind the little tear and then stood. It wasn't a perfect hiding spot but it was what she had. Carrie ordered her nerves back under control and they acquiesced to some degree. Like the hiding spot for the phone, it wasn't great but would have to do. She sat down on her bed and waited for Michael Childress to knock on her door.

9

Another golf cart pulled up to the little jailhouse and a member of the Minnewawa security force disembarked with whatever would pass as lunch for Jane Devorak and Bob Gurley. From the relative cover of the trees twenty or so yards away Lisa and Dylan watched the guy enter the building.

"Should we go now?" Dylan asked.

"We have to assume the front door is on camera. Maybe we should move down the access road and try and take him on his way out," Lisa replied.

It seemed reasonable but before Dylan could say so, his phone buzzed in his pocket. He thought it odd. If anyone were to be contacting him it would be Stas, but Stas had a radio. He checked the display and his stomach dropped. He held it up for Lisa to read.

It wasn't Stas, it was Carrie, and the text was three short words, simple and to the point: *I'm in trouble.*

"I guess we go now," Lisa said as she stood. She didn't wait for Dylan's response. Instead she gently let the strap of the backpack slip from her shoulder and it settled itself on the ground. Before it had come to a full resting position Lisa was off, making a bee-line for the corner of the building.

She pulled up before rounding the corner to the front of the building where the door was situated. She felt Dylan slip in behind her, where he pressed himself against the wall as well. She turned and saw he had the gun drawn.

She listened for any sound of the sentry exiting the building, all the while feeling the totality of their exposure. She could only imagine a staffer sitting in some basement, staring at a screen, jaw agape, having just watched them appear like wild animals from the woods. He would be stunned for a moment, but only a moment, then he would send up the alarm.

Lisa took a quick peek around the corner. The metal security door would swing outward when opened and the hinges were on the far side. That meant that when the guy left the building, based on the swing of the door, he would have a clear view of the corner that they were hiding just around. She turned back and signaled to Dylan to move. He could round the corner and take up on the far side of the door. From there he would have cover as it swung open. Dylan moved into position and they waited.

It was interminable. Lisa had wound her internal clock as soon as they broke from the trees, imagining their presence had been discovered immediately, and trying to gauge how much time that would give them. She couldn't see the door from her position around the corner so she put her back against the cool bricks of the wall and just listened. She listened for the sound of the lock being tumbled on the security door but also for any approach from the road that led from the compound to the little jailhouse.

No sound registered from either source. She measured her breath and focused. Birds called to each other from hidden spots on tree branches, the overcast sky draped her world in gray. Finally she heard the rattle of keys from the interior of the building as the guard unlocked the door from the inside.

She heard it creak as it started to open. Foregoing thought and giving herself up to action Lisa Lathrop took one last deep breath and stepped around the corner to meet the man exiting the building.

10

The Minnewawa security kid came to an awkward abrupt halt, like he'd walked into an invisible wall, as Lisa stepped out from around the corner. The door swung shut and Dylan was right there behind him. The kid recovered, struggling to find purchase at the small of his back where his firearm was surely holstered, but his dazed, stupefied eyes remained on Lisa.

He was still fumbling for his weapon when the barrel of Dylan's pistol came to rest at the back of his head. The dumb surprise drained from his features being replaced by terror as he realized the reality of his current predicament. The kid stood absolutely still. Lisa couldn't be sure but she thought maybe the young man's eyes had taken on a glassy sheen and that he might be close to tears.

For a moment she almost felt the slightest hint of pity for the kid, for that was all he really was. It didn't last long, though. Brain-washed or not, he worked for and followed people that committed atrocities and broke people's souls.

Instead of doling out her sympathies Lisa Lathrop called upon ten years of kick-boxing fitness experience and doled her fist out into the young man's face. He yelped as his head snapped back smacking into the barrel of Dylan's handgun. It wasn't the smartest move on her part. Dylan could have accidentally shot the guy, tearing the back of his head apart. He didn't, though, he kept his composure and deftly relieved the kid of the weapon holstered at his back. The kid stumbled, attempting to regain his feet.

"Back inside," Dylan said, replacing the barrel of the weapon on the guy's skull.

"Please don't—"

"Shut up," Lisa said. "Are there cameras in there?" The kid shook his head. Lisa gave him a questioning look and Dylan

278

applied some pressure to the back of his head with the barrel of the pistol.

"No cameras…but they monitor audio."

"Alright, if you open your mouth in there Dylan here will shut it for you forever."

Using the gun Dylan directed the young man back into the building and he and Lisa followed him in. The kid followed directions and kept his mouth shut. Dylan held him at gunpoint in the entryway while Lisa relieved him of his keys.

She stepped in front of the cell where Jane Devorak was being held and watched the surprise register in the woman's eyes. Then a broad smile broke across Jane's face and she shook her head. She didn't say a word but she didn't need to. Her actions conveyed her thoughts perfectly: *I should have known it'd be you.*

Lisa returned the smile and started to cycle through the keys. Jane stepped over and with her unbandaged left hand pointed out the one for the cells. Lisa slid it home in the lock and released Jane Devorak. Then she went to the next cell over and laid eyes on Bob Gurley.

Stas had made no mention of the man's shrewd eyes but they were the first thing Lisa noticed about the former sheriff. The thin slight smile turning his lip was genuine though. He clearly realized who she was and seemed pleased to see her.

Lisa opened the cell door and stepped back motioning with her arm, inviting him to exit.

11

Michael Childress escorted the girl, Carrie, to his golf cart. She seemed innocent enough and her story made some sense. Her claim was that she simply saw an injured bird a few feet into the woods and had just gone to investigate. But Childress, much like Stas, had met his fair share of liars and even though he couldn't be certain she was lying something wasn't sitting right.

He wouldn't be taking any chances, not today, not

while the bulk of their security force was otherwise engaged dealing with The Devil's Paddle. So he asked Carrie to take a little ride with him and she had come along without argument. Further review of the tapes would give them all the answers they needed anyway.

Childress turned the cart around and headed back toward the center of the compound. They had a few meeting rooms in the Wellness Building that could also be used as interrogation and holding rooms if they weren't prepared to take a subject directly to the block. They would set Carrie up there while they finished reviewing the tapes.

They had just pulled up in front of the Wellness Building and Carrie seemed to be holding up but was maybe just starting to show some signs of worry. She was fidgeting, just a bit. Childress was about to take her inside when his radio chirped and a disembodied but urgent voice crackled through.

"Headquarters to Childress, we need you back here immediately, we have a code blue. I repeat, code blue."

Jason Tolbert had decided that calling the highest level of emergency a 'code red' was too predictable and could lead to unnecessary panic if called within earshot of others, so he'd opted to go with 'code blue.' Calling one was so rare that Childress could probably count the amount of times it had happened on his fingers. This was a further development he could have done without.

Slightly harried, he looked around. A woman who'd been at the compound for ages, Maria, he thought her name was, came up the steps toward the Wellness Building.

"Take her inside and keep her in the lobby," Childress barked at the woman. She stopped and seemed confused but Carrie started up the steps past her toward the entrance of her own volition and the woman fell in behind her.

Childress hopped back into the golf cart and pushed it to its top speed as he shot across the grounds, radio already in hand.

The second that the cart was out of view around the corner of the building, Carrie turned on her heel and raced back down the steps.

"Wait…" Maria called out meekly, but she was still mostly confused and made no attempt to chase her.

Carrie put her head down and willed her legs to work harder than they ever had before as she ran toward her bunkhouse and the phone that Childress had not looked hard enough to find.

12

Dylan was just breaking from a quick hug with the woman who had been like a mother to him, Jane Devorak, when his phone started to ring, buzzing in his pocket. He returned the barrel of the gun in the direction of the young security staffer and answered the call.

"Yeah," he said quietly while attempting to remain noncommittal.

"It's me," Carrie said. Dylan was quite relieved to hear her voice and not that of some captor.

"Are you okay?" he whispered.

"For now, but I don't think you will be for long."

Lisa had stepped in close to Dylan trying to get a sense of the phone call. Jane and Bob stood side by side, waiting. The security kid remained in the corner, sitting quietly under the unnerving watchful eye of that black abyss that was the exit-hole in the barrel of Dylan's gun.

Dylan looked around quickly and signaled to Bob. Lisa handed him the weapon they had taken off the security kid and turned their prisoner over to the former sheriff. Dylan stepped outside, deciding that it would be better to be seen than heard at this point, since they'd almost certainly showed up on someone's radar by now either way. Jane and Lisa followed him out. Once outside he hit the button for speakerphone and Carrie was still talking. "Childress had me but they just sent out an emergency code and he took off. I can only assume they're on to you."

Jane stepped up to them and spoke. "Carrie, can you

hear me?"

"Jane!" Carrie's voice was choked with emotion and relief.

"Listen, kiddo, remember when we talked about the generator building?"

"Yes."

"Can you get to it?"

"I…I think so."

"Good, I'll meet you there. That building powers everything here including the small cell tower we use. We have to find a way to kill the power. We can't let them make contact with Tolbert."

"I'll be there," Carrie said, and then she was gone.

Jane handed the phone back to Dylan. "We should lock the kid up. They'll hear him hollering as soon as we're gone but I get the feeling they're already well aware that something's afoot."

Dylan nodded and headed back inside to where Bob was holding the kid to get him locked up in one of the cells.

"You need to take out this generator building?" Lisa asked. Jane nodded. "How are you planning to do that?"

Jane shrugged. "No idea, just hope I think of something between here and there."

"Well," Lisa gave her a smile, "I might be able to help you there."

Then she turned and sprinted over to where she had stowed her backpack just inside the woods.

13

The sky was still overcast but it had lightened, giving the slightest hint that the cloud cover might break at some point. Stas only noticed this peripherally as he stared across Horseshoe Lake at the shadowy mouth of the drainage pipe into the depths of which Lisa had disappeared. It felt like it had been hours since the canoe slid out of his view into the darkness, but it had only been about twenty minutes.

Tammy had wandered back up toward her car to make a phone call leaving Stas alone in her friend's backyard. That was fine with him. Her willingness to help had been amazing and he probably should be being more effusive with his thanks and the divulgence of information, but it wasn't in his nature under normal circumstances and today was far from normal.

Another couple of minutes slipped by, twisting the ball of anxiousness in his gut even further. He thought about trying to raise them on the radio but was nervous that he'd do it at the wrong time and somehow get them caught. He forced himself to restrain. The radio was for emergencies only and this wasn't an emergency, at least not yet.

That certainty only lasted for a few seconds and then the sound of multiple small explosions rippled across the lake from the direction of the Minnewawa. It wasn't a huge whomping sound accompanied by a giant fireball, just a couple of rolling cracks of unnatural thunder. Tendrils of black smoke began to slip into the sky above the tree line from over where the compound was situated.

"What the hell was that?" Tammy asked as she came jogging back down the short slope of her friend's backyard toward Stas.

"For better or worse, that was probably my friends announcing their presence." Stas lifted the walkie-talkie to his mouth but still hesitated for a second, waiting to see if Lisa would contact him first. Nothing happened and he was about to give in and press the push-to-talk button when Tammy stopped him with an exclamation.

"There!"

Stas followed the line of her pointing finger back out toward the drainage pipe. The canoe had reappeared and was being frenetically paddled back across the lake. There were only two people on board, though. Stas was quite happy to see Lisa paddling with all her might. Not only because he was worried for her but also because he wasn't entirely certain he was up to handling the business of the deconstruction of The Devil's Paddle on his own.

On the flip side, the other occupant of the canoe was causing him some further unease. It wasn't that he was unhappy to see Dylan, but he was anxious to lay eyes on Bob Gurley again.

14

The woods whipped by as they ran, their feet pounding through the brush as fast as their legs could manage. And then suddenly her hand would go up and stop them. Jane Devorak would take a few slow steps and then point out the trip-wire to Bob. He would step over with great caution, and then the race would be back on. This process repeated itself a number of times.

Of course, Jane had the little green fake ash-borer prisms to locate the wires, but she didn't really need them. She knew these woods like the back of her hand and where each and every one of them lay.

As soon as they'd taken to the woods, they had heard the approach of the golf carts on the road leading to the jailhouse. At least one of those carts would be manned by Michael Childress.

In reality the plan to destroy The Devil's Paddle and the rest of Whittier's empire should have already been thwarted. Childress should have contacted Tolbert and Tolbert should have deemed the night's run too risky. But Jane was confident that hadn't happened yet.

Sometimes dealing with the arrogance of cocky men who couldn't truly fathom their own demise was an advantage all its own. Childress wouldn't have been able to admit to Tolbert that he'd somehow lost control of Minnewawa on this, maybe the most important day of their whole cause. And in turn, even if he had, she didn't think Tolbert would be able to bring himself to cancel tonight's run of The Devil's Paddle. Not when he would be supremely confident in his own ability to thwart them. But they'd already, once upon a time, underestimated Anne Callahan. And Jane believed more and more that they would inevitably make the mistake of underestimating Lisa Lathrop as well.

Jane and Bob came to a halt just outside a small clearing where another small building stood. It was the generator building. If they could knock out the power and the small cell tower, the cameras would be down and communication between Childress and Tolbert would be eliminated.

Jane scanned the building and its surroundings. Her eyes kept moving and she didn't look at Bob as she spoke. "You didn't need to come with me, you know. You could have gotten out of here."

Bob chuckled, "If anything had happened to you after I left you here, I don't think my wife would ever speak to me again." He paused. "Course, what she doesn't realize is that you'll do a better job protecting me than I will you."

Jane turned to him and gave him a wry smile. Then it dropped away as quick as it had come and she crouched down. Bob echoed her action. She'd heard something. They crouched in silence for a long moment, then Jane gave out a sing-song whistle.

Silence.

Then the whistle was returned from the trees on the other side of the clearing. Jane straightened up and stepped out from the woods, Bob following behind her. From the far side Carrie stepped out to join them.

The two women met in the middle, shared a quick arm hug, and then turned their attention to the building. Bob stepped in next to them.

After a quick examination it became clear that Minnewawa security either didn't think anybody knew this place housed their power source or just never feared that something like today's events could happen. The door had none of the security features of some of the other buildings. It was locked with a simple deadbolt.

"Stand back a bit," Bob said as he raised the pistol that they had taken off the young security guy before locking him up. "It might ricochet."

Jane and Carrie stepped back and Bob fired two quick shots into the door. The lock disintegrated and Bob stepped forward, pushing the door open while keeping the gun trained in front of him.

Jane turned to Carrie. "You stay here and let us know if you hear anyone coming." Carrie nodded and then Jane stepped into the darkened interior of the building.

Two large generators dominated the room.

"Any idea what the best way to go about this is?" Bob asked. Jane shook her head in response. Bob walked one way around the generators and Jane went down the middle between the two.

"Hey," Jane called out from in between. "They've each got an electrical panel, like a control panel, on them. Maybe we can short them out. It seems as good a place to start as any."

Bob hustled around to meet her. As he went by, in the back corner, he saw a large breaker box. The conduit ran up and out of the ceiling. It had to be the power for the cell tower.

"How many of those flash-bangs did Lisa give ya?" Bob asked, coming around the generator to where Jane stood.

"Four." Jane was eyeing up the control panel.

"One more than we need, I think. Let's put one on each of the control panels and one on the breaker box I just saw in the back."

Jane nodded and set the backpack on the floor. With her good hand that was showing just the slightest tremor Jane removed three of the little C-4 packs and handed them to Bob to hold. One at a time, she connected the little timer detonators to the explosive the way Lisa had shown her. The tutorial had been a quick one and Jane could only hope she'd actually soaked up all the correct information. She looked up at Bob and saw that he was starting to sweat.

Jane stretched her arms across between the generators to see if she could reach them both and found she could. "Set two of them for two minutes and stick them to the control panels on the generators," she told Bob. "Set the other for two minutes and five seconds and take it back to the breaker box.

Give me a signal when you're going to start it." She had begun to sweat as well.

Bob nodded, wiped his brow, and left for the breaker. Jane unwrapped the bandage from her damaged hand and stretched her arms again ready, to press the timers.

Bob rounded the back of the generator and lost sight of her. He went to the breaker box and attached the little device. He set the timer with a finger that shook a tad bit more than slightly.

Bob Gurley took a very deep breath. He exhaled slow, centering himself, and then yelled, "Now!" He pressed the button starting the timer and ran, following Jane Devorak back out into the murky daylight.

The River...
Spring, 2017

1

The fifty-foot blade of the giant stern paddle hit the water and thrust its way through, rounding on its revolution and coming back out on the other side. Muddy river water ran from the enormous bright-red float as it circled up through the air and then back down into the river, propelling The Devil's Paddle onward.

The lavish watercraft had been built in the nostalgic fashion of the paddle steamers that had cruised the Mississippi in the late nineteenth century. The Devil's Paddle was powered by large diesel engines, though, as opposed to the steam power that propelled those early ships.

At nearly two hundred and fifty feet long and with three luxurious decks she was a sight to behold. But only a select few were ever actually allowed to take in her grandeur. The main deck housed a saloon and lounge with a full bar, dance floor and multiple sitting areas. The second was for gaming, built in the style of the old riverboat casinos. The operation of such an establishment was highly illegal. The third and topmost deck was comprised of private cabins that would also be made available to The Paddle's select clientele.

Many of the power players that were on board for these

little excursions came without their spouses and liked to enjoy each other's company. That it was just this sort of behavior that had originally indebted most of them to Cortland Whittier in the first place were ruminations most of them had long ceased to contemplate. What was done was done. And if a little of their integrity was the only price for being a part of this lifestyle and keeping their salaciousness secret, so be it.

The guests would not begin arriving for another half hour or so and the final preparations were being attended to. The women of The Council handled almost all aspects of the operations aboard The Devil's Paddle, occasionally including the entrapment of some of the new guests. They were gliding about making sure all would function smoothly. Every trip this boat made was important but today's sailing outweighed them all. The instructions were clear. Mayor Sammy Douglas was to be brought into the fold at any cost.

The day remained overcast, but the cloud cover seemed to be thinning and the air temperature above the river had shifted. A light mist was starting to form above the water.

Cortland Whittier sat sipping a whiskey on one of the couches in the saloon lounge. Sitting across a small table from him with a glass of his own was Ted Logan.

Logan had returned to McGregor the previous evening after collecting a somewhat cowed and limping Aaron Tolbert. The younger Tolbert's failings of the night before had been nearly catastrophic. But since he had managed to escape, and the car he had been using had technically been stolen, the authorities would have no way to connect him to what transpired outside that strip club. Under other circumstances Logan may have seen fit to punish Aaron further but now they both needed their focus on the night's events to come.

"In about a half hour people should begin arriving," he said to Whittier. "Olmstead will bring the first load of 'virgin' guests in an hour."

Those who had already been initiated, who had already succumbed to Whittier's powers of persuasion, would arrive on their own. They were, by now, familiar with the process. Those visiting The Devil's Paddle for the first time, though, were always brought in by Olmstead.

Whitter nodded. "But not Mayor Douglas, he doesn't arrive until even later."

"Correct." They wanted the festivities well under way when the Mayor of Minneapolis first laid eyes on the lavish ship. "Douglas and his people will arrive at Olmstead's place. They'll have a cocktail and then Travis will return and join them for a quick dinner. At dinner he'll lay out the final details and then, assuming there are no last-minute reservations, he'll bring the mayor here."

"You've done your due diligence though," Whittier said. "There won't be any last-minute reservations, will there?" His voice was stern and authoritative.

"No, he'll join us here. And once he's here, he might think he can still back out, but we both know better than that." Logan punctuated the statement with a wicked grin. "So, after dinner they'll board The Delivery and join us," Logan raised his glass, "and by tomorrow morning you'll be on the short-list of people consulted when it comes time to choose the next Chief of Police in Minneapolis."

Whittier raised his own glass and they both drank. On the water a speedboat cut through the forming mist carrying Jason and Aaron Tolbert. The speedboat zipped past them, sending a small wake curling toward the whitewall sides of The Devil's Paddle. Whittier and Logan followed it with their eyes as it continued further downriver.

<u>2</u>

The wind whipped around them as the Tolbert brothers made their way downriver. They'd come from the northern checkpoint where the river would be closed.

The Devil's Paddle's voyage would be a slow tour up and down a ten mile stretch of the river. Another two and a half miles beyond, in either direction, a Bolton County Sheriff's Department boat would be anchored and manned by trusted deputies. There wasn't generally much traffic on this part of the Mississippi anyway but tonight there would be none, unless they were there by invitation. No one without the proper credentials would pass the Bolton County deputies while The Paddle was in service.

The Sheriff of Bolton County would be present this evening but not aboard either of the boats provided by his office. The Sheriff would be reveling with the other luminaries just as he had been for the last fifteen years. Since the very first time he boarded The Devil's Paddle with Travis Olmstead, at Whittier's invitation, he'd been seduced by the ship and all it offered and had welcomed the opportunity to become a willing cog in Whittier's machine.

Jason Tolbert got to his feet and moved to the bow of the speedboat as his brother Aaron pulled back on the throttle and they eased in next to the craft that loudly pronounced along its bow to be the property of the Bolton County Sheriff's Department.

"Evening, deputy," Jason called out as they approached.

"Evening," the deputy replied with a tip of his hat.

Jason Tolbert passed over a scanner and a mock-up of the invites that had gone out for the evening's proceedings. Each invitation had a specific barcode to be scanned that would log each guest as they passed the checkpoint. With the exception of those coming in with Olmstead on The Devil's Delivery, everyone had to have an invitation. The scanner also had a slot running along the side to slide their ID's so that every single person boarding would be accounted for.

Having dispensed the scanners to the Sheriff's Department boats at both checkpoints the Tolberts headed back upriver. For the rest of the night they would continue to circle the fifteen mile stretch of river making contact with their own people posted at security points along both shores as well as with the deputies. This was standard protocol, but tonight Logan had put them on a heightened alert. Stas Mileski shouldn't know anything about The Paddle but he had continued to prove to be quite pesky, and while they had managed to keep him chasing his tail they had not managed to secure his elimination from the equation.

Twenty minutes later the first boat belonging to a guest passed the Sheriff's checkpoint on the south end of the run cordoned off for The Devil's Paddle, and the night was underway.

The Tolberts paid no attention to any of the arriving watercraft as they continued to make their laps. If they were inside the loop they had already been vetted. Jason and Aaron Tolbert focused on the shoreline, waiting at each checkpoint for the signal from their men that all was clear.

On their third circuit as they came around and passed The Paddle, it was clear that the revelry had begun in earnest.

3

Tammy delivered the trio of Stas, Lisa, and Dylan back to the marina near the Big Sandy Lodge where they had docked their boat. With a smile, she had admonished Stas one last time, making it clear she still expected a dinner and the full story at some point in the near future. Stas agreed easily to her terms. If he made it through the rest of this evening alive, he'd be more than happy to take her to dinner.

Now, as the sun neared setting and twilight was on the come, they were cruising across Big Sandy Lake toward the Sandy River and Travis Olmstead's house.

The forming mist wasn't dense on the lake, barely even there, but once they were on the little tributary that led out to the Mississippi it had begun to pool over the water. The land wasn't being affected so far, but the little bit of cover it provided on the water was more than welcome.

About a quarter mile before they hit the northern bend of the river and Olmstead's boathouse, Dylan located a sandier section of the shoreline and brought the trawler in as close as he could to the land. Stas and Lisa jumped across the small gap and darted off into the woods. Dylan remained with the boat and in radio contact.

After a short jog along the shoreline, but staying within the trees, Stas saw the looming outline of Olmstead's boathouse. He slowed but continued to creep toward the structure signaling to Lisa to hold up and wait as he did so. The boathouse butted right up against the trees so he didn't have to break his cover, but the sidewall stretched far enough out over the water that he couldn't see around it to where any of the boats would have been docked.

Walking across the yard down to the entry arch with absolutely no cover from the house was not an option. He could tell from where he stood that there was a flurry of activity up at Olmstead's residence. The staff seemed to be readying themselves for the arrival of guests.

Stas skirted the sidewall toward the river, getting as close to the water and the mist drifting above it as he could. He knew from his previous time here that the boat he was interested in, The Devil's Delivery, should have been docked just opposite that sidewall that he was squatting next to. Even though the wall extended out over the water, Stas now had enough of an angle to know that the little yacht wasn't there. Armed with that knowledge he slipped back through the trees to where Lisa was waiting.

"The boat's gone," he told her. "Olmstead must be out on the big river already. From the activity up at the house it looks like they're still expecting people though. I assume he'll have to be coming back to get them."

"We should get up to the front and see if we can find out who they might be waiting for."

Stas nodded and, staying deep enough in the trees to remain camouflaged, they crept toward the front of the house. The parking area, so empty when it had been only Stas' truck sitting alone there yesterday, was now dotted with a handful of very nice vehicles. For the moment no one was arriving and some valets were hanging out near the front entrance to the mansion. Stas and Lisa established a position with adequate cover and waited.

Twenty minutes later two Cadillac Escalades came

down the driveway into the parking area and the valets sprang into action. They met the vehicles as they came to a stop, opening the rear doors for the new arrivals. A handful of men in suits exited the vehicles. One of the valets pointed over toward the garages, directing the drivers to where they could park. The Cadillacs pulled away and Stas and Lisa had a clear view of all four of the men standing at the entrance to Travis Olmstead's house.

"I'll be damned," Stas muttered.

"What is it?" Lisa asked under her breath.

"The tall guy in the back, wearing the black suit with the purple tie." Stas paused to make sure she knew who he was talking about.

She nodded. "Is that who I think it is?"

"Yes ma'am, that's Sammy Douglas, the Mayor of Minneapolis."

Lisa made a staccato scoffing sound. "Unbelievable."

The mayor and his men entered the residence and then things outside changed quickly. The valets left their post at the door and disappeared toward the garage. They were replaced by a member of the Minnewawa security staff. Another man stepped out onto the veranda on the side of the house that led to Olmstead's study. Stas could only believe that the backyard and far side of the mansion would be manned by security as well. Unlike on the Minnewawa grounds, here they no longer made any attempt to obscure the fact that they carried weapons. Each of them had an assault-style rifle in their hands.

Stas gave Lisa a look. She returned it while drawing the Glock that she had taken from Dylan. She looked down at the handgun that now seemed quite small compared to the rifles and shrugged.

The distant purr of a motor drifted up from down by the river, taking hold of their attention. It came from the side of the bend in the Sandy River that led out to the Mississippi. Dylan was on the other side, the one that led back toward the lake. They both turned their heads toward the sound.

The mist hadn't crept up into the yard but was just

lying, light and soft, above the little river. Thirty seconds later an unformed shape appeared. Another thirty seconds and it began to solidify. Olmstead's trawler yacht, The Devil's Delivery, took form as it slipped from the mist.

They only had sight of it for a moment before it drifted from view behind the boathouse. Lisa and Stas shared another tense glance.

A few minutes later Travis Olmstead appeared in the archway that led from the boathouse to the yard. Stas had never seen him but there was no question that this man owned this house. Stas had known immediately when looking upon Willy Gustafson in that same boathouse that he hadn't belonged here. Travis Olmstead, on the other hand, exuded the wealth and privilege that had put him in a position to build this monument to excess in the middle of nowhere.

The kid with the rifle on the veranda was also looking down toward the water as Olmstead approached. Another man, presumably guarding the back door, walked out into their view and greeted Olmstead. The two walked toward the rear of the house and back out of Stas and Lisa's line of sight.

The mist on the water and the overcast sky gave the world an eerie countenance as, behind those clouds, the sun dipped into the horizon line.

McGregor...
Spring, 2017

1

After the dull roar of the manufactured thunder an eerie quiet fell over the grounds of the Minnewawa compound. Childress was shocked into disbelief for no more than five seconds before reality took hold again. That faux thunder had been an explosion. The whole world was going to hell on his watch and he was furious.

The kid that Childress had found locked in the jail cell when he arrived had been no help. He had no idea where Devorak had gone after relieving him of his firearm and locking him up. The only thing he did know was that she had help and, from the rough description the kid had given Childress, it sounded like said help may have come from Anne Callahan.

If she was here, today, back on these grounds, there would be enough hell-fire going around to be rained upon all of their heads ten times over, but Childress felt he'd get the brunt of it. It had been him after all that lost the proverbial ship, lost the Minnewawa.

He had been finishing up his quick interrogation of the kid out in front of the cellblock building when the explosion happened. He knew where it had originated from the second he heard it.

Through his anger, for half of a second, he felt a

momentary sliver of reluctant respect for Jane Devorak. She had lived here all these years, right under their noses. She had gone unnoticed. Occasionally people had disappeared and he and Tolbert never knew how it happened. And now she was back at it, being a busy little bee again, and she'd somehow managed to wipe out their power. But his momentary esteem did not last; it was gone and the fury was back. His short stint of respect would only enhance his elation when the moment arrived to kill her.

He tore off into the woods on the cart leaving his other security staff behind. He was a lone man on a singular mission now being driven by a blind rage.

The cart bumped and jerked and jumped on the path leading out to the generator building. It was not as well manicured as the other roads, being rarely travelled. He could see black smoke, getting thicker by the minute, drifting up into the air in the distance as he approached.

Minutes later he came upon the generator building in flames. And standing right in front of it were Jane Devorak and her friend, Carrie.

He let the anger consume him and he drove the cart straight toward them without slowing. Running at its top speed for so long had left the little cart in revolt and steering with one hand on this rutted track was becoming difficult. He could only afford one hand on the wheel, though. The other was retrieving his holstered firearm.

He drew and tried to sight it on Jane's forehead as he jostled along. She still held her air of confidence but he could see fear infiltrating her eyes as he closed the distance between them while showing no signs of slowing. His finger was just about to tense, squeezing the trigger, when the hand it was attached to disintegrated.

He hadn't heard the other gunshot, nor did he feel the pain until after his hand had disappeared tossing chunks of bone and gristle and a red syrupy spray into the air. The gun clanged off the running board of the golf cart before bouncing harmlessly out into the grass.

For one precious second, he thought that he would maintain his momentum long enough to strike down Jane Devorak and at least be able to derive that little bit of pleasure from this boondoggle. But as he lost control of the cart it pulled to the left, hit a bump and overturned, dumping him out hard into the gravel and crabgrass. His head hit the ground with a resounding thud.

He tried to push himself up but he was woozy and his right arm was no longer capped by a hand. It was just a gory mess and he listed to that side, slumping back down in the dirt.

With unfocused eyes he looked up and saw Bob Gurley appear in his field of vision, training a pistol on him that had come from one of his own security people.

Smoke billowed, and feeling the heat of the flames climbing the walls of the generator building, Childress closed his eyes. He felt dizzy and was having difficulty connecting his thoughts. The only thing that did remain clear was that the ship was sinking, and he was to blame.

The River...
Spring, 2017

1

Dinner had finished without a hitch. Olmstead's people performed their duties immaculately. Conversation had been light-hearted. The Mayor, Sammy Douglas, spoke throughout the meal with an air of duplicity, still unwilling to cross any legal lines out loud. Douglas was a very polished politician, but in the years that he had been working for the man, Logan had prepped him as to what might be available outside the lines, and had vetted his interest. Sammy Douglas had not come all the way up here tonight to get cold feet now.

Travis Olmstead had no worries that they would be able to close the deal as he ushered the small party across his back lawn and down to his awaiting yacht. Once they were on The Devil's Paddle it would be out of his hands. The Paddle closed deals with an unrivaled efficiency.

With after-dinner drinks in hand Sammy Douglas and his small consortium boarded Travis's yacht, and they headed down the Sandy River toward the Mississippi. Night had fallen and the mist had lifted.

The ride took about twenty minutes before the first Bolton County Sheriff's Department boat came into view. From the helm Olmstead gave the deputies a nod and they returned it. The men on board Olmstead's vessel were the guests of honor and need not be checked in. Quietly they slipped inside the temporarily cordoned section of the Mighty Mississippi.

Boats belonging to the other guests were anchored in various spots along the shoreline. Everyone but Olmstead's passengers boarded The Devil's Paddle at the southern end of her run. At first those boats were the only thing to see aside from the river unfurling before them. From the distance came the sound of a speedboat. Soon after, it materialized and Olmstead nodded again to Jason and Aaron Tolbert as the two ships passed. Seconds later Olmstead's radio crackled into life.

"They're just around the next bend about a mile or so up," Jason Tolbert informed him. Olmstead called down to the men enjoying their cocktails in the sitting area below to come up and join him. They did so and Travis navigated around the next bend.

The grandeur and extravagance that was The Devil's Paddle appeared before them lit from bow to stern. Olmstead stole a glance at Mayor Douglas and was pleased with what he saw, a shrewd excitement. That was how it always started. Tolbert had radioed ahead to Logan letting them know that they were close and The Paddle had come to a stop awaiting its very special guest.

Travis Olmstead deftly guided his trawler in next to The Paddle at its entry point. Whittier and Logan were there waiting to greet Mayor Sammy Douglas and his small entourage. They boarded The Devil's Paddle and shook hands with the men waiting for them.

Olmstead pulled away and brought the boat around. He'd head upriver a bit and drop anchor. Then he'd wait for the Tolberts next pass to catch a lift over and join the festivities.

His guests had been unloaded, but what Travis Olmstead didn't realize as he pulled away from the lavish paddle steamer was that he was not alone aboard The Devil's Delivery.

2

"Good evening, Mayor. Welcome aboard The Devil's Paddle," Ted Logan said, greeting the man who paid his salary. Logan only had one boss, whom he now introduced to the mayor. "I'd like you to meet an old friend of mine, Cortland Whittier."

Mayor Sammy Douglas took and shook the proffered hand. "It's good to be here, Mr. Whittier. Thank you for having us."

"The pleasure is all mine, Mayor. Let's get you a drink."

"That sounds fantastic." The two men shared a smile.

Beneath them the diesel engines fired and the giant paddle at the stern of the vessel began to turn again.

Logan led Sammy Douglas and his men over toward the bar. As Whittier turned to follow, he noticed that Olmstead had stopped his boat just a short way down the river. He was right in the middle, not heading to the shoreline to anchor.

It was a bit odd but Whittier gave it little thought. Instead he stepped over to where the others stood at the bar as two more men joined the group.

"Mayor Douglas," Whittier said, "may I introduce Brian Larson, the Bolton County Sheriff, and I believe you already know our former prosecutor, and now state senator, Mr. Joseph Randall."

Again, a round of glad-handing transpired.

"Senator Randall, I hear you're mulling a run for the U.S. Senate?" Sammy Douglas asked the former prosecutor of Bolton County.

"We'll have to see, Mayor," Randall replied through an easy laugh.

Logan stepped in, steering the conversation as he returned with the drinks. "Gentlemen, might I suggest we head upstairs and maybe throw some dice?" Logan knew Sammy Douglas enjoyed a toss at the craps table. Throwing dice was not legal gaming in Minnesota and it was the mayor's interest in it that originally sparked the chain of events that eventually led him to be here tonight, and in turn quite possibly involving himself in other untoward acts.

Logan began guiding the men among the other guests milling in the lounge toward the elegant circular staircase at the bow of The Devil's Paddle. At the same time, Whittier glanced out the port side and saw again what he had ignored a moment ago but which now piqued his curiosity.

The Devil's Delivery had stopped in the middle of the river but was now coming around to the back of The Devil's Paddle and trolling up along the other side of the boat. He wondered what Travis was doing, but he wasn't alarmed.

Thirty seconds later, though, when the thunderclap of an explosion reverberated from further up the river, Cortland Whittier's easy, arrogant demeanor shifted.

3

Travis Olmstead had just cleared the starboard corner of The Paddle's stern when he heard something right behind him. It was just a slight rustle but he turned and found himself staring down the barrel of Lisa Lathrop's Glock. Standing next to her with a malicious grin on his face was Stas Mileski.

Olmstead shifted his eyes back down to his console, gauging his chances of being able to reach the toggle for the radio to signal the Tolberts. He turned his eyes back to the gun thinking he would have to risk it, but even his little glance hadn't gone unnoticed and any chance he may have had to make a move evaporated.

Lisa took another step toward him and pushed the barrel of the Glock into his eye socket. She had his undivided attention but still she drove it in a little further as a point of emphasis. Olmstead's eyeball felt as if it were about to burst.

"Without even thinking about touching that radio, why don't you bring us around to the other side of that boat, Travis," Stas said to him.

Then Mileski lifted a walkie-talkie to his mouth, pressed the push-to-talk and said, "Stas to Dylan."

The little radio squawked, "Dylan here."

"It's time."

Neither of them had released Olmstead from their gaze during the exchange and Lisa had not relieved any of the pressure from the barrel of the gun on his eyeball.

There was another bout of static from the walkie-talkie and Dylan said, "Copy that, I have the Sheriff's Department in sight and in range."

<u>4</u>

Deputy Saunders was bored and ornery. For the last two hours he'd done nothing but swipe IDs and scan invitations and tell people that thought they were better than him to enjoy their night. He hated this detail. But he had gotten himself busted stealing pot from the evidence room a couple years back and instead of losing his job, he now found himself sitting on this boat every time the Sheriff went on one of these excursions.

To make matters worse he had to spend the whole night anchored here with Erickson. Erickson wasn't a bad guy but he had some kind of gastrointestinal disorder and wouldn't stop farting. So Saunders spent the night sharing in the stench of his partner's emissions while those uppity politicians shared in far better spoils.

Everyone on the guest list had arrived so now they would sit here for the rest of the night. Sit and wait for the elites to have their fun and then leave.

"Whoa, you see that?" Erickson asked, shaking Deputy Saunders from the comfortable confines of his crabbiness.

He turned and looked to where Erickson was pointing and saw the green and red lights indicating the port and starboard sides of a vessel that was practically on top of them.

"Sunovabitch," Deputy Saunders barked. "Hit the spotlight, you fool."

Erickson flipped on the spotlight and lit up the trawler that had managed to creep right up on top of their boat. It wasn't more than fifteen feet away. There was a lone man at the helm.

"Halt," Saunders hollered at him.

"Whoa! Evening deputies, didn't even see you there."

"The river's closed on Sheriff's business," Saunders said, regarding the man with a wary eye and leaving his right hand resting on the butt of his firearm. "I'm afraid you're going to have to turn around."

"Even if I have one of these?" the man asked, holding something up.

Deputy Saunders couldn't tell what the guy had in his hand, only that it definitely wasn't one of the invites.

"Dammit," the guy on the boat said. "It's backward."

He turned whatever it was in his hand around and both Saunders and Erickson recognized it at the same time. They registered the little red digital number on the detonator's timer as it switched from 7 seconds to 6. Then the guy flipped it easily and accurately through the air towards their Bolton County Sheriff's Department boat.

Deputy Saunders watched in horror while subconsciously ticking off the seconds as the little package hurtled across the space between them.

Without the need of any command both he and Erickson abandoned ship simultaneously. Deputy Saunders dove into the cold river and was still underwater when the small explosion ripped their boat in half.

5

Jason Tolbert snapped his head around, meeting the gaze of his younger brother across the speedboat. Both men knew what they had just heard, but operating with little to no resistance for most of their careers now left them in a momentary state of disbelief.

Their current location was north of The Paddle and the explosion had come from the south. Jason Tolbert was not about to panic, it wasn't in his nature. He brought his radio to his mouth and tried to raise the Bolton County Deputies at the southern end of the cordon. When he received no response his level of anxiety began to rise.

He switched to the channel that his men staked out along the shoreline were using and at that moment, everything turned. His men were in full chatter. Something had happened on shore.

"This is Tolbert, everyone shut up. Miller, report."

The order was taken, his men quieted, and then his radio squawked and Miller began to speak. "We've got a convoy of Sheriff's vehicles approaching on the closest access road to the west bank of the river. They're coming from the north, headed south. They're coming in hard, lights and sirens."

"What the hell are you talking about? We own the Sheriff's Department, they're already here."

"It's not Bolton, sir. They're all coming from Castle County."

Jason Tolbert's stomach dropped into his shoes as he was assaulted by a feeling he was utterly unfamiliar with. He was experiencing genuine panic.

Castle County was the former jurisdiction of Bob Gurley. There could be no chance of coincidence. Their presence meant that Gurley had been able to make contact with them, and that left one conclusion. Bob had somehow escaped Childress and serious trouble was now afoot.

"Get us to The Paddle," he muttered to his younger brother as he fought back the panic to make room for a burgeoning anger.

Aaron Tolbert opened up the throttle.

6

Many of the guests that were still in the lounge on the first deck, and not upstairs gaming or involving themselves in other activities, were looking to each other with questioning glances having no reference for the source of the reverberating boom. Logan ran to the rail to try to get a view downriver around the huge stern paddle at the back of the boat.

Cortland Whittier kept watch on Travis Olmstead's boat as it drifted back closer and closer to the far side of The Devil's Paddle, well aware that something had gone amiss. He turned to Sheriff Larson and Joseph Randall who were still standing with the mayor at the foot of the staircase to the second deck.

"Get me Tolbert right now." He didn't raise his voice. He didn't need to. The sheriff bolted for the bar where they kept the radios.

Whittier shared a quick glance with Logan at the side rail that spoke volumes without the necessity of a single word. Then he turned back to Olmstead's boat, which was now right alongside The Paddle. He turned in time to see a woman he remembered well leap lithely from Olmstead's vessel onto his. He had shared the bond of marriage with that woman a long time ago. He knew her as Anne Callahan then but now her name was Lisa Lathrop.

There had been something special about her. She had a fierceness that would have served him well on the Council. He should have known better, though, even then when she was young. If she wasn't with you, she was going to be trouble. When Anne Callahan had shown no interest in the Council and the life he could have provided her, she should have been eliminated.

The rest of the lemmings that made up his guests were milling about discussing possible sources of the mysterious thundering sound that had just cut through the night. They seemed perhaps a bit perturbed, but none of them quite grasped the fact that their lives were about to be torn apart.

Whittier knew better. That woman had just set foot on The Devil's Paddle and no matter how this ended it was already too far gone to be clean. They weren't getting out of this unscathed, that much was already clear. But Cortland Whittier had no problem sacrificing the lives and careers of the people on this boat.

He watched across the expanse of the lounge, through

the milling crowd, as she stuck something to the housing that held and turned the giant paddle at the stern of his most prized possession.

Their eyes met and in hers he saw a raw hate. It excited and terrified him at the same time. This was going to be the beautiful disaster he had been waiting for since the day she left. He wasn't even worried that all he'd built could be in jeopardy. They'd burned Norumbega down once before only for him to rebuild it bigger and better. Whether it played out that way again or not, if it ended with Anne Callahan's lifeless body lain before him he could make peace with that. He took a step in her direction.

At that moment the speedboat carrying the Tolbert brothers ripped by on his right, racing from bow to stern toward Olmstead's boat.

Lisa Lathrop did not hesitate. She lifted a handgun and started firing at the speedboat. There was a short, intense exchange of gunfire and then the speedboat tore away again back around the giant red paddle and out of his view.

And at last, the full scale of the madness began to erupt. The gunshots finally waking the sheep to a fact that the explosion had not. The dark night was full of wolves and the wolves were coming for them. Screams were loosed and chaos ensued.

With an intense and not entirely unpleasant rage encapsulating him, Cortland Whittier forgot about all else. He forgot about Logan, he forgot about Mayor Sammy Douglas. He was consumed by her, his hate and desire twined so tight they became one.

The quick shootout had ended and their eyes met again. They began to walk toward each other even as people ran screaming all around them. But they had only taken a few steps when another small but potent explosion ripped from the little device she had planted on the stern paddle's housing.

She smiled and behind her the elaborately decorated casing that held up that side of the paddle crumbled. For a second afterward another dumbfounded silence descended, even the screaming ceased, and still she came for him. Then the shrieking of twisting metal and cracking of lumber cut the surprised silence as the giant paddle ripped free from its tether and with an enormous rumbling crash splashed heavily down into the river.

The brief respite was over and the pandemonium resumed and ratcheted further. Cortland Whittier's eyes remained riveted on her until they were torn away as a fleeing guest smashed into him and knocked him off his feet.

7

Stas had literally hit the deck when the gunfire began, dropping to the floor of the bridge of Olmstead's boat, The Devil's Delivery. He heard Jason Tolbert's speedboat take off and he stood back up. In the few seconds that his attention was elsewhere, Olmstead had disappeared, somewhere down into the yacht's cabin.

Stas turned to track Lisa's movements and saw her starting across the expansive main floor of the giant paddle boat, but then he was derailed again. The small explosion ripped through the night dropping the enormous paddle into the river, and the displacement of water it caused pushed Olmstead's boat away from The Devil's Paddle.

Stas lost his footing and it was a lucky thing he did. A bullet whizzed past him and would have torn apart his shoulder had he been standing upright.

Olmstead had come back up from below and was in the sitting area at the rear of the main deck attempting to point a handgun in his direction. Olmstead had lost his footing as well when the boat was rocked but was in the process of regaining it and again sighting Stas with his weapon.

Stas dropped into the Captain's chair and slammed the throttle forward. At the same time he cranked the ship's wheel to the right and the desired effect was achieved. The sudden jolt and change of direction sent Olmstead reeling again, this time into the sidewall. It caught him under the arm, right at the

308

rib cage, and with a weak grunt he dropped the gun to the floor of the boat.

Stas leapt from the helm down into the sitting area, landing on top of Olmstead and crunching his already tender ribs against the sidewall again. Stas heard a satisfying crack. Olmstead howled and it was music to his ears. Stas dragged him back up into a standing position and gave him a single solid shove. Olmstead stumbled into the guardrail again and then toppled over the side of the boat and disappeared into the murky, muddy water.

Stas retrieved the gun and hauled himself back up to the helm to bring the boat back in next to the now stationary Devil's Paddle. As he did so, more gunfire erupted, this time from the far side of the boat. He looked up to try to locate Lisa again.

He could not see her anywhere in the melee that was unraveling on board. What he could see were people, dressed to the nines, beginning to abandon ship.

8

A fiery anger coursed through Jason Tolbert's veins. He got his speedboat around and behind the big stern paddle, out of the line of fire coming from the rear of The Devil's Paddle. The quick gunfight had taken only seconds but those seconds had been a few too many.

He was about to drop to a knee and assess the damages when another explosion ripped across the river from right behind him. He turned and looked up with horror as the giant red paddle burst free of its mooring on the stern of the big ship and tumbled down toward him. He jammed the throttle forward causing the boat to lurch out of its path.

With a large, heavy splash it came to rest behind him with just the topmost red floats on the paddle's apex still sticking out of the water. Having cleared out of its way, Tolbert could no longer be engaged with that disaster, he was focused on another that was far worse.

Back down on one knee it only took a second to affirm that his most terrible fears had come to fruition. The madness and mayhem that was transpiring around him and on The Devil's Paddle was the stuff of movies. But the little bit of gunfire exchanged between their boat and Lisa Lathrop had been far too realistic. A handful of shots fired from both locations and then it was over. No prolonged, dragged out scene.

Just bang, bang, bang, and his brother had dropped dead onto the floor of the boat. No histrionics, no gnashing of teeth, just one to the head and he was gone.

Jason Tolbert straightened up and sped around to the far side of The Paddle. At first he couldn't locate her but then he saw the woman about to climb onto the grand circular staircase at the bow of the boat.

Jason didn't take time to take aim, he just started firing. His first shot was true though. It would have struck her down had not some jackass running wild in the pandemonium stepped right between his bullet and the woman he wanted so badly to destroy.

Tolbert couldn't care less. What he did care about and what stoked his anger even hotter was that in those mere seconds Lisa Lathrop had disappeared up the steps to the second level of The Devil's Paddle.

2

Lisa rounded the bend on the staircase and came up into the casino on the second level. The crazed frenzy taking place down on the first deck was less because people had either broken for the lower level or had just taken cover, crouching and hiding behind and below the many felted tables.

At the far end she saw the Mayor of Minneapolis, Sammy Douglas, in a heated discussion with his men. Not far from them Cortland Whittier was doing the same with Brian Larson, the Sheriff of Bolton County. Lisa fired the gun once into the ceiling to shut everyone up.

"I suggest you all get the hell out of here, right now." She was speaking to the bystanders that were cowering about.

With an eerie efficiency the room cleared in a quick and orderly manner. People hustled down the stairs leaving only Lisa, the sheriff, the mayor and his guys, and Cortland Whittier.

Whittier leaned close to Sheriff Larson. "Kill her," he whispered in a tone that was almost seductive. The madness that formed the foundation of his empire was starting to ooze through his cracking veneer.

Lisa had her gun trained on Whittier but kept her eyes on the sheriff. He looked over to her as he started to reach under the back of his suit coat but she saw the lack of resolve in his eyes.

The Sheriff of Bolton County was a sleaze. He had committed a laundry list of crimes and was just now realizing that he was probably going to have to pay dearly for them. But he wasn't going to be adding murder to the list, not at this late date.

He let the back of his jacket slip back into place and then he scurried down the stairs as well.

The casino deck of The Devil's Paddle bore an eerie quiet, as if it were somehow immune to the mayhem ensuing below it. Lisa put Cortland Whittier's head in the sight of her gun.

"Mr. Mayor, it seems you've made some terrible choices today."

Sammy Douglas said nothing.

"A lot of people on this boat tonight are going to have large career and criminal problems tomorrow thanks to their transgressions. I think your days as a politician are over but I don't know that dragging you and the largest municipality in the state through the muck is going to be in anyone's best interests. The myriad of issues that your political peers and their constituents are going to be facing will be legendary."

The very polished Sammy Douglas stepped forward. "Ma'am, I'm not sure exactly what transgressions you're alluding to, but I'm certain we can come to some sort of understanding—"

"Shut up," Lisa barked at him. "There will be no understanding. What there will be is restitution and blood."

The polish was fading from Mayor Sammy Douglas.

"But it doesn't have to be yours," she finished.

At that moment Stas came bounding up the stairs into the casino calling her name.

"I'm here, and I'm fine," she said over her shoulder. "Is Dylan here yet?"

"Haven't seen him, but he has to be close."

"Logan?"

Stas paused then shook his head but she didn't see it. Her focus remained on keeping the gun sighted between Cortland Whittier's eyes. She seemed to sense his response but she didn't waver.

"Mr. Mayor," she said to Sammy Douglas. "I think it would be best if you and your men joined my friend here. You've had enough excitement for one day, wouldn't you say?"

Sammy Douglas nodded his head, thankful for whatever reprieve he may have gotten from this mess.

"Find Dylan and get the mayor and his men out of here," she told Stas.

"Nope, I'm not leaving without you."

"Oh, yes, you are. You have no more business here. What's left is between me and this asshole." Her eyes were locked on Cortland Whittier.

Stas looked at her, at the woman she had become, all the while remembering the girl she had been. He looked to Whittier but spoke to Lisa.

"Do what you have to do."

Reluctantly he took hold of the mayor's arm and led him down the stairway as his men followed, leaving the two old adversaries alone on the second deck of The Devil's Paddle.

10

The beautiful replica paddle steamer sat dead in the

water. From his speedboat Tolbert scoured the main deck for any sign of Lisa Lathrop. Most of the guests had now bailed and were swimming for their anchored boats. Another harried mass of people piled down the staircase and began their exodus.

Watching these dignitaries swim through the muddy Mississippi in dresses and suits that probably cost more than most people's cars might have been comical were it not for the unmitigated disaster this night had become. At that point he heard the sound of another boat speeding down from up the river. It would be the other set of Bolton County Deputies that had been stationed at the north end of the circuit.

He heard the boat approach on the far side of The Devil's Paddle and slow. With most of the main deck emptied Tolbert had pretty clear view through the saloon and lounge to the other side. He saw the deputies pull up near the boarding area but they didn't get out of the boat.

Tolbert's already unmanageable fury mounted further and then exploded as that weasel of a sheriff, Brian Larson, scurried down the staircase and ran to his waiting deputies.

Tolbert raised his gun and fired toward them through the open deck of the saloon with no care for any repercussions. His bullets found no purchase, though, and once the sheriff was aboard, they tore off downriver, disappearing behind the back end of The Paddle.

Tilting toward madness himself, Jason Tolbert opened the throttle and chased them. Logical thought had abandoned him and he let his rage prod him on.

When the giant stern paddle had ripped free, the rest of the ship had listed before coming to a stop. It now sat at an angle still facing upriver but with its bow turned slightly toward the far bank. Tolbert, letting his anger fuel him, whipped around the backcorner blind. The County Sheriff's boat was about twenty yards away and held Tolbert's entire focus. He fired a single shot.

That single shot was the only one he was able to get off. He had cut the corner tight to attempt to gain ground on them without accounting for the fact that the giant stern paddle was still sitting dormant behind the ship in the middle of the river.

When he hit the now stationary paddle, he was doing at least sixty and still gaining speed. The boat disintegrated around him, launching him through the air. One of the paddle's bright red floats caught him at the neck and ripped Jason Tolbert's head free of his body.

11

Travis Olmstead broke the surface of the river and struggled for air. Treading to keep his head up as his water-logged clothes pulled at him, weighing him down, he looked around. His boat wasn't far from him but he didn't know if it would be safe. He looked to where The Paddle had come to rest in the middle of the river and saw Mileski running toward the staircase at the bow. He had to hope that meant his boat was clear.

He hauled himself up onto The Devil's Delivery but his ribs were howling. They had to be cracked if not broken and he had to fight through the pain in order to keep from passing out. He struggled up to the bridge and found the key still in the ignition.

Travis heard something move behind him and whirled around, yelping as his damaged torso howled. His breathing settled as best it could into sharp, harsh gasps as he located the source of the sound. It was Ted Logan hauling himself up onto the boat.

The two men stared at each other, both sucking in air. Then Logan dropped, slumping into a seat under the weight of his own soaked clothing.

Olmstead looked across to The Devil's Paddle then around at the few guests still left swimming to their own boats. "What should we do?" he wheezed.

Logan looked over at the still well lit, but now quiet, behemoth ship dead in the water.

"Get us out of here, Travis."

12

"Well, here we are, just you and me, just as it was always meant to be," Cortland Whittier said through a Cheshire grin, trying to bait her.

Lisa kept the Glock trained on him and said, "I'm just glad you'll die knowing that it was by my hand."

They stood at a stalemate for a long moment. And then Whittier took a step toward her.

Lisa pulled the trigger.

Nothing happened but the slight click of a dry-fire. The Glock's magazine only held fifteen rounds and she had apparently used the last when she shot into the ceiling to quiet the crowd. Whittier's grin widened, slithering up into his eyes. He took a step toward her.

She gave him a wicked grin of her own which gave him a moment's pause. She reached into her pocket and grabbed the last of her explosives. Whittier was still at the far end of the casino deck and she was right in the middle, standing next to a structural post that ran up the center of The Devil's Paddle holding its decks in place.

Earlier Lisa had pre-set the timer to fifteen seconds. She started it now but counted to five in her head before showing it to Whittier. She watched his grin dissolve into fear and felt the most satisfaction she could ever recall. She slapped the device onto the post and bolted for the stairs.

As she approached the staircase she dropped into a slide. She hit the stairs and slid down and around the circular bend just as the timer hit zero and the structural post holding most of the weight of the third deck was ripped into a thousand pieces.

Following the ripple of the shocking sound wave came an ominous groaning as the deck above started to give way.

Lisa regained her feet and raced down the stairs. She pumped her legs with all she had as she ran for the edge of the boat and the relative safety of the river. She heard the roar from above as the third deck gave way, smashing inward down onto the casino deck.

She reached the edge and dove. Lisa was still in the air when she heard the resounding crack of the beam on the first deck letting go as well. And then she hit the water and behind her The Devil's Paddle consumed itself.

She swam hard and let the current aid her in distancing herself from the sinking, crumbling ship. When she was far enough away, she stopped and treaded water. On the far side she could see Dylan's trawler far enough away to have avoided the careening detritus from the explosion. She saw Stas and Dylan standing on the front deck scouring the wreckage for her. Stas was safe and Mayor Douglas, for better or worse, had been offloaded. Lisa started to swim toward them but stopped.

All around her debris floated. What was left of the main structure of The Devil's Paddle was now in flames. Whittier should not have been able to survive the havoc caused by the explosion and the collapsing decks, but 'shouldn't have' wasn't going to be good enough. Not this time. She had to know for sure. Lisa changed her course and swam back toward the wreckage.

She took long, powerful strokes, scanning between each for any sign of the monster that had haunted her dreams for her entire life. But she saw nothing. She pulled up, treading water, trying to decide the best course to get to the other side, when a hand wrapped around her ankle and yanked her underwater.

She managed to snatch a breath and shut her mouth before her head went under, but it was small. She opened her wild eyes and looked below her. Cortland Whittier had hold of her ankle and was dragging her toward him.

But Lisa's terror began to slip away as she looked at her nemesis and a small joy began to blossom somewhere deep within her.

Whittier had hold of her ankle but he was struggling against a large piece of the wreckage that had skewered him, pinning him to the river bottom. His blood drifted in lazy rivulets around her. She smiled and could tell by the vile hate filling his eyes that he saw it. She put her free foot on the piece of debris and pushed down, driving it further into him and propelling herself up. His grasping hand slipped from her ankle.

She stopped before breaking the surface and watched him. Lisa could see air bubbles drifting from his mouth. The bastard was screaming and had let the water fill his lungs. Lisa Lathrop felt a happy serenity settle over her even as the pain of holding her breath began to rip at her own chest. A couple seconds later Cortland Whittier stopped moving altogether.

Lisa loosed her own primal scream into the water, not even sure she still had the strength to claw her way back to the surface before she started swallowing the river herself.

Lisa Lathrop didn't rely on the strength of others with any regularity, but when she did it often came from one person, someone who'd always been there for her before and made no exception now.

A hand clamped onto the back of her shirt, pulling her up out of the river and into the night air. She spit out the little bit of muddy Mississippi River that she had taken on and, panting, allowed her oldest friend Stas Mileski to hold her.

Minneapolis...
Spring, 2017

The weathered bar top gleamed and Stas Mileski rested his elbows upon it. He waited as the bartender, Melissa, poured his beer. It was good to be back at Dusty's Bar. It was good to be home.

He glanced up at one of the two small televisions that Dusty's sported. The news was on and it looked like a press conference was about to start. A man in a uniform stepped to the podium and began speaking. The title bar at the bottom of the screen read: Ryan Tomlinson, Castle County Sheriff.

"Melissa, can you turn up the volume for a sec?" Stas asked. She did so and Bob Gurley's successor in Castle County, Ryan Tomlinson, was picked up mid-sentence and his voice filled the little bar.

"—Castle County Sheriff's Department in conjunction with the Minnesota Bureau of Criminal Apprehension will be handling the investigation into the involvement of the Bolton County Sheriff's Department in the events that transpired on the Mississippi River as well as at the Minnewawa Resort. I will read a prepared statement and then we will have a brief statement from former Sheriff Bob Gurley, who had first-hand experience on scene at the Minnewawa."

Stas chuckled to himself as the camera panned to Bob, his newest old pal, as he gave a stoic nod to the assembled media. Sheriff Tomlinson continued, giving a very detail-free report touching on the fringes of what had happened with The Devil's Paddle, and then introduced Bob who did the same with the events he had been a part of at the resort.

His report was intentionally just as full of holes as the current sheriff's was. There would be accusations aplenty, and they'd be lain upon powerful people all over the state. The officials of many counties were going to have their hands full sorting through the allegations about to be levied at some of their more celebrated peers. But the people in charge of cleaning up this mess didn't dare give up too many details until they had a better handle on the situation, and how far it might reach.

Tomlinson stepped back in and opened the press conference up to questions. The first was the only one Stas had any real interest in.

"Sheriff, is there any truth to the rumor that the Mayor of Minneapolis, Sammy Douglas, had been aboard the ship that was sunk?"

"To my knowledge, there is no truth to that statement and it is purely a speculative rumor," Sheriff Tomlinson said.

"What about 8th district state senator Joseph Randall?"

"We do believe Mr. Randall was present but we are not sure of his involvement at this time."

Stas signaled to Melissa behind the bar that she could cut the volume. He'd heard what he wanted. Sammy Douglas might not be indicted like so many of the other guests that were aboard The Devil's Paddle but he'd be resigning very soon due to an undisclosed medical condition. That medical condition, of course, being self-preservation.

Stas couldn't care less what happened to all of these politicians or their careers. What mattered to him was that Cortland Whittier was gone and his empire was in ashes. Unlike the last time, when he and Lisa had watched Norumbega burn on TV and believed Whittier's reign to be done, this time they had first-hand knowledge that it was over. This time they had laid the flame.

Stas walked over from the bar and pulled up "Ode to Billie Joe" on the jukebox. It was the song that had been playing when he had that first conversation with Bob and it somehow seemed appropriate now. The haunting strains of the opening guitar lick filled the room. Walking back to the bar with a slight swagger Stas mouthed the chorus over the intro, "Billie Joe McAllister jumped off the Tallahatchie Bridge."

Stas sat down as the professional, Ms. Gentry, took up the reins of the singing, and he sipped his beer.

Red Wing...
Spring, 2017

Dinner was finished and Tim Boyd was washing the dishes. From the sink he turned and looked out the window into Lisa's backyard. His boy, Danny, was out there with his pitch-back in his little swath of light, but he wasn't throwing. He was watching and instructing.

Brandy Redmond went into her wind-up, launched the ball at the netting, and then easily caught the rebound. Danny pumped his fist and ran to her with some further instruction. Tim smiled and returned to the dishes. Brandy was staying with them for now. 'For now' was a nebulous time period. So much about their lives was nebulous and uncertain at this point, but they were here. They were home, together.

Somewhere above Tim, upstairs, Lisa sat on the edge of the tub drawing a bath. She climbed in and slid down into the warm water. She sat there for a very long time. The water first turned tepid then started to get cold, not like the river had been cold, but still uncomfortable. There were so many things to process, so many wounds that felt like they could never be healed, and yet it was time to try.

She held her breath and let her head slip below the surface. Once upon a time she had pulled Stas from the waters of that little pond. And then he had pulled her from the river. But Cortland Whittier, he drank that muddy water, drank it until he died. And for the first time in her life, Lisa Lathrop might find her way to a restful night's sleep.

And maybe, eventually, some peace.

She opened her mouth and let the bath water fill it. Then she lifted her head from the depths and sprayed it out across the tub, baptized and ready to begin anew.

June 1st, 2019
Nordeast Minneapolis

Author's note

I would like to note a few things about this story. I prefer to use real locations in and around Minnesota but I was compelled to fictionalize a few things. Bolton County, while in basically the same location as Aitkin County, does not actually exist and is in no way associated with Aitkin County. While this story takes place in 2017, the St. Anthony Falls lock and dam that provides access to the Mississippi River north of Minneapolis was closed in 2015 in order stem the influx of the invasive Asian Carp. Those changes were made intentionally, other discrepancies are simply mistakes. I'd like to thank Mary Pat Elsen and Dennis Curley for their help in editing this book. I'd like to thank Jean Moelter for her continued support of my work. To my parents, Chery and John Day, and Elliott and Wendy Hays. Thanks to Dan Marshall for another beautiful cover photo, Ryan North, Erik Schindler and Norcostco, Erik Herrlin, Matthew and Carrie Ystad, Troy and Kate Burbach, and the rest of our Nordeast community for their support. Thanks to everyone who previously purchased *In Brigand's Woods*. And of course, thanks for all the love and support from my family, Katy, Joey, and Viv. And to you who have this book in your hand today, thank you for taking the time to go on another small adventure with me. I hope we meet again, on the banks of another river or at the edge of another wood, where together we can peek into the glowing gloom and see what mischief may be afoot there in the dark.

-B.H.

Made in the
USA
Lexington, KY